Sean Thomas

was born in 1963 in Devon. His [...] published in 1996; his second, *K[...]* time journalist, in recent years his work has appeared in *The Times*, the *Independent* and the *Guardian*. He lives in London.

Further praise for *The Cheek Perforation Dance*:

'Compelling and disturbing. Pre held ideas about male and female sexuality are turned on their head. Intrigued? You should be. This is a very intriguing novel.'   *Irish Independent*

'If you're searching for a gentle holiday read then allow us not to recommend this. The skill of this courtroom drama is in the construction: Thomas intercuts the court case with flashbacks to their love affair suggesting several disquieting notions of what constitutes modern love.'   *Arena*

'Distressingly believable.'   *Front*

Praise for *Kissing England*:

'To say this is elegantly written would be an understatement; the unique essence of England, and being English, is captured perfectly. Imbued with a delicate blend of humour and irony, *Kissing England* evokes as many personal memories as the ones it creates.'   *Time Out*

'Wry, dry, it's *White City Blue* meets *Brideshead Revisited*. Cracking stuff.'   *Daily Mirror*

'Thomas balances unremitting explicitness with acutely observed set pieces.'   *The Times*

Also by Sean Thomas

ABSENT FATHERS
KISSING ENGLAND

the
cheek
perforation
dance

sean thomas

Flamingo

An Imprint of HarperCollins*Publishers*

Flamingo
An imprint of HarperCollins*Publishers*
77–85 Fulham Palace Road,
Hammersmith, London W6 8JB

Flamingo is a registered trade mark of
HarperCollins*Publishers* Limited

www.**fire**and**water**.com

Published by Flamingo 2003
9 8 7 6 5 4 3 2 1

Previously published in Great Britain by Flamingo 2002

Copyright © Sean Thomas 2002

Sean Thomas asserts the moral right
to be identified as the author of this work

ISBN 0 00 651445 6

Set in Giovanni and Fairfield Light by
Rowland Phototypesetting Limited,
Bury St Edmunds, Suffolk

Printed and bound in Great Britain by
Clays Ltd, St Ives plc

For us, then

ACKNOWLEDGMENTS

The quotes on pages 248–250 come from *Biological Exuberance*, by Bruce Bagemihl; I have interpolated two other quotes, on these same pages: from *The Biology of Rape*, a paper by Randy Thornhill, Nancy Wilmsen Thornhill, & Gerard Dizinho, and from *The Evolution of Allure*, by George L. Hersey.

I should like to thank Patricia Parkin, Georgina Hawtrey-Woore, Karen Duffy, Sara Walsh, Mary-Rose Doherty – and everyone else at HarperCollins.

The fourteenth Veintana, Quecholli, was dedicated to Mixcoatl. The feast was celebrated by one or two days of hunting and feasting in the countryside during which the hunters adorned themselves like Mixcoatl himself and kindled new fire to roast the game. Subsequently, a man and a woman were sacrificed to Mixcoatl in his temple. The female victim was slain like a wild animal: her head was struck four times against a rock until she was half-conscious; then her throat was slit and her head decapitated. The male victim displayed the head to the assembled crowds before he himself was sacrificed by heart extrusion.

An Illustrated Dictionary of the Gods and
Symbols of Ancient Mexico and the Maya,
by Mary Miller and Karl Taube

1

—Patch, slow down

Says Joe. Patrick turns, and looks back down the sunny London street. Patrick's friend Joe is wearing a green and yellow martial arts tee shirt, and notably scuffed indigo jeans. Comparing this choice of attire to his own suit and tie, Patrick wonders how he and Joe must appear: like a banker and his drug dealer, discussing prices; like two guests en route to a mildly bohemian wedding; like the accused and his friend, walking to court.

—Don't want to be *early*, do you?

Patrick nods, assessing the truth of this. Then Patrick says:

—Guess not . . . – Thinking, considering – How about a pint?

Joe lifts his hands:

—It's *nine* in the *morning*

Patrick:

—But they're open. The pubs are open round here, because of the meat market

—I *know* they're *open* – A sigh, a smile – I was just wondering whether you really want to get lashed half an hour before . . .

Joe stops; shrugs. Patrick turns on his polished black shoes, walks briskly and authoritatively up a side street, and presses a pub door.

Inside the pub the atmosphere is already noisy, and yeasty. The Smithfield pub is full of office lads beering up before work, and meat-market porters winding down after work. Finding two stools by the sticky bar, Patrick pulls, and sits, and says to the barwoman:

— Pint of Guinness . . . – Looking sidelong – *Joe*?

Joe does another vague shrug. Patrick persists:

— *Joseph?*

— . . . 6X. Half

— Pint of 6X please

The barwoman nods and takes two glasses from the shelf above; Patrick gazes around the bar. In the corner he can see a platoon of nervy, wide-eyed student kids. The students are giggling and nudging each other as they order beers with their breakfasts.

— Takes me back

Says Patrick. Joe, a bit vague, says:

— Sorry? .

— Those kids – Says Patrick – Look at them. That was us once. We used to come here after tripping – Patrick widens his eyes – Remember?

Joe grins, and nods. Patrick returns his gaze to the students. Feeling a small ache inside, Patrick marvels at the youth displayed: the impeccable complexions, the innocent cheekbones, the naively exuberant gestures; the gold Saxon hair of the girls.

— You're only twenty-nine Patch

— I feel ninety-seven, right now

Joe sighs:

— Well. What do you expect? This morning of mornings?

Hmming, Patrick tips the beer to his lips. The Guinness is cold and very bitter. Patrick remembers how he never liked drinking this early.

— God, it's too early to drink

Joe looks at him blankly. Then says:

— Shall we go?

Manfully struggling with his pride, and with his desire to get drunk despite, Patrick nods, and rises. Together the two old college friends walk out of the pub into London: into the sweetly polluted summer air. They take a right. Then another. Their route takes them past the meat market, past the place where John Betjeman lived, past the church where they filmed *Four Weddings and a Funeral*, past the hospital ward where Mozart had his tonsils out; and past the ad agency car park where Patrick got his one and only blow job from a Muslim girl.

At the last they make a left, and find themselves staring down the boulevards of capitalism at the noble dome of great St Paul's. Joe starts walking towards the cathedral, but Patrick says he knows a short cut.

Joe nods acquiescently. Patrick steps right and guides them into a garden, then into a courtyard, then through the pink granite undercroft of a Malaysian bank; here they turn and find themselves facing a huge great building site.

—Jesus – Says Joe – I thought they'd finished London

Patrick tries to smile but fails. Patrick does not feel like smiling. He feels like turning, like going back to the pub. Patrick is thinking about what is to happen: what is awaiting him, in ten, twenty, thirty minutes. *How many minutes?*

Pulling back his stiff left shirtcuff, the cuff so diligently ironed by his mother last night, Patrick checks his watch. Its white face stares back at his white face.

9.20 a.m.

Patrick looks across the thundering street. Pensively he surveys the chaotic building site: the raw new girders and gleaming steel fire escapes; the piles of creamy new bricks.

Joe:

—OK?

With a nod Patrick says:

—*OK* . . .

But Patrick feels far from *OK*. Patrick feels so far from *OK* he wonders if he might be about to start trembling, or worse. Patrick desperately does not want this: he does not want to look scared in front of Joe.

—*Joe* . . .

—Uh?

—I think maybe I . . .

A knowing expression:

—You want to go in on your own?

—Well . . .

—Don't worry mate – Joe claps Patrick on the shoulder, and starts skipping left, into the traffic, calling out as he goes – I'll see you inside

And so Joe goes.

Alone, now, in the middle of the city hubbub, Patrick swallows and fights himself. His nerves once again quelled, he stares across at the building beyond the building site: his destination. On the top of the building, bright against the cloudless blue sky, is a statue of a woman, holding scales in her golden hand.

*Oh, sure, right. Trust a **woman**?*

Dismissing the irony of this, Patrick threads through. The pavement by the Central Criminal Court, the Old Bailey, is a tumult of chatting journalists, sweating handicam men, and young foreign sightseers knocking into people with their enormous blue rucksacks. Ignoring the crowds, hoping they are all similarly ignoring him, Patrick makes for the lowslung main door of the courts. But Patrick's boldness is holed. By the sound of a familiar car door, and by the even more familiar sound of a young woman's voice. The girl is saying:

— Yes Dad I'll call you

*Jesus. Can it be? **Can it be?** * Patrick stops still on the pavement, staring blankly at the side of a big red bus, dumbed. It sounds like her; it certainly sounds like her. Like *her*. Like his ex; like his accuser; like the truelove he hasn't seen for a year.

But. Patrick thinks again: *no, no, it can't be; doesn't make sense.* She wouldn't just be . . . *here*, standing right by him, *would she*?

— I think I've got to give evidence first thing Daddy

Unable to resist, Patrick turns, and looks. A recognisably big BMW is parked hard by the pavement. Climbing out of the back of the car is a striking blonde girl with a shortish checked dress showing long suntanned legs. The sight makes Patrick's knees infirm. Because. It *is*. It's *her*.

And now the memories engulf him. As Patrick stands and tries not to react at the sight of his ex-girlfriend, his tormentor, the principal witness for the prosecution, the best friend he allegedly raped twelve months ago, he reacts by remembering. He sees it all. The whole tableau of love. He sees: a bugle on a windowsill; a pair of handcuffs in a fridge; an Aztec history book stained with claret; a sunny Torrington Square, nearly two and a half years ago.

Two and a half years ago?

Silent, and still, Patrick stares. At Rebecca.

2

—He's still staring
—That's nice, Rebecca
—No, he is
—OK . . . – Murphy sighs – *OK* . . .

Rolling on her back, Murphy shuts her sarcastic eyes. Slightly frustrated, Rebecca gazes away from the man, and looks around the square. The late May sun is shining but the place is empty: Torrington Square is nearly deserted. Apart from a few Indian girls in flared jeans chatting by the Brunei Centre, and a small group of Japanese girls with miniskirts and superpale legs, sitting demurely on the steps of the School of Oriental and African Studies, Murphy and Rebecca are alone on the mangy bit of central London lawn between Birkbeck College and the Institute of Education. *Torrington Square*. Musing again on the man, Rebecca says:

—It's definitely him
—Uh-*huh* . . .
—I wonder what he does
—Indeed

Murphy is lying flat out with her skirt hitched up: tanning; ignoring her friend; her head pillowed by her folded pink cardigan. Murphy is using a textbook to shield her eyes from the glare. *Rebecca's* textbook. Opting not to mention this, Rebecca says:

—He's the guy I was telling you about. The one who always sits over there – Brightly – He must work round here, he's rather young for a lecturer tho, maybe he's a postgrad or . . .

phy opens her mouth:

.ebecca . . . shut the fuck up

Narrowing the space between them Rebecca snatches her textbook from its cowboy-hat role on Murphy's face. For a second, Murphy seems to scowl; then Murphy breaks into a profile of a smile. Rebecca smiles, too.

Using a grass-stained elbow, Murphy is levering herself onto her front, and visoring her eyes with a flat unwedding-ringed hand so as to look over at *him*.

A sharp, Murphyish breath.

Rebecca says:

—So? What do you think?

Murphy sets her lips; considers the question. Then:

—He looks a bit . . .

—What?

—. . . You know . . . Brutal . . . Stone Age – Another look, through the telescope of her squinting eyes – Hasn't shaved for a while

Rebecca mulls this; Murphy says:

—Just your sort. Another puppy drowner

Staring down at her painted toenails half hidden by her sandals, Rebecca demurs:

—Well

—Why don't you just wait outside Wormwood Scrubs and have done with it?

Rebecca, chuckling:

—Can't help it if I'm partial to . . . a bit of rough . . .

A Murphyish snort:

—*Bit* of *rough*? That guy's on *parole*

Rebecca slaps Murphy's suntanned thigh; Murphy does a laconic 'ouch' and then says:

—Anyway, what about Neil? Forgotten him already?

—Neil Schmeal

—Wagon Wheel

Silence. For a moment the two of them observe a Japanese girl protecting her face from the sun with an angled *A to Z*. Tucking some of her brown hair behind a thrice-pierced ear, Murphy says:

—Still hungry!

Rebecca hands over the second lunch bag:

—Here

—Ta . . .

Reaching into the shared brown paper bag Murphy takes out the last sandwich. Plastic sandwich podule open, she extracts the coronation chicken sandwich and lays it flat on the bag. Then she lifts a flap of the bread so as to examine the contents.

—Hm

Picking up the sandwich she sniffs the curry-scented, yellowish paste. Nose wrinkling, she puts the sandwich down again, plucks something from the sandwich filling, and then holds this up, in front of Rebecca's face, like a priest presenting the communion wafer.

—What's this?

Murphy is holding up an almond. Rebecca says:

—It's an almond

—*Almond*? ALMOND?? – Murphy's voice is almost a yelp – Why do they *do* this? Why do they put *fucking* almonds in a bloody *chicken* sandwich? Why can't they leave well alone? What's happening to the world?

Rebecca smiles, says nothing; plucks grass.

Consideringly, Murphy begins removing the bits of almond, diligently extracting them from the gunk, then smearing them with a wince of repugnance on a convenient bit of lawn. This done, Murphy re-examines. Pointing to another suspicious constituent of the curry-sauce-yellow sandwich filling she looks over at Rebecca, reproachfully.

Rebecca sighs:

—Raisins . . .

Murphy:

—*Raisins? Really?* Oh, for God's sake. Did I *ask* for raisins? Did I say please can you put some fucking dried fruit in my fucking *chicken* sandwich?

Rebecca's friend is making an I've-had-enough face. Rebecca notices Murphy's ankle chain. Sighing, exhaling, Murphy squints at the sandwich, looks at Rebecca, squints at the sandwich. With a decided air Murphy bags the sandwich, leans back, takes aim, and expertly lobs the sandwich bag into the nearest bin.

Clapping her hands Murphy sits up straight, cross-legged again, triumphantly laughing; Rebecca laughs, too: feeling happy in the sun. Making a cunning face Murphy does a blatant grab for the last of Rebecca's lunch; successfully filching from the other paper bag a chocolate bar. With a shrug Rebecca watches as her best friend eats the bar; Murphy is talking with a mouth full of chocolate:

—Anyway. What *about* the boyf?

—*Him . . . ?*

—Yeah. Neil. Supergeek. You gonna give him another chance?

Rebecca *moues*, as if to say: *enough said.* Sat back on straight arms Rebecca turns and glances over at the guy who hasn't shaved for a few days. He isn't glancing at her. He is busy with his own sandwiches, washing them down with a can of cola, idly flicking through his big newspaper. Occasionally he seems to look up and stare vacantly at the Fifties brickwork of Birkbeck. Trying her hardest Rebecca wills him to look at her: *look at me, look at me, look at me . . . please?*

As if commanded, he turns his face . . . and looks at the bike sheds behind Birkbeck College. Offended, rolling over, Rebecca says to Murphy, who is examining her stomach for a tan mark:

—I've seen him here a few times now

—Who invented cellulite?

—That guy . . .

—I mean you never hear Jane Austen banging on about it, do you? Did Elizabeth Bennett freak out in case Darcy saw her orange peel?

—He often eats his lunch here

—So when did cellulite start? The Sixties? I blame feminists. I reckon lesbian feminists must have invented it. To put us off getting naked with guys. Woman-hating bastards. Chop their tits off I say

—How old do you reckon he is?

—Are you *still* banging on about that . . . *thug?* He's *gross,* Becs, he looks like he'd mug your mum

—He's quite . . . sexy . . .

—You're such a slapper, Jessel

—He looks . . . interesting . . .

—Psychotic

Rebecca shakes her head and goes to answer but Murphy is checking her ironically big plastic watch. The watch with the knowingly naff boy-band motif. Looking up, tongue clicking, Murphy says:

—Gotta go

—But . . . it's not even two

—It's called *work*, girl

—. . . Stay . . . ?

A certain pause. Murphy looks over; Rebecca looks back. Rebecca notes that Murphy's face is nicely tan, her eyes green, her nose stud silver in the early summer sun. Murph[

lodges her tongue behi[

—Derrr . . . Werrrk[

—Unfair!

—What's it like [

your bikini lin[

—I do do th[

—Yeah?

With a som[

of the books that [

Murphy recites the tit[

—*The Broken Spears. The* [

Rebecca is shrugging; Murp[

— . . . Call me a stupid cow with s[

the Crusades?

—Well

—Too easy was it? Thought you'd tackle a few [

Murphy looks like she's thinking of another insu[

picks up the paperback that Murphy was reading. Slow[

the title, in a similarly stilted way:

—*Veiled Voices, an anthology of Arab women's poetry*

Murphy looks vaguely abashed; and a tiny bit proud. Rebecca say[

—Not exactly the lightest of reading . . . – Checking the title again – A[

good?

Murphy shrugs and says:

—Actually, it is . . . it's very good, kinda horny

—Kind of *horny*?

Murphy laughs:

—Well it's . . . interestingly confessional – A glance between them; then

Murphy shrugs again – O K so I'm easily aroused . . .

Before Rebecca can ask her next question, her usual question about

Murphy's love life, Murphy has barked

—*Fuck*, Becs, I *have* to go. My boss'll be chewing her arm off. Conceptual

dustbin lids don't sell themselves y'know . . .

Rebecca smiles:

—No. Hold on. I'll come with you, I've got to buy something from

Waterstone's

—K

The following is overlaid diagonal text from a torn page:

Preparing to go, they look[

—Er . . .

—Golly . . .

Hands on hips they ass[

ing their lunch spot is a[

doodled-on diary page[

scrunched-up tissue[

magazine. O K! m[

of smeared almo[

stoop to it: with[

bag the books[

grass stalks. [

checks the[

Ah we[

But [

happi[

lege[

is [

s[

around.

ess the mess they have somehow made. Surround-
airy ring of mobile phone cards, choc-bar wrappers,
, and bits of cigarette packet. And Aztec history books,
, hay-fever nasal sprays, empty mocha coffee cups, *Hello!*
gazine, Arab women's poetry paperbacks, and splinters
d. Murphy laughs; Rebecca laughs. Laughing as one, they
a burst of zeal and energy they bend to collect the rubbish,
collate the other stuff, and spend a minute mutually grooming
hen and only then do they start walking. As they leave Rebecca
corner of the lawn where he was; he isn't.

e is already just a memory, a memory almost forgotten as they stroll
y across the grass and down the steps that lead under Birkbeck Col-
This is their normal short cut: today the two old college friends' route
locked by crowds of weird people. By bearded blokes in bad Hawaiian
irts, by hairy-legged women with Marxism For The Twenty-First Century
aminate badges. Walking past a parade of temporary bookstalls set out in
the sun with an array of yellowing *Workers Power* titles, Murphy finally
stops, wrinkles her nose, blurts:

—God, they *ming*

Rebecca:

—Murf, please

—But they do. They *smell*. *Yuk*

—*Murphy*

—But why? Why do they have to *pong*? Does it say that in *Das Kapital*?

The two college friends push through one particularly gamey cell of
would-be Irish Republicans from Guildford as Rebecca explains:

—It's a Marxist Weekend, they take over the Union every spring for a
weekend and have . . . I don't know . . . conferences . . . I suppose . . .

Evidently unsatisfied by this Murphy stops short on a pavement and
starts loudly reading out the signs installed everywhere: the *Luton Comrades
For A United Ireland* poster, the *Kidderminster Spartacists Meet In The
Marlborough Arms* flyer. Then:

—Correct me if I'm wrong, Becs, but didn't, like, these people *lose*? Weren't
they like . . . *totally wrong*?

—I'm going to Waterstone's

—Yeah? Try that poetry collection, you might like it . . .

Rebecca nods. The two of them are on the corner of Malet Place. In the sun Murphy smiles and reaches over and holds Rebecca's face and kisses her on the cheek.

—And take care, ducks

With that done Murphy twists on a heel, and walks away down the road.

Still stood still, Rebecca watches her friend depart. From this vantage, the slight overfatness of Murphy's bottom is obvious, despite the pink cardigan tied around. The sight of this tugs at Rebecca. Flushed by something, Rebecca realises that it is actually this, the pathos of Murphy's self-consciousness, the pathos of Murphy's awareness of her own physical imperfections, that constitutes a large part of why Rebecca loves Murphy. Considering this, this odd fact, Rebecca gazes, half in reverie, as Murphy suddenly turns, brightly smiles, and does a sarcastically soppy wave back at Rebecca.

Observing her friend's cheery wave, Rebecca feels overwhelmed. From nowhere, she now feels an engulfing sadness, as if something soon, something looming and near, something awful is about to happen to her dearest friend that should forever change . . .

Dismissing it from her thoughts Rebecca goes over to Waterstone's the Bookshop. Pressing glass she enters. Immediately inside she pauses in the welcome cool downdraught from the doorway aircon. Where to? Travel, Cookery, or Magazines? Or Medieval History, as is proper and right? By her self-imposed schedule Rebecca is all too aware that at this moment she shouldn't even be here: she should be back at the London Uni library reading up Frankish chronicles. Disregarding her postgraduate conscience Rebecca instead makes her way slowly round Fiction, Crime and New Titles, before climbing the black metal stairs, and the second flight of stairs, at the top of which she turns and makes that guilty but familiar, wicked but much loved right turn: into Literature, and Drama, and Poetry, and Art. Her trueloves . . .

Hours pass, maybe minutes. Rebecca moves from Braque to Brancusi, from Hockney to Biedermeier. Finally she finds a book about French eighteenth-century court portraiture. The engrossing book makes Rebecca wonder how she can relate the sensuality of rococo portraiture to her thesis; she knows she can't, *but hey.*

Then Rebecca starts. Something has made her pull her head from the book: some subconscious foreshadowing, some creak in the floorboards. Some noise. Turning, Rebecca sees: *him*. It is *him*. The thug. The puppy drowner. The very real subject of her very recent lunchtime daydreams is standing in the doorway pretending to look at the book he is holding. The book is an anthology of love poetry, Rebecca notes: but the way he is not truly reading it makes Rebecca realise, with a surge, that quite possibly his real intention is to talk to her; it seems as if he really wants to be talking to her, to be looking at *her*.

So this is it; my pounding heart surcease, Rebecca thinks. For the moment he, the thug, does nothing. He appears to be about to say something, he is surely struggling for the right words, but nothing yet. Closing her eyes Rebecca starts on wondering what he *will* eventually enunciate when he works up the courage; with a pole vault in her heart she considers what cliché'd but lovely line of poetry he'll choose, how he'll opt to mark this wonderful, enchanted, never-to-be-forgotten moment in their now forever twinned and linked-together lives by saying *thou unravished bride of quietness*, or maybe *carentan o carentan* or just possibly *I have desired to go, Where springs not fail, to fields where flies no sharp and sided hail, and a few lilies blow.*

—Great arse!

He says.

3

Fleeing the sunshine and the sight of Rebecca, Patrick steps inside a low metal doorway into a tiny badly carpeted lobby, where he is scrutinised by three policemen standing half visible behind big panes of scratched, thickened glass. Patrick leans and explains, through the grille at the bottom of one pane of glass, that he is up for trial. The policeman looks blank, then mutters, then reads from a big book to his side; with a final, diffident glance at Patrick the policeman nods and buzzes a button which slides open the door of a cylindrical plastic airlock to Patrick's right. Unsure, Patrick turns and steps inside the vertical clear plastic coffin. The circular door behind slides shut; Patrick wonders why the Old Bailey gets its furniture from cheap Seventies BBC space dramas; the arc of transparent plastic that is the door in front jerks open.

Clear of the door Patrick is beckoned through a metal detector arch by the same policeman who gave him the funny look. The policeman then directs him up some steps and turns away as if he does not want to look at Patrick any more.

Patrick approaches some more steps. These are big steps, bigger steps. This is more like it, thinks Patrick. His shoes tap-dancing on the large marble steps Patrick feels a tiny frisson of aesthetic pleasure as he is guided by the dead architect's unseen hand up and out into the cool marble spaces of the Central Criminal Court proper.

—Patrick

It is his lawyer; and his lawyer's junior.

— Hello Mister Stefan

— About time!

— Yes er sorry

— You *do* remember your bail conditions?

Patrick grimaces inwardly, then outwardly. He does not feel like being ticked off, not now, not here. His lawyer seems to notice this. With a lofty chuckle Stefan places a squeezing hand on Patrick's shoulder. At the same time, Charlie Juson, his lawyer's junior, slaps Patrick's other shoulder. Patrick smiles weakly at this display of slightly awkward mateyness, and stares wonderingly ahead. The last time Patrick saw his brief Robert Stefan QC, Robert Stefan QC was in an open-necked shirt leaning back in a relaxed leather chair in his panelled chambers in the blossomy, vernal, High Middle Ages loveliness of a Maytime Inner Temple, discoursing whisky-in-hand-ishly on his wide knowledge of various sex crimes. Here Stefan is in black with a white horsehair wig on his head: looking very serious.

Back then, two months previously, when Patrick had gone to discuss his hopes, his fears, his case, his evidence, his chances of getting jail, cricket, rugby, the precise meaning of the word 'consent' as regards rape trials, Stefan had seemed to Patrick rather young to be a top lawyer, a silk, a Queen's Counsel: which was both worrying and reassuring. Now, here, in the Old Bailey, Stefan seems older and infinitely more serious; which both reassures and frightens Patrick. So Patrick stands here feeling confused; Stefan talks quickly:

— Don't worry, we haven't been called yet

— Right

— Ten thirty I think

— Yes

— But I rather think we're going to be in Court Eighteen are you feeling alright?

— Patch!

Patrick turns.

— I just saw her mother she was staring at me like

— Anderson!

— Chin up you old twat

— Was that her outside? In the school dress?

— First there'll be jury selection

— Then evidence in chief

—Talk about hooters!
—*Joe*

Surrounded by gaggles of over-sarcastic friends and an anxious-looking sister Patrick wonders, slowly. For a moment he feels comforted by this mob-handedness: after all, how can anything go wrong, with all his friends and his sister and probably his mother here and . . . and . . .

And then he remembers that if this were his funeral they would *still* be here, all of them, his friends and family, behaving precisely the same way, being chatty yet sad, feeling guilty but laughing, greeting each other merrily and youthfully and then stopping as soon as they remember where they are. And so now Patrick swoons at the thought that this *is* indeed his funeral, here, stood in the middle of the marble lobby of the Central Criminal Court of Old Newgate Jail he will be gone and never seen again; will be despatched with due ceremony; and with this thought Patrick feels himself transcend, go out-of-body, feels himself levitate above the vortex of buzzing besuited friends and black-cassocked priests-cum-lawyers . . . he is ascending . . . ascending to somewhere, to somewhere where his experience is so beyond what they shall ever experience he is beyond the reach of mutual understanding and they shall none of them ever be friends again.

—Patch you nutter I *told* you not to rape her
—As I've said, with previous convictions, the recommended sentence can . . .
—Tapir!

Crackling through the noise of his friends and lawyers like someone shouting his name at a party Patrick hears a voice come over the court loudspeakers

—**All parties in Skivington please go to Court Number Eighteen**
—That's us

Says Stefan.

Patrick breathes in, breathes out. He sweeps a gaze across the faces in front of him: his lawyer, his friends, his sister. His sister Emily. Emily looks back at him. Her Skivington-blue eyes are slightly moist, her hair slightly dishevelled; her caring for him is evidenced in the lack of care for herself. Holding her brother by his besuited shoulder Emily says:

—Good luck, Patrick
—Yeah mate

Says Joe. Someone else says:

15

— Give 'em hell, y'wanker

A couple of Joe's friends have slapped Patrick on the back; Joe has done the same. With his shoulder still smarting, Patrick is then man-handled by his lawyers, by Robert Stefan and Charlie Juson, up some more expensively shallow, lavishly marble steps, unto a marble cool corridor. Escorted by his legal bouncers, Patrick walks past other lawyers in wigs and kit, past his solicitor Gareth Jenkins who gives Patrick a thumbs-up, past a girl who seems to be crying, past three nasty-looking blokes with tattoos who are staring at the crying girl. Then they stop before a padded door which is all velvet and wood and dignified weight.

The door opens, they step through; the door closes quietly and slowly behind. Patrick lets himself be led into a wooden-railed dock. *The dock*. Patrick sits down on a crap plastic chair and gazes around Court Number Eighteen. It is a long high soft-lit soft-white light-brown-wood-panelled courtroom. A clock ticks on one wall. The other wall is taken up by a jutting gallery; the public gallery? Patrick presumes it is. Patrick leans to try and see who is seeing him from the gallery; he can't quite see. So instead Patrick looks at the royal crest, the Lion and Unicorn above the judge's big wooden throne at the end.

The judge isn't on his throne, isn't in the courtroom, but lots of other people are: a clerk of the court; what Patrick assumes is a stenogra-pher, though he isn't sure what a stenographer is; his own lawyer, now opening his briefcase; another lawyer-type, but older, (older? wiser?? the prosecution???) opening his own briefcase; his solicitor, doing nothing (*nothing?*); some security musclemen who are standing ominously nearby; a yawning policewoman; another policewoman chewing gum; another clerk of the court; and a couple of seedy-looking guys in cheapish suits who are staring him out from some of the side galleries ranked beside the dock. Journalists? Patrick shakes his head and stares at the royal crest above the judge's seat. *Honi Soit Qui Mal Y Pense*.

Something about this agitates him. In his dock, in his seat, Patrick swallows. Although Patrick knows it is a trick, a stunt, a sleight of the psychosocial hand, he feels his pulse race, his heart go fast: *the Majesty of the Law*. He might have been in courts before, but they were nothing like *this*.

Patrick is, now, suddenly, again, scared. He feels like a small boy sent to the headmaster's study. Like a schoolkid walking down the corridor, heading for detention . . . Except this time his detention will result in his spending fourteen years in a cold northern jail before having three broken lightbulbs shoved up his arse by his gay psychotic car-jacking Kurdish cellm . . .

— All Rise

Everybody in the court who wasn't standing now stands; at the back of the court beside the judge's throne a clerk opens a door and a small oldish man walks in wearing a larger wig. The man ascends to the throne and sits down and gazes around and says:

— Good morning, everybody

A good morning is mumbled back by everybody. Everybody sits down who seems to be allowed to sit down; Patrick does the same. At once people start chatting, opening folders, relaxing, moving about the courtroom confusingly but confidently: just people doing what they normally do, on a normal day. *Normal day!* Patrick sits there, marvelling. Then Patrick's lawyer leans across to chat to the man whom Patrick presumes is the prosecution lawyer, Alan Gregory QC. The prosecutor nods, nods again, and then laughs.

!

The spittle of outrage fills Patrick's mouth as he sees this open collaboration, this evidence of conspiracy. How can they be chatting? Laughing? Chatting? Jesusfuck! Patrick is outraged, helpless, stuck in his blue plastic chair in the wooden dock, palsied by impotent anger. Colluding! Conspiring! *Chatting!* Patrick wants to shout out at them: Wankers! Jobsworths! Toffeewombles!

But Patrick does not shout this; shouting out swearwords isn't going to do anything. He realises this. The judge might be a pantsucking fuckbat but . . .

The judge!?!

Patrick eyes up the judge. A good man, surely, hopefully, pleaseGod, yes. Yesyes, a good man. Yes. And so Patrick calms down, and so Patrick calms down. And so he calms down . . . until he has another spasm of panic when he realises that he can't see his friends. Where? Where! Scandal! Before it has fully dawned on Patrick that they are in the public gallery and the public gallery is virtually directly above him, overhanging him, and therefore invisible to him, some official stands up and says:

— Stand up!

Patrick looks around the court to see which idiot is being bossed in

this way. Then he realises it is him: *Patrick Skivington*. Obediently Patrick stands, and steadies his knees. The clerk, or whoever it is, says:
— You are Patrick Skivington of flat two, number thirty-five, Leominster Place, London WC1, correct?

Patrick nods and croaks a quiet *yes*. The clerk says:
— You are charged that on the night of August twenty-eight, two thousand and – Patrick jibes; was it that long ago? The clerk completes the date; then pauses, slightly, before saying – *raped* Rebecca Jessel, contrary to section one of the Sexual Offences Act of nineteen fifty-six – Another significant pause; another glance up – How do you plead?

OK, OK, **OK**. Patrick takes a grip of his thigh. *OK*. Ready. Ready-ready. Firm voice. Big voice. *This is your chance*. For months Patrick has waited for this moment, this moment when he shall express all his outraged innocence, all his innocent hurt, all his unjustly tormented truly-suffering-selfness, in two words. He has only two words, two words to say it all, all he's felt over these last months, this last year, all he felt in prison, all he felt in his cell, all he felt on remand: and so Patrick stands, and lifts his chin and looks directly at the judge, at the Queen, at God, and asseverates, with all the self-righteous self-justification he can adduce in a tone of voice:
— NOT GUILTY

Half a second passes while this sinks in. Then, nothing. Contrary to Patrick's quondam daydreams of the last year, the tone of outraged innocence in his voice fails to instantly convince. The proceedings are *not* summarily dismissed. The court is *not* in uproar. The public gallery is *not* full of hat-waving citizens demanding his immediate release. Nor does the judge glance sharply across at the clerk and say *what is this obviously innocent young man doing here, let him go at once*.

Instead the judge clears his throat and says:
— OK I think we'll have the jury in
— Call the jury!
— *The jury . . .*

Patrick sits down. Around him notepapers have been unfoldered, pens clicked on, wigs taken up. Then the main door opens, and a procession of people are led in, Indian file, one by one. Two of them are indeed Indian: a youngish fanciable girl, and a middle-aged woman in a horrible, oversized jumper. Urgent, Patrick scans these two, and the rest of the jury. Patrick tries to remember Stefan's advice not to eyeball the jurors for fear of frightening them, but he can't help himself. These people are going to be holding his bollocks in their hands, and he wants to assess their bollock-holding fitness-for-purpose.

Eight of the jury are women; only one (a man in a battered brown-leather jacket, with a wry intelligent smile) is the sort of person Patrick would consider even sharing a couple of beers with. Apart from the cute Indian girl. One of the men, a darkish, shortish, possibly foreign man, has an eggshell-blue nylon shirt on. With a glossy green leather tie.

Patrick shudders.

He is doomed.

One by one by one by one by one by one by one by one by one by one by one by one by one the jury is sworn in, each taking a bible in hand:
— I swear by Almighty God to do my best to try the defendant according to the evidence presented . . .

As the jury is sworn in, Patrick weighs up the irony of the fact that he is about to be tried by a man wearing a green leather tie. His fate is about to be decided by a man who buys his clothes second hand in . . . Azerbaijan. This pleasurably snobbish line of thought exhausted, Patrick finds that after this he is actually growing very very very slightly . . . bored. *Bored?* Patrick's sense of doom, of pointlessness, of almost-being-extraneous-to-proceedings has metamorphosed into a kind of numb dull indifference which is barely a whit away from . . . boredom. From his dock seat Patrick idly gazes at the female stenographer, wondering what her nipples are like; until he is shaken out of his maudlin torpor by the annoyingly pompous voice of the prosecutor, Mister Alan Gregory QC.

Gregory has stood up, and is saying to the jury:
— Members of the jury, the case you are about to hear is distressing in the extreme. It involves the savage sexual brutalisation of a young girl by the defendant, Patrick Skivington – Gregory does the faintest of gestures towards Patrick; Patrick thinks how much he wants to staple train timetables to Gregory's head; Gregory goes on – It is my duty as prosecution lawyer to present to you the evidence in a dispassionate and logical light, but also to convince you beyond reasonable doubt that the defendant was responsible for the truly appalling crime you are about to try – A second actorly handwave, then – The burden of proof, as we call it, rests with me. My colleague who is appearing for

the defence – He wafts the same manicured hand at Stefan, who nods, smiles briefly – Has nothing to prove, as such. His job is more to sow doubt, as it were. However I restate that it is my belief that the evidence in this case is overwhelming and conclusive, besides being . . . ah – Looking at the ceiling; looking down – . . . Very upsetting, and that you should encounter no difficulty in finding the defendant guilty – A glance, a glance at Patrick – At this stage in proceedings it is usual for the prosecution counsel to present a kind of résumé of the indictment, a summation, but as we shall be going over all the evidence in some detail more than once I shall restrict myself to a brief precis of the alleged crime – Gregory pauses, gazes down at his papers in a somehow Oxbridge way; Patrick feels his teeth grinding; he tries not to listen to his own teeth, or to Gregory; but can't help – The allegation is simply put: that the defendant, on the night of August twenty-eighth, last year, raped his ex-girlfriend, Rebecca Jessel. But, members of the jury, that bald statement barely begins to describe the true horror of the crime that, the prosecution posits, the defendant perpetrated that night. You all, I hope, have some photos in your files, these photos – Gregory suddenly and unexpectedly holds up a big photo and wafts it at the jury. Even from this distance Patrick can see a picture of his and Rebecca's bedroom. Eyes left, Patrick sees the jurors reaching in folders and looking at the same photo and nodding back at the prosecutor, who smiles so ingratiatingly and says some more stuff that Patrick succeeds in blocking out. For a few moments Patrick is successful in not hearing anything, but then the prosecutor gets a little louder, as if approaching his peroration, and the loudness forces Patrick to listen, to hear Gregory say – Nor was this just a simple case of non-consensual vaginal penetration, the technical definition of rape. No, the prosecution holds that this man, the defendant, also subjected this terrified girl to a number of other degrading acts, to coercive anal penetration, to forced oral sex, to various other sadistic sexual crimes, some of which are dealt with in the ancillary indictments – Adjusting his wig Gregory stands back a touch, as if thinking; then he looks up and goes on – I shall be bringing medical evidence to support this claim. A deal of evidence that will require a . . . strong stomach – Patrick feels his own jaw chewing, jaw-going, his jaw, jawing, hurting – And now, with the court's permission, I should like to call the alleged victim, Rebecca Jessel, to the stand

Patrick lifts and shakes his head and tries to stare bravely at the wall, at the neutral wall above the judge's head. A faint tiny prickling behind his eyes indicates to Patrick Skivington that he would probably be crying if he were ten years old and being picked on like this in the school yard.

Patrick does not cry. He stares forward.

Wasp-face! Dog-features! Badger-breath!

4

—Great arse?

—. . . Yes

—*Great arse?*

—*So?*

—Ha! This Patrick guy – Murphy picks up a pencil, waggles it – Smooth-talking *bastard*!

—It was a book . . .

—Yep O K

—I was looking at a book, of *French rococo art*

—Sure, Becs

—No you don't understand he was looking over my shoulder, at that picture by Boucher – Murphy not responding, Rebecca goes on – The painting of that girl with her bottom in the air, so you see it was really quite sharp

Murphy percusses the end of the pencil against her lips:

—It isn't big and it isn't clever

—Murf!

—I don't mind you lying to me, it's when you lie to yourself

—Ohhh

Amused but frustrated Rebecca says no more. Instead she leans against the edge of Murphy's desk: the only furniture of note in the pale-blond-wooden-floored, mostly white-matt-walled emptiness of Schubert & Scholes, Murphy's gallery.

Rebecca:

—How long *has* it been since *you* had a shag Murf?

— He just sounds rough. Very rough . . . – Murphy is twirling the pencil like a tiny baton between her fingers – Tell me about his criminal record again?

— It's nothing heavy

— Oh, only a *tiny* little bit of GBH

— He got in a couple of fights when he was at Uni

— A couple of fights. Jesus! – Murphy sticks the pencil into her hair, twists hair around the end – That's why they threw him out of his college, the University of Tesco's Car Park, or wherever it was? Right?!

— Yyyess

— Let's face it, he's a bloody caveman

Rebecca tilts her head:

— Mmm. Sexy, isn't it?

— No – Murphy snaps – It's not. It's wanky. The guy's a musclebound fuck-wit and you're all gooey-eyed. Christ! – Murphy gazes into the eyes of her friend – What about all that feminism stuff we studied at Edinburgh, what about Simone de Beauvoir and . . . that other French cow?

— You should see him when he's got a bit of stubble

— Ohhh . . . – The pencil falls from Murphy's fingers, bounces off a two-month-old edition of *Blueprint* magazine, and spins to the pale-blond-wood floor. Murphy looks down, says – I presume you've shagged him already?

— He's such a spunk

— So that makes it OK? You atrocious slut

Surveying a pile of oversized metal film canisters stacked carefully in one corner of the gallery, Rebecca says:

— Actually we haven't – Looking back at her surprised-looking friend, meaningfully – I only went down on him

A clucking noise from Murphy; Rebecca:

— Which I thought was rather restrained

— *Restrained?*

— Comparatively

Murphy:

— Fifteen minutes after meeting the bloke you're on your knees wrestling with his zipper . . . *restrained?*

— Nice and big, by the way

— ?

— And *thick*

Murphy laughs:

—Girth?

—Gerrrrrtthh!

—We Like Gerrrrrtthhhhh!!

Their chorus done, Murphy shakes her head and says:

—Just don't come running when he goes and dumps you you hairy old SLAPPER

A pause. Murphy is bending to pick up the pencil from the floor. Watching her friend bend over, Rebecca assesses her friend's shortish brown hair; her lithe figure; the cuttlefish tattoo she can see above her friend's new jeans-belt. Rebecca, idly:

—Love the belt

—Yeah?

Saying 'yeah I do', Rebecca sits back against the desk again. Looking at a grainy art photo of a power station on the wall, Rebecca says:

—Actually, we've only kissed

—Yeah right – Murphy looks sarcastic and uncomprehending and pleased at the same time – Three dates: and you've only kissed? *Honestly?*

—Honestly

—Wow . . . – Murphy pretends to get up from her chair – Do you want to lie down? I'll get you a blanket

—I think . . . he's a bit . . . inhibited

—*Inhibited?*

—Well, I told him

—*No!*

—Couldn't help it. He took me to some club he knows . . . and we started talking about sex and – Rebecca grins self-consciously – I just stupidly came out with it

—Jesus

—I know – Rebecca mumbles a laugh – Maybe it was a slight mistake

—I've told you, Becs: it frightens them

—But it's just the truth

Murphy shakes her head:

—Twenty-eight different lovers is quite a lot for a twenty-two-year-old

Rebecca, smiling:

—Rather more than he as it turned out

—Where'd he take you then?

—Thirty-one anyway . . . *sorry?*

—Your second date. Where?

—I told you, this club, he knows all these places in Soho cause of

—No, *before* the club

—Oh, some posh restaurant

—Hope he paid

—Of course. It's so awfully unfair isn't it?

A confirming grin, then Murphy says:

—Don't tell 'em – Murphy cocks a finger to her lips – They'll figure it out one day, don't let on . . .

Rebecca nods, distracted, says 'uh-huh'. Again, she looks appraisingly at her friend. Rebecca wonders if and when her best friend will get a boyfriend. Then she wonders if her own impending relationship will affect her friendship with Murphy; then Rebecca realises she has no idea what effect her possible love affair with Patrick will have, because she's never been in love before. In which case, how does she know she is falling in love now? Simply because she's more anxious than normal, more nervously upbeat? More keen to *submit*?

As if telepathically, Murphy says:

—I suppose you're going to go and fall in love with this bozo aren't you?

—No

—YES – Murphy is sighing, urbanely – You're going to sleep with him tonight and by next week you'll be texting him messages on his phone and by autumn you'll be wearing his bloody shirts and then – Murphy stops, nods to herself, decides on the rest of her speech – Then by next spring when you both walk home from restaurants you'll start looking casually in estate agents and then . . . and then . . . – Searching for the right part of London, Murphy goes on, emphatically – Then you'll move in to some stupid *stupid* flat in Clapham and that'll be it. *Finito*. After that you'll only ever ring me when he's been horrible to you and then you'll have a baby and move to Suffolk and spend the weekend wearing Aran jumpers and God it's so *annoying*

—You're jealous. Sweet

—Course I'm fucking jealous – Murphy shakes her head in amazement – Why shouldn't I be jealous. Just don't get hurt? *K*?

—You might be wrong anyway – Rebecca glances at the precious-metal watch, the watch her father bought her for her eighteenth. This makes her feel a pang of something. *Some regret* – He's a bit rough in some ways . . . – She makes a thoughtful face – Anyway I'm meeting him at the pub down the road, in a minute

Murphy, calmer:

—You did say he lives round here, right?

—Ya, it's convenient for his job — Rebecca looks out of the window, as if expecting Patrick to walk by — S'just down the road

—So that's why he fetched up every time we had a sarny

—Yes — Rebecca thinks about Patrick's flat; about the kiss on the sofa, the hand on her nipple — He's got a nice flatmate, very shaggable

Murphy looks up, helpless:

—Really?

—Really. Joe . . . something. Cute bod. Bit of a druggie

—Mmmm?

—Wears a good pair of jeans . . .

—Ooooh . . .

Rebecca starts laughing at Murphy's melodramatic ooooh-noise; Murphy has already stopped laughing. Murphy is saying:

—Hello hello

Rebecca:

—I'll arrange a drink or something. So you can meet him, he's very sweet and funny, I'm sure you'll

—sssss!!

Murphy is nodding towards a well-dressed man who has swung through the plate-glass door from the street; Murphy:

—The Christmas rush!!

Obediently Rebecca gazes across the gallery: at the expensively empty space of Schubert & Scholes now filled by a punter, a customer, a man. The man has an air of wealth, and confidence; enough for Murphy to put on her brightest, most insincere gallery-girl smile.

His hands on his knees, the pinstriped man begins examining a collection of enamelled Japanese household rubbish piled alongside one wall of the gallery. Quickly swivelling to her best friend, Murphy makes a 'sorry I'd better do some work now' expression; slipping herself off the desk Rebecca puts a fist to her tilted head and makes an 'OK I'll ring you tomorrow' gesture.

In Charlotte Street the blue sunshades are up outside Chez Gérard. A few yards further down the road couples are eating noodles outside the Vietnamese place. And on restaurant tables ranked alongside the entire facade of

Pescatori Fish Restaurant big azure-glass ashtrays are glinting expensively in the sun. Walking down this, through this, all this, along her favourite London road, Rebecca feels a head-rush of happiness. She feels a sudden sense of her youngness, her freeness, her possibly-about-to-be-no-longer-singleness. She feels almost ebullient: so ebullient, she finds she is virtually skipping down to the junction of Charlotte and Percy Streets, as she heads for the Marquis of Granby pub.

But before she reaches the Marquis of Granby pub, Rebecca clocks her watch again and realises she has walked so fast, and so ebulliently, and so nearly-skippingly, she is ten minutes early.

So now? Assessing the sun Rebecca sees that it is still slanting brightly enough down Rathbone Place to make it worth working on her tan. Taking a corner seat at one of the wooden pub tables outside the Marquis Rebecca arranges herself: she turns and faces with closed eyes the hot sun, stretching her bare legs out. After a minute of this Rebecca opens her eyes, and sees that her legs are already the subject of some male consternation. One besuited barely-out-of-his-teens drinker is openly pointing at her. For his benefit, without making it too obvious, Rebecca raises her dress an inch or two higher; thinking of Rembrandt's wife in the painting as she does so.

More heads turn. A tongue actually *lolls*. Rebecca has never seen a tongue *loll* before, but there one is, *lolling*. At her. Not for the first time in her life, Rebecca decides she actually quite enjoys *this*: the sensation of masculine eyes upon her. It makes her feel like a mid-period Picasso at a glamorous auction; it makes her feel like an attractive woman. Sitting here being sizzled by the heat Rebecca starts to wonder why some art history feminists get so worked up about *the male gaze*. How so? Why so het up about leers and oeillades? Rebecca does not comprehend it. These staring men make Rebecca feel strong, empowered, aristocratic. To Rebecca right now these men look like so many Catholic French peasants gazing at *le Roi Soleil*. Dumb, resentful, awestruck *serfs* . . .

Thinking of this, primrosing down this intellectual path, Rebecca wonders unwontedly if she can spin a thesis out of this, out of, say, the male gaze as serf-like feudal reflex. Perhaps, she decides, she could; but then, she decides, she shouldn't. All these thoughts of matters historical, and theoretical, and thesis-esque, are in fact making Rebecca feel a simultaneous twinge of *guilt*. Because she isn't working even on her present project, her Crusader thesis, hardly. At all.

Rebecca opens her eyes, worried now. Ever since she and Patrick met, she thinks, she's done *virtually nothing* towards her PhD. And this does not make Rebecca feel empowered and royal: right now this makes her feel crap, teenage, girly and feeble. God it's so crap, Rebecca decides, pulling down her dress to hide her legs: that a mere man can come along and upend her priorities, distort her intellectual life, make nonsense of her ambitions and life goals, by **not having shaved for a day or two**. How gay is that?

So she must do some work, Rebecca decides, just to show she isn't just a cheerleading troupe of hormones.

Sighing in the sunshine, putting down her pint of lager, Rebecca takes a textbook out of her bag, the ever-present, hardly-touched Crusades history book, and starts to read up. Flicking pages she comes upon the section she was deconstructing up until . . . the bit she was studying up and unto the moment Patrick walked casually through the front door of her life, like he'd had a key all along . . .

Patrick . . . ? Patrick . . . PATRICK. Rebecca wonders why it should be Patrick that finally stirs her, rather than any other. He's nice-looking, she thinks; not the most good-looking. So is it because he's like her father? Rebecca cannot imagine anyone less like her passive, diffident, tentative, bridge-playing father. Is it then because he's like her mother?

Rebecca shudders.

Then it must be because he's like neither; the opposite of both. In which case, how will *her parents* react to *him*? And how will he react to them? Can they possibly get on? Will Patrick understand the set up? Will he despise Rebecca for living at home, with her parents, at her age, for having sloped back home so as to do her London Uni PhD? Will he understand that she only did this because home was luxurious, convenient, palatial, and cheap . . .

Work!

Page opened, page corner unfoxed, Rebecca reads. She has to work. Lips firmed, she begins:

As the Crusaders trekked across Europe towards the Holy Land, they left a trail of dead. In Speyer, Worms and other German cities they butchered Jews in their thousands. Witnesses in Mainz, in particular, reported fearful scenes of panic, of terrified Jewish women barricading themselves in their houses, and throwing gold coins out of the windows, to try and distract the rampaging soldiery.

To no avail. The pogrom was savage, and relentless, and shocking, even by the . . .

—Hello?

Eyes up, Rebecca sees that: *yes!* it's Patrick. Half stooping Patrick kisses Rebecca on her grateful cheek, turning her face Rebecca turns this into a kiss on the lips. At this Patrick seems to start, then stop. For a second Patrick seems unsure again: he just stands there. Rebecca takes this chance to shut and bag her book, and also to appraise Patrick: to assess his hiply retro jeans, his cool white cotton shirt, his two days' stubble. Sensing the appraisal, Patrick makes a wry face, and a buying-the-drinks gesture, and disappears inside the pub. Two minutes later he comes out with two pints of coldish lager which the two of them sit and drink quickly, and thirstily, while they talk. After these two pints Patrick goes into the pub and buys two more pints; they drink these two almost as quickly. They are getting drunk. As Rebecca gets drunk, Patrick gets drunk, and the two of them talk excitedly and happily as they get drunk. The fact that they are getting drunk means they keep breaking into laughter apropos of nothing. This in itself makes Rebecca feel quite strange inside: sipping her beer, calming herself, she tries to concentrate on what Patrick is saying. Patrick is explaining that the small record label which he is helping to run has just bought an even smaller label which means they now have a roster of Asian ambient techno bands to promote and, *yes*, Rebecca thinks, *his tanned chest looks nice with that silver cross against it.*

Patrick has stopped talking. Rebecca makes a sorry-I-was-distracted-could-you-say-that-again face. Patrick shakes his head:

—Like you're interested

—Oh I am

Patrick laughs:

—Lying tart

—No no really tell me more about that Asian thrash metal scene

—OK OK – He chuckles – Do you fancy coming back to my flat?

Eyes on his laughing eyes, eyes on his thick, black, slightly violent hair, Rebecca wonders: about Patrick's differentness, his maleness, his foreign-ness. As Patrick makes some more noises it comes to Rebecca that his Irish-English-Britishness is as foreign to her as, no doubt, as a Jewess, she is to him. She is his Outremer. He is her Frankish knight. And this is their First Crusade.

And perhaps, Rebecca thinks, *I overintellectualise*

—Got some Kiwi Riesling

—Uhhh, sorry?

Looking at Rebecca with a cool expression, of amused bemusement, Patrick says:

—I was . . . suggesting – He slows, deliberately – That we eat at my place, I could do some food, open a bottle of white or something. You know?

Nodding demurely, saying 'sure', Rebecca sips at her lager. Then she gives up on being demure and gulps the rest of her beer down. As she wipes her lips with the back of her hand, he laughs. Rebecca sarcastically apologises and says:

—Did you not know I was a complete lush?

Fitting his empty beer glass into the circle of dampness it has already made, Patrick says:

—Come on – Holding out a hand he takes Rebecca's hand, and thereby helps her up and away.

Pleased to be holding hands with him, worried her hands are perspiring, noticing he is checking out her cleavage as they walk along, Rebecca says nothing. Together, hand in hand, they walk down Windmill Street, over Tottenham Court Road, along the side roads to Patrick's flat. *His flat*. To the bare, unpainted stairs of his first-floor shared apartment.

In the flat they stand, slightly awkward. Rebecca makes a comment about how nice and bright it is in the day, and of course how centrally located. Patrick makes a mumbling noise about how he grew up in a boring small town and therefore has a fear of living in small towns or suburbs; how living away from the centre of London makes him feel like he is dying. Dying in prison. Then he laughs and says:

—I'll get a drink

Into the sitting room, flooded with square sunlight from the large first-floor windows, Rebecca kneels in her summer dress on the polished bare floorboards and starts checking out Patrick's bookshelves. From the kitchen she can hear sounds of him, uncorking bottles, clattering plates and cutlery. The last time she was in this flat, she thinks, the only other time she was in this flat, she had been very very drunk and it was very very dark and she had not had the time to case the bookcase, to do the essential appraisal. So now is her chance.

—White wine OK then?

—Yes – Rebecca calls back, through the walls, into the kitchen – Yes please fine

So: the bookcase. Running her eyes along the spines, feeling slightly guilty about her intellectual snobbishness, Rebecca does her assessment.

De Bernières, of course; *Bridget Jones*, slightly surprising; Tolstoy, v.g.

—Dressing on your salad?

—Yes, please, whatever

Thinking for a second about the Tolstoy, pleased about the Tolstoy, Rebecca moves on.

Pushkin, golly; Nick Hornby, hmmm; Turgenev, wow; Akhmatova, even better.

Hmm.

—God I love rocket

He is calling from the kitchen again. Rebecca laughs something in agreement and completes her research. It doesn't take long. Apart from the literature and fiction titles she's seen, the rest of the shelves are stuffed with boy books: psychology, sociobiology, politics, rugby; books on fascism, cricket, anti-Semitism, sex, ant society, human evolution and Southampton FC. For the life of her Rebecca doesn't know what she thinks about the maleness of these bookshelves. Here is the intellectual equivalent of a fridge with just two beer cans in it. *Is that good or bad?*

As she tries to assess her own reaction Rebecca notices that Patrick has returned with a bowl of salad, two plates, and some cutlery lodged like a tango dancer's rose in his mouth; getting to her feet, slightly embarrassed to have been caught checking his shelves, Rebecca takes the forks out of Patrick's mouth, as he turns and produces from behind him two wineglasses full of cold white Riesling. Rebecca notes that Patrick is looking down her cleavage again as he stops to place her wineglass on the windowshelf.

They sit side by side on the sofa; eat the salad. The salad is nice, the wine nicer. Rebecca decides to ask:

—The books – She says, with half a mouthful of rocket – They all yours?

—Yeah – He answers, similarly mouth full – Mostly. The fiction tends to be Joe's, all the poetry and Russian crap

—Right

—And all the science stuff is basically mine

—Uh . . . – Rebecca says – *Huh*

They both go quiet as they eat. At one point they both laugh nervously at the same time; then they both laugh genuinely because they have both laughed nervously at the same time. Then Patrick:

—And the music's totally mine

He is gesturing behind her. Turning on the sofa Rebecca takes in, for the first time, the entire opposite wall. The entire opposite wall is comprised of floor-to-ceiling shelves holding CDs, singles, tapes, DATs, minidisks, LPs, DVDs, God knows. Thousands of titles, literally thousands. Even from this distance, with her dim knowledge of music, Rebecca can see there is a notable mixture: jazz, blues, acid house, Celtic folk, Yorkshire brass band, Karlheinz Stockhausen (Karlwho Stockwhat?), Wagner, bluegrass, flamenco. Pulled especially from the rack is a row of CDs, standing together by the player.

Setting her finished plate of salad on the floor Rebecca skips over to the row of CDs; kneeling, and wine-sipping, and gazing, she checks out the titles of these chosen CDs. What he is listening to now. Minnie Ripperton, Maria Callas, Joy Division, Nick Drake (?), the Carpenters, Elvis, Blind Melon (??), Jacqueline du Pré.

Again, despite her misty grasp on things musical, and the fact that she is now really quite drunk, quite pleasantly, happily drunk, Rebecca realises there is something odd, something almost too eclectic about this selection. With her wineglass in hand, feeling pleasantly sluttish, Rebecca is about to swivel and ask him about the music, when she feels his lips on her neck. His arms are around her waist from behind, making her feel slim. His voice is close, boozy, warm:

—Dead cred

—Mmnn?

Her voice is slurred. His voice is closer, hotter:

—You see I've had an idea we should release a CD

—Nn

—Made up entirely of music by glamorously dead people, like all those

—Realll

—Yess – He is kissing her earlobe – Cause I think there's something about music by dead people, interestingly dead people – Another kiss – Something that's incredibly powerful – Another kiss – And better and poignant and the copyright might be a nightmare but we could call it Dead Singers' Songs – Two kisses, four – And I think it would it would it might oh God Rebecca your breasts they are SO

—Here – She says, laughing – Here, you unbuckle it *here*

5

— So when did you first meet Mister Skivington?

In the witness box, Rebecca coughs. Then she looks flatly across the various heads that comprise the courtroom and she says:

— two years ago

The prosecutor nods and smiles, but his smile is uncertain. The judge intervenes:

— I'm sorry Miss Jessel but you'll have to speak up

— sorry

In the dock Patrick exhales. He wants to curse, loudly. So where did she get *this* voice? His articulate, educated, cultured, self-confident, sexually experienced, words-like-*Weltanschauung*-knowing twenty-four-year-old ex-girlfriend: where did she suddenly acquire this meek, quiet, bashful, timid, inarticulate, hushed, I-am-oh-so-innocent teenagerish voice? Cursing quietly Patrick rests his forehead on two thumbs pointing up from interlocked hands; then he looks up to hear the judge say to Rebecca:

— The jury must be able to hear every word, you see

Rebecca nods:

— Yes, I'm . . . very sorry

The judge smiles reassuringly at Rebecca, and then turns back to the prosecutor's grey wig:

— Do you want to repeat the question, counsel?

The wig nods. Laying down a pen on a desk, wrapping a hand around a black gown, gazing once more at his principal witness in her gingham-checked dress and her lambswool cardigan, the suntanned prosecutor opens his mouth and says:

— So you met the defendant about two years and two months ago?

— Yes. In a bookshop

— And you began . . . dating, soon after that?

— Yes

Dating? Patrick twitches, feels the horrible triteness of the word. He and Rebecca never *dated* . . .

— And how long after that did your relationship begin?

— A couple of . . . weeks. Maybe three . . .

— You were at college at the time?

— Yes. King's College. London University. I still am

— What are you are studying?

— History. The Crusades

— And you are doing – The prosecutor looks at his file for a fact already, quite obviously, in his head – A PhD, yes?

— A doctorate, yes

— And your bachelor's degree, from Edinburgh University – His eyes lifting – What was that in?

Rebecca shrugs:

— Art History

— And you – Gregory pauses, half smiles – took first-class honours in that, am I right?

— Yes

With a slight turn of the body towards the jury the prosecutor pauses to let this important fact take root, then says:

— OK. Now, fairly soon after this, as I understand . . .

And so it goes on. As Patrick sits in the dock and tries not to stare, hard, at Rebecca, at the side of her blonde head, Rebecca is asked to describe the inception and genesis of their relationship: from the first meeting, the first date, the first sex. *As she sees it; as she saw it.*

— I was seeing someone else but you see

— We went to a restaurant and we

— He was older than me so I

And during this litany Patrick has to admit, despite himself, that his lying cow of an ex looks surprisingly sweet, trembly and believable in the witness box. Surprisingly young, fresh, and betrayed. And raped. And in turn Patrick feels cheated, intrigued, guilty, scandalised, stressed-out, odd and libidinous. Not least because of Rebecca's get-up. Obviously she is wearing the schoolgirly dress as a deliberate move; self-evidently she chose the pale cardigan, unheeled sixth-former shoes, and the throat-exposing hairstyle this very morning – in a deliberate attempt to gain sympathy, as self-conscious props designed to assist her in her role as the wronged adolescent, the abused child-bride. Yet Patrick still has to admit to himself: the ensemble *works*. At least: it works for him. Looking at her looking all schoolgirly and vulnerable, gamine and young and quite-possibly-raped-a-year-ago, Patrick wants nothing so much as to take Rebecca into the Old Bailey toilets and press her pleading face against the cold Edwardian tiling, *hard*.

— He was in the music business. He ran nightclubs and groups . . .

— I'd never really fallen for someone like him before

— I found him interesting and

Stuck in the dock Patrick wonders. As he watches his ex-girlfriend do her evidence in chief, he has to ponder how well she is going down. How well is she going down? If he were in the jury box, the visitors' gallery, what would he see here in this pale-wood-panelled Old Bailey courtroom? Would he see a farce, or a tragedy? Or would he nip to the pub instead? Would he just dawdle a while and listen to Rebecca and then turn to a mate and say – *oh forget it, this bastard's going down. Boring.*

And what precisely would he think of Rebecca? Would he empathise? Be repulsed? Find himself moved? Would he be touched by the pale rapeable baby pink of her lambswool cardigan? Or be appalled by this lying whore of a Jewess lisping her ex-lover into court?

— So you became lovers when?

— . . . On the fourth or fifth time

— That's mid-June?

— Yes . . . I think so . . . it's . . . – Rebecca lifts her blonde head and gazes frankly at the counsel – Difficult to be specific

— We understand, Miss Jessel, we don't need actual dates

— I wish I could be more accurate . . . – She tilts her head and looks young – It's a bit . . . *you know* . . .

At this the whole court seems to nod in sympathy; even Patrick feels himself nod sympathetically, too. It *is*. She's right. It's . . . a bit . . . *you know*.

— And you continued going out all that autumn . . . and over the new year?

—Yes

—Until eventually you moved in together . . . the following spring?

—Yes . . .

—So. Let me get this right – A slight adjustment to the wig. A slightly self-conscious adjustment – By this time, Miss Jessel, would you say that . . . – The prosecutor stops again; stares at the wall behind Rebecca's head; he seems to consider something written on the wall, as he starts again – Would you say that you were in love with the defendant?

Rebecca looks puzzled. The courtroom stares at her puzzlement, rapt. Only the stenographer and Patrick are not looking straight at Rebecca. Patrick is looking out the side of an eye. Stretching out an arm to steady herself against the panel of the witness box Rebecca swallows, shrugs, looks pained, looks at her hands, says:

— . . . I suppose. Yes

—Only suppose?

— No. Yes. Definitely. Very much so

—Why?

— Why?

—Why were you in love with him? What was it that . . . attracted you to him?

— He was . . . funny, different. I . . .

—He was fun?

— Yes. Cynical but amusing, I mean . . . sort of sexy . . .

In the dock Patrick tries not to puff with pride: *sexy! Sexy and funny! I'm sexy and funny . . . and amusingly cynical!* Then he remembers he is on trial for rape. Embarrassed by himself he leans forward and listens to Rebecca say:

— But it wasn't just that about him

Alan Gregory QC:

—No? What else was it?

Rebecca shakes her head, turns her head to look at the judge; the judge smiles paternally as if to say *go on*; Rebecca turns back and goes on:

— I don't know. How can you define it?

—*It*, Miss Jessel?

— Love. Whatever it was . . . it was love – Again – We were in love

The court goes more quiet, more still. From the dock Patrick can almost hear the jury's huge enjoyment. He can sense their pleasure at this laid-on melodrama, this subsidised soap opera, its clichés withal. *His life. His trial.*

— So you definitely would say you loved him?

— ... Yes. I would – Rebecca nods, and then swallows, apparently with difficulty. Doing his own bit, the judge asks Rebecca if she wants a glass of water; Rebecca shakes her head and says no and goes on – He was ... he was ... – Head high, she confesses – As a man, Patrick was easy to fall in love with ...

Rebecca stops. Patrick looks at her and feels again an unwonted pang of pride, and also gratitude for what she has said; he wonders how difficult it was for his ex-girlfriend to say that. Then he watches, trying not to be sympathetic, as Rebecca steadies herself again. Rebecca looks, now, as if she is resisting the urge to turn across the courtroom and stare at Patrick, to turn her delicate well-bred doesn't-need-make-up face on Patrick. Sat on his plastic chair in the dock Patrick studies Rebecca not looking at him: he can see a very slight painterly pinkening around Rebecca's delicate nostrils, as if she is flushed with difficult emotions. Patrick nearly flinches, seeing this, feeling Rebecca's unspoken suffering. He feels like blushing.

But why? Why should he blush? *For-God's-sake.* Affronted by his own thoughts, Patrick sits and gazes away from her, ignoring Rebecca's words about their love. He doesn't want to think of their love. Doesn't want to think of her lies. It was true they were in love; it's lies what she says now. So how does he disentangle them? How does he unloom this skein of mendacity and veracity? And if *he* doesn't know how to do it, how does the jury? How?? HOW?

Patrick is choked by confusion. He feels like swearing. Or shouting out. Or crying. But why? He never cries anyway, or hardly ever, so why here? Because the girl he loved more than himself is now twenty yards away trying to put him in prison? Why should he cry at that?

— Miss Jessel?

Rebecca has gone quiet, she has lowered her head, and stopped talking about their love; now she is gazing across the court: gazing out. To Patrick she looks as if she is gazing out the window onto some sunlit pastoral scene, gazing at elm-shaded watermeadows, some fields where the fritillaries dance ...

Rebecca is saying, slowly:

— I loved him more than I've ever loved anybody else in my life

Pause, gown, lapel, Alan Gregory:

—And you think he felt the same way?

— I'm not sure . . . You'd have to ask him. I think maybe . . .

A pause; then, she says again:

— . . . maybe

For the first time, so far, Rebecca stops. Totally. Just for a moment Rebecca looks like she is really truly struggling to compose herself, to think of something to say. As she struggles, and succeeds, in maintaining her composure Patrick blatantly stares. For all Patrick's lawyer's stern advice *never to stare at Rebecca* Patrick is looking directly at Rebecca thinking how much *he* loved *her*, too: because she made him so desperately happy when he was with her, so desperately unhappy when not. So: what does that mean? That he obviously doesn't love her any more? Patrick is even more confused, startlingly angry: with everyone, with her, with himself. He doesn't know what he should do, he doesn't know what he's meant to think, he knows what he wants to do. Right now Patrick wants to cross the dreamy dissolving non-reality of the courtroom and take Rebecca in his arms; he wants to gather the harvest of her narrow waist to his waist, and cuddle her, and comfort her, and kiss the place where her blonde hair thins to her warm and living temple.

And then he wants to grab a fistful of hair and nonchalantly spin her round and hoist her over the sill of the dock and reach under her dress for the elastic of her panties.

—So you moved in together in February of that year?

— Yes

—And this was his idea as much as yours?

— Yes, we both wanted it

—Who was paying the rent, Miss Jessel?

— I was, mostly

—I'm sorry? *You* were paying? – The prosecutor is standing back, pretending to be shocked.

Patrick feels like laughing aloud at this. Patrick feels like openly laughing at the actorliness of this cameo; at the prosecutor's overdramatised reaction. Looking left Patrick checks out the lined-up twelve faces of the jury to make sure they saw this, too, to make sure they are fully aware of the prosecutor's phoniness.

But the jury, the Asian girl, the man in the green tie, the older Asian woman, all of them: they're just gazing back at the prosecutor, soaking it all up, taking it all in, unflinching, suspending disbelief. In the dock Patrick sighs, bitterly.

Three yards from the dock the prosecutor is making a frown – I don't understand, Miss Jessel. Didn't he *have* a job?

— Yes, but . . . – Rebecca sounds as if she is embarrassed; embarrassed for *Patrick* – You see, his business started going under . . .

— The nightclub?

— The club, yes. And the label

— Was he losing a lot of money?

— Yes. They were going bankrupt

Now Patrick wants to squirm. So what? So what's this got to do with anything? Chin on paired thumbs Patrick listens depressedly and involuntarily to the lawyer vowelling away in his pompous English way.

— *Miss Jessel*

The prosecutor is beginning to assert himself. Using Rebecca's mumbled monosyllables, exploiting to the full each tiny *yes* and *he did* Gregory is beginning to take over the court, casually laying out the truths as he sees it: the truths about Patrick's sex life, and Patrick's social life, about Patrick's violence, about Patrick's drinking. On top of the revelations about Patrick's career this comes hard. It makes Patrick queasy. Patrick feels like this is some medieval ordeal, some game with the pilliwinks and gyves. A devious and cruel sport designed to make him squeal in mental pain, and thus reveal his evilness. Patrick flinches in the dock, waiting for the next barbed question, the next prosecutorial thrust. He watches Gregory like a kid in the dentist's chair, fearfully eyeing the dentist to see what hideous tool he will choose next. Then Patrick once more curses Rebecca for bringing him to this: this profound embarrassment.

The worst of it is that Patrick can see all too easily what Gregory is doing, why he is doing this stuff, asking these questions about Patrick and Rebecca's financial relationship, their resultant arguments, the death of the nightclub. The prosecution is leading them all by the hand, along the tortuous coastal path of the evidence, to a place where the gorse of doubt will finally part, allowing the prosecutor to stand and point to where the sea of certainty serenely twinkles in the sunlight: the sea of certainty that tells them that Patrick Skivington is a juvenile fool, who, because his job went arseover, and he couldn't cope with adversity, and he felt like and indeed was an inadequate wretch cuckolded by life, came back one sad and sordid evening to rape the living Jesus out of his innocent young girlfriend Miss Rebecca Jessel, now of fifteen Goldsworthy Drive, Hampstead Garden Suburb, NW3, then of flat two, number seven Linden Street, Marylebone West One.

— Did he ever hit you?

— Yes

— When?

Rebecca looks downcast; Alan Gregory shuffles some paper importantly and confidently on his desk; grips the lapel of his gown; repeats the question. In turn Rebecca nods, pained, self-evidently pained by having the truth winkled out of her, the terrible truth:

— He hit me once . . . I . . .

— Take your time

— It was just before . . . you know . . .

— Go on

— We'd had a party. Patch

This is the first time she has used Patrick's nickname; the sound of it in her mouth feels to Patrick so painful and sweet, touching and hypocritical at once.

— Patch came home, he came home from the office with a friend. He came back drunk and he and Joe they fooled around and he was

In the dock Patrick closes his eyes like he is about to do a macho swoon, like it isn't just his nickname in her mouth but *him* in Rebecca's mouth. Patrick feels like she has him in her mouth just one more time and she is sucking him slowly, looking up at him, ominously submissive.

— He was drunk. He started hitting me . . . He was angry

Half sucking, half *biting*.

— Why? Why was he angry?

— I think . . . because . . . I was . . .

— Yes?

— As I said his nightclub wasn't working out . . . so . . .

Just *biting*.

— You mean he . . . – The prosecutor looks like he is pained by his own upcoming dip into the vernacular – 'Took it out on you'?

— Yes – Rebecca's voice goes even quieter. The judge asks her to speak

up again; Rebecca apologises, meekly. She takes in one big breath and visibly grips the banister of the witness box as she says to the far corner of the cream-painted courtroom – He hit me quite badly
— You were bruised?
— Yes
— Did anybody else know about this?
— Well . . .

Crossing his legs, crossing his arms, Patrick switches desperately off. He just doesn't want to hear this bit. The bits that aren't complete lies are the total truth: both hurt. He crosses his arm and looks at his watch, watches it tick towards lunch, as Rebecca goes on about their arguments, their fights, about the last fight before he left, before she kicked him out. Rebecca is rambling, believably; the prosecutor is gently nudging her rambles along, and Patrick is looking at his wristwatch and thinking, seriously, with passion:

Is this it? Rebecca? Where is the other truth? The real truth? Where is the love, the sex, the death, the Aztecs? Suddenly he feels like standing up and asking her, shouting: *nothing about me and Joe? Nothing about why I was angry? Nothing about my dad and your needs and my love? Your cunt? NO?*

The prosecutor is in full flow now:
— So you decided to finish it?
— yes
— How long was it before you saw him again?
— yes
— And that was when you changed the locks?
— yes
— And he took how much money out of your account?
— yes yes YES

Patrick tries not to look or listen: Rebecca is unmistakably shaken. Under this barrage of friendly but piercing questions she has stopped, to control herself. Her voice is quieter than ever, her face shakes behind the lattice of one draped hand; her lips are smeared with pink; her delicate nostrils are pinked. And her hair is young, gold, meek and sweet.

Then the court's awed and worried silence is shattered as the judge leans nearer Rebecca and says *I think we better take a break for lunch here* but Patrick doesn't really listen to this. Patrick just stares at his girlfriend, his ex-girlfriend, the girl, the bitch, the liar, the bogus emoter, and thinks:

Jesus, Bex. You loved me that much?

6

Lifting his coffee-bar-type soup cup full of takeaway Chinese soup Joe blows low; then sips; then grimaces. Patrick:
—Something wrong with the soup?

Joe shakes his head, lowers the cup:
—Yeah no . . . *yeah*
—What?
—This soup. It's that stupid *healthy* Chinese shit
—Yeah?
—With *no* monosodium glutamate
—. . . So?

Joe sits forward on the sunlit Soho Square bench, gazes mournfully into his soup:
—I like MSG . . .

Joe goes quiet, as he gingerly sips. Patrick looks at Joe. Then Patrick says:
—You know, sex is in many ways the monosodium glutamate of life

Joe:
—Oh *God*
—It makes what would otherwise be unpalatable palatable, it makes the boring samey noodles of life that extra bit
—OK shut up – Joe says, then he says – Anyway why did I *buy* soup? It's thirty degrees in the shade and I buy *soup*? Man

From his side of the bench Patrick clicks his tongue, in empathy. Then Patrick returns to his own takeaway tray of sushi. Patrick can sense Joe watching on, hungrily, enviously, as Patrick chopsticks a smear of translucent tuna belly, briefly dips the fish in a little plunge-pool of soy, then deftly drapes the result between his lips.

Joe:

—You know your gran sucks your *pants*?

—Uh-huh

—She told me in bed last night

—Right – Patrick says – Right . . . Well . . .

—Yeah?

—Your girlfriend told me your cock looks like a weasel with a goitre on its head

—What girlfriend? – Joe shakes his head, says – How is she anyway?

—Sorry??

Joe, tutting:

—*Your* girlfriend, the rich one . . . you met her in a bookshop two months ago, you've been sleeping with her ever since – Slowly – She's OK, yeah?

Silence. Patrick contemplatively stirs a few stray grains of rice around his little puddle of soy. Then he says:

—Tits are too big

Joe:

—As *if*

—No they are, too big, and too . . . *firm*

—*Don't*

—Too firm and too good, wasted on me, those big creamy

—You *cunt*, Skivington

—Oh, I forgot, you like big ones, don't you?

—Suck my cock

—Actually – Patch relents – I was thinking of bringing you in on the tits, as a kind of, breast consultant

—Kind of bomb disposal?

—. . . professional tit wrangler . . .

Together they shout:

—Breast whisperer!!!

After that the two of them grin. Then Patrick eats some more rice as he sidelong watches Joe. His friend is staring out onto the sunlit lawns of a crowded Soho Square garden. Kneeling sideways on a rare space of lunchtime grass is a young mother with her baby. Joe is silently regarding this *pietà*. The mother is kissing her baby's foot, sucking its toes. Joe seems to nod approvingly at this, then he says:

—So, are you falling for her?

Patrick, with a mouthful of salmon roe:

—. . . not sure – Swallowing – She's a package

—*Yeah?*

—Yeah. Pretty, sexy, rich . . . bit Jewish

—Nice legs, shame about the faith?

The sound of some shirtsleeved office lads arguing fills the air. Patrick looks at Joe. Joe looks at Patrick. Joe says:

—Sorry about that

Turning his face to the sun, Patrick nods and in a vague voice says:

—How about you, any progress with the redhead?

—Nah

—Not at all?

Joe shrugs:

—They all like want someone with a big car and . . . no crack habit

—Sticklers

—*Nit pickers*

—So you're wanking a lot? Bashing the bishop . . . ?

A pause. Then Joe says, in an odd voice, above the sound of a bike courier's yowling radio:

—It's true to say the upper hierarchy of the church has come in for some criticism

Patrick thinks for a while about this, sniggers for a second, then says:

—You're still missing that last girl aren't you? The last one

—Sally-Ann? *My little Sally-Ann?*

—That ugly smackhead with no arse

—Yeah, Sally-Ann . . .

A car alarm makes a horrible noise. Patrick tuts. Wiping some sweat from his forehead with a forearm, checking his watch as if he has something to do, Joe starts on a slow speech:

—Y'know, I remembered something this morning, when I woke up, alone again – Joe tilts his head, goes on – When we were, like, together, me and Sal, she used to do this thing – Joe pauses, and turns his eyes on the middle distance, as if toward the distantly heard sound of a much loved pop song – When I was asleep she would do some smack and then roll over and kiss me and blow the smack smoke into my mouth – Joe makes a wry sad face – Which meant, like, I wouldn't have to wake up, like, *clean*, so I wouldn't have to suffer reality even for a fucking *minute* in the *morning*

Patrick sits on the bench, wondering what to say to this. Not knowing what to say he joins his friend in looking out across the Square at a group of toenail-painted secretaries sharing a packet of organic crisps on the grass. At length Joe says:

—Wish I had some fucking smack now . . .

—Really?

—Yeah, really

—So why don't you? Just buy some?

As if to assist Joe in his purchase, Patrick points his Pepsi-can-gripping hand across the Square to a markedly deserted corner of the sunlit lawn. Where a gaggle of obvious drug addicts is lying, under a single big dirty blanket, like a family of Victorian street-Irish. Next to the addicts stands a stack of unsold, or stolen, *Big Issues*. Patrick watches as Joe shrugs at the prospect, as if to say 'why bother'; then Patrick returns his gaze to the tribe of drug addicts. *Like a troupe of Aborigines in an outback Aussie town*, Patrick thinks. *The junkies. They are the Abos of London, following the songlines of their addiction around the twilit streets, moving from waterhole to waterhole, moving from chemist to dealer to dodgy doctor, following their ancestral and mysterious routes around the underworld of the city . . . Which makes me*, Patrick thinks, running away with himself now, *which makes me Crocodile Dundee, a man who understands their ways yet is not of them and yet who*

—You've not shagged her yet have you?

Patrick thinks hard, says:

—Of course I have

—So why aren't you totally in love?

—Did I tell you – Patrick says – About my idea for a new hobby?

Joe sighs:

—Mn. Go on then . . .

—Well – Patrick takes a drink of his warming Pepsi, takes another shot of it. And then another shot and then a third shot before slowly burping most of the next sentence – I'm thinking of buying an Alsatian dog and a long leather coat and getting my head shaved and then going up to Golders Green Station and shouting out 'SCHNELL! SCHNELL! SCHNELL!' at people as they get off the train

—Why aren't you crazy about her then?

—OK . . . – Patrick sighs – She's got thick ankles

—*Thick ankles?* Jesus! Dump her!

—And the drug thing, her drug history, it's a problem

—The fact she hasn't ever done drugs?

—Exactly – Patrick goes quiet and pensive. Then he goes on – But that's not it, that's not the real problem. I do really like her, you know . . . I mean . . . – To fill the gap in his thoughts Patrick steps down from the bench, and goes to an overfull Soho Square rubbish bin; after carefully balancing his empty sushi tray on top of the enormous pile of rubbish he returns and sits back on the bench and says – Even though we've got less in common, or not as much as some . . . I like her . . . precisely because sh . . . sh . . .

—Sh?

—Because she's different. Smart. Cultured – Seizing the theme, Patrick runs with it – Really. She's amazing. She knows all about art, and politics, and history, it's incredibly refreshing – Examining the tan mark where his forearm meets his rolled-up white shirtsleeve, he says – Maybe I'm just too used to Soho ladettes smoking rollups and farting, do you think that could be it? – Patrick looks over at Joe; Joe nods, says:

—So it's the hooters then?

Patrick:

—No, I like them big, and I *love* the arse

—So what the FUCK?

—I know, I know . . . – Patrick sighs – I knowwww – Feeling the heat now, he unbuttons another one of the buttons on his expensive white shirt and then he slumps back to let the sun run its fingers through his chest hair. After a few seconds, feeling properly relaxed for the first time this lunchtime, Patrick admits – Actually I think I know what it is

—?????

—Yes. I think – Struggling to be honest – I think I just . . . like . . . girls to be . . . shorter, poorer, younger, and stupider than me

—She's certainly shorter than you

—Ta, Joe

—And – Joe says – She's a lot younger, isn't that enough? Not enough *dimorphism*?

Patrick stalls, does not reply. For a moment the college friends are united in quietness, experiencing each other's post-lunch metabolic low. Patrick is thinking about perhaps saying something else. Right now Patrick thinks he would like to confess to Joe that what he really needs is for Rebecca to be more submissive, because he's now realised he needs something sexually very submissive in women, something more than Rebecca has so far given him. Then Patrick decides he can't be arsed to talk about relationship stuff anymore. Instead Patrick looks idly and languidly at a beautiful girl in lowslung jeans and silver navel ring, as she swings her hips through the Square towards Oxford Street. For a full minute Patrick watches the girl's walk. Then he swerves to take in another chick just behind that one. Then he looks back at the first one. And her friend.

Stuck by lust to his bench, Patrick regards his own reaction to the girls, the parade of girls. Mostly he loves this, the constant catwalk of London, the fugue of female beauty, the sweet repetition with minor variation. But at this moment he also resents the power, he resents these girls' power and fame and the way they get in clubs for free, *like members of some manufactured boy band . . . like unwarranted celebrities with no real talent . . .*
—Dying for a smoke
—What?
Joe pats his pocket, rueful:
—Need a cig . . .
—So . . . smoke one?
—*Can't*, man
—Given up?
Still rueful:
—*Boracic*
Silence, traffic-thrum, Patrick's hand reaches for his own pocket:
—You want to borrow some cash?
—Nah – Joe surveys the Square, as if looking for a different benefactor – I already owe you enough – Joe's face is wide, sad, honest, wry – Anyway. I start some temping job tomorrow
—Shipbrokers?
—*Shipbrokers* . . .
This sadly spoken word some kind of signal, Patrick checks his watch and says:
—OK. Better get going . . . Got the lawyers round
—Going over the contracts for the club?
—Yep, some hitch with the survey
—. . . what's it like being more successful than me?
Patrick replies:
—I'm not
Joe replies:
—Haddaway and *shite*
Now the two of them are up. Now the two of them are up, out the

Square, and walking over the road towards Greek Street. Halfway across they come to a stop. Barring their way is a builder's lorry making beeping noises as it reverses. Using the moment Patrick looks down Greek Street at yet another building site: at the place where a building is going up behind a vast theatre curtain of plastic. Watching the moving girders and big yellow machines and men in red plastic hats carrying lengths of scaffolding, Patrick says:

—I remember when all this used to be fields

—Yeah?

—When I first lived in London there was . . . a meadow here, with sheep . . . and fallow deer . . .

Joe, nodding:

—God yeah, and there was, like, a little stream down there, and that's where there used to be that shepherd with his long clay pipe, right?

—Yep. And that – Patrick gestures, vaguely – That Starbucks coffee house, that used to be a little glade with crab-apple trees, and we used to make cowslip bells. Right next to that van, remember?

—Seems like *yesterday*

The lorry circumvented, the two friends cross the road and pace more briskly, until they come to the junction where they part. Jabbing his friend's arm Joe says goodbye and good luck and then angles away and then jogs down the street towards Charing Cross. Watching his friend go, Patrick thinks about his friend's drug habit for a second and then Patrick turns and walks, and sees, strolling towards him, a very pretty blonde girl, a beautiful blonde girl who gives him the usual feelings of resentment and sad yearning and powerlessness and *why don't I ever get girlfriends like that* . . . until Patrick realises it's Rebecca. His *girlfriend*.

7

— So he pinned you to the wall and said what?

Out-staring the prosecutor Rebecca says nothing; then she looks frankly and somehow bravely above his head and says:

— Kiss me properly you . . .

— Yes?

— Kiss me properly . . . you . . .

Rebecca stops. The judge's eyebrows go up. In the witness box Rebecca shrugs: a shrug that says she doesn't want to say any more. With an inscrutable glance at the defence lawyer the judge leans towards Rebecca; and says:

— Miss Jessel, I am aware this might be rather painful – The judge does an avuncular smile – But we have to have the exact wording as far as it is possible. It might well be very important, it might not, but that's rather for the jury to decide – Again the smile – So if you could tell us just as much as you can?

The smile turns into a nod at the prosecutor. Alan Gregory nods back at the judge, and then expectantly turns to Rebecca. Shifting her weight slightly in the witness box, Rebecca responds:

— Well, he . . . he . . . came across and he pushed me back and . . . then he said 'kiss me properly you . . .'

Another silence. This time, before the judge can intervene, Rebecca says:

— Jewish bitch

A pause. Half the court is looking at Patrick; the other half is looking at the prosecutor. The prosecutor:

— He called you a . . . 'Jewish bitch'?

— Yes

— And by this time how long had he been in the flat?

— About ten minutes

— Just ten?

— Yes. It can't have been much longer than that because the kettle hadn't boiled

— Yes, I see – Alan Gregory QC caresses his own chin – OK. Yes. Now – Gregory glances momentarily at the back of the court, at Patrick – Now as the defendant kissed you, did you try to push him off?

— Yes – Rebecca looks slightly offended by the question; Patrick feels he doesn't want to look at her; Rebecca regains herself and says – Yes. I pushed him away as much as I could but he . . . just laughed. He was acting weird . . .

— In what way?

— I'm not sure – Her face goes slightly blank – I remember wondering if he was drunk, I could smell beer, smell the pub

— Were you scared by this time?

Patrick can hear the big clock on the side wall ticking. Rebecca:

— Yes

— So what did you decide to do?

— Well . . . I . . . *uh*?

The lawyer turns to his notes. Says:

— I'll rephrase that. In fact, if I may – A half nod towards the judge – I'd like to go over the facts as they stand again . . . – Patrick notices the judge give a subliminal answering nod. Gregory says – Let's take stock. This is a young man you used to live with but with whom you no longer have a relationship. Is that correct?

— Yyes

— And he's only in your flat on the pretext of picking up some clothes, correct?

— Uh-huh

— Sorry?

— I mean yes. Yes that's right

The prosecutor lifts the papers closer to his face, as if to scrutinise a surprising fact more closely; then:

— OK. So. He's come round to the flat to pick up his stuff. He's been in the flat for ten minutes – A direct glance at Rebecca; Rebecca nods;

51

the prosecutor says – So he's tried to kiss you, he's . . . abused and insulted you, he's acting to say the least somewhat . . . *strangely*. And what do you do?

— I . . . I'm – Again Rebecca looks like she is aggrieved by the tone; across the court Gregory comes back with a softer, more explanatory voice:

— Miss Jessel I'm only trying to get the facts straight – A jaunty smile – Look at it this way, perhaps. Some people might say that you should have asked him to leave straight away. At this early point. You see?

Realisation seems to cross Rebecca's face. She nods vigorously like she has remembered her lines; then she says:

— Yes I see what you're getting at but you must understand. Yes he was a bit drunk but . . . he was still my ex. I still felt . . . you know . . . – She pulls her cardigan sleeve distractedly – That's why I invited him around

—And this is why you let him linger?

The cardigan sleeve is released:

— Yes. I still felt for him. I had been very much in love with him – Her face goes odd – I never thought he'd go and do . . . *that* . . .

— Naturally

The prosecutor flicks a tiny hardly detectable glance at the back of the court; in Patrick's direction. In the dock Patrick tries to stay calm. His chin resting on a fist, the elbow on a knee, aware he looks like Rodin's Thinker, Patrick stays calm and stares straight back at the prosecutor. Patrick is determined not to be fazed or angered. Patrick wants a calm detachment to enter his mind. He wants to think about something else. And so, as Rebecca goes on to describe, in tediously minuscule detail, their subsequent movements about the flat that fateful evening, that evening, the evening in question, Patrick sits back in the dock and decides to think about sex. Religion. Sex. *Religion* . . .

Patrick wishes he'd masturbated this morning. He wonders why he always thinks about sex at the worst times. Trying to think about something else, about anything else . . . about religion, Patrick recalls a conversation he had with Joe about religion. This morning. Just this morning Joe had made the point that there were really only three arguments for the existence of God, the Argument from Design, the Argument from Ultimate Purpose, and, finally, the best of all the theological proofs, the Argument from Japanese Schoolgirls.

Patrick sniggers. Thinking of Joe's comment, Patrick starts chuckling. Quite loudly: wheezily laughing. By Patrick's side the policeman looks quizzically at Patrick. Across the court the policewoman standing behind Rebecca glances over at Patrick, and frowns. Faced by these stares Patrick swiftly sobers: his chuckles become a smile which becomes a tense, engaged expression when Patrick hears exactly what Rebecca is saying. Rebecca is saying:

— So he said he wouldn't leave until – Rebecca takes a big breath – Until I let him . . . fuck me

— And you were sitting across the table at this point?

— Yes

— Why do you think he should say something like that?

— I don't know . . . I . . .

Rebecca stalls, looking excruciated, embarrassed, and at the judge. The judge flashes a significant glance at the prosecutor. As the prosecutor pauses, Patrick starts to feel sorry for Rebecca. This in turn makes Patrick feel slightly proud. Patrick feels good and proud that he himself should be so forgiving and noble as to pity the woman who tortures him; but then Patrick realises that inside him somewhere he also feels good and secretly happy that he and Rebecca are as one again, here, now: united in their shame; as one against a world which seeks to publicly bundle them in their own dirty bedlinen.

Rebecca:

— I suppose he rather thought it might . . . turn me on. I guess he thought that talking like that would be . . . arousing – Rebecca grips the stand and looks at the prosecutor, she looks him in the face – It wasn't

The prosecutor:

— And this was the point at which you asked him to leave?

— Yes

— And what did he do?

— He said he wouldn't

— Anything else?

— He said . . . he wanted to fuck me up the arse

Silence. Clock-ticking silence. Patrick looks at a middle-aged grey-haired woman in the jury who is sucking a boiled sweet with a wholly rapt expression: like she is enjoying a guiltily pleasurable afternoon at the movies.

His head in his hands Patrick sighs. Then he regains himself, looks up at the prosecutor: who is now fiddling with his papers. Alan Gregory QC has turned to his left where a seated assistant is holding up a piece of paper. The assistant is pointing to a certain passage of writing. Taking the paper the prosecutor nods intelligently, and revolves on Rebecca:

— And was it at this time that the phone rang?

— Yes

— And who was it on the other end? Who'd rung you up?

— A friend . . .

— Which friend?

— I . . . can't remember . . .

— You told the police in your statement

— Yes, I know . . .

Taking her time, Rebecca glances around the courtroom, as if to remind herself of something; for a second her upward gaze comes to a rest on the visitors' gallery, overlooking the courtroom. Patrick suspects she has probably recognised someone, one of their friends or a member of his family. Thoughts collected Rebecca turns back to the prosecutor and says:

— Freddie

— Frederick Legge?

Rebecca shrugs her lambswooled shoulders:

— Yes

— And what did he want?

— Nothing important

The prosecutor refers to his piece of paper again:

— You told him to . . . 'fuck off', is that right?

Shrugging, again; again clearly embarrassed Rebecca nods, says:

— Yes

— You chatted for a few seconds and then you made it clear you didn't want to speak to him and you put the phone down, correct?

— . . . Yes

— But – The prosecutor looks at the defence barrister and pauses and then says – I'm sure the defence counsel would raise this but for my own purposes could you tell me . . . why? Surely when Mister Legge rang this was an ideal opportunity to let someone know you were being harassed?

Another shrug from Rebecca. For the first time Patrick leans forward with keen, optimistic interest. Clearing her throat, Rebecca:

— At the time . . . I thought I could handle it all myself. I'd seen Patrick drunk like this before and I thought it was just another . . . time like that – In her dress, and her

54

cardigan, she shifts girlishly from foot to foot; then – I had absolutely no idea that straight after that he would do what he did
— I see. Thank you ... – With a flurry of black gown the prosecutor makes a moving-on expression. He says – As soon as you'd put the phone down the defendant came around the table and began trying to kiss you, correct?
— Yes
— Did you struggle?
— Yes – Rebecca looks at the wall as her face pales – But he was too strong. Too big ...
— Was he touching you?
— Yes
— How?
— He had one hand on my throat and ... one hand down my top. On my breast
— Yes?
— He'd undone the zip of my top and he was groping my breast
— Yes, of course. Was it this top? – With his left hand, the prosecutor has magicked a zip-up top from somewhere, some bag on his desk. Intent, concerned, Patrick watches as Rebecca watches the top being flagged at her. She looks surprised and shocked to see it. Finally Rebecca says:
— Yes
    The judge:
— Miss Jessel?
    Rebecca's voice is trembly:
— Sorry. Yes. Yes it was that top. That's what I was wearing – Rebecca allows herself a big long breath. While the lawyer re-bags the top Patrick finds his sympathy going unwontedly out once more as Rebecca breathes and breathes deep, fighting back obvious emotion. Rebecca Jessel gazes into the middle distance as she begins to describe: how Patrick put his hand down her jeans. How Patrick groped her breast. How she tried to stop him but he was too strong for her. How he nuzzled her breasts as she yelled. How he picked her off the chair and dragged her like a puppet over the floor and pushed her down on her back and
— And you were screaming during this?
— Yes
— And this was the point where he unzipped himself?
— Yes

— Were you . . . totally naked by this time?

— Yes

— What had happened to your jeans?

— I

— Had he taken them off, too?

— YYess . . . I *think* so

— How?

— I don't quite know, I . . .

— You're not sure how he stripped you?

— No . . . he'd somehow managed – Rebecca shivers visibly, she grips the side of the witness stand; Patrick can see her knuckles going white; for some reason he wonders if she still bites her nails as then Rebecca blurts – It was all a blur but he'd managed to get my jeans off and I . . .

In the stand Rebecca seems to shudder, she rocks back on her feet and looks imploringly at the judge.

The judge:

— Take your time, Miss Jessel

With a nod Rebecca gulps and asks for a glass of water. The court gathers itself close, takes a collective breath, as Rebecca turns and accepts a glass from the policewoman behind her. The moments pass as Rebecca delicately sips, then puts the glass down. Now Rebecca licks her newly-red lips as she looks across the silent courtroom and says:

— He forced me onto my back and held my arms above my head and then he got his penis out

— Did he have an erection?

— Yes. He was hard

— What happened then?

— He used his other hand to part my thighs

— And then?

— He held his penis in his hand . . . I think . . . and he

Patrick looks at the middle-aged juror; she has stopped sucking her sweet and her jaw is hanging open as Rebecca says:

— He put his penis inside me and began . . .

— Began . . . Miss Jessel?

Clock-tick. Patrick's heart. Rebecca's voice:

— He began to rape me . . .

— What then?

— Then he started saying things

—What did he say?

— That I was . . .

—Yes

— That I was a bitch . . . a slut . . . *his* little slut . . .

—Anything else?

— He said . . . he said he loved my dirty little . . . – The court waits – cunt

—Anything else?

Rebecca inhales, then she says, slowly, deliberately:

— He said he was going to fuck me in my dirty . . . cunt and that he was going to fuck me in my little arsehole even if I didn't like it and – She closes her eyes and visibly trembles as she recounts – He said he was going to . . . come in my face . . . and that I was . . . until I was . . . that I was nothing . . . He said I was a slut, a bitch, a sadistic bitch

She stalls. Rebecca stands back from the side of the witness box and she pauses and then she drinks some more water from the glass. The prosecutor looks at the jury, at the judge, and then at Rebecca and says:

— How long did this go on for?

Glass down, chin up, lips wet:

— Don't know . . . maybe five minutes . . . maybe ten

—And you were frightened?

Rebecca looks at the prosecutor like he has said the most stupid thing in the world. Rebecca Jessel:

— I was totally petrified

—And all the time you'd been asking . . . begging him to stop?

— Yes. I was screaming. I was shouting no . . . all the time . . .

—And did this have any effect?

—NO!

Rebecca has almost shouted. The court seems taken aback at this bitter yelp; Patrick watches as Rebecca calms herself, as she shakes her blonde head and repeats:

— It had no effect

Now Rebecca goes quiet. Looks down. The prosecutor hmms and nods, and looks at something on his desk, at a piece of paper he is pinning down with lazy fingers. A moment passes. Tanned face up, Gregory says:

—What happened next, Miss Jessel?

— He pushed me upstairs

—No. I mean . . . before then?

Rebecca looks blankly at the prosecutor, then her expression relaxes as she seems to realise what he's saying; Rebecca replies:

— He withdrew from me . . . suddenly . . . and then he

— Miss Je

Not listening, Rebecca goes on:

— He withdrew and he . . . grabbed my hair with one hand and he said . . . he said I was to suck his . . . to suck his . . . cock, to lick the . . . filthy cunt off his cock

In the dock Patrick grimaces; he can't help it; in the dock Patrick grimaces and lowers his forehead into one hand: feeling shame and pain and embarrassment and guilt; feeling guilt for everything, guilt for being male, guilt for having a sex drive, guilt for being a horrible rapist. Then Patrick grips himself and tries to rid his mind and face of guilt. He looks up, defiant.

Rebecca is saying:

— He was holding my head by the hair . . . it hurt . . . he had my hair in his hand and he was forcing me onto his . . . penis . . . forcing me to fellate him . . . to suck him, I was choking and screaming and I remember my mouth hurt and I was screaming because he was hurting my mouth as he

Patrick stares at Rebecca; despite the hell, despite the worst, despite it all he feels a tiny slight stiffening in his groin as he looks at her: her dear darling face. He is thinking of the time when he

— Forced me to suck him, and he put his hand, he put his finger in my . . . backside . . . my back passage . . . my anus and

and Patrick tries not to; he tries not to be agitated by this but it is difficult. He is forced, forced to listen, forced to listen to Rebecca describing to all these people he's never met, and all his friends in the gallery, and the unicorn above the judge's head, how he made her suck him; how he threatened to beat her senseless; how he slapped her hard; how he bit her shoulder and upper arm; how he put his cock in her

— anus. And then he said . . .

— What?

— He said that the carpet was hurting him, burning his knees . . .

Rebecca sips more water; her lips are glistening. Rebecca bites her glistening red lips and opens her lips and tells them all how he pushed her away; how he pushed her upstairs, how he pushed her into the bedroom and pushed her onto the bed and started raping her

— again and

— again?

— and again

and Rebecca tries not to cry as she tells them how he bit her, slapped her, told her to shut the fuck up; how she screamed out and scratched him; how he rammed his

— penis

inside her

— dirty little cunt

how he raped her and bit her and slapped her until she was dizzy, how he licked her face how he bit her ear how he told her she was his

— stupid Jewish tart

who wanted and needed his

— cock

in her

— cunt in

her

— arsehole

and so when he turned her

— over

and

— over

and

— took

her hard from behind and

— raped

her and

— raped

her

— and made

her cry and she just begged him and cried out and begged him and begged him and begged him and begged him and begged him and begged him not to

— come inside

Patrick can't work out which is louder: the clock, or his heart, or the sound of Rebecca's silent sobbing in the witness box. The silence otherwise is unendurable. Patrick covers his ears with his hands and stares down at the floor of the dock. He looks at a cigarette butt ground into the darkness. The court stays silent; Rebecca is still weeping; the prosecutor mumbles something but the judge intervenes and says, very quietly, as he revolves upon Rebecca, who is still covering her eyes as she stifles a gulp of tears:

— Miss Jessel, I think we are going to . . . adjourn for the day . . . so if you'd like . . . ?

Under her hands, behind her hands and tears, Rebecca nods. She nods, and then she turns and steps down and walks slowly out of the box and down the steps. But then she pauses, very near the shocked, white-faced jury. The jury members try not to look at her, but they fail. Patrick senses the jury looking at Rebecca with pity, embarrassment and fascination as Rebecca seems to pause to gather her wits. Next to Patrick's ear Patrick hears the hoarse whisper:

— The first day is always the worst

Patrick looks at his lawyer, at Stefan, who has surreptitiously moved over so as to stand near the dock, near him, to whisper this. Patrick sees that Stefan is looking a little vexed. Patrick gulps the bitterness in his own mouth and gazes silently leftwards. Rebecca is now coming towards him. With angered excitement Patrick realises that Rebecca's route to the exit door is going to take her right past him in the dock. Not knowing whether to open his eyes or close them or what, Patrick sits as still as he can as Rebecca walks right in front of him. He doesn't want to look at her gingham dress and her soft cardigan, at her walk so demure and her face *so* pale. But as she passes just close by, he can't help it. She is so close he can actually *smell* her, smell her scent, smell the scent that reminds him of her, of him; of them. Of happiness.

8

—Morning!

He says. Underneath him, Rebecca mumbles, bleary, confused:

—Z'it morning?

—Nope

—I was asleep . . . ?

—Yep

She hmms, nods, yawns. They are lying in Rebecca's bed, in Rebecca's parents' house. The pinkness of Rebecca's yawn becomes a sleepy sentence:

—Still raining?

—Yeah

—Mmmmmmmyes – Rebecca is stretching her soft naked body under the duvet, her glossy nudity – I like when it rains, really rains . . .

Then she stops. Patrick listens, but she has stopped talking. All Patrick can hear is a lonely car slashing down the wet, empty, 2 a.m. Hampstead street, outside. Patrick listens to this: to the absence of traffic, that very unLondon sound. It makes him think about traffic, their difficult traffic, the *contraflow*.

He thinks, again, again, yet again, about the contraflow of their worrying sex life: why no climax? why hasn't she properly orgasmed? wherefore not the smackrush? What is their problem? Staring at Rebecca's unaware face Patrick frets: why does he feel she hasn't entirely given of herself? why does he feel that he hasn't entirely possessed her? and why does their sex feel like an unwinnable computer game? What is this? What?

To distract himself from these not so new, always perturbing thoughts

Patrick leans out of her bed and riffles fake-lazily amongst the piles of books and papers she habitually stacks by her bed. *Aztec books,* **predictably**; *Crusader texts,* **naturally**; *some poetry,* **of course** Then Patrick finds a charity form: a sponsorship form for a half-marathon intended to publicise Third World Debt.

Picking this form up, feeling playful, bitchy, grumpy, Patrick says:

—You're running a marathon?

Beneath him:

—Yyyyeah half

His face moves nearer hers:

—For Third World Debt?

Still sleepy:

—Yessss . . .

—Hnn – He says; then he says – You know I could help you out with this? She does not reply. He says:

—I could you know, I know a lot about Third World Debt, you should see the debts I ran up in the Third World last winter

Silence. Patrick:

—Coke bills in Colombia, unpaid whores in Bangkok

—That's nice for you, darling

—Actually – On a roll now, Patrick says – I was thinking of starting a charity of my own, to help Third World Hunger – He moves his face directly over hers as she turns to stare at the wall – I was going to call it . . . International Fellatio Relief

She mumbles nothing. Patrick says:

—I'd go to Third World countries and get young women to give me head and swallow my semen, thus providing them with that valuable, hard-to-come-by protein . . .

Beneath him Rebecca turns over and buries her face in the pillow and starts singing a Celine Dion song. Pulling at her singing shoulder, Patrick says:

—Becs – Another tug – Becs? Stop singing? Bex!

At the third tug she rolls over, stops singing. She looks up at him, and grins, and reaches out a hand and strokes his unshaven chin as if to tell him to shut up. Then she tells him to shut up. Feeling a rush of responsive emotion Patrick stoops his mouth to the crook of Rebecca's pretty neck, and kisses her lovely scented Rebeccaness. Subsequently he rolls back onto his side of the four big expensive white pillows and wonders if he is as hungry as he thinks he might be: whether they can nip down to her kitchen, open the enormous brushed steel door of her fridge, and eat the ice-cold white peaches the Jessels always seem to keep on that big blue glass plate . . .

Rebecca moves nearer. With a flinch, Patrick feels her cold feet press against his legs, her feet seeking the warmth of his calves. It is as if, he thinks, she is trying to attach herself, trying to lock herself on, trying to *anchor* herself: in him, in the shifting, unreliable sands of his soul. For a moment Patrick wants to shout out *no, don't do it, don't be stupid*.

He doesn't. Instead Patrick yawns, swallows, and surveys Rebecca's room. Her frankly massive room. Her room is bigger than his mum's garden. Why so big a room? This is the seventh or eighth time Patrick has spent the night in Rebecca's room in her parents' plutocratic Hampstead mansion and yet he still feels upset by it. As he is upset by the whole setup here. Whenever Patrick stays here he is so determined not to be impressed by the Georgian silver ashtrays and the three-BMW garage and the incredibly complicated and sophisticated ways of making real coffee he starts to feel stomachy, like he's been suppressing wind for too long.

Rebecca is up on an elbow and saying:

—Patch

—Yeah?

—Do you . . .

Across Rebecca's room Patrick can see the streetlight reflected in the full-length antique Art Nouveau mirror. Patrick feels another touch of colic coming on.

Rebecca is saying:

—I was wondering

—What?

—I was going to ask

—Fuck's sake

—Well, with all that religious music you've got . . . Bach, those cantatas . . . and . . . thingy

—Yes?

—Do you believe in God?

Patrick checks Rebecca's face for sincerity. Patrick notices that Rebecca's left earlobe glints with something silver; and that otherwise she is naked. As he looks at Rebecca's nipples Patrick says:

—You know what I think

—Do I?

—Yep. You asked me this same question the second time we met

—So – She shrugs, very *girlishly* – Tell me again then

Patrick sighs, leans, kisses her left nipple, pulls back to look at his stiffening lipwork; and says:

—I reckon religion is like – Thinking of a new analogy – Nipples, nipples for men – Patrick smiles, pleased by the topicality of his insight; then he goes to explain it – Religion is a now redundant adaptation, it's a defunct psychosocial adaptation originally engendered in ignorant savages by their understandable fear of death and the inexplicable – Reaching out and holding her wrist – And of course it's wank

—Wank?

—Yep

—O brave pagan – Says Rebecca – Proud of Your Mortality

—Am I?

She giggles:

—Yep! – Still giggling – But don't worry, it's quite nice and . . . butch

Patrick grunts, wondering whether he should feel patronised. Then Patrick instead starts wondering what Rebecca's snatch looks like. He knows what it looks like – like a Hanseatic wine merchant's collar muff, like a Hudson Bay fur trapper's sampler – yet still he wants to lift back the powder-blue duvet and check what it looks like. Even though he fucked Rebecca ten minutes ago, already he wants to fuck her again, to prove that she is his, again. Fed six hundred seconds ago and already his stomach is rumbling for more, more of the never-satisfying rice diet of sex . . .

—So – She says – Shall I tell you why I believe?

—No

—No?

—Nope

Rebecca looks annoyed, and embarrassed by her own annoyance. To cover her shyness she starts butting his shoulder with her head, like a kitten trying to roll a ball of wool.

This arouses Patrick enormously. Trying not to be aroused, he says:

—Oh, go on then. Explain

Immediately:

—Well, I just think sometimes . . . there's something in me that's better than me

—Something in you that's better than *you*?

—Something kinder, nobler, gentler

He snorts:

—Oh, surely NOT, *kinder than **you***?

—I didn't

—Jesus, Becs, you really do love yourself don't you?

—No I don't it's just that

Feeling sudden anger:

—God I hate all this – Patrick feels his throat go thick with anger – All this morally superior do-gooding upper-middle-class BOLLOCKS

—OK I'm

—I fucking hate it

—Patch!

—The only thing I hate more than that is that bitch, that dead slut, that stupid fucking crack whore, what's her name – He flops back onto his side of the pillow – *Mother Teresa*

Rebecca breathes in, then out:

—Just because you are a selfish bastard, Patrick, doesn't mean the rest of us have to be . . .

—Me? Selfish? Cuh!

She ignores this. She makes a glum face. Her head is no longer playfully butting his arm like a kitten trying to roll a ball of wool. She is saying:

—Patrick you try and explain everything with evolution, with that hunter gatherer rubbish, that dreck – Waving an arm as if she is waving at his bookshelves she goes on – But I think that's just a rather pitiful excuse for being a selfish egotist

—It is?

—Yes – Her voice is now almost toneless – It is. I think you only satirise my social concern because you feel guilty about your own selfishness

—Social concern?

—Yes

—*Satirise* your *social concern*??

—Well

—So I take it you think you're better than me. Mm? – He makes an exasperated noise – Is that what you're saying?

—No . . . but . . .

—But I thought we were all the same, *all* poor sinners . . . NO?

A silence. The two of them are lying back on their pillows, side by side, staring at the ceiling, watching a light from a passing car do a slow turn across the ceiling, watching the time go. Quietly, Rebecca says:

—Patch, please, let's not argue
—Who's arguing? You stupid Jewish sex dwarf?
—OK . . . ok . . .

She snuggles nearer him; nearer, quieter, softer. Patrick notices her breasts are cold from the window downdraught. *White icebox peaches* . . .

Caring, guilty, adoring, Patrick stretches up out of the bed, reaches over to pull shut the casement, thus to stop the cool autumn rain spitting through onto her, onto his beloved. Returned to the pillow he lies down opposite this strange young Londoner, as she once again tries:
—It's just, I just believe that inside us all there is something superb, something infinitely graceful. A shard of the hologram. You know? You see what I mean? – A silence, a silence – In all of us? *Patch*?

Patrick looks back at Rebecca; Rebecca is close at hand. He says:
—You do bang on a bit
—Thanks . . .
—But don't you worry I still lu . . . – At once he stops himself; swears. A bit too brightly, Rebecca comes back:
—You still *lu*?
—*OK*
—Honestly? – She is grinning – You really really *lu*?

He pouts. Angrily. He's never yet told her he *lu* . . . He doesn't now want to say he *lu*; even though he was about to say he *lu*. So instead he says:
—Bexfuckoff

For a moment he worries this is too sharp, that she will be vexed, but she just laughs, grabs for his face, leans and kisses him. In response Patrick reaches out. He is pleased to find her right thigh still firm, smooth, well shaven. And long. Thinking about Rebecca's longish thighs Patrick, for a second, imagines her playing tennis next summer in a white miniskirt. For a second Patrick imagines them together next summer, playing tennis together. Trying not to give in to this way of thinking, this bourgeois thought, of a *long-term future together*, of *regular mixed doubles*, Patrick asks:
—Why *do* you read so much about the Aztecs anyway?
—Oh, you know
—No, I don't

Rebecca shrugs in reply, perhaps in discomfort. Slowly, she reaches over an arm, does something with a curl of his hair. Then she says:
—We're still discovering things about each other aren't we? Isn't that sweet?
—Tell me you slut

—OK . . . – Her face goes serious – I suppose . . . I suppose I can't quite seem to get a focus on what I want to do. For my thesis. What area. I sort of kind of wanted to do something about . . . feminism and . . . art history . . . but

—You chose the Crusades?

—Mmmm

—And now you are reading about the Aztecs?

—I know – She frowns – But . . . they are so totally fascinating, so enormously amazing

—Yes?

—Yes. Really – She makes an even more serious face and stares at the wall behind him – You know the Aztecs used to have a God of Haemorrhoids?

Patrick laughs, out loud. Hoping he has woken Rebecca's father upstairs, Patrick says:

—A God of *Haemorrhoids*? Priceless!!

Evidently pleased to have entertained her boyfriend Rebecca starts talking keenly on her favourite-theme-of-the-moment: on Aztec mythology and its weirdness; its strange, recondite, beautiful gods. For a long time Patrick listens, genuinely interested, but then his mind wanders and he starts thinking about the God of Haemorrhoids. This makes him consider what other gods they should have, perhaps the God of Advertising Agents with a six-hundred-metre-long ponytail; perhaps the God of Euro Federalism with a swastika on both batwings; perhaps the God of Rebecca's Breasts shaped like Rebecca's breasts.

—C'm'ere Bex

—Wh . . . ?

—I love it. The brainy stuff

—Yeah?

—Sometimes I find your intelligence incredibly erotic

She smiles:

—Honest? Really?

—But I still prefer your tits

She laughs. Grinning, Patrick reaches out and feels for Rebecca's laughing legs under the duvet; he puts his hand between her soft legs, does an expert piano scale up her soft inner thigh, up to where he's made her wet already, without really trying

—Yow – She says. He has his hand deep inside, two fingers deep inside the wetness

She is saying:

—Ouch –

and

—Mmm

and again she is looking at him expectantly, wantingly . . . yearningly . . . *Do-something-else-ishly* . . .

Patrick thinks about this. He thinks about what Rebecca wants. Then he thinks about what *he* wants. What he wants to do to her: the manhandling, the farmyard servicing, the rough treatment. He wonders if she would like it, or if she is too posh, too precious. Then he wonders about some poem she quoted him earlier on. *The lover's pinch that hurts and is desired* . . .

—Ouch

She says.

—Sorry – He says.

—S'OK . . .

—It hurts?

—Bit . . . – She says – A little bit . . . – Her face is looking at him, her eyes are shut. Again he repeats the grace notes inside her vagina; she squirms and exhales and her words come less distinct – *Just a little bit* . . .

Later, at 4 or 5 a.m., Patrick gets up from the bed and pads to the lavatory, trying not to make too much noise. *Flush, mirror, teeth, door.* Back in the bed he sits up for a while and looks at Rebecca's sleeping face. Staring at her gently snoring face he feels . . . weird. Too much. Looking at her sleeping form he feels something, something not relaxed, something worrying and life-altering; this he has never felt for a girl before. Patrick decides he is content to call it love for the lack of a better word . . . for now.

But that still leaves . . . There is still this something else, this something that troubles him. Her hunger. When they make love her face looks as if she is . . . still hungry. Still hungry. Yes, he senses her pleasure, he knows she is enjoying it, and yet. Is there some erogenous switch to flick he hasn't found? Some abracadabra to say? Some candlestick on the Gothic mantelpiece, that when he pulls will cause the concealed door to slide?

Well . . . ?

Giving up, for now, forgetting it, for now, Patrick turns from Rebecca's face to the window, to the rain-teary window. Tired, fucked, groin-aching, famished, Patrick sits half up in the bed and looks out at the damp 5 a.m.

streets of Hampstead Garden Suburb, the now clearing autumn night skies. Out there the wet empty streets are streaks of reflected traffic lights: red, yellow, and green. The colours remind Patrick of school dinners: red jam tart, yellow lemon curd, the green of lime icing.

—Constellations?

She has spoken. Rebecca has spoken. Naked, young, rich, and newly awake, she is pointing up from her pillow. Patrick sees she is pointing at the dark sky, through the window, and saying:

—Do you know them?

—The constellations? – He makes an affronted face – In the sky?

—*Yes* . . .

—Course I know 'em

Rebecca nods and smiles at this, and pulls herself upright. Sitting herself so that the two of them are sitting side by side, naked on the bed, she joins him in facing the big window. They both go quiet, as he looks up at the heavens and says:

—OK . . . That one is – Patrick narrows his eyes – Ursa Major. And that one's . . . the Pleiades – He looks harder – And that, that one over there, by Betelgeuse, that's . . . You Eating Five Bagels Last Night

She laughs, says:

—Oh yes and that one, that one's Your Frankly Tiny Penis

—The one between Orion and Our First Argument?

She giggles:

—Yep

Patrick laughs. Then he squints, again, dramatically:

—But . . . hold on . . . I . . . I can't see . . . I can't make out . . . I can't see . . . The First Time I Told You I Loved You

Her face is all white and pale:

—You can't see that one? It isn't there? *Isn't it there?*

—Oh yes – He says, looking back at her, smiling broadly – There it is

9

—What? *What?!*
—Patr
—Come on. What??

Patrick's friends are avoiding his eye. Patrick looks at them, looks them in the eye, then looks around the pub in anger and contempt. The Magpie and Stump is full of after-hours lawyers, acquitted child molesters, off-duty policemen, young girl-solicitors, and red-eyed cons' daughters; and Patrick feels as alone as he's felt all day.

Patrick is drinking away the memory of the day's hearing, Rebecca's evidence, Rebecca's tears. But Patrick is finding it hard: to forget how the day went is hard because everybody is so obviously trying to studiously not remind him of how the day went. His friends, his sister, Joe, they are all gathered in the pub next to the Old Bailey, the Magpie and Stump, and they are all evidently excited by the bizarre and groovy things they have heard in court this day, but whenever Patrick wanders near, whenever he drifts by, they all start chattering away about . . . property prices. Dishonoured, distressed, dissed, Patrick wonders if he should just go home. He can't just go home because he really wants to get drunk, and be with people. With friends and family. And really, Patrick wonders, would he really be any different? If the situation were contrary, and he was the one in the Old Bailey gods watching a friend be tried for . . . say . . . rape . . . would he, Patrick, be any less ghoulish, any less ambulance chasing? Would he resist the temptation to take popcorn into the public gallery?

Patrick wonders, sighs, sluices draught Staropramen, hears Joe making jokes about Patrick's interesting techniques for getting a blow job.

Now Patrick gets heartburn again, the heartburn he has been suffering off and on all day: engendered by the weird scenario that is his new sexual celebrity. Patrick squirms at this unwarranted celebrity. Patrick feels like he is being hyped, beyond his talent. He feels like an over-promoted stud-muffin, the Man Who Would Be King Dong.

Determinedly Patrick finishes his drink. Over his lifted glass, he observes a gang of medics and nurses come barrelling through the early evening swing of the pub door. Some of these obviously-Barts-students are dressed in fancy dress: cowboy stetsons, Viking helmets. One of the medics is wearing a mysterious blue cape with yellow plastic bananas dangling therefrom; and a yellow floppy pixy hat. The scattering of fancy-dressed medics look embarrassed that only a minority of their peers and friends have bothered to wear fancy dress this evening; except the guy in the banana coat who looks blissfully unaware. The banana man turns, and grins proudly at Patrick; Patrick wonders whether to nip back to his own flat and put on that red-and-black-striped tee shirt and that balaclava with the word RAPIST thereupon.

Grabbing his friend Nico's empty pint glass from Nico's semi-aware hand Patrick takes the two empty glasses through the Magpie and Stump crowds, past a nun, an attempted murderer, a paediatric oncologist, a silk, a Batman, a Kosovan-refugee dealer. Between two chic-yet-coarse office girls who smell of chewing gum, Patrick leans over and sets his pint glasses on the bar.

Twenty-pound note in his hand Patrick waits: waiting for the not-pretty bargirl to make her way down the line of laughing drinkers. As he waits Patrick sees a cute Asian girl looking at him from the other end of the bar. The girl is standing by a tall pinstriped young guy who is talking at the girl; but the girl is ignoring the guy and staring hard at Patrick. Patrick looks at the girl. The girl looks back. Slightly unnerved, Patrick looks back. The girl looks back. Then with another pang of acidy heartburn Patrick realises it is the jury member, the cute one.

The gastric ulcer, the gastric ulcer. Patrick winces, inhales, stands back, thinks hard. Patrick wonders what this girl is thinking; what she is thinking of *him*. He wonders if she was revolted by what she heard in court today. He wonders if she was intrigued, involved, bored. *The way she is staring at him.* Patrick wonders if the girl is waiting for him to do something: the blank-faced Asian girl is standing there staring like she is waiting for him to do something. Something authentic. Something excitingly in character. Something rapisty.

For a dyspeptic second Patrick wonders why he *is* out here, at liberty, *walking the streets.* How can it be right, be justified? Surely he is a threat, a danger, a walking hazard to womenfolk?

With maximal effort, Patrick suppresses this. But the girl just keeps looking over, as if she can't help herself. Patrick conjectures how many times this girl thought of his penis today; he ponders whether she imagined herself doing it with him. Did she imagine herself being bitten and licked, being brusquely fucked, as she sat in Court Eighteen in her Principles two-piece and discreet golden nose stud? Eh, *my little pakora? My little samosa of love?*

—Yep? Hello? Yep?

— . . .

—Yes?

—Oh, uhh

Too late. The bargirl has gone. Patrick has missed his chance. Cursing, sighing, Patrick swears at himself, then he shoulders the burden once more: leans and waits patiently. After an entire Carpenters medley from the jukebox the girl again works her way back down to where Patrick is; she nods and listens to his order, she takes and tilts the pint glasses; then gives him a smile and the pints. Carefully Patch takes up his refilled glasses, and, elbows out, tries to work his way through without spilling.

Back between his friends Patrick hands one of the cold gold pints to Nico. As he does this he notices that Nico and Joe, who were chattering away happily as he walked up, have immediately stopped chattering away. Patrick wonders if this ulcer he's got is really gastric, or perhaps duodenal. Looking from Nico to Joe, Patrick:

—Well? What?

—Uh?

—Thanks for the pint, Patch

They say nothing more. Patrick shakes his head and clucks:

—Tell me. What were you talking about?

Joe demurs; Nico drinks silently; Patch says:

—You were talking about her, right?

Shift, sip, silence, Patch:
— Weren't you?
— Man
Patrick snaps:
— Jesus you didn't *believe* her, did you?
— Course we didn't
— It's just that
— Oh. Great. Cheers, *mates*
Joe shrugs at Patrick's anger:
— Man it's . . . Y'know . . . difficult . . .
— Why?
— See it our way. She was, you know
— What?
— Not convincing as such. More . . .
— Yes?
— More . . .
Nico joins in:
— More horny
— Yeah, she's got better tits than you
Nico adds, giggling:
— Wouldn't mind bending one up her
— And when she turned on the waterworks, well sexy
Joe stops. Patrick is saying:
— You are exceptionally drunk . . . aren't you? Please tell me you're
outrageously pissed?
— And when you said – Joe's eyes are shiny, his eyes are turned on
Patrick and they are shiny as he tries not to laugh out loud – When
you, er, allegedly . . . said all that . . . stuff about her . . . Jewish cunt?
Now he laughs out loud. Nico laughs too:
— Nice one, Adolf
Patrick is silent. His friends go as silent as they see how silent Patrick
is. The pub jukebox is playing something Nineties again. Patrick looks
at Nico; Patrick turns on Nico. Nico says, more quietly:
— It's a joke, Patch
— C'mon, Patch youknowwhatwethink
— If we really thought you were a rapo would we be here?
Patrick exhales, disbelievingly; Joe:
— We're just winding you up . . .

Patrick decides to try and not be wound up. *But still.* Turned now from Joe and Nico's wry, young, drunken half smiles, Patrick lifts his own beer glass and swallows a cold quarter of a pint. Then he unmoustaches his beer-frothed lips, belches the taste of things away, eyes up the calves of a shipping clerkette. Right at the end of his beer, as Joe and Nico start arguing about Greek complicity with the Nazis, Patrick sees his solicitor Jenkins, chatting with a middle-aged woman. Jenkins and Friend are perched on brushed aluminium bar stools. The woman's head is framed by an anonymous pastel painting of somewhere Cézanney; the woman is drinking a long green drink.

Accepting his fourth pint from his passing sister, Patrick threads through the drinkers to where his solicitor is drinking. Patrick is irritated to see that his solicitor looks anxious and unnerved on seeing Patrick coming over. After a quick meaningful glance at the woman the solicitor half stands, from his stool, and grasps Patrick's extended arm. Jenkins:

— Patrick. Good to see you. Bearing up?

Patrick shrugs; Jenkins:

— Good. Just remember . . . These are early days

— I . . .

— Your pals are here? Good, that's good

The solicitor looks warily but brightly at Patrick. Patrick pauses and thinks what to say, using the pause to look up and glance at the middle-aged woman who is looking interestedly and squarely back at Patch. As the woman and Patrick look at each other, Jenkins makes a remembering-his-manners noise and introduces the woman, says her name. Patrick forgets her name. Then Patrick burps and tilts his pint glass and looks at the solicitor's cheap-looking white shirt and cheap-looking tie. Patrick wonders why, if his solicitor is so good and successful, he wears such cheap clothes. Patrick starts:

— So. Mister Jenkins

— Mm?

— How did *you* think it went?

The solicitor tilts a thinking head:

— Not too bad.

— Not too bad?

— Yes. Considering

— Considering what, Gareth??

— Everything. It was . . . Much as we expected. Actually – He smiles –
Turned on the tears of course
— And you think all that *wasn't too bad*?
— No. Not really – He smiles again – Actually, I think the school dress
was a little bit of a mistake on her part
— You think they sussed that?
— Rather
— But the jury . . . they looked . . .
    Jenkins wags his balding head, makes a weird clicking noise
— Perhaps. But. Early days!
    Patrick closes his eyes, opens them:
— But what about all the . . . kinky stuff . . . I mean – Sensing the
middle-aged woman looking at him Patrick sighs; sighing and sighing
and sighing Patrick looks at the vaguely Ottoman cornicing on the wall
of the otherwise stripped and white-walled and made-over City pub;
and then Patrick finds his thoughts again:
— I have to say it all seemed pretty fucking disastrous to me – He
returns his gaze to Jenkins's reddish, fattish, mid-fortiesish face – I mean
how d'you reckon that went down with the jury cause it sounded bloody
terrible if you were sitting in the dock? You know?
    The solicitor looks at the woman; she shrugs and looks back; Jenkins
says:
— Patrick. You mustn't get too stressed. Juries are funny things – Yellowish teeth, wideish smile – Of course. It was . . . rather an eye opener.
Of course. But – He smiles again – Shouldn't be unduly concerned.
Not if I were you
— Really?
— No
— *Really?* Even though the entire court's got me down as Hitler with a
hard-on?
— Well – Jenkins looks at Patrick. Then he looks apologetically over at
the woman; who nods understandingly back. Then he says – Patrick.
Listen – The solicitor puts his hand on Patrick's upper arm; says – I
know it's stressful. But you have to take it. Remember this is the pros-
ecution's turn. O K?
    Patrick says nothing, stares at his drink; at length the solicitor says:
— Come with me?
    Jenkins's hand is now gripping Patrick's shoulder. Using Patrick as

a crutch, Jenkins rises from his bar stool, and gently pushes Patrick away and along. Together they walk up some sauna-y blond-wood steps, up to a slightly less crowded part of the pub. Here they pause. Jenkins stands alongside Patrick, looking out of the windows.

On this upper floor of the pub, windows are wide open, open to the warm summer air, the mild London traffic noise, the as yet starless evening sky. Waving his hand at the view, the silver-grey Old Bailey walls, the surprisingly quiet, surprisingly empty, surprisingly beautiful summer-evening-in-the-City street, the solicitor says:

—You know, Patrick. This boozer's been here for . . . a very long time
   Patrick nods:
—Uh-huh?
—Yes – Jenkins sways slightly. Patrick feels the pressure of the solicitor's hand vary on his shoulder. The variation makes Patrick realise, through his own maudlin drunkenness, that his solicitor is also pretty drunk. Jenkins gestures again:
—Now. When the Old Bailey was Newgate Jail – The solicitor is tilting his head across the street, but looking back at Patrick; Patrick nods, half listening.
   Jenkins:
—When it was a prison, they used to have hangings here. Ya see? – Jenkins smiles – And when the condemned men were brought out of the jail they used to hang them. Just over there, right there – Wristwatch, gesture, smile – And people would pay to sit in these very windows and watch the executions. Like it was a performance. They'd sit right here, by this slot machine. Even Byron, once

Patrick looks at the slot machine: its Star Wars theme, its picture of Darth Vader with red lights for eyes.
—Why are you telling me this?
   The solicitor chuckles:
—No idea – Jenkins wheezes cider breath, slaps Patrick on the back; then says – Patrick, Patrick, Patrick, Patrick – Patrick half shrugs. Jenkins goes on – Patrick, you have to understand. I've represented all kinds here. All kinds
—Yep?
—Yes. I've represented people that make . . . you . . . that make your case seem . . . almost . . . humdrum – Yellow smile – I've represented a chap who tied his wife to the fridge and drank a bit of her blood

every day for six months. I've represented a guy who . . . tried to drown himself with a kitten up his backside. I've represented a guy who got so pissed off with his girlfriend's affairs – The smile thins into a grin – He raped her pet chicken. You see?

— He raped her pet chicken?

— Indeed so

— Thanks, Gareth

— So you see what I mean?

— I . . . well . . . sort of

The solicitor sways again, sighs, says:

— Just remember what I promised you – He makes a face – You do recall?

— Do I?

— Yes you do. I offered you *reasonable doubt for a reasonable price*? Recall that? – The smile again, the teeth, the cider-wet lips – So . . . that's what you'll get. O K? Yes? Happy now?

Despite himself, Patrick nods, sighs, says yes, says *maybe*, sort of grins.

Then Jenkins laughs:

— So . . . Go ahead. Get drunk. Have a laugh with your chums. But. Stop. Worrying – Half smile, half frown – And just make sure you're not late tomorrow. Alright?

Before Patrick can reply Jenkins lifts his hand from Patrick's shoulder and turns as if about to go. As Jenkins turns, Patrick feels himself start to feel very sorry for himself. Again. Somewhere quite profound, somewhere near his heart, Patrick wants to blub: he wants to let his eyes fill with Rebecca and salt.

To stop this, to curarise his heart, Patrick sips his now-warm lager-beer and gazes out of the wide-open Magpie and Stump windows. As he does he thinks about what Jenkins has said. About the executions. The executions of Old Newgate Jail. Glaze-eyed Patrick stares at the gigantic rustication of the Old Bailey walls. Dimly Patrick can imagine the crowds of costers and oyster girls barging the gallows platform, laughing, drinking gin, swearing, joshing. Stood here by R2D2 and a flashing yellow Chewbacca, Patrick can see the ranks of leaded windows full of periwigged Regency bucks, sniffing their cologne-scented hankies to keep out the smell of the mob . . .

Then.

— Gareth?

The about-to-disappear solicitor turns:

— Yes?

— Gareth . . .

— Yes?

Patrick is trying to say, trying to ask the question he does not want to ask. At last:

— Gareth . . . How much . . . how . . . much – Patrick looks at the modernist brickwork of the Old Bailey extension, its playfully bleak exterior. The tiny main door like the outfall of a medieval privy – How long *do* I get, anyway?

— Mmm – Jenkins sounds like he's stalling – Mm? What?

— If I . . . do go down . . . If I get guilty . . . how . . . long in prison?

Jenkins is eating a crisp he has found somewhere. Jenkins says, his voice slightly muffled:

— How long would you get, custodially?

— . . . Yeah

— Oh. Don't think like that. S'not going to happen

— But if it does – Patrick leans nearer his solicitor – *how long*?

The solicitor does an uncomfortable shrug:

— Just thank God you're not living in Norman times. They used to blind rapists – Sad smile – After castrating them

Patrick says slowly, and carefully, and loudly:

— HOW fucking LONG?

The solicitor makes a reluctant face and says:

— Depends. The Lord Chancellor recommends that convicted rapists should serve no fewer than five years. But as I've . . . – An even more uncomfortable shrug, an evasive cough – As I might have said. In your case . . . with your . . . form. It's. It's. It's . . .

Patrick nods, clicks tersely, says:

— I'd get *life* wouldn't I? Because of whatyoucallit . . . the two strikes rule? – Eyebrows up – Because of my previous conviction for violence and the two-strikes-and-you're-out rule . . . – Staring at his solicitor – Because of that I'd get . . . *life imprisonment*. Wouldn't I? Right?

Gareth Jenkins seems to pause, to think. Then he says:

— It's being challenged under the Human Rights Act, but . . . – Drawing breath – The two strikes rule does indicate that if you are convicted of a violent crime, as you have been, and then of a sexual crime – Pausing again – As you might be, then well . . . yes . . . – The solicitor stares directly at Patrick – Then yes you would. You would – Still staring – You'd get life

And with that Gareth Jenkins swivels on a heel.

Quiet, Patrick turns. He looks at the Old Bailey, Old Newgate Jail, where all these men have been hanged. Once more picturing the scene, imagining the tumult of a public execution, Patrick narrows his eyes. Right at the back of the mob, beyond the rozzers and laundry girls and knife grinders and sellers of hot sheep's feet, beyond the thief-takers and match-girls and pure-finders and mudlarks and tipsy Victorian poets, Patrick can make out the distant figure of . . .

himself, blinking in the sunlight, wearing his best Bond Street suit, cool in wraparound sunglasses, standing stiff to attention on the gibbet platform . . . until the hangman kicks the bucket away and the crowd goes Oooooh, and his handmade £200 shoes kick jerkily and futilely at the empty London air.

10

Thwarted on the steps of the nightclub by the jostling, joint-waving crowd of would-be nightclubbers Rebecca turns from the middle of the ostentatiously beered-up, drugged-up mob and she calls over to Murphy, who is still extracting her long legs from a minicab. Puffing, cursing, Murphy rolls her eyes at the throng, buttons her raincoat tight, and gingerly ticks through the crowd in her high heels towards her friend. Then she says:
— Popular spot
   Rebecca:
— It is the opening night
   Already at Rebecca's side is Sacha. Her oldest male friend. Sacha is sneering, and sniffing: thus to inhale the evening air, the cold late autumn night air scented with cigarettes, with Red Bull, with lager and chilli-breath and chewing gum. Sacha checks his green-and-golden watch; sighs. Feeling responsible Rebecca raises plucked eyebrows at Sacha and says:
— . . . Patch did tell us to get here early
— We ARE early
— Uhyes
— Well?
— I'm sure we'll get in . . . in a *minute*?
   Hopeful, hopeless, Rebecca stares across the helplessly large crowd that stretches ten yards up the steps to the row of impassive black-blazered bouncers. Sacha mimics her stare, mimics agreement:
— Any minute now, I'd say, Rebecca
   Murphy:

—It's not her fault
—No, it's his
—You know what I mean
—Perhaps we should come back later, like next year?
—Look. We're here for a laugh – Murphy stares Sacha out – So. Take some drugs. Anything. *Please*

Sacha shakes his head:
—Don't think *Becs* would approve

Rebecca makes a wide-eyed face, simultaneously scanning the faces of the already-in-the-nightclub people who are standing just inside the door staring smugly and triumphantly out at the crowds of not-yet-in-the-nightclub people. Rebecca says:
—I don't care what you two do

Sacha:
—Oh really?
—Really. Take E for all I care
—OK. Fine. Shall we get you some? A few uppity doodahs?

Rebecca's face shuts them both up: as she intended. Around them the crowd pushes forward, optimistically. But then a bouncer single-handedly pushes them all back, tipping the crowd three steps down the steps. Again Sacha grimaces, in an *I'm twenty-two and rich and I don't have to be here with all these plebs* way:
—Lowlifes

Murphy:
—We *are* on the guest list, Becs?
—Of course

Murphy:
—So what's the problem?
—I think . . . I don't . . . – Rebecca shrugs, she shrugs her coated shoulders at everyone around: at the giggling girls in embroidered indigo denim; at the lads with long hair and red ballroom shirts. Rebecca notices that lots of the girls are clutching the same big cardboard invites. Rebecca decides she has never seen so many dilated pupils. She sighs:
—I think *everybody*'s on the guest list, they've *all* got invites

Sacha:
—Yes yes sure but he is your *boyfriend*, he *runs* the place – Making a face – *Allegedly*

Murphy:

—You really rate Patch don't you Sacha?

—And you love him, do you Murphy?

—I think he's . . . fun . . .

—You think, Murphy – Sacha glares at the rucksack of a Japanese girl standing too close to him – That he's a gangster

—Well, maybe he's a bit of a brute, but that's what Bex likes – Murphy goes on – Why *do* you loathe him so much *anyway*?

—He's a fascist oik

—Not cause he's shagging Becs?

—Shut up! Shut UP!

Says Rebecca. Sacha and Murphy fall quiet. They all pause. Sighing, twice, Sacha tiptoes on his loafers and gazes across the postindustrial hectares of East London that stretch about them, that surround the old Victorian block with the retro blue neon Howie's NightClub sign above the bouncered door. His survey done, Sacha says:

—Charming area. Where are we exactly?

—North Hoxton

—Oh, *North* Hoxton

—South's too expensive Patch said, but Patch reckons the prices around here will go up as well so . . .

Rebecca stops, self-conscious of parroting Patrick's opinions, again. Murphy chuckles. Rebecca sighs and half laughs at herself and says:

—Well there are lots of artists, students, it's fairly low rent at the moment

—You said it

The three of them stare at the crowds. With an impatient tone, Murphy:

—You could try asking the doorman

—. . . shall I?

—YES!!!

Her two friends so obviously in agreement, Rebecca dutifully pulls away from the throng, edges round, and makes her way up the side of the crumbling redbrick steps. Rebecca can sense Murphy and Sacha watching her, as she approaches the biggest, ugliest, least evolved doorman. Girding, swallowing, Rebecca says:

— My boyfriend manages this

—What?? STOP pushing you DULL CUNT

Rebecca watches the bouncer shunt an overeager boy in the chest, forcing him back down the steps. Rebecca stammers for a second but then manages:

— uh I'm terribly sorry

—Yes? WHAT??

Rebecca wonders how to pithily explain that her boyfriend is running the whole show, is managing this opening night . . . and has spent the entire last year finding the venue, buying the property, arguing with brewers, bribing the council, organising acts who fail to turn up and, not irrelevantly, hiring apemen to work the door.

She stays quiet. The bouncer says:

—Ere! You're Patrick's bird?

Rebecca smiles winsomely. The bouncer looks her up and down:

—Inyergo

One faint jerk of the bouncer's thumb and Rebecca is inside. *Yes!*

But then she remembers her duty: trying to stifle any smug, triumphant feelings Rebecca edges back to the door wherefrom she looks down at Murphy and Sacha, at their sarcastic faces tilted back up at hers. From her lofty position at the top of the stairs, just inside the club, Rebecca shrugs an I'll-get-you-in-soon shrug and then she turns and pushes herself into the appalling crush.

Noise; sweat; neon. Dropping her coat off at the crowded cloakroom, Rebecca feels her pulse quicken in the din and energy. The noise is profound; it thrills up Rebecca's back and rattles in her head. Standing by five boys, all clutching blue beer bottles and drinking as one, Rebecca feels her heart beat in time with the enormous music: the Asian dub and Bhangra and lots of other loud percussive music. Five yards and as many minutes inside, Rebecca notices Joe amidst the crowd. He is drinking from a bottle of Indian beer, and eating a samosa, and grinning a suspiciously wide grin at Rebecca:

—Scrunchyface!

—Hi, Joe. Seen Patch?

Patrick's cute loser flatmate grins again and says:

—Not really . . .

—Where is he?

—Guess is as good as mine

—No it isn't

Joe nods acknowledgement at this, and confesses:

—Well I think he's freaked out about the council cause you know all hassle they only got a licence anyway they're in the back cause he bought some from

—*What?*

—In case they find drugs or summat, so he's probably out the back doing drugs – Rushing on – Ha anyway you heard they wanna close the place down already? Reckon they're only looking for an excuse you could try downstairs maybe he

Rebecca looks at the little flecks of white saliva in the corner of Joe's much-too-talkative mouth. *Dexedrine*, or *cocaine*, she thinks. For a second Rebecca wonders at how quickly and worryingly she's got to know the precise signs of drug abuse since she's started going out with Patch. Then Rebecca thinks: where's Patrick? And she says to Joe:

—If you see him tell him?

Joe laughs, hiccups, nods, then turns and says something loud near the ear of his drinking buddy, a girl with eyebrow studs and a tattoo on her cheek and thick black-plastic-rimmed glasses. In tune, the girl laughs and slugs from her blue bottle of beer and looks appraisingly at Rebecca. But Rebecca doesn't wait to get evaluated, doesn't want to be evaluated. Into the boom, into the throb and reverb, into the overloud laughter and opening-night buzz and drifting clouds of sandalwood incense Rebecca presses.

By a wall Rebecca finds a stairway. *Downstairs?* Downstairs. Walking past an unsteady girl leaning drunkenly against the stairwell wall, past a boy in shorts and bandanna trying to use his mobile, Rebecca pushes and jostles, and then finds herself standing next to another of Patrick's friends. *Nico*. It is Nico, Patrick's good-looking Greek friend: one of the nicer of his mates. Despite the noise Nico leans and tries to say something to Rebecca but Rebecca is not really listening; she is standing on tiptoes to look across the shadowy bobbing heads to see: at the end of the basement room a group is on stage spanking guitars and congas and electric snares. In front of the stage girls in white cricket hats and boys with bared torsos are throwing samosas at the band. Standing down from tiptoes Rebecca turns and shouts inside the ear of Nico but in reply Nico just drinks Kingfisher beer, grins, and shrugs in the noise and the darkness. Then Nico seems to work something out: he enthusiastically waves Rebecca to the rear of the basement.

Hoping, trusting, Rebecca pushes and jostles that way, past the toilets. In the queue for the Ladies are two giggling boys in Japanese tee shirts and long yellow surfing shorts. One of the boys winks at Rebecca and Rebecca smiles back. Also good-looking, she thinks.

Then Rebecca gets renewed energy: wilful and determined she thrusts herself through and between, whereat she finds herself in front of a black-painted door in a red-lit recess. It is a bit quieter here. Wondering if her hair is now a total mess, Rebecca pushes the door open and immediately she sees Patrick: he has his head down and he is sniffing the top of a refrigerator. Rebecca double takes: Patrick is sniffing a long line of coke off the top of a black-painted fridge. Irritated, intrigued, Rebecca watches: Patrick is swabbing his fingertip across the fridge top, licking his fingertip, and wincing; then he looks up and sees Rebecca. At once Patrick smiles, and gestures her into the room. A room full of saxophones, weird guitars, dressing-room mirrors, and two stoned-looking Asian girls drinking cocktails in a dim corner. Patrick:

— Hi Becs

His smile is cold. His eyes, frozen, hard; sparkly . . .

— Meet the band – Says Patrick, wafting a hand to indicate a group of languid-looking Indian guys in flared jeans and orange shirts, who are sitting on a dilapidated leather sofa. Patrick turns his head between the band and Rebecca, and says in an introducing-you tone:

— Bird, band – Turning – Band, bird . . .

The only member of the band not wearing make-up says:

— Nice to meet you, bird

Patrick chuckles at this and shrugs apologetically at Rebecca, then one of the band members says:

— Patch don't do all the fucking hooter

— I won't I won't

— C'mon, share it out

— Calm down, hoovernose

Rebecca notices that the band members are laughing, in a sycophantic way, in a sucking-up-to-Patch way. Angered by this, delighted, disdainful, envious, feeling like she now *really* needs a drink, Rebecca gazes awkwardly and self-consciously at her boyfriend. Patrick is swabbing his finger once more across the top of the fridge; this time without looking. After absent-mindedly rubbing the fingertip over his upper gum Patrick looks at Rebecca and goes to say something but before he can talk his coketalk she says:

— Sacha and Murphy are waiting outside could you get them in?

Offering the ceiling a pained expression, Patrick says:

— Not that Yiddish bum-weasel

Another band member laughs. Rebecca:

— Patrick, please

— Why d'you bring him, the tosser

— They're my friends

—He better behave himself. Only man to fail the Turing test

—Patch – Rebecca is getting very embarrassed, and angry, sensing the inquisitive contempt of the irritatingly tanned, annoyingly Asian musicians. She senses them assessing her legs, sneering at her clothes, and wondering why precisely she lets Patrick treat her like this. *God*, Rebecca exhales, *musicians*. Even their saxophones annoy her: sitting there, glittering. *Who do they think they are, musos, with their plectrums and drum machines and argot and endless streams of compliant women watching them do nothing?*

—OK. Wait here

Taken aback, Rebecca feels Patrick brush past her; for a second she smells his sweat mixed with antiperspirant; then he is gone.

So now?

Apprehensive, Rebecca sits on the edge of the leather sofa and tries to engage the band in chat. Again she senses their ardent disapproval of her: of her Hampsteady uncoolness, her rich girl uncredibility, her intellectual, postgrad, unstreetsmart, wrong-clothes-wearing heiressness. Not for the first time in Patrick's circle Rebecca feels she will never be part of Patrick's circle; not for the first time in her time in Patrick's circle Rebecca wishes she had an eyebrow stud and a small sarcastic tattoo on her shoulder and no money and a pretty obvious drug habit. So maybe she should do drugs? She has never done drugs. So do some drugs?

Abandoning the attempt to converse with the coked-up, laughing, joint-rolling members of the band Rebecca opens the fridge and grabs at the first thing she sees: a half-bottle of vodka. Unscrewing this and taking a big cold shot, she wipes her lips with a bare forearm and then pushes her way out of the dressing room and makes her fighting, angry, defiant, vodka-chugging way to the door of the hugely booming nightclub. On the way she spots Patrick's colleague, Patrick's PA, Patrick's accountant. She is surrounded. She is in enemy territory. Oppressed and hemmed in and made to feel claustrophobic by the Patrickness of her environs Rebecca takes two more largeish nips from the icy vodka half-bottle, and goes for the door. Before she can get there she finds herself standing by Murphy, Sacha, Patrick and Joe, who are all by the bar drinking from blue bottles of Indian beer as Patrick uses a beer-bottle-holding hand to point a finger at Sacha:

—Let's play a game

Sacha replies, a tone in his voice:

—Please, feel free

—OK – Patch burps, and winks at Rebecca; Rebecca notices Murphy is rolling her eyes anxiously in Rebecca's direction as if to say *yes they're arguing already*.

Patrick is saying – Let's play Ipswich

Sacha:

—Ipswich?

—Yes, Ipswich: you know how to play that?

—No

—Well it goes like this . . . – Smiling – You fuck off to Ipswich. And stay there

—You are a genuine . . . *prole*, aren't you

—My club, my rules

Rebecca:

—Please you two, not again

Murphy says:

—Come on, Becs, let's go and dance

—Why are all Nazis provincials?

—Is it because she's sleeping with me, or because you are a git?

—Oh, Murf, stop them

—I bet I come back as a marmoset

—Sorry?

—When I die

—What are you *on*, Joe?

—Or a tapir

—Stop them or I'm leaving

—I've got some E you know

Rebecca, ignoring Joe, says to Murphy:

—I don't really need to listen to this

But Patrick is spitting the words at Sacha:

—I mean do you believe that if a black guy rapes a white woman that's a racially provoked crime? Course you don't, so why is it if a white man hits a black man mm?

—That's a ridiculous question

—The weird thing is I bet you haven't got any black friends have you? I have

—Oh shut up both of you

—Yeah chill your squirrels

—Joe I want some E

Rebecca is pulling Joe's sleeve; saying again:

—Joe. Some Ecstasy

—*What?*

—Give me one?

—But . . . you don't . . .

—So there's a first time – Rebecca lifts her eyes to Joe's kind, laughing, good-natured eyes – Anything's better than listening to those two. Give me an E, please?

Commanded, Joe filches in his pocket, and pulls out a little screw of cigarette paper. Unscrewing the cigarette paper to reveal two smallish blue pills Joe carefully takes one pill and hands it over. Braving, steeling, girding, Rebecca closes her eyes, knocks back, and chases the pill with a slug of warm Kingfisher. Then she opens her eyes, and rejoins the world, and pushes near, and finds Patrick jabbing an angry hand which Sacha is angrily pushing away. The two of them are going at it. For ten minutes, for twenty minutes, Rebecca stands there dumb and dutiful, listening to the bull sea elephants head-butting each other on the South Georgia strand. Then, exasperated by the crass stupid maleness of it all, Rebecca pulls Murphy by the silky sleeve and they step aside and Murphy says:

—They'll never stop

—Why do they do this *every* time?

—You know that the prime age for a man to murder is the same age at which a man is most likely to have a hit single?

—Thanks, Joe

—Just thought ya should know

—Men and Facts, you're as bad as Patch

—Like we're interested

—Why don't YOU stop them, Joe?

Joe shrugs; sinks his beer. Joe looks back at where Patrick is gripping Sacha's arm. Rebecca sips her beer; feels the bpm of the music from the basement below; running up her calves, running up her spinal cord, making space and feeling in her brain. The music is delicious, a lovely beat. Rebecca feels a little weird. Joe is looking knowingly at Rebecca's shiny eyes:

—It's a quick come-on isn't it?

—How can we stop them

—I know Patch he'll be . . . he'll be

Too. *Too.* Very. Rebecca is suddenly feeling *very*. The music and the beer, the dazzling lights and the blue bottles of beer are *very*. Rebecca laughs and Joe laughs at Rebecca's laugh and then Rebecca feels a surge of affection for the bottle of beer in her hand, its lovely sapphire blueness, and the delicious sound of the music beating, beating. Fucking her from behind. *Fucking her from behind? Where did that come from?* The thrust of the music is fine. Without consciously willing it, Rebecca finds herself following the music and Joe down to the basement where some different band is playing, brilliantly. Almost joyous, wholly amused, Rebecca starts to dance: to dance to everything. The smoke and the sweat and the joint smoke and the epileptiform lights make her feel very alive, very in love, very much like kissing Joe.

Touching her own face with her own fingers as she dances Rebecca feels she wants to kiss Joe, the same way she wants to kiss the lights and the music. The music is so good: the way it takes her from behind, makes her spin. Rebecca is dancing so hard she is dizzy but she doesn't care because she knows the crowd all feel the same, as dizzy and happy as her. Rebecca feels at one with the crowd, she feels like a communist, like a Hitler Youth, like a North Korean, worshipping the music, the despotic dancebeat, the sweet tyranny of this gorgeous dance music, the beat; and then at just the right time as Rebecca feels all this she feels a hand on her back pressing the cold sweet dampness of her dress to her sweating back. Rebecca turns and sees: Patrick. Patrick is grinning and saying 'Joe told me' and Rebecca doesn't know what he means but she likes his teeth, the drumbeat, his mouth, the beat, his dark thick hair. Grateful and happy Rebecca feels Patrick's mouth close upon hers and she feels his chin stubble and senses her scent on his skin as they kiss, she feels the thumping bassline in her groin and she loves it; her cuntbeat, the cuntbass/cuntdrum, fuckme, fuckme, fuckme

— Fuck me, Patrick

But before she can. Theygo. Upstair. Darkness. Corrid. Here the beating music is quieter but still very loud as Patrick pushes a door, and pushes her into a kitchen. Dazed, dancey, gladdened, Rebecca notices by the wet on the windows that it is raining, the rain is running down the window; remembering she loves the rain Rebecca pushes the window open and reaches far out the window so as to feel the rain on her fingers, as at the same time Patrick lifts up her dress from behind and parts her. The rain. *The rain.* Rebecca licks the rain from her fingers as he opens her up; she presses her palm to the cold wall and her head to the cold window glass, as he enters her, as she thinks about the rain. The rhythm, the bassnote, the cuntbeat. They are having sex against the sink making the cutlery on the draining board bounce up and down, and Rebecca half shuts her eyes and squints at a glass full of knives and forks, an armoury of silver in the rain light, the cuntlight, the drumlight. The metal of the sink unit is cold against Rebecca's exposed breasts as he pushes her head down into the sink as he does her like the music, does her, drums her, bangs her in time with the delicious music in her head that she now understands oh this drug oh this drug oh yes oh yes

Patrick. Patrick. Patch. Patc. Half aware Rebecca feels him grab a fistful of her hair and lift her head back up and push her cheek against the cold sweet glass of the windowpane where she counts the rain again; but then no more, no more, NO MORE: newly determined Rebecca pushes back from the sink and she swivels on the man she loves, the man she loved, the man she has always loved, always wanted, always needed; in the sweet, sad, blueglass, nightclub-kitchen half-light Rebecca turns right round and fronts his low blue silent eyes and she says out loud:

—Hit me

And this time, this time, *this time*. This time he raises a hand and backhanded hits her hard right across the face, twice, and again, and almost at once Rebecca feels the stab of pain in her stupid face, the salt of blood in her girlish mouth; and with the shudder of a longed-for surrender she sinks to her cold grateful knees.

11

—Is it true you used to ask the defendant to hit you during sex?

Patrick leans his chin on his thumbs, looks intently at Rebecca as Rebecca pauses, demurs. The judge looks curiously at Rebecca; Rebecca stares to the wall and stays mute; the defence counsel, standing three yards down the desk from the prosecution advocate, smooths a non-existent goatee and stares directly at Rebecca. Then he says:

—Would you like me to repeat the question?

Dressed in her yellow gingham blouse and sensible long grey skirt, Rebecca turns and looks imploringly at the judge; but the judge is taking pains not to notice her. The judge is writing something down in a big notebook; the pale-silver wig bobs as he scribbles. Finally, with an air of hopelessness, Rebecca turns and says, slowly, to Patrick's defence, to Robert Stefan QC:

—At times, yes

—Sorry, Miss Jessel?

—I said, yes. At times I would ask him . . . – She sighs; then – To strike me

—And did he?

—Yes

—Always?

—Sometimes

—Was it most of the time? Would you say he hit you most of the time? When you made love?

Rebecca looks like she is trying to think through a puzzle; she frowns intensely and gazes at Stefan's wig, at the white tie ribbons of his collar, then she says:

— I suppose we did . . . I suppose I used to ask him, quite a lot. It was . . . just . . . something we did. In bed – Her eyes wander the room and for a second her gaze meets Patrick's gaze; chilled, shocked, fearful, Patrick averts his face; as he does he sees Rebecca turn back to Stefan; she is listening to Stefan ask another question:

— So when would this happen?

— Sorry?

— When would you ask him to strike you, at which point during your . . . lovemaking?

— Uhm

Stefan is calm; Rebecca is swaying. Then Rebecca seems to get a hold: she says flatly, at the defence counsel:

— During moments of passion

— And when he hit you . . . what kind of blows were these?

Rebecca looks down:

— Slaps

— Hard slaps?

— Quite hard

— Never punches, he never used his clenched fist?

— No, never

— You're certain?

— Yes. I wouldn't have liked that. That's not what we were into

— Of course – A hint of something in Stefan's voice, a faint harmonic of irony – And how often did this happen Miss Jessel? How often did he . . . *slap* you?

— I don't remember . . .

— You don't remember how many times you asked him? Or how often you asked him?

— I don't remember how many times . . . A few times. A few times at first. And then he . . . then he . . . – Rebecca stops, mid-sentence. Stefan nods, waits; says:

— And then he got the hang of it? Is that what you mean? That's when he understood that that's the kind of . . . rough sex you liked? Right?

— . . . If you want to put it that way

— And after a few weeks you didn't have to ask him any more? He'd just do what you liked?

— Yes. No. I . . . – Rebecca tilts her head; she levels an assessing stare across the courtroom. Patrick finds himself admiring his ex-girlfriend's peculiar bravery, despite. Despite the fact he wants to firebomb her house with her inside, the tilt of pride in his truelove's demeanour leaves him astir; to quell himself Patrick exhales into his praying hands and half shuts his eyes as his ex-girlfriend says – I don't remember exactly when it was that he first . . . hit me – Patrick opens his eyes as she goes on – I do remember he liked hitting me. Very much

— I see. Yes

— He used to like hitting me and tying me up

Patrick stares at the royal crest on the wall above the judge's wig

— He got off on it . . .

The crest; the unicorn; *Honi Soit.*

— It used to worry me sometimes of course how he liked it

At last Stefan says:

— And it was . . . always like this, even on the night in question?

— Uhn?

Rebecca has gone mute, a nonplussed expression blanks her face. The defence counsel adjusts his wig, straightens his gown, refines his question. As the lawyer questions Rebecca about some stuff, about the alleged incident, Patrick finds himself looking at Rebecca's fingers wrapped around the sill of the witness box. Despite his best efforts to concentrate on Rebecca's evidence, Patrick's mind is drifting, he is reminded by her fingers of the way she would wrap her fingers around the wooden bedstead of her bed in Hampstead, as he fucked her from behind so hard he could feel in his groin how hard he'd fucked her three days later. Narrowing his eyes Patrick purges these images: instead he checks the actual whiteness of Rebecca's knuckles; as he does he flinches to see the sparkle of a ring on the slender middle finger of Rebecca's right hand. It is a ring he once gave her; it looks like the silver and turquoise ring from Mexico. His own hands tucked under the biceps of his tightly crossed arms, Patrick hunches forward, thinking, thinking, remembering the ring . . .

Then he hears Rebecca's testimony:

— He was punching me, hard

Stefan:

— And this was different?

— Yes. Totally. They weren't slaps, he wasn't . . . playing. He was knocking me around, like a puppet . . . He was drunk, it was . . . frightening

Stefan nods, as if fully expecting this testimony. Patrick finds himself approving his brief's court performance: *nice and professional*. Patrick thinks, urges: *nice and professional*. In his seat Patrick sits stiffly and watches as Stefan makes delaying noises.

— Now. Yyyyesss – Stefan lets a limp hand shift some papers on his desk. Sliding sheets of paper languidly, one over the other, Stefan pauses and seems to think, then he looks up at Rebecca:

— I know we've been over it in some detail already, Miss Jessel, but if I can take you back to the . . . beginning of the alleged incident? One more time?

In the witness box, Rebecca shrugs, almost contemptuously. Stefan does a grateful nod and says:

— You say that when the accused had taken your jeans off, he then prised your legs apart, and penetrated you with his penis. Correct?

— . . . Yes

— Just like that?

— .˙. Sorry?

— He just slipped it in, just like that?

— . . . Yess

— Are you sure, Miss Jessel? You sound a little unsure

— I'm sure . . . I'm sure – Rebecca has made an I'm-sure-I'm-sure face: her shiny, intelligent eyes flash hard at Stefan, then around the room; Patrick looks away and as he does he catches the young Asian juror looking directly back at him; the girl glances hurriedly away and pretends to look at Stefan. Glancing back Patrick sees that Stefan is making a different face as he says:

— So, were you wet?

Clock, crest, unicorn, Rebecca. Standing in her box, Rebecca opens her mouth. Before she has had a chance to say anything the prosecution lawyer raises a loud voice in protest, a protest that matches the murmur of the court. Patrick looks at the judge, as the judge leans nearer to the court and says:

— Mister Stefan?

— M'Lord

— Mister Stefan . . . – Thinking, pausing – I know we discussed this line earlier . . . I just want to warn you that if you are intent on some kind of fishing expedition, then I shall be minded to intervene

— M'Lord . . . I remember . . .

The judge smiles:

— Well. Very well – Thinking; frowning; continuing – Proceed

Patrick glances back at Rebecca. Rebecca is swivelling in the witness box, looking at Stefan and the judge by turns. She looks like some oversized Victorian toy, Patrick thinks. After being conspicuously unhelped by the judge, Rebecca turns again, and says to Stefan:

— I'm not sure what you mean . . . *Wet*?

— You don't know what I'm driving at? – Stefan's arrogance verges on pomposity. Patrick finds himself thinking: *don't overdo it*. Stefan is shaking his head and saying – What I mean, Miss Jessel, what I mean is: were you receptive, was your vagina . . . *lubricated*? – He pauses, waits; waits, speaks – When the accused put his penis inside you?

Muffled noise from somewhere. Distant car noise. Rebecca:

— I don't know . . .

— But you must have been wet, for the accused to penetrate you so easily?

— I . . . I . . . wwwould . . .

— Why *were* you so wet? Miss Jessel?

— I don't know that I was. If I was. He was just being very aggressive and I was scared and it

— Miss Jessel, what had happened just before he entered you? Just before that moment?

A wisp of blonde hair escapes Rebecca's schoolgirlish chignon; she takes a second to file it behind her ear with a middle finger, and then she seems to take control as she says:

— He pulled my jeans off

— He didn't do anything else then?

— No. He just opened my legs and penetrated

— Entered you with his penis?

— Yes. I was very scared, he was very hard

— You don't remember his performing oral sex on you then? At any point?

Huge pause. Big pause. The wisp, again; this time Rebecca ignores it, her pale face is growing paler behind the dangling strands of pale gold. Glancing at no-one Rebecca swallows, swallows again, and then reaches down to a shelf inside the box wherefrom she picks up her glass of water; her pink lips are redder and wet when she puts the glass back down; when she says:

—I don't exactly recall. He might have

—He *might* have? He *might* have performed oral sex?

—I don't think . . . he did but . . . It was all very quick and I was . . . in a daze after he'd punched me so much

Stefan looks momentarily at the jury; Patrick looks at Stefan's junior, Juson; the junior looks directly at Patrick and, quite unexpectedly the junior surreptitiously winks at Patrick. As soon as he has clocked the wink Patrick can't help breaking into a smile, sensing that this is a lawyerly signal that the cross-examination is going OK, is going well; but then Patrick remembers he was told not to smile so he suppresses the smile and he tunes in again to hear Stefan say:

—That is why you were so receptive, so wet, Miss Jessel? Isn't that right? Because he had been performing oral sex on you? – Smile, sardoniċ smile – Cunnilingus, I mean

—He might . . . I . . .

—You're still not sure?

—No . . . but . . .

—It is part of your normal sexual repertoire with the accused, isn't it?

Patrick turns. Towards the judge. On his bench the judge is gazing at Stefan, hard; the judge looks as if he is about to say something. Five yards away and two yards lower Stefan appears to sense this. He suddenly goes conspicuously quiet and stands further back from the witness box, giving his witness the time and psychological space to reply

—We used to . . . you know . . . I suppose . . . go . . . down . . . on each other, like . . . anyone else would – Rebecca stops, she takes and sips more water, her tongue flicks to lick her lips; then she looks at a part of the floor somewhere between the prosecution counsel and the defence solicitor, as she goes on – He would normally . . . – Rebecca inhales, exhales – Lick me . . . and I would suck him, and I would fellate him. I imagine we did that most times . . . when we made love – Patrick is leaning nearer; in his box he is leaning nearer to his ex-girlfriend to hear her as she says – But I can't remember if we did it that night. Perhaps we did, I don't know – Her stooped blondeness is shiny in the court light; Stefan goes to say something but then Rebecca lifts her face and says – All I remember is that I was very frightened. He had penetrated me very roughly and I was terrified. I thought he was going to kill me . . .

Mouth firm, Stefan nods. Patrick gazes. Stefan nods and manages another insincere smile; so insincere Patrick wonders if his brief is doing it deliberately, smiling hypocritically like this: to unnerve the witness. Still smiling his monitor-lizard smile, Stefan says:

— Miss Jessel, would you say it was normal for a rapist to . . . 'go down' on his victims?

The court is silent, shocked into silence. Patrick looks at the startled-looking jury. The silence is broken by the sound of Alan Gregory QC rising with a chair scrape to his feet; the prosecution is gabbling something that Patrick does not catch; instead Patrick sees the judge lift a practised hand. The judge is waving at the prosecution, indicating, with an air of mild weariness, that the lawyer should sit down. As the prosecution resumes his seat in an I'm-still-very-annoyed-you-better-do-something-about-this way, the judge directs his attention at the defence:

— Mister Stefan?

— My Lord, I was merely hoping to establish that th

— I think I know what you were hoping to establish – The judge picks up his Biro. He clicks it on and off in a gruff, ominous way; then says – And I nonetheless would advise you to rephrase the question. Or pursue another course . . .

Stefan nods:

— Yes, My Lord

— And – Glancing at the courtroom clock, and at his own watch – I'd rather like to get this evidence concluded by the end of the day

— Of course, M'Lord, of course

— Alright then

The judge sits back; puts down his pen. With an abashed gesture, an apologetic expression, Stefan turns and looks at the papers on his desk, then he takes another moment, then he turns to Rebecca and says:

— Miss Jessel, did you orgasm at any point that evening?

Patrick flashes a look at the jury. The jury members are staring at Rebecca. Rebecca is calmly nodding, calmly replying:

— Yes

This direct and immediate answer seems to unsettle Stefan. As Patrick watches his brief, his brief says nothing. Rebecca says:

— Yes. I did. I came

Stefan nods. And again says nothing. Another silence overtakes them all; silence apart from muffled traffic noise. Patrick notices the stenographer has stopped stenographing. Her fingertips are paused over her machine, waiting for Stefan to resume. Patrick starts to hear his own heart beat louder and faster as Stefan nods once, and nods again, and then finally finally says:

—At what point did you reach climax? Was it during the oral sex?

—No

—Then when?

—I came when he was raping me

—When ... he was ... penetrating you downstairs, in the flat, or upstairs?

—Upstairs. When he was raping me

—Did you come just the once?

—Yes ,

—Were you surprised?

—... What?

—When you reached orgasm, were you surprised? – Stefan is regaining the confident timbre to his voice; his posture is once again a stationary strut.

Rebecca shakes her head:

—Not really ...

—No? Not really? Do you think it's a common reaction?

—Sorry?

—Do you think it's a common experience for people to have orgasms when they're being raped?

—M'Lord!!

Before the judge can respond to the prosecution Rebecca calmly says, with avowed dispassion:

—I don't know, I've no idea ... – Blouse, neck, eyes, gaze – You see I've never been raped before

Patrick glares at his lawyer. The jury stares at Patrick. Patrick clenches his fist and feels his heart race as he looks at Stefan. Stefan looks like he has been slightly thrown off kilter again. His silence gives Rebecca time to continue:

—It was just a reflex. That's all. You do certain things in certain ways and I imagine you will get a reflex. I wasn't actually getting off on him punching and hitting me

The judge is gazing intently at Rebecca; Stefan is saying:

—I see, I see, I

But Rebecca is going on, drowning him, a hint of anger in her voice:

— It doesn't mean I enjoyed it. I wasn't actually enjoying the fact that he was punching me, and raping me, and biting me, and calling me a Jewish cunt
— Of course, Miss Je
— Or biting my breasts, or forcing me to suck him, or slamming my face into the wall, or smearing his semen on
— Miss Jessel, Miss Jessel

Stefan is jabbering. Patrick finds himself urging his brief on: *say something; do something; anything.* Then at last Stefan says:
— When he was holding you down, as you say, how do you think he managed to unzip

And so he goes on: to pursue an entirely unrelated point about the whereabouts of Patrick's arms when Patrick was allegedly pinning her down: a lawyerly *poignard* that Rebecca easily parries.

Stuck in his dock Patrick sits back. Shocked and dumbed Patrick looks at the royal crest, the unicorn's horn, the petulant lion, the stylised garter belt. Patrick feels an angry, impotent despair. He feels like vaulting out of the dock and leaping across and slapping his counsel; he feels like shouting: *don't let her get away with that. She came. She orgasmed. How can you let her get away with that? Who orgasms during a rape? Who?*

But Patrick knows he just has to sit here, to take this, to deal with his brief's incompetence.

And so he sits there. Slowly buttoning and unbuttoning the top button of the new white shirt his mum bought him especially for his rape trial. Until the judge looks at the clock and the clerk of the court stands up and says:
— All rise

— What's going on?!
— Calm down
— Why???
— Because – Jenkins says, then he says – He hasn't finished with her yet. Calm down. Give him a chance
— Yeah sure great – Patrick takes a savage angry bite of his ham sandwich, stares around the Old Bailey canteen, stares at the face of his solicitor, says – He had her on the ropes
— Perhaps he did, perhaps he didn't

—She was all over the shop, the oral sex, all of it, she was losing it, then he goes and lets her off the hook . . .
—Give him a chance. It's difficult – Concentrating on his sandwich – These cases are . . .

Patrick stares, says:
—What?

Jenkins is having trouble unwrapping his Cellophaned sandwich; Patrick says again:
—What? These cases are what?

The solicitor puts down the sandwich, and pours the rest of his Orangina from its bottle into his scratchy opaque Old Bailey canteen glass; then Jenkins says:
—Well. Rape trials. They're different. They're . . . somewhat skewed
—*Sorry?*
—They're not like normal trials
—Stop speaking Welsh, Gareth – Patrick is trying to stay calm – Skewed how?

Jenkins shrugs, sort of nods:
—Um well . . . Because – Still evidently thinking about his sandwich Jenkins mumbles – Because . . . in the last twenty years they've changed the whole way rape trials are conducted. As a result of . . . feminism. Ah!

The sandwich wrapper is open. Patrick waits. Jenkins goes on:
—I imagine you want to know how?
—YES
—Well. For a start . . . they've taken away the corroboration role
—Wassat?

Through his next mouthful of sandwich, Jenkins explains:
—Courts used to be warned. You see. They were warned that they needed to ensure there was corroboration – Pause – Of the plaintiff's allegation
—And . . . – Patrick widens his eyes – That's . . . gone?
—Fraid so. And defendants used to be anonymous, like plaintiffs – He shrugs – That's gone too
—Tastic. Fantastic – Patrick is beginning to wish he hadn't started the debate
—And that's not all. Actually – Jenkins chews – This anonymity rule is really a bit rum, if you think about it – Chewing and swallowing –

I mean . . . your girlfriend won't see her name in the papers, once. And your name will be everywhere, even if she's shown to be a lying little tart and you're proved to be as pure as the driven – Jenkins half smiles.

Across the table, Patrick necks the rest of his Diet Coke. He swipes the back of an angry hand across his lips, and says:

— Anything else?

— Oh yes, oh yes . . . – Jenkins is now desultorily sifting through some papers taken from his briefcase, while he munches – What else haven't they done? Rape defendants can no longer cross-examine the plaintiff in person. And rape plaintiffs are much more likely to be allowed video links. And rape shield laws prevent your lawyer from trawling Rebecca's sexual history, establishing whether she was into this . . . rough stuff . . . with other men

— So I'm fucked?

Jenkins sits back. Sighs:

— No. As it happens – Levelling a stare – I'm actually trying to encourage you

— Come again?!

— What I'm trying to say is, amazingly, you should be heartened by all this – Still staring – The reason it's been brought in is because rape juries instinctively *do not trust* women. And despite *all* the efforts of feminists, they are *still* very unwilling to convict – Smiling – Particularly woman jurors, strangely enough . . .

Patrick goes to reply, but can't think of what to say. Quietness has descended. For a minute the two of them sit there, alone, listening to the noise of other prisoners talking to other solicitors. After a while Jenkins coughs and pulls back his cuff to reveal his watch and says *not long now*.

Patrick grunts, picks up his solicitor's Orangina bottle. Carefully Patrick tears the label off his solicitor's Orangina bottle, screws the bits of label up, and lines the bits of label on the table. Then Patrick spends three minutes slowly flicking the little bits of scrunched-up Orangina label at his solicitor.

Brushing the little bits of label off his suit, and off his trousered lap, Jenkins shakes his head and tuts, and then smiles quietly, and says:

— Did you know Leopold von Sacher Masoch was Jewish?

12

—Tits are a good move, in Darwinian terms

Rebecca laughs:

—Yesss . . .

—I mean it's better for girls to have tits on their chests, instead of . . .

—Espadrilles

—Stoats

—Tapirs . . . – Rebecca muses, *moues*, looks out the window – And . . . badgers would be a *real* nuisance . . .

Patrick chuckles. Rebecca looks over at Murphy, who is painting her toenails the colour of Rebecca's toenails; Murphy doesn't seem to notice Rebecca's attention, she just makes a concentrating noise. Turned back, Rebecca says:

—What about if you had to wear a hat all the time? What would you have?

—Oh, sombrero, definitely – Patrick is smiling, saying – What if your head was fifteen foot wide, how would you get into rooms, would you go sideways or try and poke it through the window or what?

Rebecca:

—Sideways – Then she says – Actually if you had stoats for feet that would be pretty cool. You could move about the place discreetly as long as you were wearing flares and

—Oh shut up *please*

Murphy has spoken. Either side of Murphy, Rebecca and Patrick fall almost silent, like a couple of admonished but still giggling schoolkids. Dope smoke drifts between them, rich, blue, thick, heavy. Then Rebecca says:

—If I were a Korean civil servant who could only say 'wong' all the time would you still love me?
—No. Shut up! FUCK! – Murphy is raising her face to the ceiling, as if imploring God to deliver her. Murphy's toes flex in despair. From inside her own dopey dreaminess Rebecca watches as Murphy curses, says *please no* again, then shakes her head at both of her friends and looks down at her toenails.

They are all sitting on the floor of Rebecca's expensively carpeted bedroom; Rebecca and Murphy are in shorts. A soft, ambient-trendy, Patrick-chosen song is leaking from the speakers, the smell of nail varnish mixes with the smell of hash. The expensive carpet is littered with bits of cotton wool. And from the window, open to the cold and rain so as to expel all the dope smoke, comes the soft melancholy sound of the winter streets, cars softly slicing through the leaves and rain puddles.

Murphy:
—I've never known two people talk such a fantastic amount of total crap as you two
—Thanks
—I'm *serious* . . .

Sat in the pale rainy light thrown by the open Hampstead window, Patrick makes an explaining voice:
—Becs is the only bird I've ever met who can talk rubbish like a guy
—That's good?
—Of course
—But it's only cause you've got her smoking dope, that's why she's talking bollocks
—I *am* still in the room by the way
—Isn't it, Patch?
—If your head was enormously expanded what would you call your hamster
—Bex!

Rebecca grins:
— oops
—Rover. Father Gapon. Himmler the hamster??
—Shutitshutitshutitshutit!!

Vigorous, Murphy throws a bit of damp cotton wool at Patrick. For a second Patrick eyes the cotton wool on the floor, then he picks it up and throws it back. Across the floor Rebecca turns woozily, very stonedly, to the CD player, and presses a button that skips the CD to another track.

Leaning back on one stiff arm Patrick inhales the last of the spliff Rebecca rolled; then he stubs the spliff in an ashtray; then he says:

—We do talk about other stuff don't we, darling?

Rebecca shrugs; Patrick says:

—Religion, we talk about religion don't we?

Rebecca says:

—We *argue* about religion

—Well . . .

Rebecca:

—Have you told Murphy your latest theory?

Patrick has started on assembling another joint. Looking up as he does so, he says:

—The Jesus-as-a-girl one, you mean?

Nodding, confirming, Rebecca watches her boyfriend's fingers as they do their expert artisan thing with paper and tobacco and bits of rolled-up cigarette packet. His eyes looking unblinkingly down, Patrick says:

—It's why I can't believe in God . . .

From her vantage, Rebecca notices that Murphy is also watching Patrick's fingers as they roll the joint. The joint is nearly done. Practised and confident Patrick licks the last flap of cigarette paper, smooths and pinches the spliff, shakes the spliff by one twisted end, and then says:

—You see I reckon God can't exist because if he did Jesus would be a girl Murphy:

—*What?*

—Any truly creative God would not have missed the chance to make the Saviour a lovely young woman

—*Sorry?*

—Imagine the box-office appeal, a half-naked Jewish girl being hammered to a cross, the legionnaires looking up her skirt, the white skin and the blood and the blonde hair and all those thorns in her soft lovely flesh

Murphy tries to make a bored face at Patrick; uncaring Patrick goes on:

—You wouldn't have much trouble filling the pews if that was the principal motif, would you?

—Hn

As Rebecca listens to Patrick waffling blasphemies to the brought-up-Catholic Murphy Rebecca fears for the calmness of the day, of the evening ahead; firming her yet-to-be-lipsticked lips she turns the CD louder in an attempt to distract herself and her friends from what she is hearing.

Murphy is shaking her head. Annoyedly. Seeming to ignore this Patrick gets up and crosses the room in his jeans, and scuffed boots, and expensive but fraying shirt. As he does Rebecca glances at Patrick, feeling something as she looks up at the tallness of her boyfriend. While Rebecca looks at Patrick she takes a couple of timid drags from the spliff Patrick's already given her; then she offers the reefer to Murphy who takes and drags on it vehemently yet sexily. The two of them are going quiet, quietly smoking, waiting for Patrick to finish whatever he's about to say. As Rebecca watches Murphy smoking and closing her eyes and nose-exhaling smoke Rebecca finds herself thinking about what Patrick said about her Jewishness, about Jewishness, and Jewish girls.

— Golly, all these theses

Coughing quietly, Rebecca swallows her hashish-tasting saliva and shakes her head; the room is spinning. She has definitely smoked *too much*. Trying to focus and thus clear her head she looks up at Patrick who is examining her bookshelves; finally she hears what he is saying. He is reading out the titles of some of her started-but-aborted theses:

— 'Justifiable Genocide: Faith and Violence in the First Crusade' . . .

Murphy titters; Patrick goes on:

— *Justifiable Genocide??*

Squirming inside Rebecca shrugs outside; she silently listens to him recite, as he pulls another file from the shelf:

— 'No Scrabble in Heaven . . .'

— Thank you so much

He ignores Rebecca, goes on:

— 'No Scrabble in Heaven? The Passing of Time in the Christian Paradise' . . . hmm . . . – He grins, puts the file back, says – Well. Why not. What's this? – Fearful of his sarcasm Rebecca watches wide-eyed with apprehension as Patrick pulls another couple of files down, and recites – 'Leaving the Milk: Images of Abandonment in the Poetry of Sylvia Plath' . . .

Affronted, Rebecca interrupts:

— You made that one up!

But Patrick just snorts, and ignores her, and says:

— What is it with you girls and Sylvia Plath? Anyway? What is all that rubbish about?

Despite her hashed-out head Rebecca tries to explain:

— It's because she's an archetype, the intelligent woman who yet

—Exactly – Says Patrick – She was super clever yet she still liked Ted to give her a slapping, put her in her proper place

Murphy stifles a laugh; Patrick, thus encouraged, goes on:

—Because that's what you all really want, even the brightest of you, isn't it? A big brute like Ted to knock you about a bit? Give you a seeing to? Whack you on the arse like his best milking heifer?

Cross-legged and barefoot, Murphy taps Patrick's jeaned ankle and says:

—You know it's not like that . . .

—Anyway. All this poetry – Says Patrick, ignoring them, tilting his head sideways so as to read the names on the spines of the thinnest books on the bookshelves – *Hughes, Sexton, Carver . . . Heaney* – Be-ringed hand up, Patrick pulls out a copy of some Seamus Heaney and says – Seamus Heaney?

—Irish Nobel laureate

—Right, yeah, we used to do Heaney at college . . . and Hughes for that matter

—So you have read them, you're such a liar

Standing up, tall, Patrick clicks and tssks. A few yards away Murphy flashes a wry conspiratorial *men? cuh!* smile at Rebecca before returning her gaze to her bare feet, to re-admire her toenails shining in the smoky rainy afternoon light. Between them Patrick is still gabbling away as he flicks through Rebecca's big compendium of modern poetry:

—God yes I remember this fucking rubbish, I remember Heaney and Hughes – Rebecca watches as Patrick grins to himself, as he says – All they ever go on about is *buckets* – He prepares to read out loud – 'In the slung bucket, the sun stood . . .' – Flicking the page, then quoting again – 'A cool small evening shrunk to a dog bark and the clank of a bucket' – Patrick flicks the pages very quickly – Buckets buckets buckets, watertroughs, buckets, tractors, buckets, Jesus

Murphy:

—So you *do* read poetry then?

—Buckettian, the buckettian school . . .

—You kind of pretend to be stupid don't you? But you still read poetry?

Ignoring Murphy, Patrick slips the book back in its space on the shelf, then says:

—Anyway, Plath, she's overrated

Rebecca looks for the spliff. Murphy sees her looking and hands it across. Patrick is still wittering:

—Her use of the Holocaust, bit dodgy I think . . . – Searching the shelves

Patrick finds a copy of Plath poetry, and opens it – All that Holocaust imagery, any of these artists who use Holocaust imagery, all they're doing is plagiarising Hitler
—What?
—Don't encourage him, Murphy
    Encouraged, Patrick says:
—That's what it should say at the bottom of the credits of *Schindler's List*: 'from an original idea by A. Hitler' – Patrick shuts *Ariel* and slides it back – After all it was all Hitler's idea, his conception, his Wagnerian imagination
—Fancy a bagel, Murphy?
—Why not
    Patrick, looking at the ceiling, goes on:
—No. Listen. S'true. It was his amazing, awful, evil, brilliant idea. His alone. And what a fucking conception. To kill the most creative race in Europe. To kill the chosen people, in their entirety – Patrick inhales, exhales – And not just to *kill them*. Not just to *kill* the Jews. No, Hitler's idea was to chase them down all over Europe and then drag them halfway across the Continent and install them in these special Satanic death camps with men in leather coats and trendy long boots and huge dogs. It's brilliant. Poetic. Götterfuckingdämmerung. And he designed it all. Hitler. He did the costume design, the set design, the script, chose the music . . . – Patrick is almost yelling – He should get all the Oscars and all the Pulitzers and all the Bookers ever won by anyfuckingone who's ever used the Holocaust to give any fucking power to their otherwise pisspoor artistic efforts, who use his evil genius as salt and seasoning for their otherwise bland and inane confections
—Got any biccies?
    Says Murphy; but Patrick has shut up anyway. He has crossed the floor, shrugged his shoulders, and sat down on the bit of carpet by the window where he sits cross-legged and gazes across at Rebecca who is giving the re-lit spliff back to Murphy. As Murphy says:
—Is it because it's too gay to admit you read?
—Your toenail varnish is smudged
—Especially poetry, hey, Patrick? Hmm? Poetry?
    Patrick:
—Why are girls like buckets, anyway?
—Too girly for you is it?
—Cause when they're fucked they leak

This last remark goes ignored. Clutching the spliff, Rebecca seeks around for the ashtray she and Patrick stole from the restaurant they ate in last night. It was a trendy white-painted restaurant, serving trendy offal. Thinking of this, tapping her ash, Rebecca remembers the meal in detail: the cool offcuts they ate, the cutting-edge kidney, the avant-garde faggots. Slipping into this reverie Rebecca feels the drawl of her own thoughts, thoughts of Patrick, food, last night, offal, chitterlings, middleside, the pinkredunder-cooked meat . . .

—Guest list starts about ten

—We could get a minicab

Mechanically, Rebecca reaches out for the plastic case of another CD, the first CD having just finished. As she enacts this reflex, Rebecca realises she is suddenly self-conscious about doing this: about choosing some music for herself. From nowhere she is suddenly self-conscious about her musical tastes being exposed to him, in front of Murphy. She is *so* self-conscious she is self-conscious about self-consciously looking over at Patrick to check if he has seen how self-conscious she is feeling. *Oh God. Why is she like this?* Rebecca wishes she wasn't; why does he make her at once so anxious yet turned on; why is she so in thrall to his tastes, his lower-class coolness, his manly confidence, his Clerkenwell hipness? *Why? What is she looking for from him? Freudian affirmation? Fatherly approval? A smile that reminds her of the female offal she is that he nonetheless adores?*

—They always charge fifty quid and they come from Kosovo so they don't know where London is

—But black cabs are . . .

Taking a breath, Rebecca sticks a CD in, and sits back. Her lover is arguing, again, with Murphy, as ever . . . As always. Always the two of them argue about politics, feminism, books, stamp collecting, cloud names, black cabs versus minicabs, everything. But this time it is different, this time Rebecca feels a pang of envy as she sees his blue eyes, his jazz-blue, his neon-in-the-rain-blue eyes shine and glance and glitter: at Murphy. *No. Yes.* Somewhere near her diaphragm Rebecca feels a stitch-pain of jealousy, a period pain of envy, envy for Murphy's long legs and silver nose stud and cute cuttlefish tattoo, envy and hatred for the way the two of them, Murphy and Patrick, seem to get on in some obscurely cool London-trendy way, despite the fact that they always argue. *I wish he were arguing with me . . .*

And now comes the paranoia. Even though she doesn't want to, Rebecca

feels like urgently saying something, anything, to interrupt, to stop the two of them talking, to stop the churny PMT feeling inside her stomach at the thought of her own possessiveness; her need to possess his possessiveness: to have his eyes upon her, to have him argue with *her*, to feel his eyes on *her*, the slap of his hand on *her* arse, like *she* is his best milking heifer
—Are you coming to the Seder then?

At last, somehow, Rebecca has managed to say something: she has spoken out now, so as to clear her head of these ridiculous thoughts.

After a tiny pause, Patrick says:
—What?

Patrick has turned from his conversation with Murphy to look at his girlfriend. Patrick's stare unnerves and pleases Rebecca. Rebecca:
—The Seder, *Dummkopf*
—That Jewish Christmas Easter thing?
—Yyyyyyyes
—But it's miles away, months
—Er yes but – *Say something, say anything* – But we have to know quite early

Patrick shrugs:
—Well, yes, of course I'll come if you want me to – He grins, in a kind way – It's an honour, yes?

He is moving over, he is shifting across the carpet. Where he says:
—I'd love to come, sweetheart

And he kisses her bare shoulder. Slowed, slurring, Rebecca says mmmyes, mmyesss. At the same moment as she murmurs this, Rebecca looks up at Murphy. Her best friend is looking blankly but obviously back: at Patrick kissing Rebecca's shoulder. Rebecca hates herself for feeling pleasure at the fact that she has perhaps made Murphy jealous.

Too much dope? Too much dope. With a mental shake of her head Rebecca talks to her boyfriend. Her BOYFRIEND is asking about the Seder, the Jewish festival her parents are planning; he is talking about Jewishness and then suddenly he is widening his eyes and asking her:
—Why *do* all Jewish people get more Jewish-looking as they get older?
—You mean like Bob Dylan?
—Yes. And Ben Elton and David Baddiel: they all start off looking normal and next time you check 'em out they look like Latvian rabbis

Rebecca says, from somewhere:
—Gerontology recapitulates ethnicity

To fill the ensuing silence, Rebecca looks at her watch. Clocking the time she says:

—God if we're going out at seven I'd better get ready

Half an hour later Rebecca makes her way back from the bathroom, still with the taste of mouthwash in her mouth, the prickle of the razor on her shins. Clean and happy and feeling young and in love Rebecca goes to open the door to her bedroom but before she does she hears laughter, low conspiratorial laughter. It is Murphy and Patrick; Patrick is saying some things in a special voice and Murphy is laughing after each time he says them.

Her heart pounding Rebecca struggles with her conscience, then she leans as close to the door as she can without pushing it open with her ear. She leans, gently presses her ear, listens.

With a congealing sensation in her stomach Rebecca realises why the two of them are laughing: they are obliquely laughing at Rebecca's thesis titles. Patrick is making up ludicrous satirical titles for theses and reciting them in a plinky (Rebecca-y?) voice and Murphy is laughing guiltily but enthusiastically. Rebecca listens. Patrick recites:

—'Who Pays the Gas Man: Female Selfishness and the Suicide of Sylvia Plath'

—Patch, don't

—Hold on . . . 'Gorilla in the Washing Machine: the Idea of Black Male Antipathy to Oral Sex'

—You

—Hold on, no, no, what's this one, oh God – He laughs – 'Using the Colon: Thesis Titles, Received Punctuation, and the Compulsion to Write Unreadable Shite'. Jesus I . . .

Enough. Gathering her angry wits Rebecca pushes the door open, and looks around. She hopes and expects to see them both looking guilty. But from his cross-legged stance at the other end of the room, Patrick is just smiling, just laughing, just saying:

—Hi darling, you look lovely

And across the room, Rebecca's heart lifts.

13

Lilac. Pale lilac. Aqua. Dreams are like fishes, scattered when the hand of consciousness enters the water . . .

Patrick slits his eyes. Closes them. *Mmmm. Mnngg. Must. I must . . . Open . . . ?*

Dragged from the tar pits of sleep Patrick rubs his eyes, and swallows, and unpillows his face and slowly remembers last night when he did something.

Trial!

Jumping himself down the bed Patrick leaps off the mattress and skids over the polished floor to a drawer. Late for his own trial! *His own rape trial! The third day of his own rape trial!* Shorts found, socks unballed, Patrick puts socks on, shorts on, and shifts bleary but quick as he can to the wardrobe, where he half blindly gropes. Clean shirt? Clean white shirt? *Where's his clean white shirt!!!?*

Shirt found, shirt cool on his back, Patrick looks and riffles and thinks fast and selects a discreetly indiscreet necktie, his second-most expensive suit, and the same need-a-polish shoes as yesterday. Then he trips to the door and opens it to jog upstairs to the bathroom where he makes lots of mess, noise, spittle, urine.

Toothbrush lost, towels dumped, bathroom comprehensively trashed, Patrick goes back down to his borrowed room in Joe's flat, the room which used to be his own room, where he adjusts his necktie and straightens a collar. Then he turns from the mirror and goes to a table and grabs keys, mobile, cash, another glance at a different clock.

9.22!

What would they do without him? Start without him? Forget the whole thing? Out of the door, halfway down the steps, Patrick opts to leap the rest of the steps and is already out of breath by the time he bursts out into an already lovely morning. This loveliest of mornings. How lovely this morning would be, Patrick thinks, if he weren't on trial for rape. Yes. No. If the girl he loved more than the sun on his face wasn't a lying slut who wanted to see him rot to death in prison.

Get a taxi?

— Thanks. Old Bailey please

From the back of the cab Patrick looks at the back of the cabby's head as it bobs up and down, monologuing. Not listening, Patrick looks out of the cab window at Holborn Tube station, at all the black cleaners and janitors and crack dealers disappearing home down the Tube at the same time as all the white office workers and bankers and white-trash homeless on crutches emerge into the sunlight. Idly Patrick wonders if one could tell the time in London by the average negritude of the streets, the amount of white people versus black people. A sort of race clock, like a sundial but . . .

As the sunlight from the cab window flickers strobily on Patrick's anxious face Patrick surveys the streetscape. Marvelling at all the glass, all the metal and glass of modern London, the boiled chrome and hi tech mirror walls. So much glass; how tempting it is; how easy it would be. Right now Patrick would like to smash it all. Right now Patrick would like to get out the cab and go a-wandering the streets hurling bricks and stones . . . and what a ruckus he would cause, what a lovely fiesta of destruction it would be: breaking all the windows of the condos, smashing up the Warburgs and Schroeders and Saatchis and Cazenoves and yes, oh yes, oh if only, oh if only something like that would happen, if only the Luftwaffe would come and save him, a Luftwaffe of angels strafing the City, destroying it all, laying waste to it all, erasing everything in a firestorm of forgetting.

But when he thinks of the Luftwaffe Patrick thinks about the Germans and when he thinks about the German army he remembers an image he read about sometime, when and where he does not know: of German soldiers walking jackboot-deep through sunlit fields of Romanian corn, so as to flush out the hiding Jewesses, and rape them.

And when he thinks this he wonders about Rebeccca's unJewish *blonde hair*. Patrick wonders if Rebecca's blonde hair could be an adaptation, protective camouflage, making it easier to *hide* in sunlit corn from rapists. *Hm*. Then Patrick wonders if, instead, the reason Rebecca has blonde hair is actually because her dark-haired Jewish grandmother was raped and made pregnant by some flaxen-locked Teutonic nobleman, in the Baltic pine forest, or on the outskirts of the *Shtetl*. This would help explain, Patrick thinks, among other things, why some distant female descendant might inherit, say, a genetic penchant for rough sex . . .

— Just here mate?

Clearing his head of these thoughts, these sad and belated thoughts, Patrick nods towards the cabby.

— Yeah, thanks, just here

Alighted on the sunny pavement Patrick turns, pays, tips, then walks down to the Old Bailey entrance, which is being picketed as ever by camera crews and photographers and curious Nordic tourists. Ten yards away from the door Patrick is engulfed by friends and family.

— Patch where've you been?

— About a minute left mate

— They're only letting in witnesses

— One too many wanks this morning?

Patrick looks at Joe's impish grin, and says:

— The First Lord Spiritual received something of a dressing down

— Hunh?

— What?

— Your brief's pulling his wig off

Inside the door to the Old Bailey Patrick does the Seventies sci-fi airlock thing, the airport security thing, the nod to the policemen thing. Up the steps into the main marble lobby, full of sunlit dust and paedophiles, he paces. For a moment he pauses to check a noticeboard, then he turns and finds half a bench of people he recognises sitting on the bench staring at him. Why does he know these people? Who are these people?

With a start Patrick steps back, shocked. It's the jury. *His jury*. Sitting here. It's his jury sitting on a bench staring at him. So? What should he do? Introduce himself? Run away? Act cool and innocent? *Definitely* not go over and rape any of them?

A sudden firm hand on Patrick's shoulder makes Patrick turn and as he turns he finds he is staring into the severe, bewigged, white-collared, black-gowned visage of his lawyer Stefan. Firm hand still on Patrick's shoulder Stefan says:

— Explanation?

— I'm sorry

— You did know when we were starting?

— Yes sorry, Robert, I overslept and I

Stefan's junior Juson, standing beside and slightly behind Stefan, looks swiftly over to Patrick and shakes his head as if to say *that was the wrong thing to say*. With undisguised frostiness, Stefan is speaking:

— *Overslept* . . .

— Uh . . . yes

— You *overslept*?

— Uh yeah I uh

— You overslept for your own rape trial. I suppose you think that's frightfully *cool* . . . or something?

— I

— You moron

Patrick, mouth agape

— Uh sorry?

Stefan barks:

— You do realise that if your trial hadn't been delayed this morning they would have noticed you weren't here and the police would have slung you inside for the rest of the trial?

— Ah

— Don't make a fool of me, Patch

Stefan looks at Patrick and shakes his head; Patrick makes an *honestly I'm just crap* face, and says:

— So . . . er . . . anyway

— Yes?

— What *is* happening then?

Stefan goes silent, and brooding. The junior takes pity and interjects:

— As it happens they're missing a witness or something, that Murphy girl . . .

Patrick comes back, eyes wider now:

— Murphy Reardon?

— Yeah

— She's up this morning?

— Yep

Ignoring his junior's conversation with his client Stefan looks at the gold on his wrist and then with a flick of the wrist he snaps:

— Court Eighteen, ten forty-five. Be there

— Of course

— And keep away from the jury

— Of course – Patrick repeats, glancing over to where the jury is sitting, phoning, chatting, smoking, gossiping. Some of the jurors are looking whisperingly and oo-er-ishly in Patrick's direction, like kids looking at a Disney monster in a theme park.

Turned, Patrick sees that Stefan has disappeared. As has Juson. Patrick stifles a sudden desire to bolt. To run for it. He has twenty minutes to deal with, and so he wanders down to the entrance but there he looks through an open door and sees . . . Rebecca's mother sitting in a side room. Rebecca's mother. Her mother. *Her mother?* She is sitting there in a yellow side room staring at him; he is staring at her. *Rebecca's mother. The mother of the girl who is claiming he raped her.* Now Patrick panics; his reserve of English upbringing makes him feel like going over and saying:

— Hello Mrs Jessel . . . Awfully sorry about raping your daughter

Why does he want to say that? After all, he didn't, and hasn't. Arguably. But still: the natural English urge to apologise first. Even when you didn't do anything . . .

Patrick stares at Rebecca's mother's pale, paling face as it stares back at him. Narrowing his own eyes, Patrick tries to intuit Mrs Jessel's mood from her face: from the face he remembers with great clarity. How many briochey, bagel-ish, smoked-salmon-esque brunches and breakfasts did he share with that face? As Patrick stares at Mrs Jessel he gets a flashback to that vague, evanescent, overwhelming sense of being disapproved of that he always received from Rebecca's impeccably polite, prosperous, Mozart-quintet-liking family. And as Patrick gets this big old unhappy angry feeling again he recalls how he was never able to quite work out whether – in all the times he stayed in or ate at or just picked up Rebecca from Rebecca's house – whether he was being disapproved of because he was Gentile, or lower middle class; or both. The bile of this sour memory in his mouth Patrick remembers how it used to enrage him so much precisely because it, this same disapproval, was so subtle and nebulous and Hampstead and refined and hardly there. And so now Patrick stares at Rebecca's mother in a defiant, *fuck you, I'm glad I raped your daughter* way, before coming to some sanity again. Hard-knotting his tie Patrick turns and steps back up the steps.

But as he reaches the top of the steps where the marble changes colour, from anchovy to tartan, Patrick wonders what Rebecca's mother is doing in court this morning. His friends: what did they say? They were only letting witnesses in this morning? But Rebecca's mother isn't a witness? Is she? Could she be a witness? To what? What did she see? What did she hear? What? What would her evidence be about? His ignorance of how to correctly eat artichokes? His dissing of the *Jewish Chronicle*? His insalubrious way of deliberately shagging the daughter so loud it caused the mother in the room next door to take an extra Temazepam?

—**All those in Skivington please go to Court Eighteen**

Spit swallowed, tie smoothed, suit jacket buttoned, Patrick stiffens and girds and paces down the hall and up some steps and round the marble stairwell and up some more steps and along another hall to the door he knows is the door to his court because outside it is standing the prosecution junior in her sexy stilettos just visible under her long black gown. *Black stockings?*

Pushing the door Patrick goes into the courtroom and sits in the dock without having to be asked. Then the door opens some more and the clerk and the stenographer come in, then the jury, one by one, then other people, then the lawyers, all chattering, smiling, carrying sweets, pens, books, mini Evian bottles, and switched-off cellphones. A few desultory minutes pass and then they ALL RISE in honour of His Honour. As he watches the court do its practised thing, Patrick gets a strange feeling of camaraderie. He is sensing a kind of bonding with the other members of the court, a kind of *esprit de corps*; inasmuch as they have all heard a lot of weird stuff together in these rooms and are therefore like some kind of close yet dysfunctional family, privy to the same nasty secrets. Or perhaps they are like some busload of tourists, captured and held hostage for days: by wig-wearing terrorists . . .

But this almost nice feeling of bondedness and cosiness disappears as the door opens to a shouted name, and in walks Murphy.

Murphy Reardon . . .

Sweet, tall, talkative, sarcastic, pretty, awkward, clumsy, likeable, *cuttlefish-tattooed* Murphy.

Smurf.

Seeing Rebecca's best friend walking slowly around the courtroom to the witness box makes Patrick wince. He always liked Murphy, fancied her, even. Now seeing her as a shy but brave defence witness in a trial that might send him to prison for a suicide-inducing stretch of sex criminal's solitary confinement, for LIFE, makes Patrick gulp, feel an even higher degree of fright, feel even more angry, panicked, terrifically melancholy. Yes he always liked Murphy; this same Murphy, this same sweet tall gauche funny Murphy who is climbing the little wooden ladder to the witness box of his rape trial.

From the dock Patrick feels like calling across the courtroom *Yo Murf, coming in on some gear?*

As he would have done; as he did so many times.

Murphy is in a neat black suit. Smarter than Patrick has ever seen her. Sat in his blue plastic seat Patrick finds himself staring at Murphy, thinking about Murphy's cuttlefish tattoo under that white blouse under that black suit. As Patrick stares he notices that Murphy does not stare back. She is avoiding his gaze, in fact she is avoiding his whole side of the courtroom: as she picks up the bible and does the riff, as she quietly but firmly answers a few introductory questions gently lobbed by the prosecution junior, the woman in black stockings.

Smurf . . .

As the junior and Murphy play evidential patball Patrick thinks some more about Murphy's tatt. The times he would see it when they were drunk in a pub, him, Joe, Smurf and Rebecca, when it was summer and she would stretch back and laugh her broken-lav laugh, stretching butchly but sexily in her croptop so as to show the discreet little purple-and-red tattoo and he would wonder whether a threesome, or a kumquat . . .

And now the sadness of it all comes again, the tides of sadness. Patrick feels like crying for these broken friendships, that lost innocence, the losingness of life. It is all starting to hurt a bit too much, as Murphy says all these things, all these things, these *things*.

— Yes . . .

  — Yes, he . . .

    — Yes, he used to hit her, I think . . .

      — Sometimes I dunno . . . bruises . . . I never knew whether . . .

        — Perhaps she was lying but . . .

— Oh yeah he used to drink quite a lot and . . .

— That night I was meant to be going round and I got pretty anxious you know when she didn't show . . . Is all . . . is all . . . is all . . .

Is all.

Patrick slumps. He is not looking at Murphy's side of the courtroom. He is slumping in despair and abjection, a feeling he is becoming increasingly used to during these days of prosecution evidence. Then he lifts his head from his hands to see his lawyer stand up and ask:

— Miss Reardon . . . What was the first thing the complainant, Miss Jessel, said to you when she came to you that night?

—

— That night she was allegedly raped?

— Um . . . ?

— It's here in the transcripts of your interview

Murphy looks like she is stalling:

— Mm . . . I . . .

— Shall I remind you?

— No . . . uh – Murphy swallows – No

— You do remember then?

— Yes. I . . .

— Miss Reardon?

Holding on to the box Murphy lifts her head and takes a deep breath and slowly recounts:

— She said, 'I don't know what constitutes rape, but I think Patrick raped me'

14

—trellis
—dik-dik
—... ointment
—veggie
—whooping cough
—... ff – Patrick thinks, muses, takes his hand off the wheel – fffff ...
fffffff ... Gabon
—Gabon?
—It's a country
    Across the gearwell Rebecca looks out the car window at the chariot race
of the motorway, and the hissy March rain, and the dreary South London
littoral whizzing past the car window and she says:
—Doesn't count, you're not allowed proper nouns
—Since when were there rules?
—If you can have Gabon I can have ... – She tilts her chin – Mold
    Patrick pauses, says:
—Mold?
—OK, Denbigh
—OK, Flint
—OK ... wimple!
—As if
—Wimple! – She leans across the car and taps his leg; she chuckles and
whoops – Beat that – Punching the air with a small suntanned fist – *Wimple!!*
—Right ... – Decelerating, Patrick laughs – Right, OK, if it's going to be

like that – Checking the mirror, checking the rain on the rear window in the rear mirror, the cars beyond, Patrick goes quiet; then says, quietly – Snood

Rebecca:

—shit

—Ha! – Patrick slaps the car wheel and yaws the car into the slow lane and says – Unbeatable. Snood – Laughing – How could I forget?

Silence, then:

—She does know we're thinking of moving in together? Your mum?

Slow lane, middle lane, fast lane.

—Course

—Mm . . .

Rebecca falls quiet, Patrick says:

—So. Are you worried about meeting her?

—Mm . . . no . . . no . . .

At this, Rebecca turns away evidently to think and to worry and to fret about meeting Patrick's mother for the first time; as she turns, thinks, Patrick turns to her and looks. At the swanly curve of her neck. The biteable grace of her neck. Her saying:

—This . . . must be . . . Croydon?

—You have been out of London before, Becs?

—Yes of course

—I mean you know Knightsbridge and Hampstead, and Venice, but could you actually put Bristol on the map?

—Somewhere near Ireland?

—Impressive

—Spinnaker . . . ?

I mean. Patrick thinks, looking again at her neck as she continues playing the game they have just invented. *I mean, look at her neck*. As Patrick looks at Rebecca's neck he sees just above the hem of her cashmere top, the petals of his morning's teethmarks, pink and pale violet against the white. And seeing this only makes him want to do it to her again. To plant more Alpine flowers, to add more tiny petals to the snow. *Hm*. Patrick swallows. Why does he want her to want him to hurt her? Why does he want what he least wants to do? Why does he want to destroy, to torch, to Zippo? Why does he want to burn the Warsaw of her body? Raze the slums of Krakow?

—Can we have some music?

—Sure . . .

Obedient, nodding, Patrick blindly takes a tape out of the stereo and nearly drops the tape; chucking this tape over his shoulder onto the back seat, he then fondles the glove compartment for another tape and nearly kills them by almost driving into the back of a Spanish seafood truck as he takes this new tape out. Taking up this tape, bringing the tape to his face to check it's the right tape, Patrick then takes the tape and mails it; punches buttons; starts the tape. Hissing seconds pass, a lorry overtakes, effervescent bebop fills the car. Followed by a burst of skiffle.

Patrick laughs at the eccentricity of his own taste in recorded and compiled tapes. Then he waits for Rebecca to respond to this strange segue in taste; duly she responds. She says, shaking her head at the car stereo:

— *Your taste in music* . . .

— Fascinatingly eclectic, refreshingly catholic?

— Wanky

— Naturally your thing about boy bands is different

She looks at him. He laughs. She smiles as she tilts her head and listens to the tape: a boy band is next; then some big band weirdness. Patrick says:

— I've thought about calling this tape 'Songs for Sylvia to Listen To'

— What?

— Well — Patrick taps his forefingers on the wheel, in time — Sylvia Plath died in 1963, between the *Chatterley* ban and the Beatles' first LP, right?

— Yes

— So she just missed out on the pop music revolution

— And . . .

— Well I reckon — Patrick is grinning, turning the wheel, changing gear, saying — I can't believe she'd have been depressed enough to top herself if she'd been around to hear the Sultans of Ping FC. Would have cheered her up too much, right?

Her knees up, Rebecca says, gaily:

— Hayzee Fantayzee . . . that song . . . 'John Wayne is Big Leggy', that's *very* Sylvia, she'd have *loved* that

Patrick says:

— And Kajagoogoo, if only she'd have known about Kajagoogoo, would that have influenced the *Ariel* poems, made them a bit happier?

For a moment they are both chuckling together: laughing happily and bondingly. Then a sudden sadder silence descends. Sadder music is filling the car, softer clarinet music, and Patrick feels heavy and morose at the thought of what is upcoming. The two of them are plummeting down the

M3 to his mother's house, for lunch, and the thought of this obliges Patrick to think of his mother. And his father. In different places. He always dreads meeting his divorced and almost equally lonely parents. The guilt, the loneliness, the age, the new liver spots, how he hates them. So he must try to think of things he must do, must say, to take everybody's mind off. He must try not to think about these other things.

—You know it's the next junction

—I did live here eighteen years

— *OK sorry*

Rebecca is smiling apologetically across. Looking at his smiling girlfriend, Patrick feels guilt and tension again. Because. That *smile*. Is it her special sweet *you can see me naked* smile? Or her *tell me I'm a lovely slut* smile? Or her *you really should tell me about Murphy but I'll always still love you* smile? Oh, Jerusalem. What can you do? Patrick feels a cold tender grief inside, thinking on the love, the love, the love that burns between he and she. It is too much, too fast, too exciting, too speedy, too dangerous. Sometimes when Patrick is thinking about sex with Rebecca, doing sex with Rebecca, remembering sex with Rebecca, he feels like he is hurtling down the motorway with the brakes fucked; that's what it feels like. Like the wires have snapped, the metal sheared. Trying hard to not remember how it feels Patrick reaches across the car and squeezes his girlfriend's thigh. In return Rebecca smiles and reaches over and coils a finger with some of his hair. Tickled by this Patrick thinks of Rebecca's cunt.

Turn here? Turning the wheel right Patrick takes the slip road, takes the roundabout, gets on the dual carriageway, heads on into the suburban countryside of West Hampshire.

And as he does he thinks, again, again, afresh, what else is there to think of? He thinks of what he always has to think on. Rebecca: their sex this morning. The press of her cold breasts to his face. The salty moan. The sliding and blackness; the soft and the flesh. The time he stood by the lake and gazed up at the mountains: the queenly, snowbound, glorious mountains, rose-tipped by sunrise . . .

Overtaking a lorry he didn't even really see Patrick tries to think back to a time when he didn't feel like this: devoured, banjaxed, mullahed by love. When he didn't spend all the time he didn't spend fucking Rebecca thinking about fucking Rebecca: so when *did* he start obsessing? When did it start? Is the reason he feels a strange desire to be unfaithful to her merely a result of his being so thrown by his unprecedented desire to be faithful to her?

Right. Mn. Yes. Intent, Patrick listens to a saxophone riff. Then he watches, equally intent, out the windscreen: at the sun coming out. Oh yes. Patrick watches the sparkle of new sun on the wet, glossy road, the rainy black Tarmac. Then Patrick decides that he cannot understand or fathom the

—Looks like it'll brighten up

fathom the Darwinian reasoning behind it. No: he cannot. All his life, so far, Patrick has marvelled at the Darwinian logic of everything. That's been his supreme creed. Wherever he has looked – at the beauty of flowers, the sleekness of otters, the clever-cleverness of modern novels – Patrick has seen confirmed the blind unfeeling action of Natural laws, the ruthless reason of unreasoning Evolution. Even the random mutation of shoe fashions, or the speedy global spread of successful TV quiz show formats, all these have so far merely explained to Patrick the super-efficient Darwinian processes of a wholly Godless world. These things have reaffirmed Patrick's faith in his faithlessness.

Until now. Now Patrick is confronted by – a tractor? Patrick swerves out, pushes the pedal, swerves back – now Patrick is confronted by something he cannot fit in his self-consciously tough atheistic Richard Dawkinsy outlook.

Deftly, Patrick takes a left, thinks on. How *can* he explain the depth and frighteningness of this, this thing, this deeply, disturbingly carnal love he feels for Rebecca? How can he explain his mad actions, the lunatic ardour? I mean, Patrick thinks: what's the evolutionary point in worshipping her kneecaps? Auditing her panties? Sniffing her hair when she sleeps? Why does he watch for hours the way her calves tense as she paints her toenails? Is that Darwinian? To spend his life thus? Shouldn't he be out foraging, slaying, making money, something? What fitness and survivability is inferred when he has to stop work for an hour to think about the curious disposition of her pubic hairs? What is the sociobiological reason behind his spending a morning in reverie about the slight wobble of her buttocks when he fucks her hard from behind?

—Rbecsdhfgda

—Rebeasgahappp

And now he isn't even making much sense. There is too much spit in his throat. Because he is thinking of Rebecca's pubic hairs, their disposition. He is remembering her bare knees abraded by the carpet of his car. Her little feet kicking the back of the passenger seat. FUCKTHISSAY-SOMETHING

—Rebecca

—Mm?

—Er

—Yes?

She has turned on him. This time she has turned and smiled serenely across the front seats and given him the full refulgent force of her royal beauty. The slums of beautiful Krakow. And again this does it, when Rebecca turns her lovely face and does that lovely smile Patrick feels the brakes go, again: in a rush in an almost cocainey rush he sees the tableau of this morning: fingers force-fed in her whorish mouth; fat cock stuck in her sleepy cunt; pink heels stirruped by his shoulders.

Slowly, Patrick pulls the wheel right and checks the mirror. The rain is Cyrillic on the windowpane. The sun is, however, shining. Patrick feels his heart, his heart. He feels something hurting, in the distance. In the far, rainy distance.

—Hello, Mum

His mother is wearing old woman's shoes. And nearly-old-woman slacks. Trying not to care about these things, trying not to show he's noticed these things, Patrick hugs his mum and feels the usual love-death-grief-sadness-affection-happiness as he hugs her. During the hug Patrick glances over his mum's shoulder and sees that Rebecca has got out of the other side of the car and is crossing the wet pebbly drive

—Hello Mrs Skivington

—Hello dear, you must be Rebecca

Coming around the car, scrunching pebble, Rebecca smiles and offers the bouquet of flowers and says:

—Uhm. We got you these

—Oh they're lovely

—Patrick chose them

—Really?!

Patrick's mother is laughing, Rebecca is smiling, Patrick isn't. He can't be jolly, he feels too tense. Tensed, Patrick watches the two women step up the steps and go into the tiny kitchen he remembers so well and, no, Patrick decides, he cannot laugh. Not now. Instead he watches his mother turn and pour cold water and prepare the flowers in the small chipped sink and as his mother does this Patrick feels tremendous and unwonted protectiveness towards his mother. And shame, too: shame for his mum's poor Co-oppy clothes, her chapped red working woman's hands. Close, Patrick looks at Rebecca; close, he sees Rebecca looking back. Meantime Patrick's mother turns and looks at the two of them; she reaches out and holds her son's arm as if seeking balance or support. And she says:

—You'll be staying for lunch?

Discomfited, Patrick hugs his mum, and secretly rolls his eyes over his mum's shoulder at Rebecca. But in truth he is feeling anything but complicity with Rebecca. Right now he is feeling love and stuff for his mother.

—Cup of tea first, Mum?

—It was a horrible drive, was it?

—Uh yeah

—Hold on, you sit there

—Thank you Mrs Skivington

—Sally, please

And so it goes; so it goes. Maudlin, but trying not to show it, Patrick observes the rigmarole unfold as predicted. Patrick watches as Rebecca watches the way he and his mother interact. He watches Rebecca watch the protectiveness they show for each other, unwonted. Then, out of nothing, Patrick cheers up suddenly (*blood sugar?*) and thinks *fuckit* and turns to his mother and says:

—You sure you're eating properly, Mum

—Patrick

—Wearing enough vests?

—*Patrick!*

The mother laughs at the son, the son laughs lazily and alpha male-ishly. Across the biscuits and tea-cakes the glamorous girlfriend laughs, unsurely. And then Patrick says to his mother as she transports dripping teabags to the bin:

—When are you going to get a haircut, Mum?

—I just had one . . .

—You're such an old hippy, you know that?

—And you're in the City now . . .

His mother is being sarcastic. Patrick takes a mug of tea from his mother's hand and hands it on to Rebecca, who says:

—Thank you

—How's the dog Mum?

—We never had a dog

—Oh yeah

—Drink your tea and tell me about London . . .

The conversation chugs along; as it does so Patrick finds he is sitting by the old kitchen table watching his lonely mother whom he loves so much, and that he is not sure what he is really feeling. He watches his mother as she biscuits and cakes and sugarcubes, and he feels pity. He watches her as she kettles and boils and chats, indefatigably, and he feels a kind of pride. And withal he feels: the gulf. Between. Between his small, pinched, tidy and lower-middle-class home, and the haute-bourgeois glossiness of his girlfriend. Between the woman he loves so much and the woman he loves so much.

Sneaking a look at Rebecca as she sits demurely on the kitchen chair drinking overstrong tea, Patrick allows himself to think what he has been trying not to think ever since Rebecca and he arrived here: how Rebecca-y, beautiful, and wrong Rebecca looks in this kitchen. Rebecca's newly cut blondeness; her Italian jeans; that obvious private dentistry: it does not fit. It is too much. Patrick is embarrassed and mortified by the way Rebecca looks so unable to fit in, despite her obvious efforts. Oh, Jerusalem.

Patrick broods, nibbles biscuits, watches. Leaning forward, Rebecca murmurs and asks and listens and then gets up and goes to the directed-to lavatory. When she has gone Patrick's mother looks at her son with an at-last expression, and says:

—Rather posh . . . isn't she?

—Tell me about it

—You sure you can afford her?

—Less maintenance than you'd think

His mother chuckles, takes the mug from his hand. Says:

—Did I make too much tea?

—Not quite. A gallon's about right

—Very attractive though of course

—Perhaps you overdid the biscuits. Four packs of Bourbons?

—You always liked the pretty ones

—Is that wrong?

—Like your dad

—Of course, Mum, he chose *you*

—Are you going to see him?

Patrick looks at his mum; thinks about his dad; says:

—Maybe . . . is he doing OK?

—He's still ill
—Not in hospital though?
  Patrick's mother shrugs:
—You know what he's like, you remember
—I remember, I fucking remember Mum
—Don't – Patrick's mother looks tired, and pained – It's not his fault, really
—You were too young, right?
—Yes. Too young

Tense, stiff, Patrick goes quiet. Patrick's mother goes to touch his forehead with the back of her hand as if to check he is ill. Patrick goes to push her away, but as he goes to push her away he feels the love and protectiveness inside him again and he goes to hug her; at this she smiles, and at that moment when the two of them are really hugging Rebecca walks through the kitchen door. Startled, Patrick turns away, confused and embarrassed. He does not know how to act, where to put himself; so he decides . . . to flee. Faking a cough he turns and retreats down the cheap hall carpet to the back door which he flings open onto the wet garden. The tiny wet garden. O, this garden. How he knows this garden, how he no longer knows it. The cheap little shrubs his dad planted. The place where he used to play as a kid. The stupid seat where he did his French homework. *Monsieur Marsaud travaille dans le jardin . . .*

Looking at the infinite pathos of the tiny garden Patrick breathes in the sour wet early spring air and he wonders about death, and love, and Rebecca. *Jean Claude et François. Ecoutez et répétez. Beep.* And he wonders whether he will go and see his father and he despairs of ever finding a place to be truly happy and then he wonders if his mother really likes Rebecca and then he wonders if Rebecca will have sex with him behind the garden shed.

15

— *I don't know what constitutes rape?*

Murphy is silently shrugging in the witness box. Stefan continues, more sneering still:

— *But I think Patrick raped me?*

Another Murphyish shrug. More silence. Unfazed, Stefan lifts a gowned arm, looks across at his witness, says:

— Miss Reardon . . .

Murphy raises her eyes. Patrick thinks about Murphy's surname. Stefan says:

— Miss Reardon, wouldn't you say that's an odd thing to say? Given that the plaintiff was claiming she had indeed just been raped?

— I . . . – Murphy drawls, at last – I s'pose . . . Yeah. But

— Were you surprised by it?

— Not really

— Not really, Miss Reardon??

— Well, she – Murphy looks around the court as if expecting to see Rebecca crouching weepily in the corner – She was, you know . . . very upset. Y'know. I didn't really think about it . . .

— Of course – Gown folded back, Stefan continues – And so . . . what did you do then, after she'd said . . . – Very long pause – . . . *I don't know what constitutes rape, but I think Patrick raped me?*

— Sorry?

— What did you do after she said that?

Frowning, now, Murphy says:

— I rang her father
— Miss Jessel's father?
— Yes
— And you told him that Rebecca was claiming that she had been raped?
— Yes
— But you didn't tell him . . . – Stefan looks down even though it is palpably obvious he doesn't need to – That she had just said . . . *'I don't know what constitutes rape . . . but I think Patrick raped me?'*

In the dock, Patrick feels his stomach tighten. In the box, Murphy says:
— No
— I see. And what did you do then? After you'd spoken to Miss Jessel's father?
— I think . . . – Murphy fires a look across the hushed courtroom at Patrick, a look so sharp it makes him involuntarily sit back – Yes. After that I called Patch
— You telephoned the defendant?
— Yes
— Why?

Murphy, quick:
— I wanted to tell him what I thought of him
— And did you?

Patrick thinks he can hear the tick of the watch on the wrist of the policeman sitting next to him. Murphy:
— Yeah. I told him he was a fucking sadistic bastard

Stefan, still unfazed:
— And what did the defendant say?
— Ts. Nothing
— He answered the telephone and then he said . . . *nothing*?
— Yup – Murphyish toss of the hair – Virtually nothing
— Why did you telephone the defendant?
— Because . . . – Murphy does her coolest, vaguest, I'm-just-a-fool shrug – I was angry at him. I know it was stupid but I was so angry at what he'd done to Becs
— Did you tell him that Rebecca was with you?
— Yeah
— And did you tell him what she'd said

— Yeah

— You mean you told him that she'd said – Another glance down at his notes, another sly little smile – '*I don't know what constitutes rape . . . but I think Patrick raped me?*'

Murphy glances, dark eyes, wide:

— No

— So what did you tell him?

— Stuff. I don't exactly . . . recall every word

— Did you accuse him of raping Rebecca Jessel?

Murphy levels her stare:

— Didn't have to

— Miss

— He knew what he'd done, y'know?

— Miss Reardon, I

— S'not like it was news – She lifts her head – He did it. So it wasn't exactly a BBC newsflash, shock horror exposé, you know?

Just as Patrick is about to wonder if this is all going wrong his lawyer steps back and forward and says:

— Miss Reardon. Is it true you once . . . requested sex with the defendant?

Distant voices, distant traffic. Murphy opens and closes her mouth . . .

Two or more lawyers have bobbed up. The judge lifts a sagacious hand, rhythmically lifting it up and down as if patting all the lawyers on the head. The judge intones:

— As I said . . . previously – The judge coughs, clears his throat – I think this line is permissible. You can continue, Mister Stefan

— Thank you, M'Lord

The other lawyers subside. Stefan turns and pauses, gown wafting around him. Patrick, his chin poised on two sharp thumbnails, notes how Stefan's face goes all boyish and mischievous when he is on a roll, on a line of questioning he likes. As now.

Robert Stefan QC:

— I'll rephrase the question, Miss Reardon – Importantly – Isn't it true to say you once had a . . . crush on the defendant . . . at the same time as he was going out with Miss Jessel?

— Mn . . .

Murphy is stalling, mumbling. Patrick looks excitedly around the courtroom. The jury box seems to have altered itself so it faces more directly at Murphy. The geometry of the courtroom seems to have shifted, subtly, centring Murphy and her witness box; Murphy is herself looking around the courtroom as if she is now doubly scared she might see Rebecca in the corner, somewhere, all sobbing, bitten, hissy, raped . . . betrayed. Then Murphy says:

— No

— No, Miss Reardon?

— No

Stefan's smile:

— So it's *not* true to say that on the evening of – Consulting a notebook pushed across the desk by the junior, Stefan nods, looks over, looks hard – March twenty-third, you asked for sex, full intercourse . . . with the defendant?

— . . . No

— In Rebecca Jessel's house?

— . . . – Swallowing dryly – No

— And it's also not true to say that on the afternoon of . . . March thirtieth . . . you offered oral sex to the defendant?

— No

— In the street. On Haverstock Hill? In North London?

— No

— Are you completely sure, Miss Reardon?

— Yes

— I advise you of the oath you took this morning

— I *know* . . .

— Miss Reardon?

Murphy is breathing out, exhaling too quickly. She is buttoning and unbuttoning the bottom button of her sensible black jacket. She is saying:

— None of it. It's all rubbish. It's total crap

— Really?

— . . . Yes!

— So it's not true to say that you were in love with the defendant?

— . . . *As if*

— And that you were annoyed with him when he rejected you

— Jesus no

— Because . . . because he told you he was in love with Miss Jessel?

— That's just . . . drivel. Totally. *Christ!*

— Miss Reardon . . . when the prosecutrix . . . when Miss Jessel came to you that evening, when she said . . . – Stefan glances down, pretends to read his notebook; then he looks up and his face is all boyish and smiling – *'I don't know what constitutes rape, but I think Patrick raped me . . .'* – Still smiling – Weren't you in a way angry at Patrick, but not because he'd – Stefan loads his tone with more quotation marks – . . . *raped* . . . your friend, but because you'd thought that he and Rebecca had broken up, and you were entertaining hopes of your own as a result? And that hearing they were still an item consequently made you angry? – Sly lawyerly smile – And jealous?

Murphy looks back defiantly, almost arrogantly:

— No!

— You *were* angry, weren't you?

— Nope!

— You were in love with the defendant, correct?

— God! *No!*

— But because you were in love with him you felt betrayed

— No way . . .

— Which is why you encouraged her to make this accusation

— No, no no I jus

— No further questions M'Lord

Stefan sits down; silently and precisely he sits down, leaving Murphy trying to stare, and shut her mouth. Murphy's face is almost white. The court is looking at her, regarding her with the pitiless curiosity afforded by the audience for an actress who has forgotten her lines. Dumb, face down, Murphy fiddles with the bottom button on her sensible black jacket. She looks very alone, very forlorn, and at a loss, until some new woman Patrick has not seen before steps up behind Murphy and gently clasps the witness by the padded shoulder. At the touch Murphy starts, turns and nods. From his angle in the dock Patrick sees that Murphy's usually confident face looks stressed, unhappy, almost teary, and so, despite his glee and happiness at the way Murphy's evidence fell flat, Patrick feels a huge surge of pity for his old friend, for Smurf, for the best friend of his girlfriend: as she is escorted in near tears out of the court; as the judge looks up and sighs and says to everyone:

— I think we might adjourn for lunch here

16

—It's called a . . . Seder
—A what?

Necking his mobile Patrick pulls down the cab window to feel the cold April air on his face. The air is too cold. Sliding up the window he listens as Joe repeats:
—A what?

Patrick, louder:
—Say-der . . .
—Der!
—It's a kind of Jewish Christmas
—Right
—Rebecca wants me to get to know her parents better . . . you see
—Oh yes
—Joe just clean the fucking flat will you

As Joe falls quiet, fails to answer, Patrick looks out the cab window at the speeding evening lights: thinking of their strange sadness. The wistful blueness of the Swiss Cottage cinema lights. The endless flow of regretful red brake lights.

Joe comes back with:
—What's it like then?
—What? Hoovering?
—Sex with a Jewish girl

Patrick wonders what to say to this. He wonders if he has perhaps been wittering on about the Jews too much, to provoke a question like this.

Vague, tired, drained and worried, exhausted by what's happening and not happening at work, Patrick watches the back of the cabby's head. The cabby's head bounces each time the cabby swears. Unable to resist his favourite subject, Patrick leans slightly forward and says into his mobile phone:

—I think they like sex . . . in a different way

—Jews?

—Yes

—How?

—Well . . . – Waiting, thinking, deciding, saying – Put it like this. Have you ever . . . fucked a bird . . . who wanted it . . .

He stops. Joe's phone voice sounds eager:

—Go on?

—Well, who wanted a . . . a . . .

—A tapir?

—No, a . . .

—A crayon shoved up her arse? A shag in front of *The Railway Children*?

—Nooo. I mean. Like . . . Who wanted it rough . . . I mean – Patrick looks out of the window at the city, the city. Patrick says . . . – Have you ever fucked a girl who wanted you to hit her with a tennis racquet? Who wanted you to spank her with a tennis racquet while you're wearing her dad's dressing gown?

Patch stops. Joe says:

—Who hasn't?

Patrick laughs. Joe sounds like he's laughing. Patrick says:

—No, truly, have you ever been with a girl who liked it violent?

—How violent?

—Very fucking violent

—Mebbes. Mebbes – Joe's voice is indistinct; then distinct – Y'know Patch man. I'm worried about you

—Unh?

—You're obsessed

—As if

—You are, mate, you're obsessed. You're acting weird . . . Last night you were blathering on about the Jews for three hours, when you were pissed in the club

—Really . . .

—Yes, you were mate, you kept saying weird stuff

—But I

—As I remember man – Joe's voice, even over the mobile, has a sardonic tinge – You were particularly keen on the fact that people used to get done for bestiality if they fucked Jews. In the Middle Ages. Remember saying that?

Patrick goes quiet. Joe also goes quiet, as if he has pulled his own phone away and is thinking; then Joe comes back louder and says:

—So. Get a grip. You'll lose the club if you don't concentrate. Man, you'll lose everything – Getting louder – That club is everything you worked for, everything you wanted, get a hold

Patrick sits back, thinks about his club: all those students with their stupid haircuts and overtrendy trainers and absurd arguments about guest lists. Patrick considers all those free beers he's given away to friends he's never liked. Or met.

Patrick:

—Fuck the club. Who cares. S'not her fault anyway – Vehement – You really reckon Rebecca is the reason the label's in trouble? Not the council trying to close us down?

Joe comes back, undaunted:

—Yep . . . I do. Last night you were meant to be managing the place – A breath, then – And you were so fucked all you could do was go on about her. About her tits. About tits. And Jews. Jewish tits

Patrick thinks, says:

—You know Catholics worship a Jewess?

Joe's voice has disappeared, again.

New litter, new buses, New Finchley Road. Slowly the cab slides alongside a going-nowhere bus; confused, wondrous, Patrick looks into the interior of the bus. From the lamplit and hollow interior the people in the bus stare out at him, with that special vacant melancholy public-transport stare. Returning to his mobile Patrick hears Joe come back into signal and say:

—Do you really want me to clean the gaff?

—Yes!

—But the duster's broken . . .

—Joe . . . Stop smoking. Clean

—Can't find the carpet . . .

—It's under the pizza boxes, Joe, just do it, will you? – Slightly angry now – I've got too much other shit on my mind to worry about . . . *cobwebs*

—Sure, I will . . . OK?

The bus left behind, the taxi swerves right and round; Patrick is pitched to the side. Regaining his position, Patrick says:

—Anyway, Joe, what I said about the Jews last night . . . just forget it

A brief pause. Then a longer pause . . . Patrick tries again:

—I didn't mean it . . . what I meant was . . . Joe? *Joe??*

But Joe has gone. Pocketing his phone Patrick sighs, wanly, vaguely, somehow relieved to have such a good friend in Joe. Despite.

The cab is turning: is entering the suburb, the ghetto. For a few minutes they slow past increasingly big, old, judiciously brickworked houses; then, on a whim, feeling like a walk, Patrick leans and taps the partition and says *it's OK I'll get out here*. On the pavement he turns, and starts walking the streets, these neat, dark, chilly, expensive, unique, privet-hedged streets.

The evening is cold. Tiny new leaves of limes and sycamores are shivering in the windy lamplight. Shiny new cars in every drive make Patrick think of the cold face of his Jewess: the Catholic goddess.

The what? Is Joe correct? Is he obsessing?

Trying not to obsess, to be so . . . cunt-struck, Patrick clutches close the flowers he has got for Rebecca's mum as he walks down the *haute* suburban side streets, down some more suburban avenues. As he goes he looks at the doors, counting the doors with the little angled Jewish thingies attached to the doorways. With some effort Patrick tries to compute the Jewish proportion of the population of Hampstead Garden Suburb by the number of little angled Jewish thingies on the front doorjambs. Failing in this, Patrick tries to remember when he first became aware of Jews. Did he have Jewish friends as a kid without even realising they were Jewish? *That kid at primary school, David Samuels, he must have been Jewish, right?*

And then he is there. He has reached the Jessel house, indicated by the big wooden door with the cold new shiny BMW in front, and the angled Jewish thingy attached to the doorjamb.

The bell? The bell.

At the second bell-press the door widens to reveal Rebecca looking beautiful and young. Rebecca's blonde hair is blonded further by the bright yellow hall lights behind. Her shoulders are slim in a new sexy dress. Immediately Patrick feels an urge to stoop and kiss the delicate structure of her lovely, St Paul's-educated collarbone. But Rebecca stops him with a lifted hand, and says:

—What's *that*?

Innocent:

—What?

—*That*

She is indicating his chest.

—Oh – Patrick says, looking down his shirtfront, making a shocked face and a surprised noise, as if he is surprised to see the large crucifix dangling conspicuously there – Oh. Yeah. *That*

—Thanks. You *never* wear a crucifix

—But I do sometimes

—Your idea of a joke? Perhaps?

—No, I . . .

—Patrick! Darling! Hello!!

Too late. Rebecca's mum has appeared. Looking suspicious, and affronted, Rebecca rolls her eyes and steps back and glances across as Patrick walks into the house. Where Rebecca's mum is waiting.

Angled and polite Patrick leans and kisses the offered cheek of his pseudo mother-in-law and simultaneously hands over the flowers he's been too tightly clutching for an hour. Gracious and sweet Rebecca's mother takes the flowers and smiles ably in return; then Mrs Jessel tells Patrick to come through now as they're starting. Wheeling around Patrick stares at Rebecca who smiles in a *well thank you for at least doing that with the flowers* smile. On seeing his girlfriend's smile Patrick's heart pains him with a tiny sadness. Then Patrick smiles and grins and laughs and reaches for Rebecca with a comehereandletmefu

Before the two of them can kiss properly a loud laughing shout from the end of the hall drags them back into society. Via a large open door they walk into a space where a big dining table is already surrounded by lots of Jewish-looking people: some in skullcaps, some in new frocks, some in pious smiles, some in silence turning to look at the crucifix dangling conspicuously from Patrick's shirtfront. For perhaps the first time in his life Patrick gets a pang of conscience, an agenbite at his own arch, insulting mischievousness. For the briefest of moments Patrick conjectures on how his deliberately offensive joke might actually be quite offensive to these good kind intriguing millionaires who invite him in to their lovely big Hampstead house.

OK, behave. Like a good son-in-law, Patrick shakes Rebecca's dad's soft-ringed hand. Then Rebecca's dad invites Patrick to sit down at his allotted chair at the end of table, which Patrick does. On doing this, Patrick notices however that he is far away from the important people, from Rebecca's parents. For a second the rebel yell stirs in his heart, but then he calms himself: the entire scene is too lively and interesting for Patrick to get chippy. Big candles are flickering; old people chattering; gold bangles are rattling on over-tanned arms. Patrick has never seen so many shiny new Rolexes. Girls with long noses and dressed hair are sitting next to boys with hair as black as the girls' lovely eyes. Patrick thinks of scenes from *Schindler's List*; under the table Patrick surreptitiously squeezes the thigh of his girl-friend under that lovely new dress. Happily Patrick speculates how Rebecca's thighs will have that smell of new clothes when he licks them in about . . .

how long? How long will this weirdness last? Alert, intrigued, Patrick listens as the rabbi at the end of the table stands and intones some weird Jewish words. At this signal, everybody around the table has fallen quiet, is trying to be quiet and interested. The quavery-voiced Cohen at the end of the table, who is standing between Rebecca's mum and Rebecca's dad (who are both looking proud, bored, and a bit drunk (*already?*), is intoning:

— Barry shay mischvah mischvah barry shay barry barry

Or, at least, something like that. As Patrick stares blankly at the rabbi, Rebecca's dad gets up and explains in his polished and pukka, but percep-tibly unEnglish accent:

— To all the guests we have here today for our Seder, we say welcome. We hope you will join with us in celebrating the Passover, the Haggidim – Mister Jessel is standing up properly now, is using a big barbecue match to ostentatiously light one of the enormous candles at the top of the table – In praising God we say that all life is sacred. With every holy light we kindle . . .

Rebecca's father blows out the match; proudly contemplates the candle flame. Beside him, Rebecca's mum looks on approvingly. Directly in front of Patrick a large-breasted Jewish matron is leaning forward to gaze respect-fully and interestedly up the table at the goings-on; Patrick wonders if the woman is really doing it just so Patrick can get a better look at her cleavage. It is certainly impressive.

— We praise you our God, sovereign of Existence

— When can we have a sodding drink?

— Now we drink the first cup of wine

From nowhere a hired waiter has appeared. The waiter leans around Patrick and splashes red wine in Patrick's glass. Obedient and thirsty, Patrick stands and drains the wine in a single slug with everybody else. Then he sits back down.

— Now, after symbolically washing our hands, we dip the greens in the salt water to symbolise Karpas, Rebirth and Renewal

Shrugging, smiling, going with the flow, Patrick picks up his sprig of rocket, and looks around at other people for guidance. Other people are dunking the sprig of greenery in the little cup of water set before every plate, and eating the consequently wet bit of green stuff; Patrick does the same.

— In the spring, the season of rebirth and renewal, on the Festival of Pesah, we read from the Song of Songs

Munching the rocket; scoping the tits; thinking about wine, Patrick listens:

— Arise my beloved, my fair one, And come away

Mouth tasting of rocket; hand warm on Rebecca's thigh; eyes full of the ageing but still-just-fuckable Jewish matron opposite, Patrick tries to be quiet and dutiful and a conceivable son-in-law, taking in the scene as the ritual progresses, as the dinner unfolds in all its weirdness. He sits down and listens, he stands and listens, he listens and drinks. Then he gets bored. At least, Patrick thinks, Christmas only takes two days. But this? Munching herbs, Patrick wonders if they really ate rocket in Mosaic Egypt. He whispers this in Rebecca's ear. Rebecca replies, but Patrick cannot understand her whisper. It is slurred: they are all getting drunk: all of them. As Patrick scans the table he checks out the other participants: some of them are now overtly lolling about the table. Perhaps this is not surprising, Patrick thinks: they have ritually consumed at least five cups of wine, not forgetting a couple more illicit refills; together they have celebrated the Plagues of Egypt, the Manna in the Desert, the Dominance of Hollywood . . .

— On this Festival of Pesah, preserve us in Life

Half famished, Patrick leans to the food that is being passed down the table. Quickly he fills his stomach with smoked salmon, and goulash. Soon he feels a warmth spread through himself: he feels glowy, warm, kind, altruistic. Surfing a wave of fellow feeling, Patrick decides he likes it all, likes the house, likes Rebecca's mum, the goulash. Patrick especially likes the youth of his girlfriend sitting next to him. Yes, Patrick thinks: this could be him. This could be his new family; his new home; his new life. He could fit in. He is one of them. He might buy a skullcap.

Feeling content, a bit sleepy, Patrick sprawls on his seat. As he does he vaguely notes that he is experiencing his third erection of the evening. Consequently, Patrick leans to Rebecca, and thinks about suggesting they skip the end of the dinner as he'd like at least one more fuck before he dies.

But before Patrick can get his mouth round a suitably sanitised version of this suggestion, everybody seems to sense that it is *over*. The rabbi has risen and said:

—*Shalom*

and other people have said:

—Next Year in Jerusalem, Next Year may all be Free!

At this signal, Rebecca hisses *come on* and grabs Patrick by the hand. Happy and woozy, pleased to be emancipated, Patrick gets up and lets Rebecca pull him down the napkin-strewn length of the dining-room table. Outside, in the huge Jessel hall, Patrick notices there is a cold breeze blowing from somewhere: it comes from the open front door where servants are standing, smoking. Before Patrick has a chance to properly appreciate the black miniskirt and white blouse of the youngest hired waitress standing in the doorway, Rebecca has pulled him up the stairs. At the top of the stairs the two of them turn, and kiss, and laugh; then they both press and open and tumble into Rebecca's bedroom. There to fall onto the bed. Softly Rebecca falls, like a gamebird despatched by a Burgundy chasseur. Exultant, Patrick snatches at his girlfriend's exemplary breast, at the same time as he tries to stop the room doing a country dance around his head. Slurred, vinous, red-lipped with tannin, he murmurs:

—That was OK

She looks up at him, says:

—Several hours too long

—No. Really. Judaism is a cool religion

—ShutupandkissmePatch

—Say some poetry first babe

—Fuck me hard as

—Proper poetry

—O love be fed with apples while you may – She leans up and kisses him hungrily – and and feel the sun and . . . go with royal array

—Yes!

Thinking *yes!* Patrick looks down at the red and white sweetness of his girlfriend's soft mouth. Drunk and happy he revels in her gleamy teeth; her little snub nose; her slurring lips; her wine-hot breath; her thick ankles; her dress that is hard to slip off, but so good to slip off.

—Go on go onnn . . .

She murmurs, he pulls; she says, he undresses; she giggles, he laughs; she recites:

—Oh this man what a meal he made of me
—How does this undo?
—Are you a man, are you Ardent Aardvark?
—*What?*
—It's John Fuller; the hook's at the front
—Go on
—Tie me up!
—Who wrote *that?*
—*Like we did last night*
—Babe I can't find the
—Daddy's ties!
—What?
—Use his ties, his neckties! Upstairs!!!
—His neckties?
—*Mazel tov!*

Stepping urgently back into his strides Patrick steps to the door; peeks out, peers. From downstairs he can hear muffled babble; the sounds of diesel-engined taxis, of goodbyes and departures; upstairs he can hear nothing but his pulse rate racing at the thought of Rebecca totally naked and twenty-two and awaiting him in the bedroom behind. So. So. So. Barefoot and Don Juan-ish Patrick skips across the landing. Bare-chested and shirtless he bounds the stairs and goes into the master bedroom. Here he looks at the mirrors, the big furniture, the expensive big perfume bottles. Three soft black cashmere overcoats are lying on an enormous bed. Into the nearest wardrobe Patrick looks, seeks, and smells: he smells French aftershave and old gold watches and clean linen shirts. Beeswax. Leather. Rich man smell. Still-wrapped dry cleaning. *Ties!*

Taking a fistful of silk ties Patrick stuffs them in his pocket and freezes at a noise: the door is opening!

b?

b!

barefoot, bare-chested, naked and possessionless but for his strides and a pocketful of looted foulards Patrick turns and looks and sees . . .

nothing.

It was the breeze.

The breeze of April coming through the window!

Quickly Patrick skips, out, down, along, and into the bedroom where Rebecca is on the bed: looking at him. Naked. She is still gloriously naked.

Patrick looks at her supine nudity. Tufts of beautiful black pubic hair are daring him to look at them. With a tiny smile Rebecca opens her legs. The black panther snarls; Patrick steps nearer; the ties come out.

— Use the Dolce one

— Like this?

— Yes. Tighter

— Here?

— There!

— Say . . .

— Oh glory be to God for

— Bec?

— . . . *dappled* . . .

— Bec?

— *Shit*

O the bitter herbs, O the charred symbolic lamb . . .

Patrick swallows. Feels like swooning. Thinks.

The door behind has opened. The door has opened and Rebecca's father is standing at the open door, staring at them. The door has opened and Rebecca's father is standing at the open door of Rebecca's bedroom, staring at them; as they lie thwart on the bed, mid-fuck.

Feeling his back turned to fragile cold glass Patrick curses, shuts his eyes; he has stopped licking Rebecca's pink cunt but he is still squatting with his mouth a few inches from her cunt. Angry, sad, frustrated, bewildered, Patrick senses Rebecca's dad not moving, just standing in the obloid of light made by the open bedroom doorway. Finally, unable to endure it, feeling like a hyena caught at his carrion, like a miser found gloating over gold bullion, Patrick turns from Rebecca's glinting cunt and squints and gazes at the silhouetted father in the overlit doorway.

As Patrick does this he computes; he tries to think what Rebecca's father can see. Can he see his naked daughter lying tied up on the bed? Can he see Patrick's wilting erection? And can he see the glitter of Patrick's dried cum on Rebecca's twitching cold face?

At last, at some signal, for some reason Patrick does not care to figure, Rebecca's dad walks away. He goes: vacating the bright wide space of the bedroom door. At this wordless departure of her father, Rebecca says nothing. The reigning silence is despotic. Only the bed makes a noise as Patrick shuffles barefoot to the door and closes it, and then turns to look at his girlfriend.

— shit

Rebecca says, again. Patrick looks at her. She regards him. She flexes her left hand, still neck-tied to the bed. Then she says – Scratch my nose?

Dutiful, Patrick leans over; scratches her nose.

Rebecca nods, says thank you. She sighs, and sighs, and looks like she is about to cry.

Then at last she looks down her naked self and says:

—I suppose you'd better untie me

17

The jury is thinking about Rebecca's cunt. As is the judge, the clerk, and most of the lawyers. As they all think about Rebecca's cunt, Stefan turns to the female police doctor in the witness box. Stefan pauses. Meanwhile Patrick looks across the court and sees the oldest male juror staring with absolutely rapt attention at the doctor as she prepares to discuss Rebecca's cunt. Patrick feels turbulently aroused by the idea of everybody in the court considering his ex-girlfriend's cunt. Her cunt. Her exposed sea creature at low tide. The ground floor of her Venetian palazzo, where she stores her furs and cinnamons. Her *cunt!*

Stefan is standing; the court is waiting; Patrick is concentrating, concentrating on anything but the idea of the world speculating about his ex-girlfriend's vagina. Because: *it turns him on*. The idea of these disinterested people picturing his ex-girlfriend's privates affords Patrick some weird churning feelings that are not far from arousal.

Patrick sweats at this idea. He squirms. In a white shirt that smells of his mum's fabric conditioner Patrick sweats and shifts and looks at the fine cloth of his trouser material and tries to stifle all these painfully unwholesome feelings; half successful he shifts in his seat in his elongated wooden box in Court Number Eighteen the Old Bailey so as to give his erection more room.

Picking up the doctor's report, for about the fifth time today, Stefan taps the end of his pen against the big sheaf of A4 paper, and he wafts it in the direction of the police doctor:

— It is true to say, isn't it, Doctor . . . – Stefan seems to forget the name for a moment, then seems to remember – Doctor Bradley . . .

Doctor Bradley shoots a cuff under a sensible blazer. A strangely masculine gesture, or so it appears to Patrick. For the third time this day Patrick wonders if the good doctor is lesbian. That she is a police doctor *because* she is a sadistic lesbian who enjoys looking at pretty young girls with their knickers down crying.

Patrick stoops his head, listens. Stefan is saying:

— Doctor Bradley . . . would you say it is true that in most cases of non-consensual sex one would expect to see bruises to the . . . – Levelly scanning the courtroom – Perineum? The area between the anus and the vagina?

The doctor sort of nods. She takes a professional second to gather her thoughts, then:

— Where there has been resistance . . . *usually*

— Yes?

— One might expect to see bruises

— And?

— But not always

— And this – Stefan says, seeming to ignore the doctor – And this bruising would be because the accused . . . would be trying to gain entry – He taps a pen against the cover of the file – To use the penis as a kind of battering ram?

Doctor Bradley:

— As I said . . . usually

— Very well – Stefan is sounding authoritative. He puts down the pen and uses the free hand to riffle some pages – But there weren't such bruises in this case? Were there, Doctor? At least you don't mention them in this report, do you?

— Perhaps . . . no

— If you might glance at your report, Doctor Bradley?

The doctor swallows and shakes her head in a small way; she picks up her own copy of her report; she reads on for a moment, does a tiny grimace, then stares expectantly across the court at her interrogator.

Stefan comes in:

— Did you in fact see such bruising in this case?

A pause, a frustrated sigh, Doctor Bradley:

— . . . No

—No? Would you say not at all, in fact?

—Not . . . *at all*

—Thank you – Stefan is flourishing the report again – So when you examined the complainant's genitals there were in fact none of the bruises we would normally . . . associate with rape

—Not there . . . but . . .

The doctor stalls, Stefan comes back:

—In fact wouldn't it be true to say that the complainant's . . . *perineum* – The lawyer flashes a glance between the doctor's report, and the doctor's lesbian face – Showed all the normal signs we associate with *consensual* intercourse?

The doctor does a discomfited shrug, then sighs:

—Perhaps

—Thank you – Acting satisfied, Stefan looks down to his junior, his magician's assistant, who pushes across a sheaf of what seem to be photos – Now, Doctor, if I may take you through some of the photos . . .

. As if reminded of something, Stefan glances at the judge; the judge nods, and says:

—For the jury?

—Yes, Your Honour, please – By Stefan's side the junior checks a note and whispers upwards to his boss; in turn the defence counsel says loud, and authoritative – We'd like the jury to see photos 3a to 3d . . . if you will

—Thank you – The judge turns to the clerk, says in a soft voice – *Could we . . . ?*

The clerk of the court nods. She peers in a big plastic bag, lifts a hand in, and takes out envelopes seemingly full of more photos. From his panelled box Patrick leans to see these photos. As the clerk begins sorting the big slippy photos into a coherent pile, Patrick sees: a glimpse of golden shoulder, a flash of soft white thigh, a bruised and female upper arm. He sees the famous arc of Rebecca's lovingly scratched back.

Patrick swallows the saliva of lust. These photos of that body he loved so much: these pictures of Rebecca's wounds: they are a map of his guilt, an atlas of his sins, proof of his butchery, his wickedness, his hopeless masculinity. And they are even now erotic. What chance?

While the photos are sorted, numbered, organised and slowly handed over to the jury – one copy of each for two jurors to share – Patrick slacks his head and gazes remorsefully at the grainy wood panelling of his box. He remembers: when he first saw these photos. When his lawyer brought them in to him on remand in prison. At the time he could hardly bear to look at them: these golden Polaroids of his golden girl. As he'd sat there in the prison visiting room, watching his lawyer go through photos of his girlfriend, naked, beautiful, blonde, young, beaten, Patrick had felt sick, desirous, desperately in love, yet also desperate to take these photos back to his cell . . .

Patrick clenches a fist, uses the fist to prop a determined chin. Brave and firm-chinned he watches all the courtroom having a lark, a gas, a veritable giggle, as they all pass these jolly photos around the jolly courtroom like they're shots of someone's white-water rafting trip. Slow. Calm. Slow. Patrick's heart does a thing. Sends a nervous signal to his groin. Fast. Slow. Calm.

Calm!

Somewhere in the court they are talking about bruising. Again. The defence counsel and the doctor are arguing over the exact extent of bruising evidenced in each shot. During the exchange, Patrick tries to remember the exact amount of bruising he occasioned that last time he loved Rebecca, the last time he had his fist up her. How much do, can, should these photos really show? Can they show the noises, the words, the love? Do they show the way she deeply breathed his name, the way she yawned with pleasure, the way she turned dark liquid eyes on him and murmured *harder, harder* . . .

— You're telling me, Doctor Bradley, that these . . . blemishes . . . this mark I can hardly see, that is your idea of a contusion?

— It appears that way

— It appears that way?

— I mean they appeared that way during the examination

— Very well

— You see – The doctor gazes level and equal at Stefan and goes on despite Stefan's attempt to interrupt – When I examined the plaintiff the marks were larger than they appear here. There must have been a considerable lapse of time between. That's the only explanation

Stefan is making unimpressed noises:

— But surely given the amount of trauma you describe, some would still be visible?

— Well . . . It is

— *It is?*

—Yes

—Er . . . – Stefan's pen is poised over one of the photos of Rebecca –
Where? Doctor Bradley?

The doctor holds up a photo of Rebecca's buttock and says, pointing
with a be-ringed finger:

—Here

Stefan theatrically doubletakes:

—*Here?*

—Yes

—Can we?

The court can. The whole of the court can and is looking closely at
Rebecca's arse and trying to see something.

Stefan half chortles:

—So. You mean this blemish here, the one I just accidentally wrote
over with my pen and totally obscured?

—. . . Yes

—This is the blemish you call a . . . 'significant bite mark' . . . in your
notes?

—. . . Yes

Wide-eyed, Stefan looks at the doctor, looks at the jury, looks at
Patrick's teeth marks in Rebecca's left buttock. Then he says:

—I've no more questions

But as he sits down the prosecutor jumps up and says:

—Just a few more questions

The doctor sits back; the prosecutor, with his wig and gown and
most confident demeanour, is already saying:

—You are a doctor of how many years' experience, Doctor Bradley?

Shrug, frown, nod:

—Fifteen, maybe sixteen . . .

—Sixteen years. And – The prosecutor smiles, seriously – In that time
you have examined, roughly, *how many* rape victims?

—Pff – Doctor Bradley exhales – Mmm, I suppose . . . – The doctor
thinks, thinks more, then seems to agree with her own calculations –
At least a hundred, perhaps more

Wig, gown, smile:

—Thank you. Now. In that time, Doctor Bradley, I imagine you must
have heard of the adage 'you can't thread a moving needle'

A wince from the doctor; then:

— Of course
— Could you explain it?
  The doctor nods again:
— Yes. It's one of the most pernicious rape myths there is. It presumes that if a woman is struggling a man cannot gain penetration. And that if there were a struggle there would have to be a huge amount of bruising to the vagina and labia
  Alan Gregory QC:
— And this is, as you say, rubbish?
  The doctor snorts:
— Absolute rubbish. Total and utter rubbish
— Right – Gregory glances at the jury, the jury glances back. In the dock Patrick tries to think about lunch – Now, if I may cast your mind back to photos 2a to 2f – The prosecutor turns slightly to the judge – I don't think there's any need for the jury to see these again . . .
  The judge nods; the clerk shrugs; the prosecutor goes on:
— I mean these are the same photos of the plaintiff's face I'm referring to, so . . .
— It's O K, I remember – Says the doctor. The prosecutor nods gratefully, then continues:
— Thank you. O K – Lifting his head – Would you say, Doctor, the bruises on the face we saw in those photos, the bite marks and bruises – The words hang in the air – Would you say they were consistent with an . . . extremely violent sexual encounter?
  The silence is heavy. Patrick slips a forefinger between collar and neck; then feels guilty about the guilty-ness of the body language. The words are still resonant in the air as the doctor takes long seconds to decide what to reply. The doctor coughs, then says:
— I would say there is no other explanation. Apart from an . . . – Patrick blinks, Patrick swallows, the doctor goes on – Extremely violent sexual incident – Patrick stops blinking. The doctor concludes – I would say there is no other explanation for the bruises and other marks in these photos, other than . . . a . . . very brutal . . . – Deep breath – *rape*

Do you
    Do you think
    Do you think I'm

— Do you think I'm guilty, Mum?

His mother makes a motherly face as best she can:

— Patch . . . darling . . .

— Mum. I'm serious – He makes a very serious face – Do you?

She looks at him. Says nothing.

They are sitting in the canteen at the top of the Old Bailey. Patrick's mother looks suitably pinched and public sector amidst the public sector drabness all around: the crap sandwiches half eaten; the cups of cold machine coffee; the policemen in nylon shirts sweating dark-blue patches. His mother does a fearfully aged smile which makes Patrick flinch at the deepness of her wrinkles, as she smiles and says:

— I've never thought that, Patrick darling, you know how much I believe you

And so his mother goes on. And as she does Patrick looks at her, at her sadness, and tiredness, and oldness, worst of all her bravery, and consequently he feels the pangs of guilt, the pangs of guilt at having put her through this, the pangs of guilt at his being innocent but still stupid enough to end up here, the pangs of guilt that he might just possibly get a guilty verdict . . . And as he thinks this, Patrick thinks how much he is hurting his mother because he loves her and that makes him think something he's been thinking for a while now: how all love seems to be a process of hurting people you love, how the amount you love seems proportionate to, maybe even predicated upon, the amount you can hurt.

In which case . . . In which case, Patrick decides, he must love Rebecca more than anyone.

— You know I might go down for this, Mum. *For life*

Silence, frown, wrinkles, silence. This is the first time Patrick has mentioned aloud this possibility and Patrick wants a reaction. The reaction is silence. His mother does not start but nor does she refute the concept. Inside Patch feels like crying out. He stares at his mother. *Flesh of my flesh*. He thinks of her crying and dying without him, with him in prison.

Then she speaks:

— Look my boy you've got a good lawyer and all your friends believe you and just because that silly nasty girl can't get her

my boy?

Patrick listens to his mother's outrage, her defiance, but he senses that they both feel that there is something wrong, something wronger then before. The confidence they were able to fake hitherto is beginning to ebb away. And as the final moment, the moment of truth approaches, the naked fear is showing through. Patrick wonders how much his mother must resent him, somewhere, for his putting her through this.

Then he thinks of something even more painful: how much she has learnt of the kinky sex. How much? How much of that evidence has she heard? How much have they told her? Pained, agonised, Patrick tries not to think of his mother hearing the gruesome sexual details, the biting, the tying, the handcuffs, the buggery. The idea of his mum hearing of his sexual peccadilloes is, to Patrick, like the idea of actually having his mum standing by with fresh Kleenex while he's noisily copulating. It makes Patrick feel embarrassed, resentful, nauseous, dirty, sinful, bad. Not least because: if his mother has never done or heard of sex like this, like the pretty fierce sex described in this courtroom these three days, then his mother will be upset, scandalised and humiliated. Which would be bad. But perhaps worse would be if this kind of sex her son is having does *not* upset and scandalise and humiliate Patrick's mother: because this would mean she had heard of, perhaps even done, such sexual things . . .

Patrick gazes at the sad cup of weak tea his mother is sipping. Maybe, he thinks, maybe an entire lifetime in prison wouldn't be such a bad option. After all.

18

—Oooh, tricky
—Exactly
—So what did he *say*? Afterwards?
    Rebecca chuckles, says:
—Nothing!
—He saw you doing it, tied up and everything – Murphy's wide eyes widen even further – And he said *nothing*?
—Yep
—*Golly*
    Rebecca:
—I just hate it when parents say . . . *nothing* . . . Don't you?

Rebecca is looking brightly at Murphy. Murphy shakes her head and gives up on the dialogue, she just whews smoke into the sunny, dusty air. They are both sitting on the unpolished floorboards of the furnitureless flat. After a final puff on her cigarette Murphy leans sideways, and uses a middle finger to drag back an ashy saucer, into which she aggressively taps more cigarette ash. Then she says:

—So that's why you've moved?
—Sort of . . .
—Just because of your dad finding you naked and tied up by your ex-convict boyfriend with his own Armani ties . . .
—Dolce
    Another smoky drawl:
—Golly goggles

152

Rebecca smiles:

—Thank God it wasn't my *mother*. Can you imagine that?

—NO!!!

Murphy is slapping her own forehead. Rebecca half smiles, half grimaces. Letting go of her forehead, Murphy looks around the flat, at the unpainted walls, the greasy skirting board, the paint pots with rough sticks protruding. Her nose tilted upwards Murphy sniffs the damp and musty air, and says:

—Needs a tiny bit of work . . .

Rebecca:

—You hate it don't you?

Murphy wags her head:

—It's a fucking hovel

Rebecca smiles, shrugs:

—But . . . a brilliantly located hovel – Still smiling – Anyway. How else do you think we got it so cheap? In this location?

Murphy nods, says:

—So Patch has given up his flat?

—Yep

—But he liked that place – Murphy thinks – *I* liked that place

—You liked Joe, Murphy

—Mmm, spunky Joe

—He's got a new flatmate already I think

Murphy looks thoughtful, says:

—And . . . this is . . . – She surveys the room – All this is what Patch wanted?

—He *said* he wanted it. He said his and Joe's flat was a tip

—Mmm . . .

Rebecca looks firmly at her best friend:

—OK, tell me. You think it's a big mistake don't you? Our moving in together?

—No no no no NO – Murphy shrugs – Yes

—Yes?

—No I'm joking

—No? It isn't? What??

Murphy makes an exasperated noise:

—Look, no, yeah, it's a great idea? *K*?

—Really?

—Rilly. Specially if you . . . – Murphy grins, leans back, admires the turn-ups on her own jeans – Seeing as you and the . . . caveman are gonna be doing freaky sex, tying each other up and the like, it's probably good you get your own place, right?

—Thank you, Murphy

—No probs

Rebecca narrows her eyes:

—Do remind me of that threesome you had with that guy from the . . . carpet fitters? Wasn't it?

—You Munter

—And what was that spit roast thing you told me about? When he got his friend and they put in that

—Spark plug, he put in my spark plug – Grinning – He was a mechanic

Rebecca laughs. Murphy chuckles. Then Murphy gets up. In her dark jeans and clingy jumper Murphy stands and turns and crosses to the grimy window of the flat. Without a further word Murphy flings up the grimy sash window: sunlight and wind and Marylebone traffic noise come in. Across the room Rebecca imagines the view Murphy must be enjoying from the open window: the tattooed taxi-drivers leaning bare-armed in the springtime sunshine, as they stare slack-jawed at the miniskirted Portuguese *au pairs*. Murphy:

—It is an *amazing* location

Rebecca envies Murphy's long figure in the frame of window light. Rebecca looks down; says to the floorboards:

—He refuses to live outside the centre, anyway

Murphy turns:

—Who? Patch?

—Yes . . .

—So it's *him* that forced you to rent this hole

—Oh. It's not so bad

Murphy seems to think about this, then she says

—What else do you two do in bed?

Rebecca tsks. She looks at the watch on her wrist, checks the time, checks the faint marks of handcuffs beneath the watchstrap, says:

—Murphy. You're a voyeur

Her friend is whining:

—. . . tell me? Pur*leeze*?

—Really?

—Yes?

—Well . . . Sometimes I like him to . . . like him to . . .
—Mm yes go on go on DON'T STOP
  Murphy is padding back, enthusiastic and barefoot, to where Rebecca is sitting. As Murphy folds her long legs under herself, and sits down on the floor opposite, Rebecca looks at the silver ring on one of Murphy's toes and Rebecca says:
—I like him to say your name when we do it
  Murphy stops. Says:
—What?
  Rebecca:
—I'm not telling you what we do, you'll just go all judgmental about it
  Murphy:
—He hits you, doesn't he?
  A Rebecca-ish *moue*, then:
—Wouldn't call it hitting, *precisely*
—So sorry – Murphy clicks a tongue – Perhaps *thwacking* would be better? Or *clattering*, or . . . how about *smashing your stupid head in*
—Anyway I ask him to
—Y . . . ? W . . . ?
  Her friend all quiet and shocked-looking, Rebecca smiles again:
—*I ask him to hit me*
  The sound of a motorbike being over-revved comes through the window. Then Murphy says:
—Why the fuck would you wanna ask someone to hit you??
  Rebecca ponders whether to say what she wants to say. So she says:
—It's a girl thing?
—Fuck it is!
—No. I think maybe it is. Maybe
—Derrr? Hello?????
  Rebecca laughs and says:
—Perhaps it's possible, you know? That some women are inherently masochistic?
  Murphy's face is pink with outrage:
—Fucking medieval drivel, Bex, I'm a girl and I don't like people beating me senseless
—No?
—No I bloody *don't*
—But – Rebecca grins, very slightly – Don't you ever dream of some great

big . . . hairy . . . man coming into your bedroom with his antlers and pelt? And spanking you?

—Wow!

Rebecca laughs openly, goes on:

—Bull elephant seals, I had a dream about a bull elephant seal the other day . . .

—Antlers, stags, zebras. Jesus. What's wrong with car mechanics?

—Grease monkeys?

—Ha – Murphy laughs – You're a bloody freakshow, Rebecca Jessel

—Least I'm not Vanilla Girl

The two of them stare at each other, outraged, amused, curious. After a few seconds Murphy lifts her slim-fingered gallery girl hand and says:

—So. Let me . . . *No* – Talking loudly through Rebecca's protestations – It's my turn, let me get this right . . . – Working it out, Murphy says – You ask . . . *him* . . . to **punch**

—Slap

—Slap, punch, decapitate you during sex cause . . . for some weirdo reason . . . some reason no doubt connected with your dad . . . these kind of carnal shenanigans, they turn you on?

Rebecca does her best unashamed face:

—Yes

Murphy:

—Jesus I'm boring

Rebecca beams:

—Don't be too hard on yourself

—No. It's true. Have to face it. Haven't lived have I?

—What about the Spark Plug Incident?

—Don't patronise me

—Well that was a threesome you told me and . . .

—Spark plugs were too small anyway

Running fingers through her dusty hair Rebecca tilts her head and says:

—You don't truly disapprove then?

Murphy sighs, looks long and kind and soft at her friend, and says:

—Why should I disapprove, babe? Whatever turns you on – Still looking she says – Just don't get hurt, K? Like, please? – She ruminates, then says – So is Hoxton Man into all this freakiness? Bet he is . . . Right?

—Well . . . he . . . actually . . . – Rebecca looks at her own trainers; looks at her pleasingly old jeans. Rebecca likes the fact that she is in old dusty jeans and old jumper so as to be prepared to strip out, and kit out, the new flat she's going to share with her boyfriend. *How wholesome is that?* Then she says – At first he was a tad chary

A lorry reversing outside nearly drowns out the sound of Murphy delightedly mimicking Rebecca:

—**At first he was a tad chary??????**

—Think I might have corrupted him

—Flip!

As Murphy starts laughing, Rebecca hears a key in the lock. Downstairs. At once Rebecca jumps:

—It's Patch!

—*Bex . . . !*

Ignoring the strange look on Murphy's face Rebecca skips to the sitting-room stairs. Descending with a hop and a laugh she leaps to the opening front door and pulls it completely open to see Patrick saying:

—Hiya scrunchy

He is standing there, smiling, door key still in hand. He is half shaven, he is silhouetted by sunshine. The chic, busy, agreeable streets of Marylebone are doing their subtly wealthy thing behind him. Gazing at the pastel-seascape-blue of her lover's eyes Rebecca smiles and feels her heart lift; rapt, devout, self-consciously in love, she watches with a smile as he lifts up a brown-paper-wrapped package and says:

—Er, I was going to get a wok

Rebecca looks at the package, she looks at Patrick's inscrutable smile, she looks back at the package. Then she takes a step back and with a giggle she runs forward, jumps right into him, straight up into his arms. Seemingly winded by this, he drops the package, staggers back, manages to keep hold of Rebecca, but nearly knocks over the Japanese restaurateur from next door. This near accident makes Rebecca laugh but she still keeps hanging on to her boyfriend; half in his arms, half falling out, she kisses him full on the lips. In an apparent effort to save them from teetering into the Linden Street traffic Patrick topples forward through the front door of the flat, thus carrying them both into the stairwell, where he stoops to drop her gently to the floor. But they are so unbalanced they both collapse headlong into a shiny, slippy pile of glossy property freesheets and pizza chain flyers. For a few giggling moments the two of them sit there, on the carpet, looking at each other, laughing, regaining breath.

Then he says:

—But they didn't have any woks

Feeling the scratch of the nylon pile of the cheap hall carpet in the small of her back, Rebecca strokes Patrick's unshaven chin. She kisses the chin, smells something expensive, some expensive soap or balm. Then she remembers the package. Leaning, giggling, she picks it up, shakes it, feeling agreeably like a kid with a Christmas present. He kisses her neck; she pushes him away; she wriggles free of his embrace and kneels on the scratchy hall carpet and uses both hands to properly tear open the brown paper wrapping and Sellotape.

Inside is a shoe box. Rebecca opens the shoe box and lifts out

—A trumpet?

—A bugle

—A . . . *bugle*?

Lying back, unshaven and languid, against the lowest stair, he smiles and looks sheepish and says:

—I was gonna get you something sensible . . . like a toaster . . . but . . .

—You thought a small trumpet would be better?

—Yeah

—Mnnn. OK

—OK? Bex?

Rebecca, cod-shyly:

—I suppose we could play it . . . after sex?

—Before, during, instead of

—Wake up the neighbours!

—You like it then??

Rebecca grins, gets to her feet. Standing on the bottom stair she reaches out a hand and lifts her boyfriend up by the hand and when he is standing over her, the two of them close and kiss, expertly, and then she says:

—What more could a woman ask than a brand-new . . . bugle . . . for her house?

— second-hand

—Murphy's upstairs!

Holding hands, they climb the stairs and they go into the bright, paint-smelling, sunlit, unfurnished sitting room. Rebecca waves the bugle at Murphy, who is changing the tape on the portable tape-player. Seeing Murphy's surprised, what-the-hell-is-that expression, Rebecca explains:

—It's a bugle. Patch bought me a bugle!

—Nice

—For the kitchen!

—Good thinking

—So, Smurf – Patch strides into the sitting room, casting an eye over his own decorating efforts at the same time – What do you think of the new flat?

—Great location, really great

—You think it smells, right?

—Hums

—That's why it's so cheap

—I know – Murphy says, getting to her now-shod feet – Bex told me

—Well I don't care I love it

Says Rebecca. Murphy and Patch look at her; Patch goes over and puts an arm protectively around his girlfriend's shoulder; Murphy cocks an eye at the two of them, and says quietly:

—Ahh the golden couple

—You do like it, Murphy?

Sardonically, distantly, Murphy says:

—Course, it's lovely – Sliding past them towards the door – OK, I have to go, enjoy your bugle

And with a semi-wave Murphy exits. Standing side by side Rebecca and Patch listen to her departure: the stairs, the door, the traffic, the door.

Listening to the echo of the doorslam, Rebecca considers. Standing beside her taller boyfriend in their new empty flat, Rebecca considers how the two of them must look now: like a just-wed couple in an advert for mortgage lenders. As she thinks this Rebecca finds herself thinking how pleased she is by this, how strongly, purely, properly glad. And then, despite herself, Rebecca feels the further tug of these thoughts, the insidious temptation. Looking around the flat, feeling Patrick's arm around her shoulders, Rebecca scopes the dusty floors, the empty walls, the rolls of discarded carpet, the bin bags full of rubbish, the paint pots stacked in a grimy corner and she sees not these but the future. The Future. In her mind she sees big churchy candles, old silver on a polished dining table, elegantly smoking friends; in her mind she sees bottles of balsamic vinegar, washing in a big wicker basket, doodled-on Sunday papers piled carelessly next to empty bottles of wine. And then Rebecca sees the final image. Gazing at the space by the door to the kitchen she sees an annoyed but happy young mother nibbling a fingernail while reading Thomas Hardy in a second-hand Penguin edition while standing over the crib of her gorgeous baby.

—Rebecca?
—Mm?
—Why on earth are you crying?

19

—And this was, *when*, Doctor?
—About three thirty
—In the morning?
—Yes – Doctor Lewis looks down at her notes, looks across at the silvery wig of the prosecution, at the Seventies-style downlights beyond – I arrived at Paddington Green police station at about two o clock, and the accused was escorted into the cell for examination – The doctor glances at her wrist, as if checking her watch – I think about half an hour later

Lawyerly nod; solicitous smile:
—Did you notice anything about the accused?

Air conditioning. Cough in the gallery. Doctor Lewis:
—I . . . ?

The new witness is looking blankly at the lawyer. Alan Gregory QC lifts an eyebrow and says:
—What was he dressed in?
—The . . . paper suit
—Yes. Can you explain this to the jury?
—Of course. Forensic need to examine any . . . clothes in such cases, so the . . . accused . . . uh . . . persons – The doctor seems to shrug at her own grammatical infelicity, then goes on anyway – Well. They are given a kind of disposable paper jump suit to wear, a white paper jump suit. With a zip

—And as a result Mister Skivington's clothes were taken for forensic examination?

—Yes

—Have you read the forensic reports on the clothes, Doctor Lewis?

—Yes – She smiles, professionally. At her smile, the judge nods, the lawyer nods, the jury rolls a communal boiled sweet round its mouth and leans forward; and Patrick shuts his eyes. Patrick opens his eyes again to see the prosecution whisper something to his assistant, who subsequently lifts up a see-through plastic bag and takes out a pair of dark-blue frayed jeans. Seeing his clothes, the clothes he wore the night, that night, makes Patrick want to close his eyes again; the jeans were trendy then, he muses. The lawyer's assistant is taking out a pair of Patrick's shoes, the shoes he wore then, followed by Patrick's top. *Nice top*, Patrick thinks, watching intently as the asistant reaches in the bag one more time and rummages for a second and then extracts . . . A pair of Cross of St George boxer shorts?!

Someone in the jury laughs as the prosecutor lays the Cross of St George boxer shorts on the courtroom table beside Patrick's jeans and top and shoes. The jury stops laughing as the prosecution counsel wipes his hands on a tissue provided by his junior, balls the tissue, then gestures the cleaned hand over the pile of clothes and says:

—Was there anything of significance in the reports, about these clothes?

—There was semen staining on the jeans

—And anything else, did you notice anything else, any other stains?

—The boxer shorts are stained

—With what?

—It appears to be coffee – She nods at her own remarks – It's faint. But it's older than the semen stain – The doctor puts her reading glasses back on and looks down at her notes and says – The tests indicate it's about six weeks older than the semen stain. Six weeks before the alleged rape

Taking off his tee shirt Patrick climbs naked apart from his Cross of St George boxer shorts into bed, beside Rebecca. Then he leans back out of the bed and lifts up one cup, and then another cup of shop-bought coffee. Twisting in the bed he hands the heavier cup to Rebecca who takes her cup, peels off the plastic white lid, and peers like a squirrel at the milk foam.

—Cinnamon?

—Yep

—Decaf?

—Yep

—*Apricot croissant?*

Patrick leans over and picks up the bag of pastries and hands that over too. He sighs:

—And I got the magazines. And the post. And the new mortgage. And an obsidian blade from Veracruz and a

—Thank you, darling!

Bright and blonde in the morning sun streaming through their Marylebone window, Rebecca is grinning. She is grinning and kissing him on the lips; she is naked as she lifts herself and leans across. The touch and smell and proximity of his girlfriend's naked skin makes Patrick's naked skin tingle deliciously as she leans over him to put her half-drunk cup of coffee back on the floor beside his side of their bed.

—Too hot – She laughs, licking some capp foam from her finger. Snuggling down under the duvet with her apricot croissant half eaten in her hand, she eats more croissant, and says through crumbs of croissant:

—Love spending Sundays in bed

—S'Thursday

—Really. God – Wriggly, in that wanting-attention-way, she says – What are you going to do today then?

—Tsch

—No. What?

—Dunno

—You're not going into work then?

Patrick turns the page of his *Telegraph*. Reads the weather headline. Says lowly:

—Can't be arsed

—But you've got to, they need you there

—Fuck 'em. Anyway I . . .'ve got to go and see my dad

She pauses, breathes twice, says:

—Are you really going to go and see your dad?

Weather map, weather in New York, weather in Ecuador . . .

—Nah

Croissant finished, Rebecca takes the pastry bag, scrunches it, and throws it roughly in the direction of the stereo. Then she says:

—Patch you *have* to go and see him

—Why?

—DUH because he's

—Dying?

—No! Because he's your dad. And he's . . . not very well! – She shakes her head – God! Why don't you give him a chance before you start nailing down the coffin lid

—He's dying – Patrick sucks air through his teeth, as he reads the paper – But yes sure course I'll go and see him sometime soon. Maybe next week – Patrick lifts up the newspaper – Anyway, let me read my paper, please?

—No!

Rebecca is giggling; her hand is snaking down under the bedclothes, where she is doing something to his boxer shorts. Pretending not to notice Patrick breathes in and out and reads the same paragraph about Arsenal's share price five times over, while his girlfriend tussles with the elastic of his shorts. Finally frustrated by this elastic, it seems, Rebecca lifts the duvet and stares down her semi-naked boyfriend's torso at his Cross of St George boxer shorts. Pause. Rebecca speaks:

—Patch . . . ?

—Nn?

—You've . . .

—Babe?

—You've got the Nazi pants on again

—My patriotic jocks? Sure. Why?

—Patch – Rebecca sighs, lifting the elastic of his shorts and letting it ping back onto his stomach, painfully – Why do you wear them?

—Cause they annoy you

—But they don't though

—They make you think I'm a Nazi

Rebecca:

—Have I ever told you how much those shorts really *annoy* me

—Yeah. Sorry

—*Please* forsake the Hitler underwear again please it's kind of sensitive for us

—English in the drawing room, French in the kitchen, Jewish in the bedroom, that's the ideal woman

—Don't ever wear them again?!! Please??

Rebecca's little scrunched-up nose is near his bigger nose, her big eyes are near his staring eyes. Marooned, compassless, scorbutic with lust in the seas of love, Patrick gazes into his girlfriend's green-and-brown eyes, feeling his heart and his groin doing a jazz duet. The Patrick Skivington Duo, performing 'My Helpless Love'.

Rebecca asks:

—Does my Jewishness really turn you on?

—Yep

—Why?

—Because you're exotic, different. You're like . . . – Patrick thinks – Olives. Jews are like olives. I never had an olive until I was twenty – Patrick pulls the duvet up and snuggles nearer his naked Jewess – Never liked olives at first either

Rebecca half slaps, half caresses his shoulder. The boyfriend looks down, at the duvet, goes quiet, then says:

—When was the duvet revolution, when was it that sheets and blankets went out?

Rebecca leans and whispers loud and hot in his ear:

—Call my cunt that name again?

He looks at her, says:

—That name . . . of that programme you never saw?

—The kids' programme, yes

—Really? You want me . . . ?

—To say it!

—You want me to say the name?

—Yes!!

—. . . Show me your . . . *Pogle's Wood?*

—Oh yes

—Oh yes?

—Come on you bastard!

—Do you want to see my Woodentop?

—Only if you put your Woodentop in . . . *Hector's House?*

Out loud Patrick laughs, lifts the duvet up and looks down at his naked girlfriend's long but short body. It is slender but curvy; tiny but generous; beautiful but terrifying. It is Crystal tips, but Alister.

—Time for bed

Says Patrick.

Urgent, nodding, giggling, Rebecca reaches down under the duvet, reaches for his shorts, slips her fingers around, and finds Patrick's hardness. Patrick shuts his eyes. He senses her lovely fingers, her lovely, nimble, expert, grade eight, Für-Elise-playing fingers, as they slip inside the slit in his jocks. Then he hears her say:

—God Patch I love your fucking cock

—So you took a penile swab?

—Yes

Doctor Lewis puts her glasses on again as she reads from her notes:

—I took a . . . penile swab, nail parings, and hair clippings from the accused

—And the result?

—The swab indicated that intercourse had taken place maybe two hours before

The tiny silver ribbon of horsehair at the back of the prosecution lawyer's wig bobs up and down. Patrick starts counting the ceiling-level apertures of the complex air-conditioning system. Then he listens again as the doctor describes his nail parings, his hair clippings, his penile swabs – and how she inspected Patrick's body.

—He seemed to me quite a fit young man

—Strong, would you say?

—Yes

In the box Patrick feels a mixture of pride, resentment and violation. He tries to feel calm. They are evidently trying to make him out as a superfit, physically well capable rapist; how nice, Patrick thinks, to be described as superfit, as physically *well capable*.

—What else did you notice?

The doctor pauses, computes, and says

—There were two large abrasions on Mister Skivington's knees

—Both knees?

—Yes

—Can you describe them?

—They were large red patches of raw skin, where the skin had rubbed away, with a certain amount of bruising

—And these ... abrasions ... were they – The lawyer taps his closed mouth with a pen, goes on – Were the abrasions of recent provenance ... were they fresh, as it were?
—Yes. The skin was raw
—What do you think they were, Doctor Lewis?
Doctor Lewis looks briefly at the judge; Patrick looks briefly at Doctor Lewis's chubby red thirty-something face. The doctor says:
—I think they were carpet burns

—Not on the carpet, hurts my knees
Rebecca listens to her lover say this and she thinks in a Northern accent *give over* and then she thinks *why isn't he taking me from behind yet?*
As if commanded by her thoughts Patrick lifts Rebecca up and turns her around and starts taking her from behind and as she feels him slip hard inside she feels a bliss and a resentment, a sense of pride, and a sense of violation. She thinks of the witches they tortured; she thinks of the croissant she ate; she thinks of sexual dimorphism in animals and how she likes his bigness, his biggerness. His tallness and hardness. Yet she also likes his relative roughness, his maleness, his coarseness. So? Tasting the apricot-and-pastry flavour on her lips Rebecca wonders if sexual dimorphism can be applied to wealth and intellect and class background and credit rating. Can she be turned on by the fact he can't get a mortgage because of his police record? Rebecca thinks of his lovely cock inside her and she lets out a strange sound.
Erkkgkkaka??
His hardness. Oh *them*. Together. Working. Having her boyfriend inside her Rebecca loses herself in the pillow beneath and she finds herself wondering when was the last time they laundered the pillowslips and then she thinks of his cock. Pillowslip. Patrick's cock. Pillowslip. His cockerel. Little red rooster. These animals. O these wee beasties. These her witch's familiars ohGod ohGod ohGod, Rebecca half swoons, does he love her little black cat? Her sweet greedigut? Her little vinegar joe?
Do it now!
He does it now. She is turned over again. Face to face, Rebecca feels raw air, and his raw unshaven chin on her soft open face. Rebecca lets her mouth do a Kiri te Kanawa; she opens and closes; she chunks her hands in his lovely dark soft sweet hair and kisses his shoulders until his dark dark

hair disappears down the bed to start the examination. Of the wytche's boddie; for blemmishes and wenns. O yea, Rebecca swoons, will he pryck her or burne her? Will he strip her nakedde, for to see the devil's marks, on her snowie breast?

— Were there any other marks on the accused?
  Doctor Lewis says:
— There were lots of little . . . cuts
— What sorts of cuts?
— Small lesions and abrasions on the back and shoulders
  Gregory looks down at his own desk, and says:
— Consistent with . . . ?
— Well, there are several possible explanations . . . – Spectacles in hand, Doctor Lewis looks across at the prosecution and says – The explanation I most favour is scratches – More emphatically – Yes, I would say they are scratches
— Made by human fingernails?
— Yes
— As if in a struggle?
— . . . Possibly
— No further questions
  The judge leans over his desk and his dais and looks lofty, old, kind and downwards at the doctor; who turns and looks sweet, young, submissive and like a Jane Austen daughter up at the judge. The judge says:
— Doctor Lewis? Was there anything you wish to add?
  The doctor *moues* a yes. The judge smiles; the doctor adds:
— It appeared to me that the scratches had been formed over quite a long period of time . . . not just on one occasion. There were hundreds of them

— Ouch
— Sorry
— Don't fucking scratch so much
— Sorry
— Don't say that, say

—OK do me harder Patch fuck me till

—Till it fucking bleeds, I know

Patrick is sweating as he ties guitar wire around his girlfriend's lovely ankles. Pausing for a second to kiss the lovely instep of his girlfriend's foot, he then leans back and ties the rusty guitar wire around her ankles, thus trussing her feet, her little trotters, her little feet together. His girlfriend suitably squeals and says *it hurts*. Patrick says *I know*. She says *I love you*. Beneath him she now nods dumbly and submissive at him; he rolls her like a carcase onto her front; as he does she rolls into the half-full Caffé Nero coffee cup and it goes spilling over the carpet and his clothes and his shorts.

But he doesn't care. Instead he takes her hands and roughly he holds them together. Reaching back he grabs the last steel guitar wire, his trusty D string, and he takes her slender white wrists and he twines them together with the rusty guitar wire. She groans. Momentarily Patrick wonders if he is hurting her too much; he hopes he is hurting her enough.

Patrick looks at the coffee on her breasts; he wipes some sweat from his forehead with an arm, like a workman. He has been working so hard he is sweating hard; he has been working so hard his erection is nearly gone. Patrick uses the natural pause to take a breather: he sits back and looks at his handiwork: at his trilingual girlfriend trussed with dirty guitar wire by the ankles and wrists. She is bound so tight she may well start bleeding. Gazing at this Patrick wonders if he is really anti-Semitic. He remembers the only time he was ever a bully at school. *That kid, David Samuels.* They used to torture him every day. They used to put little Dave on the janitor's ladder and force him to climb the ladder onto the roof where they would leave him all day. *God*, Patrick thinks, *David Samuels? Might as well have called him Dreyfus.*

Then Patrick thinks about putting people on the roof. Then Patrick thinks about putting Rebecca on the roof. His erection returns as he leans and gets to work again, as he hoists Rebecca up and over his shoulder. As he carries her through the little door and up the stairs, she says *ow* and *stop*; but he ignores her, the same way he ignores her slaps and yowls as he punts open the door to the roof terrace. Outside it is bright. In the sunlight Rebecca moans and sighs and says *what are you doing*?

Patrick stays silent. He puts Rebecca down on the roof terrace in the warm sunshine, dropping her onto the gravelly flooring. Then he puts his hands on his hips feeling like a Smithfield butcher after a hard morning's toil, and looks down at her. At her cunt. He looks. Then he kneels and squats and pushes apart her thighs. He can feel the windows of the nearby office blocks staring down at him but he does not care. He pushes apart her thighs and he feels her wetness inside. She is wet enough, more than wet enough, so he positions himself so that he can enter her. Using his own wet hand he slippily undoes his flybuttons and then he leans and makes a little noise as he enters her soppy wet cunt. Then he starts fucking her. Now he is fucking her. He is very aroused; he can feel the wind on his face; the sun on his arse; the office workers of Zenith Media staring at his bucking arse. He does not care. He is so aroused. God, the guitar wire. The sunshine. The violation. He is thinking that he is fucking her on the roof in the middle of the day even though she is bound up with rusty steel guitar wire and he is thinking God I love her. I love her. He is thinking *God I love her I love her. How I love her. Love Her.* **Love her**.

— Doctor Lewis, thank you

The doctor steps down, and crosses the court. As she passes a few yards in front of Patrick she shoots a strange surreptitious glance at him. And a tiny but definitely there smile. Then she passes on, passes out of the courtroom. A silence ensues. Patrick sits in the dock pondering the doctor's glance, until with a shiver of mild shock he realises that the doctor *fancied him*.

Alone on the roof, alone on the gravelly roof terrace, Rebecca lies there, tied up by guitar wire, by her ankles and her wrists. The guitar wire is digging into her flesh; as is the gravel of the roof terrace. Lying on her side, as she is, Rebecca can feel the pressure of the gravel on her hips, her hipbone, her cheek. She wonders where Patrick is. Where he's gone. *Mnnn, Patrick.* She feels woozy. She feels woozy, and warm. From above she feels the sun beat down from the early summer sky; she feels this sun on her cunt. It is nice, almost hot. It is healing. As she moves and wriggles to rid herself of the gravel irritations Rebecca feels Patrick's semen trickle down her inner thigh like melting ice cream; like Häagen-Dazs on an infant's sunburnt arm.

The sun beats down. Rebecca lies there, blinking. She senses the office buildings around her. She wonders if the office workers have pulled up the sunblinds and seen her lying naked and tied up on her own roof terrace.

The thought of this makes Rebecca orgasm, again. The thought of all these people seeing her naked, and fucked, and trussed with guitar strings. Inside herself, Rebecca feels the pulsing, slowly, she feels the noonday, the Patrick, Cherry Garcia, cherry and black. Slack.

Just as Rebecca is about to fall asleep she hears a door open and she senses someone; then she senses muscly arms pick her up and she smells Patrick's skin as he hoists her over his Viking shoulder, and carries her back down, out of the sunshine, back down the stairs to their bedroom. Where he kisses her on the lips: once, three times. As he lays her out on the bed.

The wires are taken off. Rebecca relaxes, spreads. Her eyes shut, she rubs her wrists, her painful wrists. Then she half opens her eyes and looks up at her torturer, her rescuer. He is looking down at her. She smiles and opens her legs and relaxes, and with her eyes still shut, she senses his head go down between her thighs again, again again again again.

He is so hungry, so thirsty, so famished without me, she thinks. He is so poor, so impoverished, so homeless, so needy.

So have me, she decides, have me again, take what you want, have my money, rob me blind. For I shall climb up to the second storey of my house in Mainz, and lean out of the leaded window, and shower the young Crusaders with my Jewish gold.

20

The Dying Father. Thinking that this sounds like a Michelangelo sculpture or a lit crit archetype or something Rebecca might have written a thesis on . . . Patrick slides his car into a slot between two crappier cars, and steps out into the warm, lovely, early summer air of the hospice car park. Car door slammed, Patrick stands, and taps his pocket to check the car keys are his. Then he strides towards the warm friendly sloped-roof vernacular of the Nineties building, checking out the suckable sweet colours of the jolly wooden window frames as he goes.

Patrick smiles, snidely, at the building. He wonders whether the architects of the building know that They're Not Fucking Fooling Him. The place might look like a posh nursery school near Highgate, but Patrick can see the redbrick, Auschwitzy chimney tucked away at the back.

As he approaches the wide glass door of the hospice, Patrick contemplates the truth and potency of this Holocaust metaphor. Standing here in his cool white shirt and brown strides, flattered by the lovely sunshine, Patrick considers how this place, this hospice, is indeed the Auschwitz we are all headed to. *We are all on the cattle-train*, he decides, *we're all slowly making our way to these places, these nondescript places on the outskirts of town. Even if we choose to ignore the evidence, even if we spend our lives in determined ignorance of the uncanny smells on hot summer days, of the browny-grey ash that sometimes floats through the streets . . .*

—Yes!

It's a nurse. A pretty, young, almost World War I nurse, in stiff starched cotton, holding a parcel of towels, has just turned at the door, and smiled through the door. At Patrick? Patrick smiles back. Patrick stands in the sunlight smiling at the nurse. The hospice doors close, reopen, close, and then Star Trek open again. The nurse grins. Then goes.

Eros having thrown Thanatos to the ground, and spat in his face to boot, Patrick turns off his mobile phone, and enters the hospice. Inside he is at once engulfed by unsettling feelings. There is an air to the place; it all has a slightly different smell to hospitals. Quiet, pensive, resigned. Fear filling Patrick's mind again he walks up to the reception, where a middle-aged lady, in an apricot blouse and black plastic name tag, sits, looking rather dreamy. Patrick opens his mouth:

—Er, I'm here to meet . . . Mister

—Yes

—David . . . um . . . David . . .

Patrick does again his newly mastered impression of an idiot as the lady stares at him. The lady tries to look kindly and understanding:

—Do you have a surname?

—Yes. Of course. It's my dad . . . it's *Skivington*

Assessing her list of names with a pursed-lip nod, the woman scans down, looks up, and says:

—Room one seven-two . . . just down there

The fears and the horrors filling Patrick's heart, he nods abruptly and he turns, trying not to think about old times with his dad. His old drunken cunt of a dad. His warm-hearted sarcastic old man. *The Dying Father*.

Trying not to look in the separate barracks, at the skeletal Jews and the sunken-eyed Gyppos and the various Polaks and Slavs and *Untermenschen*, trying not to peer voyeuristically at the dying, at the soon-to-be-gassed, Patrick looks anyway in the wards and sees one room is inhabited by a seven-hundred-year-old skeleton of a woman, who seems to be staring at a picture of Jesus pinned to the wall. Jesus? *Jesus??* What's that about? Patrick speculates. Why this shrine to the fucker who's doing this to them? Were there portraits of Hitler on the walls of Belsen? Suppressing the urge to march in the ward and spit on the religious poster with a cackle of contemptuous laughter Patrick coughs and walks and . . . indulges in a mild sex fantasy about Rebecca as a naked Belgic slave in the slave market of a sunlit Roman town. But then he has to think about his dad, the Dying Father, because he has pushed open the door to his dad's room and he is now staring at his dad. Half asleep; half dead.

—Dead? I mean . . . *Dad?*

A stir. A twitch of skin under an eye. A twitch of old thin skin, rosy with the sunsetting light of life behind it. Lampshade skin. Turning and twitching, Patrick's Venetian-paper-skinned dad opens his eyes. Slowly, prehistorically, David Skivington turns and looks at Patrick through the festoons and swags of tubes, pipes, catheters and thingies which Patrick now notices are positioned next to his dad's bed for the purpose of pumping stuff into his dad's wrists and torso.

—Dad?

The Benetton poster that is his dad, the moving piece of unflinching modern photography that is Patrick's *dad, my dad, my dying dad*, blinks and smiles wanly at Patrick. Patrick swallows, stiffens, finding it hard to accept that this, this really is Dad, this really is his father, this is his smart, drunken, funny, savvy, unfulfilled, this-is-a-boat-don't-drown-you-stupid-kid (was that on holiday in Wales?) *dad*, looking like nothing more than an old sad ill person, like someone's dad dying.

Quickly Patrick says:

—Dad

His dad's eyes open wider, but slowly, but slowly. His father says:

—Thought you'd never make it . . .

—Oh. You know. Worried about my inheritance . . .

The Dying Father croaks; he actually *croaks*. Then he opens his dry-looking mouth and Patrick can see that buttoned up to his father's throat are some pathetic pyjamas with paisleys. The pathos of these night things makes Patrick feel very very very sorry for his dad and he doesn't want to feel sorry. Especially not for his father; his boozy, lecherous, pitiably brilliant father.

His father speaks:

—Inheritance?! A fucked-up old motor . . . some debts?

—Yeah, why not . . .

—I have got a bottle of Scotch in the cupboard, you can have that

—Fine. I'll take it

His dad shakes his head:

—You got anything for me then?

—Oh yeah – course

—Don't give me any fucking grapes. No fucking grapes! – Eyes watery but sparkly, his father looks up above the bed at something floating in the middle of the room. And says – I'm thinking of having a sign over the bed. No Fucking Grapes!

—I haven't brought a thing
—Good
—*Dad* . . . ?
—How's your sister anyway she still with that idiot boyfriend with the suit and the car and the constant adding up?
—He's an accountant
—He's a boring little tit, is what he is
—She loves him – Patrick smiles, despite – He doesn't hit her, she likes that, you know
—I loved your *mum*, Patrick
—Dad . . .
—What?
—I'll just go and get some grapes . . .
—Sit down, Patrick

Patrick's father is shifting in his proneness. It looks painful; at once Patrick goes towards the bed to try and help, but his dad waves him back almost angrily as he uses a thin elbow and a thinner arm to try and lever himself up a bit. The tubes rattle against the metal stand; Patrick feels something weird in his heart and his stomach as he watches his dad not really being able to move. Appalled, Patrick turns away and swallows spit and stares at a wall painting by some kids. *Kids.* Again the nursery school thing, Patrick thinks, again the infantilisation; again the beckoning of the womb, the reversal of time's arrow.

—Jesus what a place! – Says Patrick. Patrick's father nods, says nothing; then the older Skivington says:
—Yerss . . .

And with a pang Patrick recognises the old intonation, his father's old sarcastic let's-have-a-whiskey way of saying *yes.* Patrick remembers this; remembers it all. *Yersss Patrick I'm rather afraid I'm fucking off down the pub because your mum's a total cow.*
—Things could be worse, Patrick
—How's that then?
—Could still be living with your mam
—Right . . .
—You know they say I've got about two weeks but I'm gonna show 'em. I'm gonna see the rugby and then fuck off in my own time: you see . . .

With a mouthful of angry words Patrick goes to say something but his father's eyes, his father's still-proud eyes, silence him. The rattle of the tubes and the sound of trolley wheels and various medical engines beeping distantly fill this silence. Otherwise there is silence.

—See the pretty nurse?

Patrick grins at his father: a fake grin, but a grin nonetheless. Patrick says:

—The one with the arse?

—Cruel it is . . .

—Nice legs, as well, right?

—*Vraiment!*

—She gave me a once over at the door

—Good – His father smiles – *Good*

Patrick looks at his father. The Dying Father appears to be laughing, sarcastically; Patrick says:

—Was it because Mum is a bit stupid? Is that why you were the way you were?

Pyjamas, bedsheets, catheter, laughter:

—Yerss . . .

—Is it?

—Maybe

—Or was it just the women? All the women?

Patrick's father goes to speak but Patrick blurts:

—Tell me, Dad. I want to know – Patrick pauses, wondering; then he goes on – You *were* seeing that blonde one, weren't you, your secretary I mean? All that time?

A fatherly breath, then:

—Course I was

—Hah – Patrick smiles sadly and says – Well. Sod it. Can't blame you . . . I fancied her too

His father slowly eyes him:

—You were six, Patrick

—Tits to kill for, right?

—Yersss . . .

—And a bit of an accent . . . ?

David Skivington nods, as much as he can nod. Then he says:

—She *was* from Gloucestershire . . .

—Yeah . . .

—Very strange people from Gloucestershire – David Skivington's hand moves, as if unsuccessfully seeking out a cigarette. For a moment Patrick

sees his father as he was, in the pub, his local, the Bricklayers, being funny
with his mates, always smoking. Seeming to give up on the futile cigarette
quest David Skivington clutches the hem of his bedsheet and says – Yersss,
Gloucestershire, they're all mad there. You can see it in their village names.
Bourton on the Water, Stow on the Wold, Father on the Sister

Patrick says:

— I've heard that one. You told that joke *years* ago

David:

— Did I? Oh well. Thanks for not bringing me any grapes, Patrick – A
glance over – You know you're the only one I can rely on not to bring me
anything when you eventually come in and see me after I've been a year in
hospital . . .

— In fact I can remember when you told that joke, I can remember exactly
when it was

— Your sister was in last week

— You were drunk at home. You remember that? – Patrick glares at his
father's grey-white hair – You always told bad jokes. When you were drunk
– Patrick thinks, goes on – You always used to march around the house
frightening all mum's friends and saying 'See my nipple and fear me' . . .
remember that?

A silence. A rueful stare at the ceiling. David Skivington chuckles:

— I remember

— And then one day you were saying it in the Brickies, and some bloke
came up and said 'I'll see your nipple, and raise you a penis'

David laughs. As he laughs, the tubes rattle; the catheters sway. Grinning
properly, proud to have made his father laugh, Patrick puts down his bag
and casts about for a chair. There is a pause. David says:

— The blonde nurse is alright as well, you should buy her a coffee son . . .

— Nurses, schmurses

— Stockings, they always wear stockings

— Not any more, Dad

— She's better than that black bitch keeps trying not to knock me out. She's
a right old death camp *Kommandant*

— It's good that you've mellowed

— How is your sister?

— She's fine

— Nmm. Don't let that black one near me. She'll hit me with a shovel I
tell ya

—Christ! You aren't allowed to *say* that, not any more
—Really?
—Really
—Ah well

Patrick listens to his father. Not to his words, but to his voice. The voice is the same. It's still *Dad's voice. That teaching-me-to-swim voice; that shouting-at-Mum voice; oh fucking hell Dad don't fucking fuck off you fucking fucker.*

—Why did you drink so much, Dad?

David Skivington looks across his own supine body; at his son. Patrick is again searching for a chair; the chair found Patrick considers at what angle he should position the chair: face-on to his dad seems to Patrick to be slightly too much a sad, serious, last-ever-meeting type of approach; side-on seems excessively casual, in a kind of hey-let's-pretend-you-aren't-dying way. And completely facing away from his dad is probably not the thing either.

Turning the chair halfway around Patrick leans over the chair's back. And listens to his father say:

—Want some of my morphine?
—Is it a pump?
—Yerrs. I'd give you some if I could

Patrick chuckles:

—I'm off the drugs, Dad
—And you aren't chasing tail either, of course
—No. Actually!

David leans up:

—What about that posh bird I heard about, Rebecca . . . Jewish name, you still seeing her?
—Jessel. Still seeing her
—Good breasts?
—To kill for
—See my nipple, and fear me!
—I'll see your nipple – Patrick wishes he could give his father a cigarette; could smell his father's smoking again – And raise you a penis

Another pause. David:

—God, Patch son. Could murder a fag
—Shall I sneak some in?
—They've got alarms and stuff

—Who gives a fuck

—It'd be my last gasper – Smiling at his own joke David says – Do you love her? The Jewish girl?

—Too much

—She's bright isn't she, I heard she was bright? – Staring at his son's nodding face, Patrick's father goes on – You know I loved a bright woman once: she'd read *Ulysses* in French, the stupid tart, I mean what's the point in that? – Still going on – The trouble with bright ones is that they are always mad I think it's because you can't have a womb and a brain working together. Something to do with the circulation – Patrick's dad looks like he would like to properly chortle, if there weren't a tube going painfully through a hole in his throat, a hole surrounded by yellow and bandages and bromine and Sellotape.

Coughing, Patrick's dad says – Girls always have circulation problems it's their cold feet. Hm. At least your mum was honestly dim, dim as hell that woman . . .

—She put me up last night, she's doing OK since you ask

—Yeah? – His father sighs – You know I think we should have had a dog, always thought that

—Mum didn't like dogs

—Hmmm – The father looks at the son and says – Actually I think she didn't like living things, your mum. Make too much of a mess

—God Dad, she's OK. She's not that bad. A decent old stick, you used to say

—A decent old stick? Did I say that? Hm. Old stick. Sticky old stickettystick

—Why did you marry her, Dad?

—Fantastic arse yer mam

—Please!

The Dying Father is smiling. The Surviving Son is shaking his head, and smiling, and listening to his dad as his dad breathes. The rattle of Patrick's dad's breath chimes with the rattle of the tubes which chimes with the rattle of the door opening. A black nurse pushing a trolley has entered. The black nurse looks at them both; Patrick's dad winks at Patrick as the nurse says to the room:

—How're we, David? You filled in your lunch form now?

David Skivington dad looks at Patrick; and smiles; the father looks at the nurse and says:

—Yes nurse thank you nurse I'll have a dry sherry

Patch turns to the nurse and says nothing; Patch turns to his dad and mouths *dry sherry*?

His dad smiles and says:

—They let us have sherry don't you Nurse Wilson?

—You filled in the form David? Have you? Have you filled it in?

—I can hear you nurse yes has that old git next door snuffed it yet?

—Don't talk like that David we gonna move you outside in the rain . . .

—Give me some fags you old trollop

—The doctor is coming any moment

With another rattle the nurse leaves and Patrick says:

—Stop winding them up! God!

—What little pleasure I have. Other than trifle . . .

—What about the *sherry*?

—Sweet British sherry oh it's great, and perhaps some cribbage. What a hoot

—It really is a bit of a knees-up in here isn't it?

—How's that club? You making any money, son?

—Mmmnn

—Well? Areya?

Patrick shrugs, looks at a figure silhouetted in the frosted-glass pane of the door, a doctorly white-coated figure; Patrick shrugs again, says:

— mnnnnn

—Make money, Patrick: that's the only way

—Like you you mean?

Patrick knows by his dad's face that his father is about to get more sarcastic, more cynical, maybe even angry and hectoring, but his dad's usual moody spiel is instantly interrupted by the doctor coming in and wordlessly and summarily pulling down the bedclothes of his dad's bed: to check the stigmata of hospitalisation; the catheter wounds, the intentional vaginas. A silence reigns as Patrick watches this: the embarrassing horrible awkward physical underwear-soiling reality of his father's hospitalisation and impending death. Instinctively Patrick averts his face: he stares at the floor, the carpet. At the wall, the floor, the doctor's expensive shoes. *Nice shoes.* Then Patrick raises his eyes and looks at the doctor as the doctor turns to Patrick and says:

—Don't tire him out too much

—No no of course, Doctor

—He's easily tired now

—No I'm not you silly bastard

—All right, Mister Skivington, I'll be back in shortly

—Go and kill someone else you stethoscoped fuckwit

Patrick snorts a laugh; suppresses it. Patrick tries to look serious and says:

—Why do they let you stay here, Dad?

But the doctor is laughing anyway, the doctor is laughing and saying:

—I'll be back THIS EVENING – Turning to Patch – Nice to meet you

And so the doctor goes, the door swings, the door shuts; a kind of silence comes over. Patrick thinks of his father, his father's health. He thinks of haemorrhoids. Then he thinks of the God of Haemorrhoids.

Then he says:

—Do you believe in God, Dad?

His dad makes a scoffing noise:

—That miserable cunt? Nah

Patrick's dad looks like he wants to scoff some more, to go on, but instead he has started on a cough, a long cough, a long, rolling saga of a cough that Patrick tries not to listen to; to listen to; to listen to. Listening to his dad cough, and then sigh, and then recover, sort of, Patrick thinks on God, on how if God existed, which He doesn't, but if He existed, which He doesn't, but if He did, if He existed . . .

Patrick thinks how God, if He existed, *would be like a doctor, a doctor who takes pity on the fact that you are seven years old and nervous and puts a fatherly arm around your little shoulders and says Come in come in sit down . . . and then, when you are inside, when you are sitting in the big chair in the surgery with your short trousers, and your battered satchel on your lap and your feet hardly touching the floor, then the doctor turns and smiles and says Oh I'm terribly sorry but we've had the results and you are going to die . . .*

And then just as you are about to start crying the doctor grins and says, Oh yes and your mum's going to die, and your dad, and your sister and all your friends at school, and that nice teacher who does Art, and the girl down the road, and the entire Leeds United squad, they're all going to die, to die, to DIE!

—Dad???

The coughing has done it. His dad's fallen asleep. Or at least into a morphined stupor akin to sleep. Scraping the chair, Patrick stands, and looks over. Then he goes over and looks closer at his now sleeping, now dying dad. The last time? *Is this the last time?*

His eyes CS gassed again, by the Italian riot police in his head, Patrick wipes a stupid wetness from his eye, and stoops very close to his dad's face. From this far away Patch can smell the chemicals, the preservatives; at this proximity he can sniff the bromides and linctus and TCP and bandagey stuff. A very different smell to what Patrick remembers. No more the Jameson's and the fags, the whiskey and tweed. No more. It is as if his dad is fading away, even olfactorily . . .

Patrick leans over his father's barely breathingness, his pitifully belittled form. Patrick's eyes are filled with the wetness of that holiday in Wales, the boat that never went properly, his dad laughing in the pub with a Scotch, his dad saying 'see my nipple and fear me'; here and now Patrick gulps back the gulfingness and he kisses his dad in the face and says:

—Bye, Dad

And then, before he can get done over by the nasty cops, with their baton blows of sadness, their rubber bullets of regret, Patrick pushes the swing door of the room and paces inappropriately fast down the corridor past the kiddyish lower-case signs saying **exit** and **way out** and **the bourne from which no traveller returns** and by the time Patch has reached the sunny, warm, flowery, lovingly tended Macmillan Hospice car park Patrick has convinced himself he's not crying even though his cheeks are red and wet, he has convinced himself there is no Holocaust, even though he's seen the chimneys and the gas chambers, he has convinced himself he does not love his dad, never loved his dad, didn't feel for his dad so much, even though Patrick feels already an emptiness inside him like a huge black steel box that must never be opened, **ever**.

21

—So that's it I'm afraid Patrick the club is pretty much kaput
—Right
—The council's intervention was the last straw
—OK . . .
—If they hadn't intervened in the noise abatement proceedings well then there was a chance that you could get by on bar sales, but the revoking of your late licence, wellll . . .

Patrick looks at the lawyer. Patrick looks at the lawyer's butter-fattened features, the cool open shirt collar: this shirt collar so lacking a tie. Square behind the insultingly tie-less lawyer is an open window. Through this comes taxi-door arguments, scooter noise, French tourist-kid chatter: evidence of the cruelly vibrant, cruelly sunlit world that goes on, outside, that goes on despite the crashing and burning, the looting and despoiling of Patrick's dreams, herein . . .

The first lawyer's colleague, another tie-less lawyer, is talking now:
—Best option is actually therefore to sell up the club, maybe convert to flats, that way you might just cover your most pressing debts and the bank might not foreclose
—Buh
—And of course you'll have to sell off the back catalogue
—But I
—Then you can go back to the bank and maybe they will extend the loan until you can get out the office and
—**You know my dad died last week?**

The lawyer closes his open mouth. Says nothing. Then says:

—Sorry?

—Of **cancer**

—You . . . er um – The lawyers are exchanging looks – Er

—Look – Says Patrick – Listen. See that? – Patrick is waving at the shelfload of CDs to his left, to their right. The lawyers look blankly yet expectantly back at Patrick, as he goes on – That's what we do. *Music*. We do *music* and *clubs*. What do you suggest we do if not that? – Widening his eyes – What else? What should we do? Make rubber bands? Chocolate euros?

The first lawyer, his gelled hair shining silver in the sun, does a firm nod and says:

—Patch I see what you're driving at but you see we're not suggesting you shut up shop *completely* – The lawyer looks sidelong at the other lawyer, who looks affirmingly back; the first lawyer turns to Patrick and says – It's simply a case of . . . reining things in, of doing . . . *not a lot* . . . for a while . . .

—Not a lot?

—Not a lot. At the moment

The pencil tight in Patrick's hand, Patrick says:

—But we will have to sell the labels, the back catalogues, fucking everything?

Unabashed, the other lawyer comes in:

—Well. No . . . Not *everything*

—You mean we can keep the *pencil sharpener* . . . ?

—Patch, listen . . .

Not listening, not wanting to hear, Patch feels the prickle of sweat, and panic, and despair. He despairs: and wonders. *So is this it? Is this what it comes to? Is this all I get? A bathetic, sad, unobserved death behind the lines? A stupid fall off the duckboards of solvency, into the drowning mud of bankruptcy?*

The lawyers are chuntering on. From his desk, Patrick pretends to nod sagely at them, to absorb the good advice they're still giving, to understand how crap and sad his life is going to be from here on in. But instead Patrick opts to click into his computer. Instead of listening to the lawyers do their lawyering, Patch ducks behind his screen and clicks into the Net, clicks into *History*, clicks into a website.

Ah yes. The comfort of the Web. Yerrs. Looking up briefly at the lawyers and smiling at them Patrick turns his face back to the screen they cannot see, and mouse-clicks . . . Patrick waits. Patrick sees. Patrick half listens. *Self-assessment. Chancery. Vine Street Magistrates* . . . **Tokyo Puppies** . . . *Noise Abatement. Hackney Council Magistrates Record* . . . **Schoolgirl Panty**.

Ahp! Startled, Patrick realises the lawyer has suddenly moved: so that he is standing on Patrick's left. The lawyer is leaning over Patrick's shoulder like a teacher checking coursework and is staring at Patrick's computer screen. Onscreen is a wide image of a buxom Japanese schoolgirl being spanked on her arse by a ponytailed Bavarian sous chef.

—Cool!

Says the lawyer, laughing. Patrick grips his pencil so hard it snaps.

—Helps me concentrate . . .

The lawyer laughs, again. Moments pass. Patrick glares hard at the tie-less lawyer until he gets the message: looking uncomfortable, the lawyer retreats around the desk and rejoins his colleague.

Once the brace of lawyers are sat on their giant toadstool, looking neat in their little lederhosen, Patrick sighs enormously and says:

—OK. Would you mind if I thought about this overnight?

—Of course not . . . no probs

The lawyers rise, say goodbye, go; but Patrick has already turned away. He is already thinking about the Net again, he is already thinking of losing himself in the Web, of finding some solace there, of maybe searching out some images . . . of . . . nude . . . Taiwanese . . . sixth formers . . . *being shagged from behind by their big negro games teachers.*

—So, Mister . . . Blackburn

Joe nods; Joe nervously glances at the public gallery of the courtroom, at the spectators Patch cannot see. Then Joe nearly looks at Patrick but instead looks at the prosecuting counsel.

The defence counsel, Robert Stefan, is cross-examining:

—Tell us about that afternoon . . .

—The time in May?

—Yes, May fifteen

—Well – Joe says. Patrick wonders how Joe feels; how torn; *how does it feel to be giving evidence in your best friend's rape trial?* – Well – Joe says again, looking pretty uncomfortable in what is obviously a borrowed suit – I could see he . . .

—He?

—Patrick, I could see Patrick was . . . very agitated, you know, that morning

—Why?

—Well you know I mean he'd just lost his club and – Joe blushes, fingers a borrowed collar – His dad had died and he and Rebecca were arguing and well . . . anyway I went into the office that morning and he'd had the lawyers in and he'd been drinking and

The judge:

—Slower, please, Mister Blackburn – Smiling in a soft way – This is important

—Joe?

Joe is stood at the door of Patrick's soon-to-be-someone-else's office. At Patrick's welcoming wave, Joe comes over and puts a flat hand on Patch's desk, and stares around Patrick, at Patrick's computer screen. Joe looks at the computer screen, at the image of a mammacious Japanese schoolgirl being vaginally examined by a presumably lesbian doctor. Joe grins:

—Hootermania?

—White Socks dot com

—Uh-huh – Stood back now Joe puts hands on hips as he appraises the image, then Joe says – *Nice wombats!*

Lifting his beer can Patch toasts the computer image. Then Patrick burps and uses his unbeer-canned hand to click the mouse and make the computer image larger: thus to enlarge the view of the petite, white-toothed adolescent.

—Yeah – says Patrick, wiping the beer wetness from his lips with a side of the hand.

Joe nods at the beer can:

—Drinking already?

—Why not?

—It's ten to eleven

—Don't grief me out, Joe, I've had the lawyers up my arse all morning

—REALLY nice tits

Says Joe. Patrick turns from his own problems to once again contemplate the sweet Nipponese girl on his monitor. Joe is stroking a sagacious chin; Joe goes on:

—Ten-inch woofers

Patrick:

—Nice tweeters too

Joe strokes:

—She's the *spit* of Rebecca

Patrick:

—Naturally. Who else?

—Why do you do it?

Patrick says, distractedly:

—What?

—You're shagging Rebecca. She's lush. Why do you surf the Net for porn as well?

Patrick thinks. Says:

—I like wanking as well

—You're a perv – Says Joe, leaning to scrutinise the image – Actually, the tits are a bit different

Now Patrick does the swivel chair thing:

—What?

—The girl, on the screen . . . her . . . buffalo mozzarellas – Joe is shrugging – Much better than Rebecca's

The ensuing silence lasts long enough for them both to hear someone's mobile phone beeping the arrival of a text message, in the sunny Soho street outside.

Patrick:

—Rebecca's got the best tits. Ever

—Yeah.

—She fucking well has you shipbroking Geordie budgie fucker

—Sure . . .

—She *has, really*

A smile, a shrug, an annoyingly dismissive wave. Then Joe stops smiling and says:

—Hey. I'm . . . really sorry about your old man . . .

—Fuck my dad

—Patch . . . ?

—You don't believe Rebecca's got the best tits in London?

—*Patch*

—I'll jolly well show them to you

*   *   *

Robert Stefan does the usual pause, the standard gown-lapel clutch, the obligatory melodramatic smile; then he says:

—And this was unusual?

But before Joe can reply, Gregory interrupts:

—My Lord . . .

The judge turns to Gregory:

—Yes

—M'Lord . . . I'm just wondering where this is going?

The Judge. The Defender. The Prosecutor.

Robert Stefan says:

—As we discussed, M'Lord . . . ?

The judge looks at Stefan. Stefan looks at the judge. The judge lets Patrick's heart beat once, twice, thrice, then nods and says:

—You can continue, Mister Stefan

The two of them are walking down the office stairs, past the office looker behind her desk:

—See you later, Trish!

—Bye, Patch!

Patrick hiccups as they walk out into the Soho sunshine; into the early summer smells of Soho. Joe sniffs these smells, spilt beer and Thai curry. Then, together and as one, the two old friends look long and appreciatively at the sweetly hotpanted arse of a teenie girl sashaying past. Patrick whistles:

—Goodness me

Joe exhales, agreeingly:

—Amazing – Joe looks across at his friend and says – Patch I believe you, I believe you about her tits

—I'm sorry. You've still got to see them

—No, please, drop it

—No? You mean you don't *want* to?

—Well yes, of course I do, but – Joe tsses through his teeth, says – It's just . . . You're pissed, you're having problems with Becs, you've lost the club, and your . . . – Joe puts a palm towards Patrick's face – Can't you just leave me out?

Mid-pavement, Patrick stops. Patrick says:

—You *are* still my best friend?

Joe:
—That's unfair
—But you are? Yes?
—Course yam but
—Then do this. For *me*. Please?
Joe looks unhappy. Patrick goes on, more emphatically still
—Please Joe? Just do that? Just check out her headlamps just once for me
no I haven't got any FUCKING change
The two of them step gingerly over the junkie, and his filthy sleeping
bag. Then Joe says:
—What *are* you on, Patch? Really? We all like a wank on the Net now and
again but . . . wanking on the Net for five hours a day it's . . . bonkers
Patrick shrugs. Patrick walks on up to Oxford Street. Turning to look at
a homeless girl with bleached spiky hair and a surprisingly pretty face,
Patrick says to Joe, as Joe catches up:
—You know . . . I was walking up the Cally Road the other day and a tramp
pointed at my hair and said 'you should put some gel in that'
Joe laughs; Patrick sighs a burp; the two of them walk on: through the
garment district; the BBC district; the doctorly purlieus of Harley Street,
where they have to step off the pavement to get round an old Arab man
sitting seemingly stranded in a wheelchair by the Wimpole Street watch
shop.
Finally the two of them are approaching the door to Patrick and Rebecca's
flat. Patrick looks at the door, at the dusty door, then at the African res-
taurant opposite, then at the Japanese noodle café beside, then at the pub
where the local *au pairs* drink. Patrick wonders how and why he ended up
here: dadless. Clubless. Cashless. Jobless.
—Rebecca . . .
Joe gives Patrick an I'm-still-your-friend-but-this-is-wank expression:
—Nuff's enough, Patch
—But I want you to do this
—Nope. This is rubbish
—But I mean this, please
—Just sleep it off, can't you?
—No, soon, *come on*
The two of them cross the road, overtaking a woman with a Waitrose
bag, and a pair of Korean girls sharing a copy of *Hello!* Then Patrick says:
—S'weird, isn't it?

Joe, his voice edged with impatience:

—*What?*

Patch clocks the edge; opts to ignore it:

—Love. It's . . . weird, it's like . . . – Stroking his own jawline, he says – A lover is like a friend . . . whose piss you have to taste

—Skivington!

—. . . And a girlfriend who you really love is like a friend who demands you put your finger in their arse

Joe is silent. Patrick gathers himself, determinedly he pushes himself and his friend towards the door. At the door Patrick taps his pocket, uses his key. Side by side the two of them push the door, heaving against a snowdrift of post.

—Fan mail

Stepping over the parking fines, tax demands, notifications of bankruptcy, bailiffs' letters, and a single holiday postcard, the two friends climb the stairs.

Upstairs is empty. The bugle shines in the sun on an undusted windowsill. Three uncleared wineglasses sit on a glass table showing dusty white lines. Patrick looks around, feeling he should be surprised by the squalor and mess of his and Rebecca's flat. Then he says:

—She's still asleep . . .

—. . . then he said he reckoned she was still asleep

—And then?

Joe reaches to his right for a water glass. Patrick looks at the purple cotton-knot cufflinks in Joe's shirt cuff.

Somehow reassured that Joe is taking this so unseriously as to think it not worth borrowing proper links, Patrick lowers his chin to his supporting fist and watches, tense, from the dock, as Joe gulps some water; twice. The glass set down, Joe turns, smiles wanly at the prosecuting counsel, and says:

—He went upstairs and then he . . . – The court leans forward; Joe goes on, slightly quieter – Then he called me up. So . . . I went . . .

—You went upstairs?

—Yeah

* * *

From the top of the bedroom stairs Patrick looks down at Joe as Joe reluctantly climbs the stairs. At the top of the bedroom stairs, Patrick steps back to allow Joe ingress to the bedroom.

At once Joe hisses, looking over at the bed:

—She's fast *asleep*

Ignoring, burping, tasting again his morning's beers, Patrick grabs his friend by the arm and firmly leads him over to the bed, to where Rebecca is lying. The duvet cover is a deep, desert-noon blue. Patrick watches Joe as Joe looks, half aghast, half curious: at Rebecca's blonde sleep-tously hair: all that is visible of Patrick's girlfriend under the duvet. Patrick tries to grin, casually, although his heart is racing. His friend looks now like he is going to quit, to run off, so Patrick keeps a tight hold of Joe's arm, as with his other hand Patrick reaches over to the top of the duvet.

Slowly, as slowly as he can, Patrick lifts back the duvet and pulls it down and away, down to Rebecca's waist.

Rebecca does not stir at this. She twitches, moans tinily. Patrick feels proudly possessive.

They are both staring at Rebecca's breasts. Her breasts that are so . . . *there*; so in front of them. Patrick looks at his girlfriend's glorious, firm, sizeable, nipple-tipped breasts, thus revealed. Something about Rebecca's snoring makes these lovely large breasts even more beautiful. *The unselfconscious beauty*. Patrick feels his mouth go dry and his stomach tumble as he looks at Joe looking at his girlfriend's cold bare breasts. Rebecca snores again, a small girlish sound; then Rebecca turns, slightly, her lips wet, half a centimetre apart. Joe whispers:

—OK man they're fucking excellent can I go now?

—Hold it!

—No, Patch, c'mon

—Just hold on. Just . . . *Stay there*

Patrick is lifting the duvet again. Joe breaks free from Patrick's grasp and says:

—Enough!

But Joe does not leave. He does not go. Joe stays at the foot of the bed as Patrick pulls the rest of the duvet down down, away, down: to show Rebecca's hips, her legs, her feet.

And her cunt. Patrick looks in rapt fascination at his girlfriend's exposed . . . *cunt*. Its cuntness. Its being-looked-at-by-Joe-ness. Staring down at the coils of hair, the mysterious thing, Patrick feels an inexplicable upsurge of desire, fear, self-hatred, pride, nausea, as he senses Joe also staring with rapt plebeian admiration at his girlfriend's . . . cunt.

The two of them keep staring. Transfixed. Patrick's girlfriend stirs slightly, and moans, as if sensing the cold air on her skin; she shifts her legs apart until her suntan thighs are apart enough to let the two men see inside her cunt. To see the TV snooker pink, the inner flesh, the violin case interior.

Patrick swallows.

Oh God: the cunt, his girlfriend's cunt: this cunt, this cunt. This Aztec Playstation; the Devil's Christmas present to men. Look at it. At its black and pink. Its plush de luxeness . . .

—Touch her, Joe. Go on. She's asleep. Touch her

Patrick is taking Joe's hand, and pulling it towards his girlfriend's loins, towards her cunt, the cartwheeled rose . . .

—Go on go on go . . . go on . . . do it, touch it . . .

But no. Joe snaps his hand away. Turns. At the very moment Patrick and Joe reached towards Rebecca, Joe has turned. And run. And disappeared.

—I ran off . . .

—Just like that?

—Yes. I'd had enough

—And . . .

—It was all too much. His obsession with her . . . With Rebecca – Breathing deep – I couldn't, like, handle it

Stefan nods, grimly. He looks down at his desk, although it is empty. Then he looks up again and says:

—Thank you, Mister Blackburn

In the bedroom Patrick looks at his girlfriend, her naked five-foot-threeness, so shapely on the sheets. Then his girlfriend opens her eyes and says:

—He's gone?

—Yes

He smiles sadly at her. She smiles, strangely, distantly, and says:

—Poor Joe . . .

Patrick laughs, tasting bitter tastes in his mouth . . .

—Well, maybe

Stretching, shaking her head, Rebecca looks directly at Patrick, and says:

—God . . . what are we *like*?

—What are *you* like you mean

—But . . . it was Your Idea – She grimaces – Bad idea? Maybe?

—My idea? Mine?! It was *yours!*

—We *shouldn't* have, Patch . . .

—You didn't enjoy it of course, oh no . . . *God* no

—Nnno! I didn't!

—Oh Jesus

Patrick feels too much. Sad, angry, aroused, unmanned. He is thinking too hard; worrying how this will affect him. This little scenario. What will he think of what has just happened: in the future? What will it mean? Will this mean he will now always have to deal with this, with what has just happened? Will he always want to masturbate about it, always try and forget it, even though he will never be able to forget it? Will he always bear the neocortical scar of this traumatically arousing incident, this disturbingly erotic scenario, even as Rebecca, in that womanly, unobsessed, grounded, not so hypersexual way, will pretty soon forget it?

Then Patrick says:

—Stupid Jewish slut

and he slaps her, hard, across the face.

22

—He's drinking too much

Rebecca says. Murphy nods, stands, goes to the window. At the window she pouts smoke from her cigarette, exhaling professionally, like a Slovenian whore in a Mayfair hotel bar. Rebecca looks at the smoke her friend is fwwwwing into the air; the imperial featherplume of blue; Murphy says:

—And the drugs?

—Some

—Just some?

—He says – Rebecca shakes her head – He says sex with me is the best fun you can have . . . without a rolled-up tenner and a mirror

Murphy looks down at her friend:

—Christ you really do love him don't you?

Rebecca looks up:

—What do you think?

Murphy:

—I think what ARE you gonna do?

Rebecca shakes her head and stops looking up and says:

—Oy oy oy oy OY

Murphy is now looking out the window, at the road. She is saying nothing. Rebecca regards her friend and says nothing. Then Rebecca looks up again and says:

—Sit *down*, Murf

—Uhn?

—You're doing the tall thing again

Shrugging, Murphy turns, and says:

—K

And she sits down.

Sat opposite, Rebecca watches as Murphy folds her legs beneath her hips, so as to sit cross-legged. Rebecca sees Murphy's unshaved ankle exposed under the flared hem of her plastic strides. Rebecca says:

—You really need that boyfriend, Murf

—K

—No. You do. Make you shave more often

—Ooh – Grinning – Coughed up any furballs recently? *Mee-ow!*

Rebecca smiles. Says:

—You need someone to . . . *you know*

—Bring his best mate round to look at me in bed naked?

Rebecca leans back with her bare arms behind her, her palms flat on the rough carpet, the knee-burning carpet . . .

—It was just a game

—Oh. Just a game, just a game like Cluedo then only with your breasts as . . . Colonel Mustard in . . . the kitchen? That kind of game?

—Just a game, a game I invented, actually

Murphy tuts, then says:

—God, Rebecca, can't you just get over him a little bit?

—Why?

—Cause it's too intense. It's virtually, like, *morbid*

—*Morbid?*

—Rebecca . . . it *is*, it's morbid. You are morbidly obsessed with each other – Vehement, now – God's sake you've just been complaining about him for months. So finish it. Why not?

Murphy pauses for breath; Rebecca looks blank at her friend; Murphy shakes her head and looks away and says:

—Really. For a smart woman you're a bit *blonde*

Accepting, unaccepting, Rebecca shrugs. Then Rebecca thinks about her blonde hair. Rebecca wonders if Patrick still loves her hair as much as he used to. Again Rebecca pulls some of her blonde hair to her side and looks at the ends. *Split ends?* Rebecca puts the hair in her mouth and tastes her own hair. *And his cum?*

Inhaling hard Rebecca struggles to her feet and gets to stand, and walks across and leans out of the open window, breathing in the sweet summer air that feels fine: nice and affluent, full of southern smells of coffee, perfume, hot cars . . .

Whispering a poem to herself, Rebecca looks up and down Marylebone High Street, feeling a vague nostalgia. From behind, Murphy says:

—I suppose we oughta remember he is going through it

—?

—Y'know I mean his dad did just . . . die . . . I guess so maybe

—Well, exactly . . .

—And he's been ill hasn't he? And it must have fucked him up, the club and stuff and . . .

Window-struck, still, Rebecca shrugs another yes. She is looking at the crap French men's clothes shop across the road. She is thinking of French men, French clothes, male plumage. Female plumage. *The feathers and greenstone we wear. The tiny white shells around our bare ankles.* Looking at the shop window with its terrible French versions of Barbour jackets Rebecca thinks of the imperative of sexual display, the imperiousness of female display. Rebecca thinks how much it is like Aztec display, *how it is designed to impress the brutish Spanish soldiery: to impress them with the headdresses and the turquoise masks and the golden piercing pins, with the barefoot dances in the plaza and the circles of the eagle warriors, with the strange blood-letting rituals, and the piercing of the genitals* . . .

and *enough*, Rebecca thinks. Still staring out of the window Rebecca wonders if she is pregnant; she sits back down, opposite her friend, and says:

—Tell me about that Tuscan poetry course?

Murphy looks at her:

—Nah

—OK . . . – Rebecca shakes her head, and smiles – OK – Still grinning – What's the biggest one you've ever seen then, anyway?

Murphy narrows her eyes, assessingly:

—Must have been . . . ooh . . . *nine*?

—Golly!

—Perhaps even *ten*

Frowning slightly, Rebecca:

—Was it Andy?

—No, it was that Iranian guy

Rebecca, mouth open:

—Oh, my God. The Drakkar guy? *Really?*

—Khomeini more and I'll die
  Rebecca giggles:
—God yes! God yes I remember him!
—Like you could forget
—But – Rebecca is nodding, vigorously – Do you remember when we spent
that *whole* day squirting water at his friends in their car and they
—On Keats Grove, yeah
—And then there was that guy with the enormous head who you called
You With The Head
—Fucking hell!
  Murphy is laughing aloud, Rebecca pauses, then says:
—Must say though. Nine inches is a tad *excessive*
—Slightly flashy
—Almost showing off . . .
  Murphy makes a thoughtful face:
—He used it pretty well tho. Like a Jedi sword, *zhoom zhoom*
  Murphy is doing a Jedi lightsword impression, waving the imaginary sword
around the flat; Rebecca is laughing too much to reply, so Murphy says:
—Which is the biggest one *you've* had anyway?
—Seven and a half, but Patch's is the *thickest*
—Really, he's really thick?
—Yep. He's got the girth
  Murphy:
—*He's got the girth! He's got the girth!!*
  Both of them are laughing. Then Murphy stops laughing and looks very
sober and says again:
—But you do have to get over yourself, B. You have to stop thinking this
way about him. It's unhealthy
—Can't – Rebecca is shaking her head, saying – I can't. Can't help it
—Rebecca you've a degree and a . . . *car*. You're all grown up now
—Yes *yes* – Rebecca looks slightly sadly at her friend – I . . . can't. I *would*
. . . but
—But *nothing*, ditch him
—O Murphy – Rebecca's eyes are fast on her friend's face – Murphy. I
love him. I can't help it. I wish I could but I can't – Eyes bright, eyes wet,
eyes shiny in the sunlight – You have to *see* that?! He just . . . he makes
me come and he makes me laugh. What more could a girl want than that?
Someone who makes you come and makes you laugh?

—Someone who doesn't make you sit on all fours and show your private parts to the newsagent?

—He hasn't done that

—Yet

Rebecca shakes her head:

—I'd die without him

Murphy makes a noise:

—Listen to yourself! Jesus! You ARE gonna fucking die darling you are gonna DIE with HIM – Getting louder – You two are like one of those pervy couples who should never get together cause when they do they get on so well in their perversity they do weird shit like Fred and Rosie West or the Bulger boys or Bonnie and Clyde or

—Hitler and Germany?

Murphy comes to a stop. Rebecca shrugs as if to half apologise for what she's just said. Murphy shakes her friendly head and says:

—See you are losing it, those are his words his thoughts all that Jewish race crap just try and get a handle. Jesus – Murphy reaches out and grabs her friend by the head; her hot palms feel very hot on Rebecca's hot cheeks, as Murphy says, louder – Look at me Becs! This is all wrong! You have to leave him! It's out of hand!

And as Murphy holds Rebecca's face Rebecca faces her friend who is looking so friendly and sincere and loving and Rebecca starts to feel like crying; to prevent this she gulps back the tears and she tries to think of other stuff; not him; not them; not their doing it; not her and Murphy sitting here talking about their doing it. So instead she thinks about . . . the emperor . . . in his blue featherwork headdress, piercing his genitals, showing the blood to the dumbstruck Castilian pikemen.

—How bad is it at home then?

—Bad

—How bad?

Turning on his friend, his shorter, kinder, *seen my girlfriend's cunt and not mentioned it since* friend, Patrick clicks his teeth and says:

—Remember, years ago . . . That day we spent at the Millennium Dome?

Joe's eyes go wide:

—You don't mean . . . ?

Grimly:

—Yep. It's . . . *almost* as bad as that

—Jesus

Patrick goes to explain:

—It's been like this ever since . . . well . . . – Patrick tries again – I dunno . . . She's hardly spoken to me, for weeks. I know she probably wants to finish it, wants me out . . . – Staring down Marylebone High Street, as if at his bleak Rebecca-less future, Patrick goes on – All we do is shag. And read. And shag. We don't talk

—That's a problem?

—Yes

Joe looks across:

—Never thought I'd hear you say that

Patrick comes right back:

—The weird thing . . . The strangest thing is: she's in control – Eyes on his friend, seeking, asking – Although she's the one with the bruises . . .

Another pause. Joe looks over at his friend. For the first time this afternoon Joe looks like he's taking Patrick's troubles with proper seriousness. Patrick observes Joe as Joe appears to think hard. Finally Joe says:

—Golly

And after that Joe falls quiet, strolls on. Catching up with Joe, Patrick laughs and shakes his head and says:

—That's it? That's your advice: *golly*?

Turning, Joe says:

—Why don't you finish it yourself

Patrick:

—I can't. I love her. I love the fucking bitch. And the sex is so good – He smiles, vaguely – The most fun you can have without a sheet of tinfoil and a lighter

—OK, so . . .

—D'you really think I should do a runner?

—Maybe

Patch:

—I will arise now and go, and go to Innisfree . . .

—Good idea. Fuck off to Innisfree

—God I don't know though. Her cunt – Patrick looks at the sky – I'd really miss her cunt, I'd miss the way – He fixes his eyes on the hot sunny sky and speaks to someone, anyone, to Joe – The way the soft little hairs coil out . . . and the way she looks up at me when I come all over her face . . .

and the way her stupid little nose wrinkles when she comes and the way she makes that eeky eeky noise when she goes down

—eeky eeky?

Patrick nods, sadly:

—Eeky eeky . . .

—You two are *doomed*

—And because we're not talking it's even worse . . . – Patrick looks ahead, down the street, at the taxis queuing on New Cavendish corner, seeing an image of himself and Rebecca, her low sleepy eyes and her fiery tongue and her endless taking, taking, taking. Gazing at the rich people, the rich streets, the richness of the West End, Patrick sees a sudden and shocking himself as he probably is now: the pitiful gambler, making his furtive visits to the casino of sex, sitting down to the endless losing poker game of their sex, taking his place at the tables he cannot leave, cannot leave, cannot leave

—Oh God, Joe – Rueful, really rueful – Reading her books doesn't help either. All those Aztec books. They do your head in

Joe nods, and sighs. Stood on his sunlit patch of West End pavement, Joe sighs and shakes his head and reaches into his corduroy pocket for his packet of cigarettes; as Joe does this Patrick looks down at the sparkle of the Marylebone kerbstones, sparkling in the sunshine.

They are walking on. Towards a Japanese girl at the corner of Wigmore and Marylebone High with little blue and orange bobbly bits tied to the ends of her lovely hair; as Patrick approaches the girl reaches to adjust her hair and Patrick looks at the lovely white softness at the bend of the girl's bare arm.

Patrick turns to Joe, says:

—I'm wanking too much as well

—On top of all the shagging?

—Yes

—So is this why you've been ill? Are you wanking yourself ill? – Half grinning – Dude! You told me it was a throat infection . . .

—It's serious, Joe. I don't do anything else. You know I've been wanking on the Web at the office?

—Yyyyyeah . . .

—Well – Patrick stops, goes on – All I do is surf for pictures of girls that look like Rebecca, I wank all day over girls that resemble *her*

—On the Web you say?

—Yeah – Patrick shrugs, confessingly – Jap girls. Upskirts. Hours a fucking day . . .

Joe nods:

—It's another addiction, isn't it? Wanking on the Web . . . ?

Patrick sighs:

—Yep. And it's not easy either. I mean, how do you wank in front of a laptop?

—Sit back with a tissue?

—Gets on the keyboard . . .

—Kneel in front?

—Tried that – Patrick nods sideways – I tried that but I got housemaid's knee from kneeling too much – As they walk along Patrick glares at the upmarket kebab shop; he stares at the big white-green onions sitting in the window, between the racks of uncooked skewered lamb, the trays of minced lamb, the knitting needles threaded with chunks of meat and big red tomatoes. Patrick says – I thought of inventing something to help when you're having a wank on the Net – They are walking on. Past Topkapi, Starbucks, NatWest – In fact I thought of inventing a special Rubberised Wanking Cassock

Joe laughs:

—So like you could like kneel in front of your laptop and not get . . . bunions on your knee?

—Exactly . . .

Patrick falls quiet. He is bored of the laptop-wanking thing now, but is also determined to keep the shark of conversation moving. Lest it once more stop, and look up and see him, alone, in the sea, floating, vulnerable, *alone* . . .

—Funny word, bunions

Says Patrick. Joe ignores him. Patrick goes on anyway:

—You know when I was ill last week – Looking over at Joe, meaningfully – When I had *tonsillitis*

Joe sighs:

—I remember

—Well I was looking it up and I found out on the Net that suppurative tonsillitis is also known as . . . quinsy

Joe, half listening:

—Yeah?

—Isn't that quaint? Quinsy? – Patrick stops and smiles at Joe who is gazing along the High Road towards the Conran restaurant – Isn't it cute to get an illness that sounds like an Old English Pudding, don't you think?

Joe half nods; Patrick goes on eagerly:

—I'm just glad I didn't get Raspberry Cobblers. Or Plum Shuttles . . . – Watching Joe's response, Patrick goes on – Huckle-my-Buff would have been interesting tho . . .

Joe mms, and nods, and flashes an unappreciative smile; Patrick:

—Laugh you miserable trouser-biter, that was my best joke, took me ages

—Yeah, haha, can you see that chick up there? – Unlit cigarette lodged between two fingers, Joe points – *Tits* on *that*!

Patrick turns to see; Joe is looking almost angry:

—Christalive – Joe says, hissingly – Why is she trying to smuggle a couple of East German skinheads . . . *under her tee shirt*?

Patrick puts his hands on his hips like a North Country butcher, and says:

—Fookin' asylum seekers – The accent unsuccessful, Patrick goes quiet. Then Joe says:

—God, I can't hack it any more

—What?

—Another summer of *this*

—Sorry – Says Patch.

Joe:

—Can't handle it. I can't. Another summer of *this*, of like, having to constantly look at tits and stare up dresses and stuff, it's . . . knackering

—True . . .

—S'like a sentence of hard labour, from puberty to old age, you know? – Joe curses – God, sumtimes I just wanna read the paper and have a coffee, I don't want to have to look at some stupid girl just cause she's got a tiny netball skirt on you know? I'd rather have a pleasant conversation not spend every minute checking out cleavages

—What chance did we have – Says Patrick, beginning to laugh – We're cursed from birth . . .

Joe:

—You know what I'd like to do? I'd like to give women testosterone, just for one day

—Yeah?

—Just to let 'em know – Joe stops and stoops to quickly light his cigarette, Patrick watches this, feeling an urgent desire to smoke again, for a second, to feel what it's like to light a cigarette in the sunshine; as they turn and continue south down Marylebone High, Joe continues between drags on his cigarette – I'd like to let feminists feel what it's like to have testosterone coursing through your bloodstream every day having to think about pussy every five seconds, they fucking bang on about how they want to be men well they could be a man for one day and see how they like it – Blue smoke exhaled, Joe says – It would be like that Greek thing, the sword of Damocles, except this would be with a scrotum, they'd have a hairy scrotum hanging over their heads instead of a scimitar

—A big pair of testes to symbolise masculinity and its perils?

—Yep

—The Scrotum of Blackburn?

—Yes!

Patrick laughs loudly, and says 'Scrotum of Blackburn' again as they pause on the sunny pavement outside Waitrose supermarket. The two of them are looking inside: at the Jewish matrons buying big jars of sweet yiddish cucumber from the kosher counter; as they do Patrick shrugs. The sun is hot and delicious on Patrick's coolly summer-shirted arms; Patrick wishes he had a jacket to joyously swing over his shoulder. Patrick turns and says:

—How do you get away with your name anyway?

—Uh?

—I mean it's racist. Joe *Blackburn*. They should call you . . . Joe *Tragic Racist Incident*

—Can we not talk about race again?

Patrick goes on despite:

—You know I never know which word we're allowed to use for black people, is it coloured, black, what is it? Is it negro now? Or fuzzy wuzzy? Cocopop? – Thinking aloud – I'd like my coffee African-American please . . .

Joe is staring into the gleaming and affluent brightness of Waitrose; Joe says:

—Isn't this where you get your cheese?

—Yeah. They do a mean Lanark Blue

Joe:

—That the Irish one?

—Scottish. And the Gruyère is good – Patrick is thinking aloud again – Jesus Joe what am I like? She's turned me into a girl banging on about supermarkets and worrying about cheese counters

They approach the door and Joe says:

—You have started to sound a bit like her too

Patrick pushes the door as he says:

—Really?

—Yep. Sometimes, when you talk about Aztecs. And religion. History. Those are her obsessions, it's like it's *her* talking

Patrick shakes his head; they go into Waitrose; Patrick says:

—They've got a fine fishmongers here as well, superb langoustines

Joe laughs; turns to the cheeses, says:

—Patch?

—Yeah?

—What's mountain Gorgonzola?

—Dunno – Patrick shrugs – Sounds good, try some. And try the Colston Basset Stilton. That's great . . .

As Patrick says this he looks at a girl on the checkout desk; she is speaking some Asiatic language to the girl on the next checkout desk. Hundreds and thousands, hundreds and thousands, thinks Patch, then he smiles. He is entertaining the possibility of buying some quince cheese; though Patrick is not sure what quince cheese is. Deciding against, Patrick says:

—By the way Joe what did you think of Rebecca's cunt?

23

Sitting around the expensively white-tableclothed Covent Garden restaurant table, the night before the last day of his rape trial, Patrick scans the faces of his solicitor, his brief, his brief's junior. His solicitor Gareth Jenkins is looking at the menu. With an incredulous tone, Gareth says:
— Laminated menus?
— Americans like them
— It's like the caffs back in Cwmbran . . .
— Thanks for doing this, Robert
  Head in the wine list, Robert Stefan murmurs:
— Don't worry about it. Please – He lifts an eyebrow – I always like to
. . . have a chat with my clients . . . before . . .
— You normally do this on the last night?
— Mmmyes – Stefan's eyes are intent on his wine list – God that's pricey . . .
— A condemned man's last meal sort of thing?
  A tie-less Charlie Juson steps in:
— Hey, Patch . . . stay cool
  Jenkins nods:
— Grace under pressure man
  Stefan seems to wake up:
— Sorry, so sorry – He lowers the wine list – Terribly rude. Of course you are worried, Patrick, and you've got questions, yes?
  Patrick sighs:
— Well yeah . . . Yes I have – Trying not to fall over his own words

Patrick says – I'd like to know . . . What's it going to be like? I mean, when I go in the witness box . . . tomorrow, are you . . . are – He is starting to stammer – You . . . are

After swiftly ordering some red, Stefan turns back and says:

— Patrick. Relax. You'll be articulate and convincing, I'm sure

— You can't be any worse than her anyway, that *dress*!

— And the voice!

Says Jenkins.

Patrick looks at them all, and feels . . . trusting, but contemptuous. Hopeless, but dependent.

— Let's order . . . ?

— What about the partridge . . . ?

— Wrong season

Says the junior; Jenkins looks at Charlie Juson. The junior shrugs, then turns to Patrick and says:

— Hey, did you check out the girl doing the coats?

— The blonde?

— Was she blonde? Didn't notice her *hair*

At Juson's tepid quip Patrick smiles; Patrick also feels a twinge of pain. At this moment Patrick feels too guilty about, and distanced from, his masculinity, to happily join in any laddish banter. *Not tonight*. So instead Patrick looks down at his big plastic menu, tries to think about food rather than rape trials. Then Patrick says:

— snipe?

— Sorry, Patrick?

— snipe, uh – Patrick is trying to be interested – What's snipe?

— It's a sort of . . . aquatic pigeon. The lamb should be O K

Charlie:

— Tiny little fuckers – The junior does a relaxed, out-of-hours laugh, then explains – Snipe. They're small even for game birds

Patrick goes to try and add something, anything, about snipe; Stefan turns and looks directly at Patrick, and adopts a storytelling tone:

— There was a duke, in the mid-nineteenth century. He went to stay with a friend, who was a notorious miser. The duke was served half a snipe for dinner, just half a single snipe, and the duke said 'I'm prepared to share most things with my friends, including my wife, but I draw the line at a snipe'

At this, at last, the four of them laugh. This mutual merriment makes

Patch feel a tiny bit more relaxed and normal. So Patrick laughs, and laughs more, as he slugs some of the cold new white. Patrick is aware he is probably laughing too long, too much, but he does not care, he'd rather laugh inappropriately than ... think about tomorrow, rather embarrass himself by getting drunk tonight with his lawyers than ... think about tomorrow.

TOMORROW

Sighing, Patrick thinks about tomorrow. The terminal rigmarole: when he's got to stand in the dock and be examined. Be cross-examined. When he's going to be examined, cross-examined, re-questioned, dismissed, docked, summed up, adjudicated, adjudged, sentenced, grabbed, slammed, taken, shoved, carted, decanted, stripped, hosed, pushed, locked up, forgotten, forsaken, and garrotted as a nonce by some Largactil'd sex murderer from Galashiels.

The beef?

The beef.

After ordering the beef, Patrick pushes his chair back, rises from the table and turns and threads through the hubbuby restaurant. At the back of the restaurant he climbs stairs; he finds the shiny white urinal; unzips; sighs twice.

Back downstairs, Patrick tries to remember where they are sitting; as he is about to sit he notices the girl at the coat-check that Juson the Junior mentioned: the blonde with the breasts. The girl with the breasts is young, and smiley, and she indeed has nice big breasts. *Ohf*, Patrick sighs, looking at the breasts. How bitterly desirous they make him feel, how reluctantly admiring.

And how much these breasts also make him think of and yearn for *Rebecca's* breasts. Her tits. *God yes*. The pair of them. *God yes*. Patrick wishes they were here now, all three of them, reunited; in fact Rebecca could come too. In his present sad and anxious state Patrick decides he'd like nothing as much as to sink his lonely face against Rebecca's big lovely bosoms, feel their soft forgiving cool. O those perfect Hampstead breasts, O the Lost Breasts of London.

As Patrick approaches the table he hears Jenkins, who appears to be finishing off a story:

— So these Japanese soldiers would keep lockets of the pubic hair. Cut from the Chinese girls they'd raped. In Nanking. In. Er ... Mm

— Patch ... ?

Deciding not to be fazed, Patrick sits. As he does they all go quiet, so as to concentrate on their eating. Their food. Their dinners . . .

Creamed leeks, pink beef, horseradish?

While the four of them silently eat, Patrick wonders why he chose such a stupidly wintry, roast beefy dish on such a humid summer's evening. *Comfort grub?* Sidelong Patrick notices that Stefan is eating a more apt and elegant dish: between mouthfuls of chilled white wine Stefan is forking cold salmon, green beans, new potatoes. Ignoring his own food Patrick watches, kind of fascinated, kind of jealous, as Stefan eats, chats, laughs, and points his lazy fork. Then Patrick realises the QC's fork is pointed at Patrick. Stefan is explaining to Patrick why he is not calling any witnesses for the defence; witnesses other than Patrick. His fork pronged with very pale-orange salmon, Stefan leans past the lofted fork and says to Patrick that he believes Patrick is good enough on his own: a better witness on his own: more convincing in his isolated pitiability. Eating the salmon, setting down his fork again, Stefan picks up his wine glass, swallows some cold Sancerre, nods at the taste, then puts down the glass and explains that he feels additional witnesses might merely confuse the jury, blur the narrative, *as it were*.

Juson joins in. Halfway through a mouthful of pork chop, the junior adds his own advice, the same standard advice about Patrick's keeping his answers short and sweet, and preferably monosyllabic. Dumb, Patrick nods and drinks some of the burgundy chosen by Stefan. Dutifully, Patrick drinks, and drinks, and drinks and . . . drinks, and . . . tries to eat some more of his Galloway beef with mustard. But the mustard is so strong, especially when mixed with the horseradish: it makes Patrick want to sniffle. And anyway Patrick is not hungry. He can't find it in himself to eat. TOMORROW is like a big cold jade-stone toad squatting in his stomach.

Salmon finished, Stefan starts talking again, quite loudly, above the restaurant-goers, the honeymooners, the Americans, the sommelier. Stefan is loudly confessing that he does not usually get truly curious apropos his clients but he feels a certain mystification. With Patrick's case. *You see.*

—You see . . . – Stefan says – If I can put it this way we *are* all men of the world . . .

Juson:

—I'm not

Stefan turns his silvery-black head to his junior, and laughs. Then he turns back to Patrick, who is self-consciously napkinning a mustard sniffle from his nose. Tilting his wineglass in Patrick's direction, Stefan says:
— I'm interested on a professional level, you see
— Yes?
— Yes, it's my field, these . . . psychodramas, the psychosexual filigree of relationships
— OK . . . OK . . . – Says Patrick, wishing this weird dinner would be over; wishing it would never end – So – He feels for the words – So . . . yyyyyyyyou want me . . . to talk about Rebecca . . . ?
— Yes. Because it's a puzzle – Uncharacteristically, Stefan looks at Juson as if seeking moral support, Juson mentions he might have the bread and butter pudding. Stefan shifts back and says, directly:
— I confess it mystifies me why you and Rebecca split up. After *all* you *appeared* to be in love right up until the . . . alleged incident – Patrick shrugs and says nothing. Juson looks at Stefan. Stefan is going on – So what, if you don't mind my asking, what was it? Why *did* you break up?

Pointing to the summer pudding entry on the menu, Patrick hands the menu back to the monochrome waiter and turns back to Stefan and says:
— Well . . . – Patrick is aware that it might come spilling out if he is not careful; he is also aware he wants to spill it out, to regurgitate – Well I'm . . . I don't know . . . I don't know even now . . . – Patrick is staring at Stefan; staring at the deer's head on the wall behind, the stuffed red grouse on the dusty yellow shelf; then Patrick says – I guess we just got too into sex, too much. We never talked, we just shagged . . . – Thinking – I remember the last night, before she chucked me out, a month before the . . . – Patrick sighs. Do they know? – It was a month before the incident . . . – He shuts his eyes picturing it – Anyway that night we went too far, too stupidly far. In bed. And even though I knew she still loved me, I kind of agreed – Patrick opens his eyes again; gazes at the faces around the table – Perhaps we just had nowhere else to go. Perhaps we'd done it all . . . Or nearly all . . .

Patrick falls quiet. Stefan nods, as if he is impressed by, and understanding of, this sadness. Juson says nothing, possibly embarrassed. The mutual silence allows them to finish their puddings, coffees and

Sauternes, in short order. After that they pay the bill, get up, and push glass and wood into the mild evening air.

Emancipated into Covent Garden's warm, gutter-sweet, opulent, old-fashioned streets, Patrick feels a weird dizziness, an urgent headrush, a night-before-the-battle upsurge of life force. He feels a desire to dance, or to do a comedy routine, or to sing. He also feels sick. And he feels full. And he feels like he is in a film. A musical ... He feels he is in a musical, that musical, *My Fair Lady* ... and that tomorrow he has to perform, to perform like Pygmalion ...

— Patrick? – Gareth is slapping Patch on the back – You alright? Patch?

Shaking his head Patrick says:

— I'm fine

Making some shall-we-get-a-cab gestures at Juson, Stefan says:

— O K we'll see you tomorrow, Patrick

— O K ...

— Try and get a good night's sleep, if you can

— And remember, keep it brief, mate

— I remember

— Nine o'clock sharp?

— Yes

— Goodbye Patrick

— Bye Patch

— *Bye*

Standing alone on the corner pavement of Maiden Lane and Tavistock Patrick watches as his saviour *manqué*, and his saviour *manqué*'s junior, sit back in their cab, which goes sailing down towards the Strand. Then Patrick continues watching the space where the cab was, which is now filled by a spectacularly pretty girl, high heeling past them. Summer-dressed, firm-calved, neatly ankled, suntanned, the girl is sexy. The girl is pukka. The girl is, in fact, a classic twenty-two-year-old West Fulham damsel *in oestrus*.

The familiar ache, the helpless desire, roils in Patrick's groin again. He feels like a black in antebellum Tennessee, looking at some moustache-twirling blue blood. He feels weak and poor, and helplessly envious. What chance did he have, he thinks, what chance do men have. *Men are demons, helplessly fallen, cursed by fate, cast into eternal perdition by their love ... for the daughters of men ...*

With a start Patrick notices that he ain't alone: Jenkins is standing beside him. Jenkins is also, mournfully, watching the coltish Fulham girl, observing her as she finally disappears into the mobs of Covent Garden market. Into the crowds of clubbers, kids, Kiwis, Afrikaaner cricketers.

— Classy – Jenkins says. Then he turns – Good man, Robert Stefan
   Patrick shakes his head, shrugs a yes:
— Yeah, good bloke
— Bit stiff, at first tho
— Yes . . .
— Not so sure about Charlie Juson
— Aii. He's OK – Says Patch. The two men, the client and his brief, have turned and are walking down towards the night buses and the Tube, towards the Thames – I know his type – Says Patrick, quietly – We used to get 'em in the club, young lawyers on the make – Patrick does a soft smile, remembering better times – They're often like that, posh but laddish . . . Good fun in their own way . . .
— Nmm, look you

Says Jenkins, aping his own Welshness. Patrick chuckles. Then in silence the two of them walk on, turning right and left and right, past the Savoy, past the road to Savoy Chapel, past the site of old Northumberland House, down to where the great old river slides silent and bronze between the sombre grey office blocks.

24

Stepping out of the blue-painted door into the humid slightly dank air of Linden Street Rebecca looks up and down at the cars waiting for a cab; as she does her mobile goes. Lifting the phone out of her Sloane Street handbag Rebecca puts the phone to her ear and the mobile says:

—Hey. It's me. Where are you?

—Murphy?

—*Yes*. Derr. Why aren't you at home?

—I'm just getting in a cab hold on yes please the British Museum please

—The British Museum? What?

Settling herself in the taxi back seat and absent-mindedly looking at the adverts on the backs of the flipdown seats in front, Rebecca puts her head to the phone again, and explains:

—I'm going to the new Aztec gallery

—Yeah?

—I'm . . . meeting . . . *him*

The taxi swerves along Wigmore Street. The stucco cherubs playing flutes on the side of upmarket pharmacies give on to the Robert Adam splendour of half-ruined Portland Place, which in turn segues into the cardboard-boxy bustle of the garment district.

Rebecca listens to Murphy saying:

—Why the *fuck* are you doing that?

—Because . . .

—You throw him out for being a drunken idiot and now you're seeing him??

—I . . . miss him

—Oh you miss him right sure course — Murphy is spitting the words —
Like you miss having black eyes and constant rows and his hairdresser round
the flat lifting up your skirt
—He only hit me . . . when I asked him — She pauses — Generally

A silence. Great Portland Street; Great Titchfield Street; the old ITN
headquarters.

Murphy shouts:
—You stupid stupid stupid . . . *bird*
—I miss the fun, he made me laugh — Says Rebecca, looking at her own
knees. Looking at her own bare knees makes Rebecca wonder whether
Murphy has a boyfriendless shagless . . . Patrickless agenda of her own;
trying to dismiss this train of thought Rebecca says to Murphy:
—Murphy has any of this to do with the fact that you haven't had a boyfriend
in two years?

The next silence lasts the length of Foley Street. Then.
—Ow

Rebecca says nothing; Murphy says again:
—Ow!! That hurt!
—OK I'm sorry
—OhFuckyouRebeccaJessel

The mobile has gone dead. Regretful, angered by herself, Rebecca puts
the phone back in her bag, as the taxi crosses over into Tottenham Court
Road, as Rebecca gazes out the window. The disconsolating summer drizzle
is coming down again, making tourists in shorts run under the newsagents'
awnings where they turn to stare uncomprehendingly out at the English
summer. Touching her own face for some reason, Rebecca keeps looking:
she stares through the taxi window at the unspoken colonnade of Gower
Street; the untouched yet somehow sterile Georgian-ness of Bedford Square.
Then the cab swings viciously left and deposits Rebecca at the place where
the man sells hot sweet chestnuts in the winter.

The cab driver paid Rebecca checks the weepy sky for a moment, then
she skips in her trainers across the retouched rain-blacked plaza that fronts
the Museum, to the crowded-cause-it's-raining portico. Pressganged by
French kids, American kids, by Japanese kids and Nordic kids all shouting
together Rebecca forces her way through the hubbub into the open but
glass-covered square in the middle of the renewed Museum. The harle-
quined glass arches over the covered square; it is an undulating carapace
of grey lozenges. Patch is in front of her.

—Hi

He says, diffident, unshaven, not obviously drunk.

—Hi

She says. Also diffident. Their being separated by three yards and a month, she looks at him, appraisingly. She still fancies him but she wonders if she fancies him as much. Then he smiles and says something funny, and she knows she fancies him even more; then she thinks she catches the smell of beer on him and she knows she is glad she is trying to end the relationship. But then she looks one more time, just one more time, and she sees some tiredness in his pale, sad blue eyes and she feels an enormous pity and empathy for him: for losing his father, his money, his club, her, for being so obviously in need of her body which she can see he is looking up and down remembering.

—Nice skirt – Patrick says, adding – Short

Rebecca smiles at this; feels resentful. She takes his hand and squeezes it and says:

—Shall we go in?

—Why did you dump me, Rebecca?

—It's just over here

—You aren't going to have my kids then?

—What do you think of the reading room the way they've done it it's quite nice with the café and

—I'm a fucking mess without you Bex – He moves nearer – I'm sleeping in . . . bus stations

She turns:

—No you're not

He admits:

—No I'm not

—So shut up then

—But I am . . . *emotionally*, I am living in a . . . Victoria Coach Station. Of loneliness. Without you – His hand is now tight on her hand – Jesus you're still cute you know – She smiles; he responds to her smile – Fuck Bex come here please I need you

He tries to squeeze near, to kiss her soft and wet on the cheek. Rebecca wants him to do this; she dreads his touch; she wants him to still desire her; she is afraid of that desire. As they walk through the new Africa Galleries and turn right towards the just-restored American Galleries Rebecca shrugs her shoulder as if exercising a painful twinge. By doing this she manages to prevent him kissing her; but as she succeeds, as she repels him, he looks so hangdog she is obliged to squeeze his hand even harder; and then to lean and kiss him on the stubble.

At once he brightens. Says:

— So you haven't seen these galleries before?

— No

— I thought you'd seen just about everything to do with the Aztecs

— Not this gallery. It's new

Together they push the double swing doors and go into the slightly darkened room, where sculptures and artefacts are looking glamorous and evil in the atmospheric half-light. For a moment they stand there beholding a screaming baby being hastily carried out of the doors by a harassed-looking father. Then Patrick says, his hands in the pockets of his desirably old leather jacket.

— Bit small?

— Small but . . . perfectly formed. It's one of the very best collections in Europe

— O K. You're the expert

They start. They start by bending their heads, and looking at Olmec axes, Maya glyphs, Toltec knives, and little ankle chains of conch shells from the Isle of Sacrifices. Next comes a picture of a big wooden cudgel with a serrated row of large black obsidian razor blades stuck in it the same way broken glass is cemented on top of a high wall.

— That's a *macuahuitl*, a sort of Aztec sword

Says Rebecca. Patrick nods, looking more interested than he ever used to when she used to witter on about Mesoamerica. Or Crusader history. Or sixteenth-century witchfinding. Or their relationship. Rebecca warms to this unexpected responsiveness, and hence starts explaining what it, the sword, was used for, how it was used in battles, how it was used in the ritualised gladiatorial battles of Xipe Totec, the Feast of the Flaying of Men, when in front of the assembled nobles and dignitaries and feather-headdressed royalty of Tenochtitlan a captured young half-starved nobleman from an enemy tribe would be ankle-tied to a huge round circular stone and after being gorged on psychedelic drugs would be forced to fight the chief jaguar warriors of the Aztec city, forced to fight even though he would always without fail lose the battle as the skilful Aztec warriors slowly sliced him to death by chopping his hamstrings and slicing his tendons and stripping the sweating skin from his back until it hung in ribbons down his bleeding torso.

Rebecca stops, takes a breather. Patrick is looking at her with fascination and surprise, with nodding curiosity, and understandable-over-keen-ness-because-he's-trying-to-be-nice. But Rebecca doesn't feel any pride at her own eloquent display of knowledge, she feels a reflux of self disgust and revulsion welling up in her throat. She feels sick. Even the *names* make her feel sick. Cinteotl. Huitzilopochtli. *She of the Serpent Skirt*. Rebecca feels dizzy: thinking of the humid summer air; of Patrick's unshaven face between her legs. Getting hold of herself Rebecca bends and looks at a Toltec pot with the inscribed glyphs for extruded human hearts. But this merely makes her wonder why she has this unhealthy fascination with pre-Columbian civilisation. With its flayed skins, its human bones, its cannibalism and collections of fingernails and its platoons of priests with their long black never-cut hair matted with human offal.

Why? Of course why. Rebecca at once sees what all this reminds her of: of serial sex-murderers, rapist killers, Hannibal Lecter, Fred and Rosie West, Denis Nilsen. For isn't this what sexual psychopaths do? Make grisly collections of human remains? Just like the Aztecs? Little stamp collections of innards and eyelids and dried penises and the like? Little collections of things that look like dried sealife so that when the police crash in the door in the night and flash their torches in the fetid black corners of rented rooms in provincial towns they will see . . .

— Go on – Says Patrick – More. Please. I'm interested

— No . . .

Rebecca waves her hand. She waves her hand so as to wave some air in her face. She is trying not to be sick; trying not to feel sick; she can't help thinking of the cold fridgy handcuffs around her wrist; and the bruises on her thighs; and the blood on his fingers. Her blood. That he wipes on her cheek and kisses away . . .

Where were they going with this? What did it mean once?

— You OK?

— Yes . . . – She sighs – yyyyesss

They walk on. Around the corner. As a couple they lean to the stone lintels, lintels Rebecca remembers reading about in one of her books; they are stopped short when an electronic beeping shrills out across the room and several Chinese-looking youths stare over. Patrick:

— Oops?

Rebecca points at the side of the wall at a small black hole. Says:

— Electric light beam

Thus warned and chastised they both lean more gingerly, to scrutinise the first stone square with its stylised picture of a lady with a nose ring in her nose kneeling in front of a man with a lip plug in his lip. The lintel is decorated with lots of wavy lines. And lots of stone symbols of human hearts. Rebecca knows what all this means. Patrick presumably doesn't. He leans to the little cardboard panel on the side of the lintel and starts reciting:

— 'Lord Shield Jaguar and his wife Lady . . . – He pauses, gazes at the next words, then says – 'Lady Xoc'? – He is looking over at Rebecca for approval, she nods at his pronunciation; so he smiles and goes on – 'They engage in a bloodletting rite . . .' – Patrick stops, again, and half smiles and Rebecca looks at his still handsome face and wishes he wouldn't smile, as he goes on reciting – 'The king stands on the left brandishing a flaming torch to illuminate the drama that is about to unfold. Kneeling in front of the king wearing an exquisitely woven *huil . . . pil . . .* Lady Xoc pulls a thorn-lined rope through her tongue. This rope falls into a woven basket holding blood-stained strips of paper cloth . . .'

Patrick stops and hmms. He puts his hands on hips; turns to Rebecca. And then he winks. *He winks!*

Rebecca stands back. *He winked!* She feels like slapping him for the wink, for what it meant, for winking after reciting that card; but because she does not know what to do other than slap him, she reaches out and holds Patch's hand, the hand that has done . . . so much to her . . . Blithe and unaware, Patch points:

— This sculpture? Isn't it in one of your . . . books?

— Yes

— You know I remember you telling me about this bloodletting thing months ago so anyway why did you chuck me Rebecca?

— Please. Don't

— I still fucking love you

— **Don't**

Letting his hand drop, Rebecca turns and quickly leans to the next lintel. Intent, she looks at the image, the image of the Aztec emperor piercing his royal penis with cactus thorns, while he contemplates the image of the God Yat Balam. Rebecca feels sick. She feels that waviness inside her, again, that swallowing smoke feeling, that inner nausea. This is not helped when her ex bends his stubble to the museum wall and recites from another panel in his beginning-to-annoy-her way:

— 'Many smiling figures of Classic Veracruz may be dancers, with their hands raised in a praying position. Musicians and dancers occur in the art of West Mexico, and the anecdotal groupings include . . .' – Patrick pauses, reads on without talking, then he says – Jesus Bex look at this – He recites aloud again – 'and the anecdotal groupings include scenes of a *cheek perforation dance*, in which a stick may pierce two different performers' cheeks, binding dancers together in . . . pain and bloodletting'

Patrick has stopped. Rebecca stays quiet. She is thinking: God help us. God help us. Yat Balam, Yat Balam, Yad Vashem, Babi Yar. Rebecca shakes her head, looks across: Patch's eye teeth are sharp, white, and too wet as he grins, as he looks at a turquoise Aztec mask with graphite ball eyes and human skull underneath, at a lampshade made from human skin. *A lampshade made from human skin?* Rebecca shakes her head. She watches as Patrick turns his head and looks with self-conscious interest at a mock-up of Tenochtitlan city, the Aztec capital. Patrick is examining the pyramids, the sacrificial centres, the manufactories of death, the Auschwitz and Treblinka of the pre-industrial world. *The Auschwitz and Treblinka? What?*

Rebecca frets, feels anxious, self-hating. She remembers what Patrick used to say about people obsessed with the Holocaust, people who were kinky for the Holocaust, who liked the kiddie porn of the Holocaust. She remembers how he dissed Sylvia Plath, and other artists, for using the Holocaust. Plagiarisers of Hitler, was that what he called them? Rebecca recalls this, and feels respect for his insight, and revulsion at her own obsessiveness. Because somehow in her head it now all connects, her obsession with Nazi-like Aztecs, the Aztecness of sexual killers, her obsessively hypersexual love for him. Here now it seems to make sense; and Rebecca doesn't like the sense it makes. She has to ask herself: *is* it her at fault, then? Is it her that's morbid, perverse, corrupt? Is it her that's corrupted him? That's ruined and poisoned their love? Is it her that's taken them to the place, to the little darkened room at the top of the pyramid, where the unspeakable things happen?

— Rebecca?

Rebecca is pacing out into the easy air of the glass-covered central court. She is half running out, half running over, she is queuing for a coffee at the café and maniacally counting her change, trying not to think too much. As she enumerates her change she tries not to look at Patrick as he walks over with concern on his face, as he watches her sit at the long grey table and gulp her coffee though it's too hot. After a while he sits down opposite her; the two of them sit together. Rebecca notices there is a Roman statue right behind her boyfriend. The statue is chaste and cream-coloured in the chaste cream-coloured great space at the heart of the great Museum.

Swigging the last of the coffee, Rebecca wishes to God, to Yat Balam, that she'd put some sugar in. Across the table Patrick watches her as she downs the coffee; he looks at the coffee; tries to say something funny about her drinking so much coffee. It fails. Consequently Rebecca feels sorry for him again. She hates feeling sorry for him; would rather hate him. Yes, *hate him*. With his stupid unshaven face and blind blue eyes, his big male hands and trendily retro leather jacket. The way he sits there trying to please her. Lord Shield Jaguar? *Fuck off.*

Rebecca feels like crying and Patrick seems to notice this. He goes behind her; she hears him speak very slow pidgin English to the Spanish cafeteria girl; he returns with another cup of coffee. Two cups of coffee. One for her and one for him. As one they sip their coffee and look at each other between sips, wordless. She remembers the pool party; how much she loved him then. She remembers how much she loved him and she resents him for the fact that she does not seem to love him that much any more. Christ, she hates this feeling, the *chagrin d'amour* . . .

One sugar, two sugars, three, fuck it. Sipping her over-sweetened second coffee Rebecca looks at Patrick as he talks about the Aztecs about how he really really appreciates

—Oh shut up, Patrick

—Sh . . . ?

—Just please. Shut up

—But you . . .

But everything. But everything. But all and everything he does treads on her toes; interrupts her; turns her over at the wrong moment. She wishes she could wish the last year and a half away; wishes she'd never met him. And yet, and yet *something*. Through it all Rebecca feels inside that she will never be able to forget him and that somehow he is right for her and that it is her that has ruined it all. Which makes it all the worse and maze-like. Again the wavy lines, again the smoky mirror, again Rebecca stares into the polished obsidian, unseeing, uncomprehending. Then:

—So what the fuck do you *want* me to do, Rebecca

Good question. Very good question. Coffee finished, caffeine doing its thing, Rebecca looks at the chiselled white stone of the north portico. Crowds of people are walking cultural widdershins around the oval of the reading room. Very good question: what the fuck *does* she want or expect him to do? How can he know? When she has no idea? No idea what's gone wrong, or why she hates him because she still loves him even though she hates him because she still wants him?

—I'm sorry . . . Patch . . . I really . . .

Empty words, empty words. He gazes back at her in an understandably empty way. Then he says, dry, more distant now:

—Do you remember that time in Greenwich Park?

—When I went barefoot?

—We made love on the Iron Age tumulus

He pauses, goes silent; she feels sad, feels happy; she feels her loins; she nods and laughs quietly and says:

—I called you Stig, didn't I?

—You called me Stig . . .

Her boyfriend, her ex-boyfriend, he looks at her, with his assessing blue eyes, his scientific blue eyes. She stares back unscared and then for some reason he says

—No

Then he reaches in his pocket and pulls out a box. A little jewellery box. Rebecca's stomach churns. Patrick flips the blue box and looks disdainfully at the flashing silver torc inside as he takes it out and says:

—It's Mexican, solid silver . . . antique

Clasping her left hand Patrick slips the ring on her fourth finger and it fits; he looks down at the prettily be-ringed finger and he says:

—It's pretty, isn't it? I was going to . . . you know . . .

And then he stands up, looks at her. He looks tall again. After a pause he slowly leans and kisses her on her sweating forehead.

And then he just turns and nobly walks away, adorned by the quetzal feathers of his self control; attended by the Toltec princelings of his dignity; Lord Shield Jaguar once more.

25

—Death's not so bad

Says Patrick; Joe nods and puffs as the two of them sprint across Gray's Inn Road. Traffic avoided, they stop to catch breath by the cute grey dragon marking the City's boundary. Patrick goes on:

—I mean, it's only annihilation of the soul. And destruction of the body. And entry into a night of infinite bleakness

Joe:

—You're right. I dunno why they go on about it

Patrick:

—They obviously haven't read contemporary women's fiction . . . *that's* bad

The two friends watch the traffic, then watch more traffic. As they walk on, Joe says:

—You OK man?

—Sure, fine

—I mean . . . apart from your suicidal urges?

Patrick nods and says:

—Apart from those, yep

—Excellent

The pace quickens; Patrick ranks his last pair of stiff white shirt cuffs, suitable for the last day of his rape trial, as they stride on past the Ely Place roundabout, as they traverse the trafficky roads that lead to Holborn Viaduct. At length Patrick looks sidelong:

—Thanks for sticking with me, Joe. All through

— No problem – Joe looks down, turns a wrist, looks at his watch – You'll never guess pal – He grins – We're *early*

Patrick tilts his head, thinks about the fact that he is early. Then he wonders why he is early, why he is keen to get started, to get put in prison. For life.

To use up mental space, to distract himself from what gives, Patrick stops and leans two hands on the taffrail of Holborn Viaduct, watching the rush-hour traffic below, the dirty white butcher's vans queuing to turn right into Smithfield. The white-and-green ambulances from Bart's hospital.

— Er . . .

Says Joe. Patrick turns, says:

— What?

— Have to ask, Patch man

— What?

Joe clears his throat:

— Well like . . . I've been wondering all week

— Yyyess?

— Well

— Yes?

— Well, like . . . – Exhaling – *Did* you . . . ?

— Did I what?

— *Did you do it?*

A plane comes over, goes across. Joe makes a face and raises placating palms:

— Joke! I'm joking!

Patrick looks at his friend. They are within a bus-hop of their destination. Patrick turns, eyes the bright sun, and says nothing. So Joe says, jauntily:

— You seen the paper?

He is evidently trying to change the subject, after his naff joke. Patrick half smiles, half shrugs. In response Joe reaches a young friendly arm in his Waitrose plastic bag and pulls out a copy of a middle-market tabloid and reads out from a middle-of-the-paper page:

— 'A society beauty told the court this week how she was brutally assaulted and sexually abused by her club-owning ex-boyf'

The paper grabbed, Patrick reads, maniacally. Amongst a thousand other *Daily Mail* words Patrick reads the words: *beautiful, West End, racist, passionate, harrowing, kinky, heiress, long blonde,* and at least three or four *Patrick Skivingtons.* But no mention of *her* name. Instead there's a picture of him walking towards the Old Bailey smiling. Smiling? Patrick notes that his suit looks a bit crumpled. His tie looks nice.

Closing the paper, Patrick shakes his head and laughs at the traffic. Then he stares sideways and hard at Joe; Joe seems to clock the expression. Joe stammers and gabbles:

— Hey. Dude. It doesn't mean they think you're going down

— No?

— No, it's the opposite, think they're running it now cause they think you're going to get off . . .

— Naturally

— No really, Patch

— Joe. I'm fucked

— No no n'no NO

— Yes. And maybe they're right, maybe I should go down – Walking on, Patrick says – My head hurts, Joe

— You're not sodding guilty, Patch

— Well maybe I am

— No you're NOT

— I feel sort of sinful

— Christ. Jesus. You have to get a handle man

— I just . . . – Patrick stares ahead of himself, at a turning bus, an advert for jeans thereupon – I just . . .

For a few moments they are both quiet, amidst the noise of the city morning. Then Joe looks at his watch again.

— When's she due back?

Joe stops looking at his watch:

— Told you, any time this afternoon

— I *hate* waiting for drugs

— So have another beer

Patrick:

— I already did, I'm bored of beer

Joe, with the infinite patience of the true junkie, shakes his head and says:

— First thing you learn is that you always gotta wait

— Yeah, if you're a total stoner

— Thanks

— Well – Patrick picks up the pint glass he has already drained, tilts it meaningfully at the approaching barman – You do do too many drugs. Same again please. Why do you do so many drugs?

— Why are you a twat?

— Your hair's looking nice, Joe

— Cup hands here comes cuntbury's

Patrick laughs, says:

— You know you look like a member of Metallica after seven years in a hut?

Joe also sniggers; then he turns to the barman, indicating he too would like another drink. Using the lull, Patrick stares around him, surveying the old Victorian pub on the most important corner of the main street in Kentish Town. Patrick reads Irish soccer posters, adverts for Broccoli Bake at £2.99, he sees the winking slot machine and the young Dublin lads sluicing Murphy's by the pool table. Then Patrick stares out at the hot late-summer's day that is today's Kentish Town. Three red buses are stalled nose to tail. Taxis are simmering behind and between. *Laundromat. Kleen Machine. Taste of Empire Curry House* . . .

Despairing of the horribleness of Kentish Town, Patrick wonders how often he has found himself in Kentish Town lamenting the end of relationships.

— Why do all relationships end up in Kentish Town?

— That might be her van

— They start in Soho . . .

— Looks like her dog in the back!

— They peak in Richmond, when you have sex in the park

— S'not. Soddit . . .

— But they always seem to end up in Kentishfucking*Town*

— Nother voddie and Red Bull, what did you say?

Patch watches as Joe orders another drink. Patrick leans in and asks for another drink for himself, another vodka chaser to go with his beer. Patrick is getting very drunk. To ground himself he reads more stuff around the pub. *Killer Pool Sunday. Odessa Vodka. Trio Minted Lamb Cutlets £3.99.*

— Whoops. Hold on! *She's back!*

—Calm down, Joe
—That her van?!
—*Christ* . . .

Turning and staring into the Rebeccalessness of his vodka glass Patch thinks about his ex-girlfriend, his dead father, his defunct club, and he wonders whether he would like to become a junkie too. Now he's lost everything. Well why not. Why not become a junkie? How does one become a junkie?

—How does one become a junkie?

Says Patrick. Joe, disappointed to see a builder climb out of the van, half turns and shrugs and says:

—How should I know . . .

Joe is pouring some more Red Bull in his vodka; smart and deft Joe downs half of the lot; then wipes his lips, and says:

—Change of subject?
—Can't
—Try
—OK – Patrick says, changing the subject – Tell you what . . . I . . . can't help wondering, you know, whether we're still . . . evolving. Us. Humans. Are we? – Seizing the theme – My big worry is what might happen if we *stop* evolving. You know? We might get overtaken by other species if that happens . . .

Joe chuckles, his tee shirt says COORS; he rubs his red baggy plastic trousers and says in reply:

—What, you mean like we might wake up and find . . .
—Don't say tapirs
—We might find tapirs ruling the show?

Patrick lifts his glass as if in a toast:

—Or dik diks. Or . . . caterpillars. Think about it, the shame, being blind-sided by *caterpillars*
—I think her curtains just moved

Patrick:

—God, Joe, your dealer is OUT!
—No no she might be there she might have just woken up dude they're not known for rising at nine I'll try her mobile again

Setting down his glass, Patrick sighs and orders a fourth vodka chaser as he tries to stop seeing two versions of Joe, Rebecca, Joe, Rebecca, of Joe ringing his dealer on his mobile for the fortieth time this afternoon. O this stupid drunken afternoon. This stupid drunken afternoon when nothing will happen except that he will fail to score some drugs to take his mind off Rebecca.

Rebecca. Rebecca. Rebecca. Broccoli Bake £2.99.

Joe, loudly:

— Patch! Where you going?!

Patrick continues to the door of the pub; he says to Joe, without turning:

— To see my ex

— No more questions

Stefan sits down, Patrick breathes out and relaxes. Then Patrick looks over from the witness stand to the desk where his defence team is sitting and he notices that Juson is doing him another surreptitious thumbs up. Presumably this is to indicate that he has done well under interrogation from Stefan. Patrick relaxes more and feels happier; then Gregory the Prosecutor leaps to his feet and smiles at the judge and says:

— Mister Skivington, I'd like to go straight to the day in question

Patrick grips the wooden rail of the witness box and nods:

— Yes

— You had been drinking all day, hadn't you?

— No, not all day

— No?

— No

— How long then?

Patrick looks swiftly at the impassive face of Stefan. He looks back at the wig and gown of Gregory:

— Three hours, maybe four

Gregory:

— Oh, do forgive me, not *all* day. Only four hours?

Patrick feels like bopping Gregory with the judge's gavel; for his laboured sarcasm, his pedestrian sardonics; instead Patrick remembers what Stefan said about staying monosyllabic and Patrick says:

— Yes

— You were pretty drunk, anyway, would you say?

— Not that drunk. Just a bit

— Well. Then. OK. To clear this up could you tell the court how much you'd drunk that afternoon?

Gregory is waving a hand at the court, at the policeman behind Patrick, at the swollen bunch of journalists to the side and the invisible public in the gallery above Patrick's head. Patrick does a shrug; realising that a shrug is not enough he says:
— I suppose I'd had maybe four pints, maybe five . . . and a couple of vodkas
Gregory is smiling again:
— Thank you
Pushing back the folds of his robe as he stoops to a notebook, Gregory lifts up his face and says:
— And at about five o'clock you decided to go and see Miss Jessel, your ex-girlfriend?
— Yes
— Why?
Patrick:
— . . . Why what?
Gregory:
— Why did you decide to go and see Miss Jessel? Suddenly? Just like that?
Patrick thinks, puts his hand to the knot of his tie, wonders if this gesture looks guilt-ridden; he puts his hand back down, and says:
— I missed her, I wanted to talk to her
— To talk, that was all?
— Yes
— And what happened when you got there? To the flat you used to share?
— I pressed the buzzer
Exhaling, calmly:
— And?
— And I told her who it was, and that I wanted to pick up some stuff
— And then?
— . . . then she came down and answered the door . . . And . . . she let me in
Someone in the gallery covers a laugh with a cough; Gregory looks sternly at the public gallery above Patrick's head; before looking back at Patrick:
— And what did you do then?
— I went in . . . and we talked

—Just talk, just conversation? That was all that happened?

Patrick nods:

—Yes

—Then what? Could you tell the court what happened then?

—Rebecca made some tea

Gregory sighs, as if he is disappointed in a once favourite pupil. He looks directly at Patrick and says:

—OK. At what point did you first . . . *kiss* . . . Miss Jessel?

—After about half an hour

—Half an hour. Really?

—Yes

—Are you sure?

—Yes

—Not ten minutes?

—No

—How did it occur? This first kiss?

—. . . We were sitting drinking the tea by the window and she looked at me and she said

—You don't fancy me any more

Patrick looks at Rebecca's beautiful hair, the colour of . . . of Russian corn in the summer of 1941. He giggles at his own analogy and burps beer and says:

—Course I fucking do

—Patrick you're drunk

—No I'm not

—Yes you are

—OK OK yes I am and OK yes I mean it yes I love you

Drunk, Patrick leans and puts his face to his ex-girlfriend's lovely hair and inhales the scent, the honey and smoke. Drunk, still in love, Patrick trails his slave-running fingers through the silent Circassian blondeness; then he leans his face to her cheek, so close he can sense the warmth of her blush as he says:

—Rebecca I love you God I love you

And he pincers her sweet lips into a pout and twists her untwisting head and he says:

—Kiss me

—Patch
—Kiss me go on kiss me kiss me now *bitch*

—Did you say 'kiss me you Jewish bitch'?
Patrick looks at the wall slightly to the left of Gregory's wig. Then says:
—No
—No? What did you say?
—Nothing. We just kissed
—I see. And that was it?
—Yes. That was it. Just a kiss. Like you do. You know
Gregory winces, then says:
—You didn't say *any*thing?
The court is silent. The unicorn rears. The lion roars.
—No. Nothing. We just kissed . . . without words

—Take it off!! Take it OFF
His hand down her top Patrick grabs her beautiful breast; he feels like shouting out, he wants her so much; she struggles in his grip like a precious wild animal he has captured for the zoo; like a young Jewess in the Belorussian snow; like Rebecca, now. The zip scratches his hand and she says:
—Patrick please, please don't
But he senses a struggle lessening and he knows that she wants him to take her now; to fuck her roughly as she likes; to do it again; to rape her again; to do what they like. Then he wonders if he is too drunk to get it up; if he will disappoint her. She is saying:
—No Patrick no
And as she says this she struggles, lifting herself away from him. This elevation allows him to put his hand in, further, into her unbuttoned jeans, down to where her cunt is as wet as he can remember

—Did she say no?
—No
—Did she say anything?
—No

—You just took her clothes off – Looking up at Patrick – Without a struggle?
—Yes

He is trying to rip her jeans off; she struggles and sighs; he struggles and bites; she groans; he holds her tight; she slacks. Then he lifts her up and pulls the jeans down, along; allowing him to look at his handiwork, the flag of her body unfurled. And the cunt; of course; the cunt that he loves. O that, O the warning black triangle; O yes. Now Rebecca is lying back and moaning and saying:
— kiss me

Commanded, he leans his face to her face and kisses her deeply, on the lips, on the sweet little lips that tremble that go O that match tongue with tongue, like a candle flame, like a moth's wing, flickering; she is like a moth against the leaded window. This brilliant kiss done he breathes her smell and lifts her up and feels her body draped like a sack of looted corn in his hands; hungry and desperate Patrick stoops and kisses her breasts the white breasts he worships; adores; is scared of; detests; he is drunk on. He is Wordsworth in the Alps of her breasts. He is drunk, he is Red Bulled, he is hers; he is saying:
—God I love you you fucking slut

—I told her I loved her
—I see
—And that I'd always loved her
—So you didn't call her . . . – A Gregorian pause – A slut?
—No
—Nor a bitch?
—No
—Nor a – Glancing at the jury, the judge, Patrick again – Little dirty cunt? A little cockteasing slut?
    Patrick sways, hands on rails:
—No . . .
—And this was the point that you dragged her upstairs?
—No
—No? Really?

Patrick shakes his head; abandoning his restraint:
— No! That's not what happened, not then, that's when I went down on her, when I went down on her and

licking her out Patrick looks up above the carrion before him and he sees her face swaying from side to side as he licks at her cunt; Rebecca is biting a bent forefinger in her own mouth and is saying:
— No no no no no stop stop stop stop stop stop stop stop no no no no no no no no no no

And so he goes on; thus encouraged he goes on; keen to pleasure her more than he has ever pleasured her, he licks and he licks at her, at the unresisting cunt; the beseeching rose; the helpless thing; the infinitely gentle infinitely suffering thing; the cunt he adores. Helpless, careless, Patrick prostrates the Jesuit novice of his body and soul before the God that commands; the cunt far above him; the despotic tyrant; as she says:
— Oh Patch stop oh Patch stop oh Patch stop

He can sense her wetness inside; taste it; he stares; he loves her, he hates himself for loving her; he hates her for making him love her; he hates this cunt that transfixes them all, this source of all joy; this computer game he cannot win, this inescapable fate; this Aztec goddess, this heathen idol with its feathers and fur: this beautiful horrible thing that he stares at rapt and adoring like, like, like, like Ruskin staring at the narthex of St Mark's Cathedral.
— Stop stop stop – she is breathing near orgasmically, the words running on – stop stop stop stop

— Did she at any point say – Gregory's eyes narrow – 'Stop'?
— No
— You expect the court to believe that . . . that despite everything we've heard . . . she at no point said . . . 'stop'?
— That's right
— Really?
— Yes – Patrick stands back a few inches and stares at the ceiling counting the ceiling tiles and then he says again – She didn't say stop, ever
— So what happened next?

— We had sex. On the floor
— Just like that
— Yes, she was wet. She wanted it
   Gregory smiles; stands stiffer; says:
— Could you repeat that for the court, a little louder?
   Patrick shrugs; wondering what Gregory's about; whether Gregory is actually as crap as he appears to be; Patrick says:
— I said . . . she was wet. She wanted it
   Gregory:
— Thank you.
   Patrick feels like saying 'no problem', but doesn't. He stays silent as Gregory stoops to read something from some scattered papers; hand hanging from black gown lapel as seemingly taught at lawyers' RADA, Gregory then looks up with an air of resolution and says:
— So at what point did you say . . . – Gregory does a special I'm-quoting-now face – 'I'm not going to leave until you let me fuck you?'
   Patrick stares at Gregory's left ear, just visible under the wig. Patrick:
— I didn't
   Gregory appears to flinch with amazement:
— You didn't??
— No
— Not once?
— Nope

— I'm not going to leave until you let me fuck you
   Rebecca looks up at him. Her face is impassive, her cheek twitching slightly. She looks at him with her head back on the carpet looking at him. He gazes down, and thinks. How he loves her moorland peat-pool brown eyes, so wet, so wide, so glistening dark.
   Full of love and desire Patrick looks at her gorgeous blonde hair; he has to run his fingers through it one more time, one more time. Doing this, one more dance of his hands in the hair that he loves, Patrick craves to sleep now, to fall asleep in her hair, to lose consciousness surrounded by the scent of her loveable otherness. Stooping his face to her face Patrick breathes her scent, her warmth, her youth and aliveness, and it makes him want to stop because it is too good. Too good. So he pulls his nearly crying face away; feeling the wet of her cunt dry on his lips . . .

Patrick bites his lip because he doesn't quite understand. The juices are drying on his lips; his kisses are now dry on her breasts; the sad sad song of love is playing endlessly in his drunken head as he opens her unresisting legs, as he holds himself and then he enters the place he misses, the happy family he never had, the coralline exhibit at that museum where his dad took him. And now he is inside her. He is sailing out the harbour on that sunny day. She is the wind in his hair, the sun in his eyes, she is him as a seven-year-old with his dad tousling his hair and jesus oh jesus oh Rebecca oh Rebecca ohRebec oh my father and mother

— I got carpet burns
— That's why you went upstairs?
— Yes
— Where you continued to rape her
— No
— Could you explain to the court what happened next . . . – Heavy-duty emphasis – In your own words . . .
— We went upstairs
— Did you push her?
— No
— Did you drag her?
— No
— You're saying she went of her own accord?
— Yes
— She didn't struggle at all?
— No
— At what point did you ask her – Gregory's eyes are open and yet half shut – To . . . – He stoops and seems to read from some paper – To . . . 'lick the cunt off my cock'
— I didn't. I never said that

— Lick my cock
Rebecca shakes her head, dumbly, like a child. She is on the bed naked and beautiful and his: already fucked. Patrick's knees are hurting. He looks at her and puts his hand in her hair; he fists the hair and drags her face to his cock and forces her face next and around; then he feels the gorgeous

wetness and warmth as her lovely-soft mouth opens and yields and is all around. But it is too good: he nearly shudders straight into orgasm, so he has to pull her face away. Away.

Loving, angry, grateful, he looks down at her face, puts her face back round his cock. She is sucking him. Suck suck suck like the endless tireless sea on the shale of his lust; his manliness; his helpless rocky promontory. Mute, he looks down, sees the sea of femininity that will always win, will always erode, will always destroy. Some reason Patrick thinks of his night-club. Of his dad. Feels like crying; that sailing holiday. And God she is beautiful. Yanking Rebecca's face away he looks with curiosity at her face and yes it is the face of an angel, a Botticelli angel with golden curls. So serene. When he slaps her, she just smiles. Ohyesohyes. How much he loves the altarpiece-gold of her hair, loves the beauty of it all. He would buy this painting if he could. Angel Sucking Cock, Unattrib., 1567. Naked Girl on Marylebone Bed, oil on wood, 1450.

And her breasts! Patrick looks, exulting, marvelling. He is stupidly happy to be near those naked breasts. They make him happy; and anxious. He reaches for her silent sullen nakedness again, pulls her by the ankle next to him; hard and angry he slaps apart her thighs, but she just yawns with silent pleasure as he parts the softness and enters again.

Angel In Orgasm, fresco, 1247.

— She came
— You claim she . . . orgasmed?
— Yes
— How do you know?
— I'd been going out with her for a year – Flattening his voice – You get to know

Gregory looks at Patrick and says:
— You're not telling the truth are you?
— Yes I am
— This is a complete pack of lies, isn't it?
— No
— This is a complete and utter fabrication, isn't it?
Christ, Patrick sighs, *what's this? How crap is this?*

Patrick folds his arms and tilts his head and then wonders if this looks arrogant and cocky, so he unfolds them and says again:

— No it's not lies. It's the truth

Gregory nods curtly. He takes a piece of paper from his junior and scans it, puts the paper back on the blonde-wood tabletop next to his clear plastic half-litre bottle of Evian water, and says:

— If we can recap a little

Patrick shrugs. Gregory:

— At no point did you call her a 'Jewish cunt'?

— No

— At no point did she say 'stop', or 'no', or 'go away'?

— No

— At no point did you force her to fellate you?

— No

— Nor did you – Gregory scans the courtroom quickly, looks back at Patrick – Nor did you ever use the terms 'bitch' or 'slut' or 'tart'?

— No

— Nor did you drag her upstairs or throw her onto the bed or anything like that?

— No . . .

— So you claim you didn't rape her?

Big sigh, big breath, Patrick raises his chin a fraction and also looks at the jury and says as loudly and defiantly as he can:

— I didn't rape her

— No further questions

Gregory has sat down. The lawyer's conclusion is so abrupt Patrick opens and shuts his mouth. Patrick feels like shouting: *no further questions? Ask me how she liked it! Why she liked it! Please!*

— I'd like to ask something

Stefan has risen. Patrick feels relief. The interrogative Gestapoid light on Patrick's face has been switched off and now he is gazing at the friendly, smiling face of his own lawyer. Cleverly, professionally, Stefan is lobbing him questions, easy questions, patball stuff. Relaxing, Patrick answers them clearly and lucidly, these questions about his and Rebecca's love life, their sex life, their home life. Then, just as he is getting in the swing of things, Stefan nods at him to step down.

Obedient, silent, Patrick starts walking around the courtroom, back to the dock. As Patrick paces from the box to the dock Stefan turns to the judge and says he has no wish to call any more defence witnesses. So the judge says they might as well hear the concluding statements, as they still have an hour and a half before lunch. So Stefan stands up and makes his statement.

In the dock, slightly bemused by the pace of it all, Patrick props a chin on a fist and listens intently:

Bruises, doctor, consent, sex games, school dress, betrayal, never . . .

Stefan sits down; Gregory stands up. Gregory makes his statement. Patrick feels exhausted, totally drained of life and energy. Almost fatalistic and resigned. But he still listens as Gregory turns his verbal tricks:

Alcohol, ordeal, police, protect, tragedy, condemn, punish . . .

Patrick sits and listlessly stares up and counts the ceiling tiles. They are arranged in grids of eleven by eight. Gregory sits down. There are twelve brackets supporting the public gallery above. The judge is now doing his own summing up. Patrick looks at the clock as it ticks the minutes, he tries to estimate how wide the clock is – ten inches, fourteen? – as the judge does his speech:

Assess, balance, believe, consent, reckless, alcohol, sex games, corroboration, unanimous.

Quiet, sad, Patrick stares at his shoes and thinks about his dad's funeral. He breathes in and out as the jury is dismissed to consider the verdict. One by one the jury departs; then the clerks file out, the journalists scamper out, other people disperse. Almost alone, now, Patrick finds himself staring at the face of Stefan, a foot from the dock. The courtroom is otherwise deserted . . .

— OK how did I do?

Patrick steps out of the dock. Stefan throws an arm around and says:

— I think . . . pretty good

— *Pretty good?*

— Yes. Don't worry

— Oh sure

— It's out of our hands anyway

— Hm . . .

— Really, try and think of other stuff

— But – Patrick looks at Stefan like Stefan is his dad; they walk towards the courtroom door – But . . .

Stefan once more grips Patrick's shoulder; says:

— I never guarantee anything, Patrick, you know that

— So . . . ?

— I think you did pretty well

— Really?
— But just remember juries are funny things
— OK ... OK ...
— Best get a cup of coffee. You know you can't leave the building ...
you know that; right?
— ... Yes ...

Patrick tries to smile and nod but his head is hung too low. Stefan lets go of his shoulder as they single file through the door and out into the echoey marble lobby.

Outside in the cooler air of the Edwardian atrium the sound of cellphone conversation surrounds them as Stefan turns and goes. Patrick also turns, and walks, alone, upstairs. He walks up stairs and more stairs and finds himself in the Old Bailey canteen, where journos with laptops and tabloids are sitting around a crisp-packet-strewn table, laughing. Some of them look at him. Patrick feels very very alone. He goes and sits down at a table and tries to twiddle his thumbs. *Ridiculous: why do people twiddle their thumbs?* Getting up again, trying to ignore the adrenaline surging through his system and the awful gut-killing tension in his heart and lights, Patrick approaches the metal tray-slide of the counter. *Steak pie? Beef crisps? Choc bar? Suicide?*

Turning from the unhelpful choice Patrick paces to the door and as he does he looks at his watch and is surprised to see that half an hour has passed. Where did it go? Pushing the glass and cheap wood of the canteen door he walks to the steps and leaps the steps, trying to be youthful and careless. Then he wanders some corridors for a while. List Office. Robe Room. Press Office. Jury Members Canteen.

Done with corridors and people looking at him suspiciously, Patrick turns a left and a right and he finds himself in a huge marble round place underneath the main Old Bailey dome. Tiled in a vaguely Byzantine way to the ceiling of the dome is a series of admonitory and elevating mosaics; gold inscriptions; mottoes. Patrick swivels about as he reads the old inscription in tiny mosaic tiles: **Right Lives By Law, Law Consists In Power, Praise The Cause In Justice Equal Scales**.

An hour and a quarter, an hour and a half. Still feeling his heart pounding, Patrick leans his cheek to the cool of the marble wall and swallows and goes into a form of reverie.

Two hours, two and a quarter hours.

Sitting down now, Patrick rubs his face. Two and a half hours have elapsed while he's just stared out of the window at the cloudy summer sky, at the hint of rain to come.

— **All parties in Skivington to Court Eighteen!**

OK . . . OK. Rifle, kit bag, bayonet. Standing back from the window, thrusting back, Patrick wills himself across the tiled marble floor and down the steps to the floor of his court; he sees the journalists going into the court, the lawyers, the hangers-on, the policemen; some of them notice him and they step back to let him pass, like he is the Oscar-winning star at the press conference; momentarily famous he passes between and he enters the courtroom, where, after a flurry of nods and whispers and policewoman's coughs the jury foreman is standing in his unevolved leather jacket listening to the clerk of the court. As she intones:

— Have you reached a verdict on which you are all agreed?

The jury foreman says . . . Yes. Patrick's heart is doing jazz percussion. The clerk nods and makes a note somewhere, and then she says:

— Do you find the defendant guilty or . . . not guilty?

A pause. Patrick stares at the momentarily silent, note-reading foreman. Patrick balls his fists, and stares, and thinks . . . *Go on then. Get it over with, send me down then; go on. Please. Now. Just make it all go away, get it finished.*

Because after all, Patrick decides, *because after all they are probably right anyway, all of them: I'm just another one, just another man, just another one of them, another you-know-what-they're-like.*

Right?

Right. I'm just another racist, another Klansman, another Serb in the bedroom, the General Pinochet of foreplay, aren't I? Aren't I?

Yes I am. Yes. Yes I am. Yes I am yes I AM. I'm just another Loyalist psycho, another moustachio'd heavy, another secret policeman with a penchant for the cattle prod; I'm just another swamp-dwellin baccy-chewing nigger-baitin unterfuckingmenschen rapo with a clawhammer.

The foreman opens his mouth. Speaks.

Two Years Later

26

Staring at her own brown eyes, Rebecca winces, and looks away. Stuck in her old room, listening to the sounds of the house, to the summer breeze in the sycamores outside, Rebecca looks across at her cigarette balanced on the edge of her dressing table. Taking the cigarette, she smokes and exhales, and then balances the cigarette again; then she gazes back into her old dressing table-mirror.

The mirror reflects herself reflecting on herself. Leaning forward Rebecca wonders. She analyses, scrutinises: tries to make out what her face says about herself, her life. Has she got older, because? Her eyes do still seem the same, soft brown; her cheekbones are still emphasised by the rouge of youth, maybe. But her complexion is definitely paler; paler because no longer marked, not any more, no longer reddened and violeted by his love . . . maybe . . .

A slight tremor in her hand makes Rebecca drop the hand that had been touching her cheek; she lets the hand fall to her lap, and gazes around her old room: her old bedroom. She has not slept here in so long and for the second or third time this day she feels that this place is no longer where she will ever truly sleep again: it is no longer her ultimate domicile, the default option, home.

It has been emptied: of her. On the walls are square, lighter-coloured spaces where her art posters used to be, on the shelves are dusty rectangles that mark the slots where her feminist textbooks used to slide. She has been moved out, thrown out, under the pretext of redecoration. And so Rebecca turns, and thinks, her lips slightly ashine in the setting sun slanting through the window; and so she remembers: this is the bed where she used to be in love, where they used to make love, her and Patch, when his chin stubble was abrasive on her inner thighs, when their hands used to interlock like the branches of trees in a wind, when he used to stuff her Paddington Bear between her lips to muffle her orgasm, making them both laugh so much afterwards she woke up her parents, anyway.

Rebecca picks up the Paddington Bear. Puts it down. She remembers when she came: with him. When she came she used to talk, to babble, she used to make those weird noises. Rebecca recalls this. He would always claim she came in German, long long incomprehensible compound words with lots of Ks and Ichs. This, she would assert, was due to her Yiddish heritage. And when she said this he used to say *yum* and lick the rise of her stomach and call her cunt his little ghetto, his adorable Shtetl, *the squalid slums of beautiful Krakow* . . .

Remembering this now Rebecca remembers how much she used to love Patrick for this: how he was always exciting and wrong, at the same time: like sex, indeed. His charming tongue. Sometimes he used to positively *schmooze* her cunt . . .

Feeling tired, gloomy, Rebecca picks up the cigarette from its nearly-burning-the-dressing-table situation and sticks it between her thick red lips: where she lets it dangle from her mouth, Ute Lemperishly. Again she stares into the mirror at her unbruised, bitemarkless face. *The face he loved, bit, slapped, kissed: a million times.*

Whatever. It's hot: too hot. Standing, moving, creaking the window fully open to the cooler air Rebecca leans in her summer dress, and gazes out over the perfect hush of the evening Suburb. Suntanned elbow on a wooden windowsill she surveys the fake arcadia of her childhood: the red-slate mansard roofs, the artfully lichened walls, the redbrick Arts and Crafts cottages, the neo-Queen-Anne chimney stacks, the butterflies fluttering through the lime-tree-scented air to Little Wood.

The sun is going down; the kids are coming out. Leaning further into the still-hot humid summer night air Rebecca sees and hears a shiny new racing green BMW roadster throttling down Meadway. The car is being driven by a laughing Jewish *principessa* with too many bracelets waving to a boy in a Fiat. Brushing a coil of blonde from her eyes Rebecca squints to espy and recognise the girl's face but as the car revs to the distance Rebecca is distracted by the numberplate of the car: 8EEN.

8EEN?

Eight-een. Of course. Eighteen Years Old and driving her eighteenth birthday present. Of course.

And *only here* Rebecca thinks. Only in the Suburb; this Beverly Hills with crow's step gables. Only in this cradle of the cul de sac; this place where nothing bad could ever happen. Except what happened.

Rebecca muses. She has always found this place, the Suburb of her youth and upbringing, reassuringly prosperous, luxuriantly safe, somehow uterine. Today, staring across the roofs and gardens and bay windows to the cod-medieval town walls of Hampstead Heath boundary, she finds it claustrophobic and unbearable. A prison by Ruskin and Morris. Rebecca wishes fervently there were a great big motorway running through it, a great big tube station right in the middle of Central Square. If only.

Through the window Rebecca sees 8EEN again, reversing backwards and taking a different route. Then she sees a Jewish guy with skullcap and two corgis resting against a wall. Fuzzy white stuff is riding the air. Clover drifts from the Heath; scents of grass cuttings.

This scent breathed in, Rebecca is brought back, perforce, to a memory. This is the smell of her A levels. Of being 8EEN. This lovely cut-grass cologne perfuming the streets is the smell of hot afternoons with no more exams, those wonderful nothing-to-do days at the end of her upper sixth when she and her friends would spill out of school. When they'd skip laughing through the grey-and-redbrick portals of Henrietta Barnett's and run to where Murphy had parked; where they'd lean their bare arms on the hot metal of Murphy's driverside door and gossip, and chat, and wonder whether to walk down the road to Rebecca's to raid the fridge for juice and white peaches, or jump in the car and shoot off to the Freemason's Arms.

They were her best friends; Murphy was her best friend; Murphy was the very best of friends. Sitting back at her dressing table Rebecca picks up the cigarette and gauntly inhales a last Rebecca-full of her Marlboro and then stubs the cigarette in the empty cigarette packet and chucks the packet in a bin.

Stretching out a long soft arm, tanned apart from a white band where her watch should be, Rebecca plucks a photo of her and Murphy from where it was stuck in the frame of the mirror. Other photos of her on holiday, of her parents, she ignores; Rebecca takes instead the photo of her and Murphy and holds it up to view. With a pang Rebecca wishes most of all she could talk to her best friend. But she can't; she feels too guilty. So she can't. Not yet, at least . . .

— Re ye si gu

— *Ca ye su gi*

Her parents are arguing downstairs. Rebecca can tell they are arguing because they are trying to keep their voices unnaturally quiet. And not succeeding. From two floors up Rebecca can hear her father's weak and languid vowels, can sense her mother's shrill aggressive silences. Then Rebecca hears a pause, of true silence, then perhaps a footfall, on the stairs. Holding still, Rebecca listens hard, wondering if her mother or father are going to climb the stairs, to come and see her, to come and ask her the troublesome things: why she hasn't had a job for two years. Why she hasn't moved out the flat. Why she's done this, that, and . . . The Other Thing.

But no. Her parents are not coming, it seems. All there is is the breeze, riffling the photo. It is an evening breeze: true evening must be falling. Breathing in the base notes from the open airy window, the barbecue smells and monoxidey pollen, Rebecca looks around; then she sighs and falls back onto her bed, where she lies and surveys the ceiling. Silent and thoughtful Rebecca watches a shaft of car light slide across the darkness, as a car goes by with voices laughing. Rebecca watches, and hears, in quiet. She wants a cigarette, she wants to forget. The sense of summer-night London *en fête* around her, just outside the window, only compounds her isolated sadness, her melancholy apprehension, only makes her remember the nights. The nights like these. When he would throw her white body onto the bed, her body a stripe of white car light across the bed.

Patrick?

Patrick.

Laid on the bed, Rebecca opens her lips, so as to silently pronounce his name to the ceiling, to the window, to the wall of her bedroom, to the last Klee print thereon, next to where her MOMA poster was. Laid here, laid out, Rebecca thinks of him, what made him, the taste of him, the taste of her on him. She thinks of the garlic and oil that they were: the sweet mayonnaise: the aioli of her cunt on his fingers that he force-fed her to stop her crying his name to the ceiling: aioli, aioli, eloi, elohim. Patch.

Patch?

Rebecca picks up her ringing mobile phone; it says MURPHY.

Murphy? Please not. Rebecca doesn't want to talk to Murphy; she hasn't spoken to Murphy in weeks; the last person she wants to speak to now is Murphy. Thinning her lips, Rebecca presses a button on the phone, deadens the ringing noise, then flops back on the bed and thinks about Patrick.

Where is he now? She wonders where. What is he doing now? Is he suffering, tense, sad, thinking of her with grief? With regret and anger? Is he thinking of her as she thinks of him now?

Reaching for her favourite old hairbrush from her bedside table Rebecca sits up, and brushes her hair, brushing the sadness of Patrick from her still-long hair, brushing and brushing, as she gazes out of the leaded window half open to the air. Then Rebecca checks the watch her father gave her; replaces the brush on the wood. On a new whim she gets up, crosses her room, goes to the place where her old textbooks are boxed in cardboard boxes ranked alongside the wall: ready for some familial move she does not quite understand, appreciate, care to consider.

Crouching nearer the boxes Rebecca reaches in the first box and takes out a history of the Renaissance. Then a monograph on Bosch; a book of Victorian photographs. Then Rembrandt, Hockney, the Venetian Renaissance. One book gains closer attention: holding the book in her hand Rebecca gazes at the cover: it is a reprint of one of Hockney's swimming pool paintings. What does this remind her of? It reminds her of . . .

The pool party! Gazing into the blue of the picture Rebecca closes her eyes and sways on her crouching thighs as she holds the book and pictures: yes, of course, what else: she can see Patrick's eyes of chlorinated blue: blue behind his laughing fringe, his unshaved chin, his sweet dark hair roughly but lovably tousled. At the pool party.

Patrick. Patrick. Patrick. Patrick. Too much. Too much. Too much.

Half slumped, Rebecca tries to distract, not to think about it, tomorrow, about the law, the police, it all. Flicking through and down the piles of books Rebecca knows, however, it is inevitable. Everything here, everything now, everything she sees will remind her of him; of what she's done; of what they did; of whether she's done the right thing.

Rebecca cocks her head, and listens, listens to the oh-so-slow-to-wind-down clock of sadness still ticking in her head.

Pat-rick, Pat-rick, Pat-rick.

Fresh cigarette between her lips, Rebecca lights, draws, inhales gauntly. Marlboro-ing her cheekbones as she inhales, she nostrils two plumes of blue Virginia sadness down into the second cardboard box.

She has found and stopped at another book. *Against Our Will*. By Susan Brownmiller. It is a book on rape. It is her book of rape. It is *the* book on rape.

But of course.

Sighing, wryly smoking, Rebecca takes up and opens the once-famous book on rape. Riffling the pages Rebecca remembers how she read and reread this book when she was seventeen, eighteen, nineteen. This after all was the book she liked above all other feminist texts, this was the ancient feminist primer she pressed closest to her heart, this book on rape was the old book on rape she thought she had most understood and knew and truly learned from.

Until Patrick.

The old Penguin paperback flattened under one hand, on one crouching knee, Rebecca flicks through the pages as she smokes with the other hand.

The pages send her. The writing spins her. Reading once more the well-wrought text, the serious but sensuous tenor, the exhilarating scholasticism, the intense but feminine intelligence of this book that Rebecca now remembers so well makes Rebecca wince: at the book's determined naiveté, its wilful innocence, its brilliant simplisticness. Rebecca feels outrage at herself: how could she have bought this so totally? Rebecca winces again. This book was the reason for a lot: was the reason Rebecca became studious and feminist, not least. And now? Rebecca flicks, reads and exhales smoke over the paperback pages: yes the book is well written; yes it was necessary; yes it made her, Rebecca, a better more self-aware young woman. But was the book ever *right*? Ever as right as it thought?

Stopping, checking, Rebecca moves from a crouch to a kneel to sitting flat on the carpet as she loses herself in her old self that loved this old book, her little red book. Rebecca is remembering, realising. Reading the annotations in the margins of this book makes Rebecca sadly conjecture how long it has been since she cared so much she used to write in book margins.

Then one phrase catches Rebecca's eye. On page twenty-seven, she reads

No zoologist, as far as I know, has ever observed that animals ever rape in their natural habitat, the wild.

Vff, Rebecca thinks. Mpfff. Tapping a tarry chunk of left-to-burn ciga-rette ash into a bin, Rebecca takes and inhales and smokes and holds smoke, and then exhales, and sits back, and thinks about this. Yes, she understands why a Seventies feminist might say this. Might allege that

No zoologist, as far as I know, has ever observed that animals ever rape in their natural habitat, the wild

because she understands the thinking behind it. Even if she didn't have A levels in Philosophy and Law, an MA in Feminism and Art, and a PhD in Aspects of Aztec Mythology, Rebecca thinks she would know and understand the necessity of thinking this particular thought. She sees. She sees it is necessary for Brownmiller to believe that rape is not found in nature, that

No zoologist has ever observed that animals ever rape in their natural habitat, the wild

because Brownmiller could not otherwise support her central thesis: that rape is uniquely human, uniquely horrid, uniquely organised and wilful, that men are uniquely rape-intent, singularly sexist, are biologi-cally unique in their oppressive and predatory sexuality, and that rape is . . . is what? . . .

Rebecca checks the blurb for the famous phrase; finds it. On the back of the paperback she reads that

Rape is nothing more or less than a conscious process of intimidation by which all men keep all women in a state of fear

Cogitating on this, more-than-thinking, Rebecca smokes, taps, smokes, and half listens: listening to the minicabs in the street outside, listening to the minicabs offloading giggling summer-night partygoers. Then she is struck with a thought.

But is it true? *No rape in the wild?*

Rebecca remembers something, a book she still has: a book on animals and evolution Patrick once gave her, to settle an argument they were having. *Yes.* Seized with her old scholastic glee, the thrill of the intellectual chase, the feeling she used to have researching Late Titian, Frankish Chronicles, Medieval Misogyny as Evidenced by East Anglian Witch Trials, Rebecca returns to the first cardboard box, searches through, and with a sigh of satisfaction takes out the book she remembered.

Biological Exuberance. Animal Homosexuality and Natural Diversity.

Smartly Rebecca starts filleting the book. She does not have to search for long: a few pages from where she begins, she comes to the section headlined 'The Chimp'. In 'The Chimp' she reads that, in Chimps,

> *sexual relations are less than amicable: males occasionally try to force females to consort and mate with them by threatening and even violently attacking them*

So? Rebecca nods, stubs out her cigarette, nods, lights yet another. As she does she wonders: did she ever used to smoke like this? Not caring to answer her own question Rebecca seeks out the section on the Orang-utan. What about the Orang-utan?

Rebecca finds the page, she reads that, in the Orang-utan

> *heterosexual relations are sometimes characterised by aggression and violence rather than pleasure and consensuality. Young males often chase, harass and rape females. During such interactions, which may account for the majority of copulations in some populations, the male may grab, slap, bite, and forcibly restrain the female, who struggles violently while screaming and whimpering*

A pause; Rebecca smokes. She blows a semi-smoke ring at the wall and returns to the book. She reads that in the Savannah baboon

> *Hamadryas males often threaten and attack females, biting them on the neck to prevent them from leaving the group. Adult male Savannah baboons sometimes rape younger females*

Nodding, absorbing, Rebecca turns pages and reads that in the Bonnet Macaque

Nineteen per cent of sex is non-consensual

and that in the Pig-tailed Macaque

Forty-eight per cent of homosexual mounts between females are non-consensual.

She reads that in the Squirrel Monkey

females often form group of COALITIONS during the mating season to chase off males who are pursuing unwilling females

and that gangs of male Bottlenose Dolphins have been known to

harass adult females, chasing, herding and even 'kidnapping' and attacking them (e.g. with charges, bites, tail slaps, and body slams) in an attempt to mate with them.

Rebecca stops; pauses; listens. She listens to her father listening to Mahler downstairs. Then Rebecca stoops her head and keeps reading. She reads that during mating, Northern Elephant Seals

routinely bite, pin down, and slam the full weight of their bodies against females (bulls are five to eleven times heavier than females)

and that, in the same species

a female may be pursued by groups of males as she leaves the rookery, sometimes being raped three to seven times as she tries to escape.

Paging on, she reads about Wild Cheetahs, where

adult males try to mount their mothers

and about the Peach-faced Lovebird, where

there is considerable sexual antagonism between the sexes in heterosexual pairs

as well as Grey Squirrels, where during

mating chases, as many as thirty-four males may pursue and harass a single female

She then reads about Snow Geese, which take part in

gang rapes

where

males gather together in large 'spectator' groups – sometimes containing as many as twenty to eighty males – to watch and perhaps even join in

and little Anna's Hummingbird where

males pursue females in high-speed chases and sometimes even strike them in mid-air, forcing them down in order to copulate . . .

The book is nearly done, nearly finished. Only the section on Insects remains. Filing through these last pages, Rebecca comes upon genus *Panorpa*, the Japanese Scorpionfly. First she reads that, in the Scorpionfly

female body design has selected for elaborated male genitals because females have desired increasing amounts of vaginal stimulation through ever larger areas of physical contact . . .

and then she reads that 'forced copulation' in the Scorpionfly

is in no way abnormal or 'aberrant' behaviour, it is an aspect of the evolved behavioural repertoire of individual males that is widespread among species of the genus **Panorpa***.*

*　　*　　*

Cigarette done, Mahler finished, book shut, Rebecca takes the book and drops it back in the box; then she gets up off her legs and crosses the floor to the window, and creaks the window further open. She is keen to lay the yashmak of cool air across her face, keen to enjoy the soothing mantilla of the night breeze.

The stars, the headlights, the gloaming.

Rebecca wonders.

She wonders that if . . . if all; if . . .

She wonders: where does all this leave her? Does this leave her anywhere particularly different? Does this mean she's done the right thing? Maybe, maybe not, maybe it doesn't. Standing at the window, Rebecca calms herself, as she tries to work it through. Just because every animal is guilty, she thinks, every animal a sinner, every animal worthy of prison, or worse, that does not exonerate her ex-boyfriend. Does it? No. Rebecca decides. It does; it doesn't. Just because Brownmiller was wrong in this does not mean Brownmiller was wrong overall. Right? Wrong? What?

Right, Rebecca thinks, right. Just because Patrick is a Grizzly Bear, a Pronghorn Stag, a Bull Elephant Seal, that does not release him from responsibility for what he did.

But then, Rebecca thinks, if Patrick *is* just a Mohol, a Bonobo, a Hanuman Langur, what, and why, and where; where does that leave her? Standing in the windowed streetlight, Rebecca wonders, almost aloud, she almost mouths to the street, the warm summer-night air: then what was I, Patrick, was I your Anna's Hummingbird, your Peach-Faced Lovebird, your Aztec Parakeet?

Or was I genus *Panorpa*? Your Scorpionfly?

A knock at the door: it is Rebecca's mother.

Rebecca looks up as her mother puts her head around. Something about the way her mother looks as if she is trying not to look intrusive and careworn makes Rebecca think her mother is about to broach The Subject.

Sure enough:

— Um, Rebecca . . .

— Mum?

— About tomorrow . . . – With a careworn sigh her mother sits on the bed next to her eldest, blondest, once-most-favoured daughter; then Rebecca's mother says – I was . . . well . . .

— Go on Mum

— Well um . . . we all know . . . roughly why you . . . did it

— Why I withdrew the charges?

— Yes

— *So . . . ?*

— Well of course um darling we know *why* – Obviously struggling – It's just that when . . . the police come round tomorrow to interview you you really don't want to . . .

— What, Mum? Incriminate myself? Tell them I lied? *What?*

— Yes well yes . . .

— Oh, *Mum*

The two of them are six inches apart on the bed; Rebecca wishes she were in Edinburgh. Far far away, far away from all this. There is a pained silence; then Rebecca's mother seems to abandon any pretence; she looks at her daughter's Klee poster and says, loudly, to the wall:

— Why *did* you do it, Rebecca? If you still think he's guilty? Why? Why do that to all of us? Why put us through this?

— Because. You know why

— Tell me again!

— Because he got life, Mum, Patrick got *life imprisonment*. I wasn't remotely expecting *that*

— But . . . – Rebecca's mother's eyes are still on the poster – But that was because of his previous convictions . . . and anyway that's nothing to do with you, darling – Rebecca goes to stand up, to get far away, but her mother puts a restraining hand on her arm – No, Rebecca, darling, listen, is it because of those letters he sent you? All that pleading? Is it because you still love him? What is it? *Tell me!*

Forcing herself free of her mother's hardening grasp, Rebecca rises. Then she goes barefoot to the window and stares at the road where 8EEN was. The evening is enclosing. Rebecca looks at the orange and charcoal of the sky; the westwards view across town; the black needle of Highgate Church. Her mother is still bleating from the bed:

— You know they're letting him out of prison tomorrow

— I know, Mum, that's why I'm here

— What do you think he'll do? Then? Mmm? Come here? Come to see you? With a thank you present? *Rebecca?*

—Mum ... – Rebecca leans further out the window, speaks to the polleny air – I don't care. He didn't deserve life in prison. That's all. Whatever he deserved ... he didn't ... deserve that

A door slams. The mother has gone. Rebecca turns to the night air, to feel the mourning veils of night air so cool on her face. Her eyes shut, Rebecca listens to the distant car music.

27

Later, shifting listless about her room, Rebecca listens to her parents doing their evening things, moving around the echoey house: she can hear her mother sorting stuff into the dishwasher; her father switching off the TV and selecting some music. Then a tap being turned; a kettle being boiled; two quiet phone calls taken one after the other. In her room Rebecca's breathing is one with the mild breeze brought by her open casement window; the warm summer wind is bringing the Heath into the house.

Opening her eyes Rebecca hears: again: her mother's voice from the hall: raised, tense, wired; the voice is answered by her father's lower, softer, equally indistinct tones. A phone clicks up, and then down, and then the conversation resumes. Rebecca cannot quite hear what they are talking about but she thinks she knows they are talking about her: she can just about make out the words: *tomorrow, the police, Patrick, Rebecca.*

What else is there to talk about?

Her sudden retraction. Her change of heart. Her emancipation and exoneration of her rapist ex-boyfriend. Her ineffable stupidity; her incomparable selfishness.

The house is quieter. Rebecca can hear Richard Strauss and her parents' urgent murmuring. Feeling the cool air blown in through her open window, Rebecca strains to listen. She hears her parents move from hall to sitting room to kitchen, still conversing, still debating. She hears them both pause at the foot of the stairs and talk in hushed tones;

and this time she can hear the phrase 'shall we tell her?' After that she hears her father's slow unurgent footsteps, as he climbs the stairs, crosses the landing, approaches the door to her bedroom.

Tensed, alert, agonised, Rebecca waits. Her father is standing on the landing outside her room. Rebecca stares at the blankness of her bedroom door. Her drying eyes do not blink; she stares at the door, staring hard, as if with effort she can see through, see her father standing beyond. Rebecca wonders what her corduroy-wearing oh-so-diffident Anglo-Jewish father is thinking; perhaps he is thinking about his daughter's shameful and embarrassing retraction. Perhaps he is thinking about the possibility of Rebecca's being charged with wasting police time. Perhaps he is thinking about replacing the landing carpet.

Whatever her father wants to tell her, Rebecca doesn't want to hear. She is glad when her father seems, typically, to change his mind; when she hears him turn and pace downstairs again.

So?

So: enough: get out. Taking a pair of sandals from under her bed Rebecca kicks back a heel and slips her sandal on; she sits down on the bed to shoe the other foot; then she picks up a bag filled with her keys, some money, her mobile phone, and she gently nudges open the door.

Judging by the subdued noises, Rebecca's mother and father are now watching TV in the distant kitchen. Quietly Rebecca shuts her old bedroom door and descends the stairs into the hallway darkness; quietly she opens the front door, steps outside, clicks the front door shut behind. Then she walks into the hush and the aromas of the garden, stepping between the trees, between the sweet deep throats of the night flowers.

Rebecca walks on, out of the garden, down the lamplit road, past the redbrick walls of the Heath boundary, and onto the Heath extension. Here, the moon shines over the yew trees; here cars are parading down the distant roads, their lights turning slowly like pairs of lanterns carried by dancers in a distant gavotte. Rebecca watches them as she pauses at the edge of the grassland, as she gathers her courage like her cardigan around her shoulders. Slowly she walks across the dark urban meadows, smelling that smell of cricket matches, cut rye grass, lime trees, summer-evenings-when-she-was-a-girl. *It is good to be out of the house; to leave behind . . .*

At the road Rebecca stalls; cars and bikes pass up and down. Rebecca waits. The evening traffic is doing things in a leisurely way; the traffic is heavy and persistent. Rebecca watches a police car, a tee-shirted girl on the back of her boyfriend's motorbike, a council cleaning truck full of shirtless men; then she sees a space between and she crosses the road and re-enters the Heath; the Heath *proper*.

Now she is near Kenwood, near the rhododendron lanes, although their colours of red and pale violet and purple are bleached away by the darkness. Rebecca crosses through the colourless groves and takes another path into the oakwoods.

There, then, somewhere out there, Rebecca senses a bush rustling; through the gloom she spies a figure. Blithe, benign, seduced by the tranquil warmth of the evening, Rebecca follows the figure with her idle gaze; it is a man, disappearing. Curious, Rebecca looks, and sees another man, following. What?

Wondering if these men are what she thinks they might be, Rebecca passes out of the little wood onto a dais of grass; here she turns and surveys the south and she sees . . .

London. From here Rebecca can see the city stretched out on its carpet of jeweller's velvet. She can see the sweet dark apricot of the city light tinting the sky; she can see the wheels and towers and domes of night-time London, lit up. London is looking like a city ripe for bombing, vulnerably lovely, *en fête*.

Finding a dryish piece of grass Rebecca sits and rests her chin on paired knees and looks out over the spread-out city lights; at her town.

And – yes – all – *the – people*. Rebecca thinks on them. Out there, living, breathing, dying, smiling; all the Londoners. All the Spanish girls in Bradley Street, the Aussie boys in Ealing pubs, the Americans everywhere. Rebecca thinks of them. The Asian girls with pink saris, in Southall dance halls. The murderers lifted away, in Wormwood Scrubs. The skinheads sluicing snakebite in old Chelsea taverns; the clerics eyeing the gold-tooled books in Lambeth Palace library; the E'd-up clubbers funnelling money into Dean Street jukeboxes. Yes, Rebecca sees them all: the Kiwis, the Londoners, the Belgians, the Georgians, the Armenians, the Cockneys, the Welshmen; the Arabs smoking hookahs on Edgware Road; French bankers downing Ferrari cocktails in South Ken; the fighting Irish in the Town & Country; alcoholic Wimbledon housewives opening bottles of Cab Sauv for themselves alone; the

Turks and Cypriots selling smack in late-night Stoke Newington grocers, while black-tasselled Hassidim walk on by.

And Patrick. Amongst them all, Patrick.

Wishing not to feel this, Rebecca walks into the woods again. Through a fence-and-tree bottleneck Rebecca crosses a lawn into a woodier part of the Heath; here the moon is a scatter of silver dollars on the underwood floor, coined by the leaves of the full-summer oak trees. Rebecca smells a scent, hears a noise: some nervous laughter. Her blonde head turned Rebecca sees: another young man, standing by a bush. He is smoking. The cigarette he smokes glows redly, each time he draws, gauntly.

He is a signalling firefly in the cypress groves.

Closely Rebecca watches: sees another man walk across the dim smoky lawns. The second man ignores or fails to see Rebecca: he walks purposefully: towards. Rebecca thinks; sees; watches. She thinks of jaguars, night herons, flamingos, ocelots, parakeets, lyrebirds, roseate terns. She thinks of herself: a night heron winging its way across the waters, across the moonlit ria of life. She thinks of the warped but ineluctable evolutionary urge that forces these men; that drives all these night birds together, towards risky sex, towards beauty and death, towards the head of the salmon river.

The other man has now crossed the short expanse of Hampstead lawn: he has crossed to meet the other younger man, attracted by the insect pheromones of the younger man's smoking. The bleached-out blue of the younger man's collarless shirt somehow matches the show of the younger man's instep inside his chic leather sandals. Rebecca squints at the younger man, his leather sandals; the young man stands by the gloom of the night-time trees: nonchalant, cool, somehow very Noël Cowardesque and Twenties; like he has just returned from a game of long-trousered tennis.

Rebecca squints through the pixilation of her night vision to see the older man wrap his hand around the back of the younger man's head and french him, unshavenly. The younger man vigorously returns this kiss; Rebecca stands wondering whether she should hide herself; whether the two gays have seen her and this sexplay is for her benefit; whether they haven't seen her and this sexplay is for her benefit. In the dark Rebecca just about sees the clutch of a kiss; a white hand go down; the flash of a silver belt buckle. Then Rebecca hears jeans being sloughed; ardent murmurs, laughter. A cigarette is flicked away: spiral-ling red and then nothing. Rooted, Rebecca thinks. So here are the aliens, she thinks, here are the foreigners, here are the Aztecs of North London: with their freaky rituals, their strange cannibalism, their bloody rites: their joyous passing of the desert thorns through their penis-heads.

And as Rebecca watches the older man bend the younger man around and over so as to fuck him, she cannot but think of the gay male sex that she and Patrick used to have: the desperate, cottagey sex they used to have: even when they were safe and private, even when they were alone in her bedroom. Almost whenever they did it they did it like they were stuck in the urinal, like they'd met just then on a train, like the walls were covered with graffiti and blood. She would hoarsely whisper the wrong name; he would french her and thrust her jeans to the grass; she would bend round and let him bugger her, fuck her, whatever, *just do me*.

— She can see us!

— Jesus!

— How long's she been there?

Jaguar eyes pierce the jungle undergrowth; Rebecca has been spotted, and she panics. Should she make a stumbled apology for watching the men's sexplay? Or *what*? Rebecca coughs, a timid cough, as if to convince them she is just standing here accidentally and she has not noticed they are having gay sex; then she hastily backs down the path and backs down some more, stumbling backwards on a tussock, tripping over a trailing root. She hears footsteps behind her; gaining on her. *Gaining*.

But not. At the last she turns, exhales, runs on, and pants out loud as she rounds a copse and steps out and finds herself out on another lawn once more; she listens acutely: the noises behind her have stopped.

A path lies before. Rebecca breathes and breathes easier as she walks the pathway, as a cool breeze from Highgate or Crouch End makes her shiver, makes her wrap the cardigan a little tighter.

Phone?

Rebecca reaches in her handbag and takes out her trilling cellphone. Of course . . .

MURPHY

This time Rebecca answers her phone. She says:

— Yes, hello?

There's a surprised silence at the other end; then Rebecca hears Murphy yelp:
— BEXX?!!
— *Yes?*
— Where have you been we've been Jesus your parents they're freaking
— Murphy . . .
— They're freaking out and I've been trying to get you for weeks and you've not been answering and
— I'm on the Heath. I went for a walk
— Sorry? On the *Heath?*
— Yyyyes
Murphy yelps again:
— Bex you're not, like, going to the flat, are you?
Rebecca pauses, looks at the sky, says:
— No . . . *but why?*
— Just don't go there
— Why? I don't understand
— . . . *He* might be there
— Who, Murphy? *Who?*
— PATRICK!
— *What??*
Surprised, shocked, furiously working this out, Rebecca leans against a metal railing and slowly asks her heavy-breathing friend:
— Murphy . . . please tell me . . . *what* are you talking about?
— Rebecca . . . they told me
— Uhn?
— Your parents, I've just rung them, they told me you dropped the charges
Feeling relief and despair at once, *so it's out, it's known,* Rebecca gets an urge to sit down on the grass, despite the dew. The air is cool. Murphy is gabbling:
— Why Rebecca? Why do that? Why the fucking hell did you do that?
Rebecca thinks, replies:
— I don't want to talk about it
— Oh golly, Bex
— Please
— But why, Becca darling? Fucksake
— *Please??*

— Rebec

— Please!

At last: a pause. Murphy sounds like she is sorting something in her head. Then Rebecca's best friend comes back, still gabbling as fast as before:

— Look anyway, sweetie, it doesn't matter now what matters *is* they've let him out *early*

— Who, Patch?

— Yes! Patrick! They let him out of prison this arvo, today, early, by mistake or something – Still gabbling – And so I think the police rang your folks this evening to tell 'em and when your dad found you'd done a bunk they asked me to ring you and . . .

— So where . . . is *he* . . . then . . . ?

— Where *else*, Bex? He must be going to your flat, no? Where you lived? Where else would he go?

Lifting herself away from the railing, Rebecca walks towards the edge of the Heath, towards Hampstead High Street. Murphy is now burbling on about revenge, about: Patrick, prison, two years, rape law, knives, and who-knows-what-he'll-do. Rebecca listens, half dazed, half distracted with thoughts of her ex. *Patrick? Patrick?!*

Stalled by the weight of traffic, Rebecca stands on the curve of Heath Street, counting the taxi lights, not really listening to Murphy.

Then she hears Murphy say:

— So what the hell did you retract the charges for anyway?

Thinning her lips, Rebecca kills the phonecall; and walks on.

28

The moon is slung low over Rosslyn Hill, a white geisha-face beyond
the skiddy clouds. It is a lamp hung up to show Rebecca the way
downhill towards Belsize. The way she intends to take to their flat,
towards Linden Street.

Why not? Because her phone keeps *ringing*?

Bag down, phone extracted, Rebecca lifts the maddened mobile to
her face and irritatedly reads the read-out. It says MURPHY.

Murphy?

MURPHY . . .

This is the fourth time Rebecca's friend has rung since Rebecca spoke
to Murphy on the Heath. Staring down at her phone, Rebecca watches
her phone ring and flash, ring and flash, hypnotically. What is it
that makes Murphy keep ringing so? Ring, flash, ring, flash, ringring,
flash . . .

Aware that a couple of American tourists with white sneakers and
very pale-blue jeans are watching her as she stands here looking at but
not answering her phone, Rebecca waits for the thing to quit ringing,
then she slips the phone back in her bag, continues walking down the
lamplit High Street, down Hampstead High Street.

The High Street is a George Grosz painting: crowded with drunks
and Jewesses. Girls in lip gloss, sequiny skirts, flip flops and Italian
woollens are standing and smiling sarcastically outside the pizzeria;
boys in expensive loafers and cotton strides are getting off on the girlfriends' sardonic laughter. Further on, a fey English boy with a black

rucksack is standing beside a Coke sign written in Arabic as he squints at couples eating red stuff with pitta bread on tables set up outside the Moroccan restaurant.

Stepping around a young Hispanic drunk kid, who is standing on a red and wickerwork faux-French-café chair so as to abuse his equally Hispanic friend, Rebecca looks inside the open doors of the faux-French café and sees drunk German tourist families drinking espressos, shimmying waiters in black and white aprons, phoney Michelin tyre signs all metal-yellow and rusty, and shiny-foreheaded girls with pinned-up blonde hair serving big blond frothy glasses of Alsace beer to shouting American students . . .

Gazing into the interior of the café Rebecca can also see, right at the back, a young couple.

The girl is in black, with a soft, costly jumper slung about her shoulders; the boy has a brown leather jacket and absurdly tousled hair. As Rebecca watches, rapt, she sees the boy stoop a beery, stubbly jaw to nuzzle the girl's neck; he seems to whisper something to the girl's collarbone. Rebecca keeps watching, still rapt, as the girl sighs and smiles and creases her ticklish shoulder, and giggles in a fatuous, naive, innocent, coquettish, joyous, not-yet-raped way.

Aiiii. Rebecca steps back, aghast at *her* own stupidity, nostalgic for *her* own happiness. She was always like this with him, wasn't she? Always ready to melt and swoon as he looked at her and joked; as he did fingery things with her hair, and kissy things with his lips, as he did the sexy things, the Patricky things . . .

But why? Why was she like that, with him, and with him *alone*? Why was it only to him that the rose-heart of her would open, why was his the only wind to which she would bend? Perhaps because . . . she so enjoyed the way he patted her arse after they fucked. Like she was a difficult but lovely new boat he'd just successfully berthed.

But: why? Still: why? Why did and does no-one else make her feel like that? Trying, squinting, shivering in a summer-night breeze coming up the road from Chalk Farm, Rebecca pulls her woollen around herself and tries to think of all the first nights and last nights, the first-and-last nights she's had since, all the OK dates, all the nice sex, all the mild romance, all the blond, loving, kind, young, pleasant, tediously-insistent-on-foreplay men she's seen in the two years since *then*. Is it Patrick's fault that she is now unable to pin down a proper, wholesome relationship? Or is it her fault, and Patrick simply the kind of lover she likes?

Shivering, although there is no breeze now, Rebecca wonders if she is sick, ill, mismade, marred.

PHONEPHONEPHONEPHONE

OK! Impatient and irritated Rebecca snatches the shrill and insistent cellphone with HOME flashing on and off on the little screen, and she makes it go quiet, by pressing it into Silent mode.

Then Rebecca turns and continues walking, trying to forget her recent linkage of thoughts. Onwards, and downwards, she walks. Past the King of Bohemia pub, all purple and neon, past the smell of crepes from the little stand across the way. Curious, nostalgic, remembering her own youth, her own good times spent in Hampstead, Rebecca passes the lines of yellow- and lime- and loganberry-coloured sports cars all full of rich Arab kids laughing and taking their shirts off as they shout at the tan-ankled Jewish girls kitten-heeling down Downshire Hill.

Kitten-heeling? Caught by the sight of some pink-and-sequin shoes in the richly glowing L.K. Bennett shop window Rebecca pauses, looks, breathes, covets: and remembers. How Patrick used to delight in her shoes, her clothes. He used to love the way she spent hours choosing clothes, buying clothes, selecting knickers, wielding lipsticks, rubbing perfume into her elbows and wrists and other places. He loved it so much she used to find herself overdoing things, overemphasising the girly behaviourisms. Sometimes she used to dawdle at her dressing, take hours putting her panties on, flick languidly through fashion mags with her dress halfway up her thigh: merely to wind him up, and to relish the sight of him all wound up. Sometimes she would walk barefoot when it was too cold; let fall a dishonest dress strap before breakfast; lick her already lipglossed lips when they were only nipping to the bank, just because she loved the way it gunned his engine. She would accentuate the feminine so as to inflame the masculine in him. Make him crazy. Make him need her like air.

Outside Rosslyn Chapel a girl in mules and short skirt is tilting on her toes to kiss her tall blond white-tee-shirted boyfriend but he is pushing her away and looking at Rebecca.

Guilty now, a little sick and guilty of all the sex, all the sex everywhere, all the evidence of sin, of sinning humanity, Rebecca walks on, turns right, turns left, walks quicker. She walks through the streets of Belsize

Village, where green plane trees are gilded by lamplight, where crack willows flourish outside yellow-lit bay windows, where, in an unkempt front garden, a florid old rose glows cream and vermillion: like a barmaid bursting out of her red satin blouse. Yes. This place calms her. Rebecca knows and likes these affluent middle-class streets; she loves these streets of South Hampstead and Belsize and the Finchley Road as she loves herself: because in a way they *are* her, they are *hers*, they are her past, her childhood; from Belsize Square Synagogue to the gates of University College School, this is where so much of Rebecca's past unfolded.

Even Avenue Road is populated by her . . . and by . . . Patrick.

Staring at a telephone box Rebecca ruefully recalls. This is where she once had sex with Patrick. In that telephone box. And down the road is where she once parked the car and . . . had sex with Patrick. And over there in Regent's Park is where she and Patrick . . . once had sex.

Oh God. Rebecca condemns herself. Why does everywhere remind her of them; every street in London have some blue plaque? Some little shrine? With candles?

Rebecca doesn't want to know. Running across the street Rebecca runs from the endless upset of these memories, the difficult questions, towards the inviting blackness of Regent's Park. As soon as she is over the lowslung railing, she starts to feel better. The park is hushed and darkened, welcomingly tranquil; the trees are a dark silent green in the lamplight, in the far car light. Calmer, cooler, Rebecca strides on, using the distant red lights of Telecom Tower as a skymark.

Right in the middle of the blackness, Rebecca pauses, and looks up at the dark dark sky. Here, in Regent's Park, she thinks, is one of the only places in central London where you can ever see stars in any true way, see the constellations. But as Rebecca looks up at the constellations she wishes she hadn't. Yes, she can see all the constellations they made up, all the constellations they used to lovingly title, she can see Using The Phone On Avenue Road, or Borrowing Dad's Tennis Racquet. But she can also see others, too; new ones, new constellations.

Rebecca blinks; Rebecca blinks again. From the square of dark green that is Queen Mary's Gardens at night, Rebecca can see scattered across the dark Heavens of London entire new constellations. Constellations like: Patrick And Me Arguing, and Patrick Being Led Away By The Cops, and I Still Fucking Love Him.

And then, quite near the Pleiades, north east of Orion, Rebecca spies the constellation she perhaps always knew was there, but never really wanted to acknowledge. Due east of Sirius B, hard by the Great Bear, not far from Sagittarius, Rebecca can see He Never Raped Me.

29

At the junction of Marylebone Road and Baker Street Rebecca pauses for the traffic. A large black car is turning left, throwing a bridal veil of white car light across Rebecca's darkened face. When the car is gone, Rebecca crosses, turns left, walks south.

All is silent. The 3 a.m. city is quiet around her. Nearby she can just about hear a streetlamp buzzing; like there's a hornet trapped inside. Rebecca turns and half looks at these buzzing lamps and lights, stretching down the High Street. Red, Yellow, Green, Yellow, Red. The darkened street lined with streetlamps is the nave of an Orthodox church, she thinks. Here are the Byzantine colours of the city's mosaic; here are saints' haloes glowing around the halogen bulbs.

Steeling herself, Rebecca walks on. She is very near now, she is very close. She can see the bookshop, Waitrose, the upmarket kebab place. And their street. She is at the corner of their street. The street with the flat they shared; the flat she still lives in; the flat she should perhaps have quit years ago. Just around this corner is the door against which they slumped, that time . . .

Thinking of the bugle, of the flat, of them, Rebecca remembers; she remembers it all. As she stands here, stuck, afflicted, rooted to the pavement, Rebecca remembers the lot. She remembers the handcuffs in the fridge; the sea bass he cooked once so badly. She remembers his smile; his aversion to umbrellas; when they were in the country with her niece and they chucked snowballs. She remembers him in that stupid coat; buying him a new coat; the time they were throwing water at each other like lovers in an advert for car insurance; his eyes of marlin-fishing blue; the way she once shaved him and he blew foam from under his nose and they laughed together; the way he held her around the waist that time when they walked to Selfridges to buy some smoothies and it was hot; his eyes always above her; his eyes; looking up at him like she was looking at her father as a child; her sweat when they fucked; the sun of his love above her that made her sweat; two buttons he did up for her; her doing his bow tie for a dinner they hated but he kissed her when she did the tie; crap songs they both liked; the tape of Dead Singers' Songs he made for her and they sang it together in her garden; reciting Yeats to him; the Aztec book he bought for her only he wrapped it so badly she knew what it was; her kissing him in a phone box and it was awkward; his hand on her breast when she took him to the opera, once; that muscle on his upper arm one time when he was trying to fix the fridge; the twin tattoos they planned; the one single time he kissed her like he was about to ask her to marry him and didn't; the dances they tried to learn that night when they drank grappa; the way she was too embarrassed to take her tampon out in front of him; the way he took it out anyway; the weekend in Paris they never went on; a poster she saw once of a tropical island with couples on it laughing together and she had thought I am as happy as that and I'm just on Euston Road and it's raining and I'm happy because of Him; the smell of his hair when he washed it in her shampoo; the way he lied to her then always laughed and admitted it immediately; his blue shirt; his eyes; an argument about politics which ended with him fucking her rapily and she liked it; sharing toothpaste for the first time; him; his eyes; the presence of him in her life; the ballet of sex with him; the sultry tango of their fucking; the fascist jitterbug; his eyes; his whisky breath; the suit he wore that day; the underwear she so lovingly and slowly chose because she knew it would make him happy and the fact that she was doing something that made him happy made her simply simply simply *happy* and that was enough and for the first time and the only time in her life *love* had been *enough*.

Tears? *Here?* In the *street*?

Rebecca can't help herself: she feels like giving in; like crying, even sobbing. Maybe she even feels like ululating, like really wailing like some bereaved Palestinian mother.

Instead she swallows and looks across the road. At the door.

30

Key in the lock, shaking a little, Rebecca pushes open the door, ignores the mail, climbs the did-he-rape-me-here stairs to the maybe-he-raped-me-here sitting room. Then, after a quick anxious scout, she takes more stairs and makes her way to the let's-face-it-he-never-raped-me-anywhere bedroom.

Dust everywhere: no Patrick. Rebecca glares at the bugle sitting on the sill, the dark uncurtained window, the fulsome moon, Marylebone. There is no evidence of Patrick. No mug for a late-night coffee; no noise; no bags, no shoes, no clothes chucked carelessly the way he liked to in a corner. The room is *sans* rapist. What was Murphy talking about?

As soon as Rebecca remembers her friend, the cellphone starts vibrating and trilling and Rebecca lifts her cellphone to her ear and hears Murphy:

— *So?*

— What?

— Are you there?

— Yes, Murf. I'm at the flat . . .

Silence. Fraught silence. Then Murphy exhales; then she says:

— Look, you mad cow, it's your life, your choice

— Thanks but

— I'm not going to do anything, I'm not going to ring your parents, I just . . .

— Great, thank you

— I just want to know if *he's* there too

— Murphy – Rebecca gazes around – He's not here. Alright?

The mobile is quiet again. Then Murphy's disembodied voice says:

— Yer sure?

— Yes

— *But Becs . . .*

— But what, Murphy? Why are you so adamant he'll be here anyway?

— *Because* – Rebecca's friend's voice sounds angry, yet confused – Because I just . . . rang the flat and . . . – Murphy stalls. Rebecca can sense her friend thinking. Then Murphy says – OK. I'll tell you . . . *He answered*, Rebecca, Patrick *answered*, I'm *sure* it was him

A mutual pause. Rebecca inhales, gazes flatly ahead

— Well he's not here now

— But, Becca

— Look, Murf, I'll ring you back, alright?

Re-bagging the stifled phone Rebecca stares ahead of herself and tries to assay her turbulent feelings. What does she feel? She now feels grief and sadness that Patrick is, seemingly, apparently, *not* here. Two years gone, two years he's been in prison, two years she's been torturing him, and now she really wants nothing so much as to have him back, to see him, to explain to him, to ask him things, to make love to him, to simply have him back in the flat, black-haired and unshaven and derisively laughing at the French clothes-shop shopkeeper across the road while he eats Rice Krispies noisily at three in the afternoon.

Rebecca shakes her head. She wants not to cry, but the flat is making her feel the wind of her loneliness: as if she has stepped outside the night and into this bleak and solitary room, into this flat so redolent of their love; it all makes her shiver, feel cold.

Totally alone, it seems, Rebecca wanders about the half-dark flat, listlessly gazing out each window in turn. The windows they used to gaze out of together are dirty. Ticking a vague to-clean list in her head, Rebecca walks over to the stairs, goes down the stairs, walks across the sitting room to the black table, where she hears a noise that makes her jump.

Patrick?

She says it aloud:

— *Patrick?*

Her grievous voice is answered by nothing but the noise of the fridge doing a shudder. Steadying her nerves, Rebecca breathes, breathes again, then picks up a plate from the table and carries the plate into the kitchen. Angling the plate into the sink she turns the tap and watches water, then she turns the tap off and turns to the fridge. Fridge door open she takes out a carton of juice from the otherwise empty, definitely handcuffless fridge. But the juice box is bloated, nearly gone, the juice is almost fizzy, so Rebecca swivels around and finds the rubbish bin she remembers their buying, and she drops the days-old juice carton in the bin.

Out of the kitchen and into the sitting room, she looks at the corner of the room: where a box full of her stuff sits: evidence of her half-hearted attempt at leaving the flat. Peering over, Rebecca looks into the box and there right on top of the box is a smaller, lidless, Selfridges shoe box full of his letters to her from prison.

She really means not to take out any of the letters and read them again; so she takes out just the top letter, dated, what . . . a month ago?, and she unfolds and she reads:

Rebecca I'm sorry. I've had enough. I cannot believe what I did how I hurt you. What I did. When I left you lying. How could I have done

Scanning down the letter, appalled at the candour and contrition, once again, Rebecca reads some more:

sometimes in here I get religious. I don't want to feel Godless any more. Don't laugh Bex but I sometimes see my soul as like some sixth former some English girl with long blonde hair, some girl who longs to matriculate, to go up to Trinity

Still scanning

but maybe we should be blaming God, you know? Sweetheart? Cause maybe it's Him, after all. He's the kiddie fiddler, the one who likes to look at us naked, his children, and maybe it's Him who's the sadist, the rapist, maybe He's the one who forces us all to do stuff we never

Enough; enough; far too much. Going to fold the letter Rebecca hears her phone. Again. Setting down the letter, she picks up the phone.
—So is he there?

— *No*. He's not
— You sure?

Rebecca does not even answer this. She falls silent. Undeterred, Murphy barks:

— So anyway you pulled the charges what the fuck for?
— Mn . . .
— Two years later??
— Because
— Why, Bex? Why?
— Because I love him, because he didn't do it, because . . .

With outright anger in her voice, Murphy:

— You're mad! Aren't you? Jesus! What do you mean he didn't do it?
— He didn't do it
— Do you want to be a total cretin?
— No I
— Jesus, Rebecca, he *did* it, I *remember*. You *told* me

Rebecca starts saying:

— He didn't and even if he did what does it matter. He didn't do it . . .

But then she stops short. Rebecca doesn't want to talk; she wants to hug someone. Someone? *Him*. At this moment she wants him to be here no matter how angry he is. She wants him to come round the kitchen door in that dark-blue shirt. She wants to fold her face into his unshavenness, his rough tousled funny angry brutal soft ironic cool dismissive manliness. His eyes the blue of that sky when she was in Crete as a teenager. Like that iridescent dragonfly hovering over the ponds in Hampstead when she was six.

— What is this?
— Sorry?
— Jewish guilt is it?
— Murphy, I *love* him
— He's a monster!
— Oh, get over it. He's not. He didn't do it. I *lied*
— You . . . *lied*?
— Maybe, yes. Maybe I lied what does it matter now and maybe
— What?
— Maybe it's all rape
— What? Duhh? – Breathing quickly, almost panting – What? The? Fuck? Are? You? Saying? That all sex is rape?

—Yes ... If it's good

—Listen to yourself! REBECCA!

A pause. Rebecca holds her mobile a few inches away and stares blue at the window. The many stars beyond. *A young girl longing to go up to Trinity* ...

Murphy:

—God! We all believed you!

—Well ... don't

—And we still believe you!

—Well ... *don't.* I don't want anybody to believe anything for me ... don't believe anything please, ever again

The next long silence is punctuated by another fridge-shiver. Then Murphy speaks:

—OK, Rebecca. Lookie here ... – Murphy is talking slowly, sounding patient, angry, patient, angry – It ... doesn't matter what happened ... we can sort that out later ... – She sighs, sounding like she is about to get angry; but she says again slowly, says again softly – The important thing is ... he must be *there*, or heading back there. He was there earlier on. K? So get out *now* – Rebecca goes to say *but*, but Murphy says – What if he reacts? What if he's, like, just a tiny bit pissed off that you put him in jail? What if it isn't all 'oh what the hell it was only a life sentence'? What if he says ... – Murphy changes her accent slightly – 'Why don't I go round and kill her for making me do two years in jail?'

—I ...

—You?

—Murphy I just couldn't bear to think of him in *there*

—You couldn't bear what? Fuck!! Bex have you been looking at his crazy letters again? – Even louder snort – *Oh* God

—Sitting there thinking he did it. I couldn't bear that

—They'll prosecute you ...

—Maybe – Rebecca thinks – Maybe

—Just get out NOW

—In a minute. I want to see him. It's all rubbish and ... wait ... What's that noise?

—Rebecca? REBECCA?

A noise has made Rebecca drop the phone. A different kind of noise. *Him?* It has to be him. It can only be him. *Who else?*

But the noise is upstairs? But it *can't* be upstairs, upstairs was *empty.*

No. It *is* upstairs: there it is again.

The . . . roof terrace? The roof terrace . . .

Rebecca stands, paralysed. She wonders what to do. The roof terrace . . . ?

Rebecca moves nearer the stairs, the stairs to the bedroom. She wants to go up and she wants to run away. She wants to think about God, about rape, about love, about dying, about fear of death. Is he up there? And if he is up there what is she going to say? Is she going to blame him, or kiss him, or something else? Rebecca listens for the noise again, while she thinks about God. Maybe God *was* the culprit . . . handcuffing them all to the bedposts of lust, putting the gimp mask of orgasm on every human face . . .

Again: the noise. Unmistakable. *It is.*

Following her own darkest wishes, Rebecca takes the stairs. Dignified, dutiful, feeling like the innocent wife of a cruel Tudor king, she lifts the train of her thoughts and makes a slow sombre route up the stairs, into the bedroom. Here Rebecca crosses the floor of the room to the other door. The door that leads to the roof terrace. Up?

Up. Panting a little with the exertion, stooping her head in the confined space of the little stairway, Rebecca climbs all the way to the roof space.

Starlight, lamplight, office light . . . blinking in the fresher air, Rebecca looks out into the blue humid softness of the evening, seeing the first lineaments of lighter blue dawning over Welbeck Street. She can see a blanket, a bag, two books . . .

And then yes, then yes, then yes, indeed: she sees Patrick. Patrick Skivington. Patrick Skivington G4628. He is sitting on the edge of the roof swinging his legs over the side, looking down the three-storey height to Marylebone High Street. From the side Rebecca can see his unshavenness, his pale face, his prison face: thin and cheekboned.

He turns. She spies blue eyes. Does he have a knife?

— Be careful . . .

She says. He looks at her; and does not move. He says nothing. Two years? Three?

Rebecca goes over. She does not know what to do, whether to run away, or ring Murphy, or call her mother, or go over and let Patrick throw her off the top of the building as perhaps she ought. So she goes over to him. Very carefully she goes over and sits down next to him, dangling her two legs down next to his; now the two of them are both kicking their heels against the guttering.

— I . . . – He says – I . . . – He says. His voice is older. But still: it's his voice. Rapt, frightened, devout, unsure, Rebecca watches as her ex-boyfriend sighs and puts his head back and looks fairly handsome again as he looks up at the stars. She watches as he reaches for her hand without looking; as blindly he takes her hand in his hand; as with a crushing grip he lifts her hand to his lips and kisses it.

Their hands clasped together, he stares up at the just seeable summer stars and says:

— Look, the constellations

Rebecca nods, and says, slowly:

— You In Prison?

— Me In Prison . . .

She pulls her hand away, and says:

— And . . . Me Accusing You Wrongly

Patrick laughs, a little strangely, then goes quiet. Then he says:

— What did you think of the trial then . . . bit of a lark?

She wonders what to say. She says:

— You looked sweet in the dock

— Like a rapist?

— Like my *boyfriend*

— A rapist . . .

— Ex-rapist *manqué*?

He says:

— Fucking hell, Rebecca, I was scared – He is turning to face her full-on. His face is wan but not unhappy, she thinks. Inscrutable. What does he want? She wants to know. Does he want to kill her? To kiss her? Rebecca stares into his eyes seeking an answer as he says:

— You know I never stopped loving you I always kept wanting you: have you slept with anyone else?

— . . . Not . . . really

— You know I wanked about you six times one day

— Six times?

— Maybe seven

— Well . . . my shower head needs replacing

He laughs, again. More like the old laugh. Then he says:

—Oh fucking hell Rebecca I hate you

Rebecca says nothing, says shh, feels weird, feels strange frightened sad but alive. So is this what? Is this when? Is this why? Is this true love? If love is forgiveness, who has more to forgive of each other than them? But where does the sex go then? What of the *sex*?

Still sitting next to him, still sitting on the edge of the roof terrace sixty feet above the empty pavements, Rebecca feels very very tired. Blonde and wordless she leans and rests her tired head on his shoulder. In response he rests his head on top of hers, likewise. Then they go quiet; then they both gaze over the Marylebone streets. Beyond them the quiet Georgian townhouses stretch towards Fitzroy; somewhere out there the gingkos of Cleveland Street flutter their leaves, in the tress-lifting breeze.

—Do you still . . . ?

—What?

—Nothing

Taking his hand she lays his hand between her two hands. His soft hand, his soft innocent not-exactly-a-rapist hand. *God.* Where does she wanted now? As she lifts his hand and kisses his soap-scented hand she thinks: How does they go now? Why does love unhappy? Where is she happy to? She is not happy; she is not scared. She wants to laugh and slap him at the same time. Because, because, because

—Going to be a lovely day

Says Patrick, obviously.

Rebecca nods and says, also obviously:

—I'm tired

Patrick nods and says:

—Here

And he leans back indicating he is making space for her to lie on his lap. Nodding, obedient, still impressed by him, after all these years, Rebecca nods and does as she is told. Right on the edge of the roof terrace she tucks her legs back up and to the side, then leans and awkwardly rests her head on his lap and from this dangerous-but-horizontal vantage she also gazes across at the starry dawn sky. She senses with some relief how he could just tip forward: tip her to her death on the streets sixty feet below.

And then he says:

—Tell me about the Aztecs

— Really?

— One more time . . .

— What do you want to hear?

— Anything

And so she thinks. With his hand curling the hair of her temple and his kissing lips occasionally warm on her cheek Rebecca ignores the wet tears on her face and thinks what say. What to say? Thinking wildly and laterally she wonders whether to tell him about the Tarascan Empire, or the demon women known as Tzitzime, or the hallucinating jaguars sacrificed on the Templo Mayor. But before she can say this, he touches her face with a hand and leans over and says down to her horizontal cheek:

— Sorry for raping you

— You didn't

— Yes I fucking did

— So what if you did . . .

— So I did then?

— No you didn't – She says, firmly – Rape me anyway

— Shall I?

— Yes. Forever

He pauses, says:

— Really? Do you want me to rape you forever?

— Till death us do part, Patrick

— Then I shall – He says – I'll never stop raping you

— Thank you

She is nodding, determinedly. He is exhaling, as if relieved. Feeling his breath on her cheek, feeling a strange warmth inside, Rebecca kisses his thighs beneath her face, she squeezes his lap to her face; and then and only then does she turn towards the sky and decide what to tell him. She has decided to tell him about the fate of fallen Aztec warriors, who spend the afterlife as golden Monarch butterflies, as creatures of the sun: wholly without memory, without knowledge, mouths always full of sweetness; floating about the sun-lanced cloud forests, entirely bereft of desire . . .

But she doesn't. Before she goes to say this Rebecca has a change of heart, and she decides to be quiet, to shut the fuck up, to say nothing. And so instead they just sit there, the two of them: with her head in his lap, just a few inches from the edge of the roof terrace. And then for what seems like hours they gaze into the eastern sky, where dawn glows soft indigo over Holborn, and the Inns of Court, like a choir screen of turquoise in this dark nave of night.